DARK RIDER

The dog began to bark, alerting me. Someone was walking along the lane, leading a horse, moving something back and forth ahead of him, almost as if sweeping with it like a blind man with a stick.

The dog was going berserk now, three times as upset as he'd been when he'd first scented us. *Lizard*, I thought. A hound would know. The figure took something out from under his cloak, something that might have been a short saddle musket, and pointed one-handed at the dog. But there wasn't any bang, just a thin line of light that found the dog and silenced it instantly.

Then the horseman scanned around, taking in house, barn, fields. Finally he started on again, still sweeping the lane with whatever it was, and passed the barn.

I moved along behind the thing crouching low behind the fence on my side, certain that my comrade was keeping pace. About sixty or seventy meters down the lane, the Lizard stopped again, and I stopped too. He stood there for a moment, staring back at the barn. Suddenly the Lizard turned and spurred directly toward me. I held very still.

JOHN DALMAS

THE LIZARD WAR

Copyright © 1989 by John Dalmas

A Baen Books Original

Baen Publishing Enterprises
260 Fifth Avenue
New York, N.Y. 10001

ISBN: 0-671-69851-6

Cover art by David Mattingly

First printing, December 1989

Distributed by
SIMON & SCHUSTER
1230 Avenue of the Americas
New York, N.Y. 10020

Printed in the United States of America

I've had the good fortune to work for or otherwise know some exceptional people at important, formative periods in my life. This book is dedicated to two of them:

Dr. Alton A. Lindsey
Emeritus Professor of Ecology
Purdue University

and

Art Heiberg
Logger (retired)
International Falls, Minnesota

Both were employers, friends, and tutors. Both had and have my admiration.

PROLOGUE

The narrator of this story had a very restricted, if highly personal and intense, view of the events he was part of. To provide the reader with perspective, four documents with very different viewpoints are provided here as prologue. The first of these is one with which the narrator was familiar, but which he did not consciously connect with the events and thus barely mentions in his debrief.

The other three documents, indeed two of the other three viewpoints, he was totally unaware of.

From the *HOLY BIBLE: THE BOOK OF RENEWAL, CHAPTER 1*

1 The second millennium had passed since the birth of the Redeemer, and the Lord GOD looked at what man had wrought upon the Earth. 2 HE saw the waters and the air fouled, greed rewarded and virtue scorned. 3 Liars were empowered, their voices entering every home, and their pictures which moved with the semblance of life. 4 And the cities of man were beset with murderers and thieves, tempters and corrupters.

5 Great armies there were, and fleets of warships that fared upon the sea and beneath it, and there were

1

other fleets that flew swiftly in the air. 6 Still other fleets flew above the air, and these were the most terrible, for they had in them such power that a single one of them could destroy a great city and all its people, and poison whole regions of the Earth.

7 And even as HE watched, GOD saw the armies of man move and clash upon the Earth; the fleets on and under the seas destroyed each other, and the fleets that flew in the air wrought havoc upon all they flew over.

8 Then those other fleets were launched which flew above the air. 9 And when they came to earth, the walls of the cities fell as less than rubble; fire and great winds reaped the people like mighty scythes; the sun was masked with blood and the moon hid its face; days became like nights; myriad were the dead, and loud the cries and lamentations.

10 And the Earth in its sorrow was cold beneath the pall of Death, so that the corn did not grow; hay rotted in the windrows and potatoes in the ground.

11 And the armies of man were without rule, sacking and killing, and the children of man were without bread.

12 Pestilence and famine spread across the face of the Earth, even pestilence that was sent not by GOD but by the hand of man, so that few remained of man's multitudes. 13 And bands of the wicked wandered the waste place the Earth had become, murdering with knife and gun, bow and club, stealing bread from the widow and blankets from her children, making slaves of them and violating them.

14 And many men raised their faces to GOD, crying aloud for mercy, but only a few there were who fell upon their knees, calling out to GOD that they repented, and saying that all which had befallen them was just.

15 And among the Host of Heaven were those who spoke to GOD saying that man was too iniquitous, that the time had come for the final judgment, and that the Earth should be cleared of man and all his works.

16 GOD listened to the hosts, but also HE listened to the supplications of those men who were righteous. 17 And in His infinite mercy and His infinite justice, GOD stopped for a space the passing of night and day on Earth. 18 HE made the suffering and dying and life itself to

pause and wait, while HE renewed the Earth, recreating it. 19 And on the renewed Earth, HE left few works of man; simple tools whereby man could have shelter and bread by the sweat of his brow.

20 For GOD did not return man to the paradise of Eden and the innocence of the beginning. 21 Instead HE took the remnants of the nations of man and divided them into small portions, and sowed those portions separate from one another in distant places, mingling them, and caused them to forget their pride and their shame, and much else. 22 And charged the Church to teach man to love GOD and his fellow men.

Report of hostile encounter in restricted Varnis-4 Reserve Zone. GPV 1207-34-29643

A vessel of ISWS Class 7V entered the Varnis System at 3174.29038.1592.4911 under cover of an FB cloak. A Varnis-4 Sentry Unit detected the faint emergence wave and tracked the intruder to its nearest approach, then challenged it. Intruder promptly fired S-pulses, then despite a G-field distortion of 0.493 mG, began to generate a warp field. Sentry Varnis-4 fired penetration pulses in an unsuccessful attempt to disrupt the nascent warp field. Intruder escaped, leaving neutron fog indicating critical generator strain.

Parameters of the emergence wave indicate intruder source in Vekktalos Sector.

Parameters of departure eddy indicated 5° departure cone centering on 5214.49960.812275.

**Memo fac, Cultural Oversight Bureau
GPV 1207-34-30427**

◗ Operations Director, Monitor Service
◗ DEB COB, via Intelligence Filter
Bogey report

Maqq,

Suggest you call up and read *Report of hostile encounter in restricted Varnis-4 Reserve Zone* GPV 1207-34-29643.

Per Intel Eval, this intruder is probably (P<0.10) fun-and-games crazies out of LZ world Kelgorath-5. Consider sending a Sec-C warning to all teams in the 5° departure cone given in Report of Encounter.

In this Era of Fiscal Responsibility, I appreciate that sending warnings to so many receipt points will play havoc with a tight comm budget. If you decide to do it, and I hope you will, I am authorized to transfer up to 5×10^4 credits to your budget to ease the pain.

Brand

**Memorandum of transmittal, dated GPV
1207-41-93126**

Furg,

The official account of this mission is already in agency files. You may have read the abstract.

I realize how unusual (unprecedented?) it is, without a Committee of Evidence request, to send up an ultrarecall debrief of a project personnel, let alone a very junior project indigene. But that's what I'm doing. Obviously it is good promotion for the Sol Three Project, and therefore self-serving. And equally obviously, if that were the only reason for sending it, it would be severely counterproductive. But given the conditions on this planet, and our operating strictures here:

1. I believe it will be enlightening to HQ administrative personnel to read this. Too many have only the most general notion of field work in the boondocks. Very few will have had experience on anything like a 5-C Spec world.
2. You may also consider it desirable and appropriate that this be made available to COB, to promote the Service.
3. And finally, it may be useful in recruiting, whether by showing it to prime prospects or publishing it broadly.

Besides which, I like this young man, and obviously believe he can have an important future in the Service. This will establish a file on him at HQ.

Regardless of whether this debrief ever gets beyond your desk, I trust you'll enjoy reading it for the memories it'll stir up, from the years before they made an office slave out of you.

Tahmm

ONE

I'd been dreaming about a war with the Lizards. Some of the time we were in the woods, and sometimes the woods became a village, my home town of Aarschot, although it didn't look like Aarschot. Sometimes the Lizards ran around on four legs, looking something like the gator I saw once in a traveling show. Other times they had lizardy faces and ran on their hind legs, with long skinny tails lashing around behind them. And sometimes they looked more like people carrying pitchforks, but had froggy faces, in spite of fangs that showed when they opened their mouths. In any case they had horns on their heads.

Sometimes we were actually fighting, usually with swords, but other times I'd be talking with them and drinking coffee. It was always their coffee, as if they were rich.

I woke out of it and opened my eyes. And saw the wolf sniffing at my feet. I suppose I jerked, maybe even yelled. Anyway, the wolf leaped backward and disappeared, and somehow I was on my feet with my sword in my hand. I don't know just how I managed that. I can visualize myself getting up like a steel spring released, but I still haven't imagined how I got my sword at the same time. At the moment it all had a feeling of

7

unreality, as if it were part of the dream, but I knew it was real.

My knees were honest-to-God shaking, too. I couldn't see the wolf any longer, but then, I couldn't see very much else either. The forest roof cut out most of the light from a lopsided moon.

My heart slowed from a gallop to a trot, and I became aware of the mosquitoes on my face. I squashed them bloody with one hand, then squatted down by what was left of my fire: a few coals showing faintly ruddy through a blanket of white wood ash. I'd left dry broken branchwood in easy reach. Working right-handed, with my sword still in my left, I took a twig, brushed ashes off the coals, and laid a few smaller, brittler twigs on top of them. Then I raised my eyes and scanned around again, listening hard.

Seeing and hearing nothing, I crouched forward and blew long and gently on the coals, brightening them. I took another deep breath and blew some more. Twigs flared suddenly, and I heard a sound as if a heavy body had jumped back, startled. After adding larger twigs, I laid several pieces the thickness of my thumb and bigger across them, then stood up to scan the woods again. Back a ways, three pairs of yellow eyes reflected the firelight—a she-wolf and two yearling cubs, I'd have bet. Unusual for a wolf to make so bold, especially with young; at least back in Mizzoo it would have been, but this was wild country along here.

Gripping my sword, I stepped around the fire toward the eyes to see what they'd do. They disappeared. A dead branch snapped, as if they were leaving too fast to care.

The moon's height said well past midnight, maybe two or three of the clock. I squatted down with my back to the log I'd been sleeping against. The air was damp and still, and beginning to be smoky again. I put on three or four more pieces of branchwood and watched the fire grow. The smoke made my eyes water some, but the mosquitoes stayed away.

Feeling in my pack for the johnnycake, I opened the cloth it was wrapped in, ate a crumbly piece of it, and thought about walking on. I can most always go to sleep by lying down and closing my eyes, but I didn't feel sleepy anymore, and it wasn't more than a couple-hundred meters to the road. I'd only left it far enough to put a low ridge between my fire and possible night travelers who might otherwise see or smell it.

Not that I'm a worrier, but Ohioans had spoken ill of the Kingdom of Allegheny, and sometimes local prejudice is right.

I raised my wineskin for a single swallow—creek water now, with scarcely a tinge left of grape—and decided to stay where I was. Till either dawn or the mosquitoes woke me again. I had some green wood on hand, and laid it on to make the fire last and add to the smoke. Then I put my sword where I could grab it, lay back down against the log, and closed my eyes. The wood popping in the fire had me asleep in no time.

TWO

With morning there were clouds, and toward noon, thunder. I was getting out of the wild border country then, to where there was an almost continuous string of fields on my right, between the rutted road and the river. Hills of potatoes or glossy green corn stood in rows, and here and there people were out chopping weeds or picking potato bugs.

Then it got really dark. I heard the rushing sound of rain crossing forest, loud enough to be a hailstorm coming, and people took off running for the woods. Forest hung over the road from the off side, and I ducked under cover myself, swung the pack off my shoulders, and took out my oilskin poncho. I'd hardly got my pack back on when the rain came galloping down the road, the big first drops hitting so hard they splashed up dust. There wasn't any hail; it was just raining that hard. Even under the eaves of the woods, I hurried to get my poncho draped over my pack and me. In seconds, looking into the rain was like looking into a waterfall.

I kept on walking then, passing field workers hunched wet and shivering under the trees, which by now weren't keeping much water off at all. After a few minutes, though, it eased to a steady fall. A wagon came along,

drawn by two horses past their prime. Its driver stopped
and looked down at me from beneath the dripping hood
of his own oilskin. He must have seen that I carried a
sword; it would have shown, even with the poncho. But
it didn't seem to worry him.

"Would ye be carin' to ride?" he asked me.

I told him I would, and climbed to the seat beside
him.

"Me name's Shamus Finnigan," he said. The hand he
gave me was small but thick and hard.

I shook it. "Mine's Luis Raoul DenUyl," I told him.

Finnigan's Merkan had an accent, a sort of lilt, sounding as if part of the time he spoke another language
entirely. Not that that was unusual, of course, but his
accent was new to me. Most all districts, during the
great shuffling, were settled with folk from a single far
place, and mostly they held to their old language, learning Merkan as a second tongue, at least the men, to
trade and otherwise traffic with outsiders.

Where I was from though, two different peoples got
planted together, plus a few Old Merkans who'd been
drifting around in a daze. The Vlaamsch had been the
most numerous at home, and the Espanoles next, but
the Old Merkans, few though they were, had been kind
of depended on. They'd known the country—what to
plant and when—that sort of thing. That was more than
a hundred years ago, and since then both the Vlaamsch
and Espanol languages had died out there. Mostly all
they left were names. I could remember my daddy's
grandparents using Vlaamsch when they wanted to talk
privately, but even so, there was generally enough
Merkan mixed in that us kids could sort of guess what
they were talking about.

After we'd shaken hands, Finnigan started up his
team. Water streamed off their rumps. "Ye're no soldier oi take it," he said, and when I looked surprised,
he grinned, misunderstanding. "Yer sword's not all that
shows. Oi could see your breeches and brogans below
yer raincloak."

Brogans? That must be what they called boots here, or maybe shoes. What surprised me, though, was that anyone would comment, or think to notice, that I wasn't a soldier. "You're right," I told him. "I'm not. Are there many around?"

"Not now. But there were, these weeks past. And trouble enough, too, before they went back to Kings Town. 'Twas the king sent 'em 'round, pressin' young men into service, ye see." His eyes withdrew, and he licked thin lips, shaking his head. "There's a war off east. And talk of devils . . ."

He shut up then, as if the devils he'd mentioned were on his mind now and he didn't want to talk about them. His devils had to be the Lizards, I supposed. Pretty soon the rain petered out to spatters. Finally Finnigan asked where I'd spent the night.

"In the woods," I told him. "I don't have enough money to spend it needlessly, and I'd have lost two hours' travel if I'd stayed in the last village. Gorky that was."

"Gorky." The wagoner nodded. Gorky was in Ohio, on the west bank of the Ohio River. "Ah well, ye didn' miss much. Gorky folk aren't friendly to strangers, oi suppose ye noticed, and their whiskey's not fit to drink. They're pagans, too; worship a false god they call Lenin."

The rain was down to occasional spatters, and Finnigan had pushed his hood back. With his face more exposed, his eyes showed green beneath carroty eyebrows, and they looked me over again. "Where might ye be from?" he asked.

"Mizzoo. County called Aarschot, near the Mississip."

"Ah! The Mississip! Oi've heard of it. The Ohio'll take a man there, they say, if he stays on it far enough. Our county here is Connemara. Where might ye be goin'?"

"On east." It was a put-off.

"Lankster?" he persisted.

I shrugged. "Never heard of Lankster. Have you ever wanted to see the ocean?"

Finnigan nodded. "When oi was young. But oi never did anything about it."

More than a few young men got the wanderlust and went to see the Ocean, or the Sweetwater Seas off north. Or back home, maybe the Great Grass Sea to the west, where people lived on horseback, herding cattle or following them, and sometimes were hostile to strangers.

"If ye go to see the Ocean," Finnigan suggested, "steer off south. Well before ye come to Lankster. Down through Jinnia, south and then east. *North*east is truly dangerous; it's full of devil worshipers up there."

The green eyes peered keenly at me as if watching to see how I'd react. I don't think I did, though somewhere along the way, talk of devils would start being more than just talk. As for avoiding northeast—that's where my mission lay, where the cloth map in my pack was leading me.

"I'm new this far east," I told him. "Maybe it's time for me to stop a day or two. See what I can learn. In times like these, a man likes to know the road ahead a bit, and the people."

Finnigan nodded. "God willin'," he said, and crossed himself. I did the same, with feeling, and we made small talk for a while. One of the things he told me was that on east from here it wasn't a good idea to sleep out in the forest. What I didn't tell him was that, for me, inns could be more dangerous than the woods, though I stayed in one now and then for the comfort and to scrub up.

The valley had been getting wider, and the farm fields bigger. The hamlets where the farmers lived were closer together. We passed occasional wagons, and now and then a horseman, or someone traveling afoot. No one was in the fields now, nor would be till after noonmeal, when things had dried out some. The rain quit entirely and the sun came out. We took off our ponchos and let it dry our clothes where water had leaked through or trickled down, or crawled up the legs

of our breeches. Things didn't look much different now
than back home in Mizzoo, or most other places I'd
seen.

After a bit we rounded a corner of woods and I could
see a village ahead, almost a town. It must have had a
couple-hundred houses. The ridges that walled the
valley closed in there, their trees well spaced from a
long time of grazing and firewood cutting that had
thinned the forest almost to parkland—the way it usually was near so many people. Above the village, the
valley really got narrow, with steep sides, and on a
hilltop I could see a big fort made of stone, maybe even
with cannons on its walls. This had to be a county seat.

"There she is," Finnigan said pointing. "Galway Town.
Father Hannery, our priest, knows as much of the
world as any man. Many a traveler stops with him for
bed and supper, in return for tellin' what they've seen
and the news they've heard."

He clucked to the horses and they moved a little
livelier, as if oats and a rubdown were practically in
sight. Close up, Galway looked and felt different than
Aarschot. For one thing, most of the roofs here were
thatched; I'd seen other places like that, here and there
along the way. And between the vegetable gardens
growing around them was something I'd never seen
before: waist-high fences of stacked stones, some of
them overgrown—looking tied together—with vines.

There were more children than I was used to, too,
playing in puddles or around and behind the stone
fences, or hoeing or weeding in the gardens. Some
were clearly not all right, as if the people here didn't
cull their infants as strongly as the Pope commanded. I
saw a cleft palate, a stunted arm with a hand that was
little more than a wrist with nubs on it, and a clubfoot
that would curse its wearer with a limp all her life.
Hardly made in the image of God, and any children
they got would carry the curse too. It made me wonder
about the priest here, or whether these people might
be heretics. Or maybe it was just the distance from the

Holy See; Galway had to be more than a thousand miles from Norlins Town at the mouth of the Mississip.

The main street was cobbled, though, with river stones, which was more than I could say for most villages I'd passed through. The church was near the upper end—a church of stone blocks, with a taller than usual bell tower. Just below it, two roads branched off, well traveled, going off up two side valleys, one in each direction. A sign in Merkan pointed east to the inn.

Father Hannery was out of town, and just now there was no assistant priest. His wife made it clear that she wasn't free to take in strangers not of the cloth. Certainly not young, sword-carrying strangers, unless they were in sore distress. Finnigan frowned at the door when it closed, and shook his head, muttering something in his own language that didn't sound like flattery.

I could have shown Miz Hannery my medallion of course, but Finnigan would have seen and heard. And anyway she might not know of my Order, or might have heard bad things about it. Father Hannery would have known it of course, and taken me in whether he approved or not. For it's well known among the clergy that we stand high with the Pope.

"Me wife and oi've got only a small cottage," said Finnigan, "and four young in it, or oi'd offer ye a bed. But oi've a barn, if ye're willin' to sleep in the hay and take a bowl of stew with us. Otherwise there's an inn at the upper end of town—you saw the sign—no doubt with travelers that could tell ye more than oi about things in the east."

I didn't have to think twice. "That's a generous offer," I told him, "and I'll take you up on it, with thanks." So I went home with Finnigan, helped him unload the barrels from his wagon into a shed, then rubbed down and curried the two horses while he went in the house to tell his wife about the noonmeal guest he'd brought home with him.

The meal was nourishing enough, and since leaving

Aarschot, I'd gotten used to underspiced food. It was like most of Merka didn't know about garlic and peppers.

Finnigan's wife was as red-haired as he was, and the children too. Four was a good-sized brood, and none had been drastically cursed, though the oldest was cross-eyed enough that at home the priest would probably have done away with him at his second winter solstice.

Moira Finnigan didn't speak much Merkan, which wasn't unusual for a woman. But if you didn't mind freckles, she was pretty for someone probably in her thirties. And her teeth still seemed good; apparently their priest did his duty in teaching hygiene, at any rate.

I ate more than a single bowl. The Finnigans urged a second on me, and a third, with a goodly stoup of beer and then another one. Finnigan was a pretty good brewer. Back in Mizzoo I'd have handled it all without blinking, but my stomach had shrunk since I'd left, and afterwards, talking, I got drowsy. When we'd talked ourselves out, I thanked both of them, went back to the barn feeling full as a tick, and fell asleep in the hay.

THREE

Evening sunlight slanted flat and dusty through the hay door when I woke up. I climbed down from the loft, irritated with myself for sleeping so long in the daytime. I wondered if I'd slept through supper. The horses were gone though, and the wagon, which seemed to mean Finnigan was off somewhere, hauling something for someone. He probably hadn't eaten yet.

Whatever. It occurred to me I'd accepted about all the hospitality I should from the Finnigans. I'd gladly spend the night in their barn, but I shouldn't be putting my knees under their table again. So I stopped at the cottage and spoke to the oldest boy—asked him to tell his mother I was going to the inn, to eat supper and learn what I could about the country off east. He nodded and said he'd tell her. I wondered if he'd remember, and what things looked like through those crossed eyes.

I didn't go straight to the inn though. My father was a constable, which in Aarschot was a job with status. And in what time she had between the kitchen garden, cooking, sewing, keeping house, my mother was a scribe, with a fondness and talent for words and poetry. And a love of the Church. So I'd been well brought up, and just then I was dirtier than I cared to be in a public

17

place, given a choice. I walked to the river, and up it to a willow copse, where I took off my clothes, leaving them where I could keep an eye on them. Then I waded out into the water and bathed with the tin of soap from my pack.

I'd have washed my clothes too—soaked them anyway—if there'd been time to dry them. As it was, I rubbed myself partly dry and stood around naked for a while in what was left of the daylight, which wasn't much. Then I beat my clothes against a tree trunk to knock the worst of the dust out, and got dressed again. My hair was still wet, but it was cropped short enough that it didn't much matter.

The inn, made of planks, was at the upper edge of town a little way above the church. It was bigger than you'd expect for a village the size of Galway, probably from the crossroads being there and getting a fair number of travelers.

Altogether there were maybe fifteen customers inside. Ten or so of them looked like local people—not dressed for the road. There was an open space that seemed to be for dancing, but no musician just then. Most of the people were eating or drinking, and talking of course.

One was a tall, rawboned man, greasy-looking and swarthy, wearing a uniform—yellow breeches and green tunic, cavalry boots and a cocked hat. The jacket had brass buttons on it. He wore a saber, too, and two pistols stuck in his sword belt. And an arrogant, loose-lipped smirk beneath a big black mustache that needed more tending than he gave it. I decided he was someone I didn't want to know. He was standing, talking with a couple of locals. Actually he was doing the talking while they did the nodding.

The innkeeper had a girl of maybe thirteen, and a younger boy, helping him serve; children of his, I supposed. I went over to the bar and asked for a beer. While he drew it, I told him I was traveling east. "To the Ocean," I said, lying straight-out instead of being coy, and I asked him what the news was from that direction. It seemed to me an innkeeper would hear at least as much as Father Hannery, though he might be less careful about accuracy.

Handing me my mug, he shrugged. "Oi don't listen much to what's said," he told me. "Oi'm too busy. But oi do hear bits o' this and that." He shrugged again. "A man should be free to go where he wants, especially when he's young and has no family to care for. That's what youth is for, or part of what it's for. But east? Meself, oi wouldn't go much east of Galway Town if oi didn't have to. And oi don't. Nor would oi set foot east of Allegheny under any circumstances." He crossed himself. "It's one thing to die if ye go to Jesus. It's somethin' else if the Devil gets his claws in ye."

That wasn't the kind of information that helped much, and when he'd finished drawing a pair of mugs for his daughter to take, I asked him who among his customers might have come from the east. He motioned toward two men who looked like chapmen, sitting by a window, talking while they ate.

"Any others?"

He shook his head. "That's all oi know of. There's others here not from Connemara, but whether from east or west, south or north, oi wouldn't know. Ask around."

On an impulse, I asked, "How about him?" and thumbed toward the soldier in the green tunic. "The one with the pistols."

The innkeeper shook his head, his face going sour. "He's from the fort. He'd know nothin' but hearsay. And lie about that, oi have no doubt."

I went over to the chapmen then, one of them middle-aged, the other still young, both heavyset. They looked up sharply when I stopped at their table. My face isn't that ordinary, even at home, and their eyes reminded me that it didn't fit in around here, any more than it had, say, in Gorky. It's a narrow face with strong cheekbones, a face for someone slimmer than me. And dark, though my hair is light-colored. My nose is narrow too, and curved like an axe blade. Add to that eyes as blue as any you'll see anywhere—"the mark of the Vlaamsch," they call them at home—and I'm someone people notice, in Galway and most other places. In my profession that can be a nuisance and even a hazard.

"Excuse me, sirs," I said. "Have you come from the east?"

"Ve haff," said the oldest one. "Vhat iss your interest in us?"

Deutschers, obviously. "I plan to travel northeast," I told him, "and I wondered if you had information or advice you could give me. About the traveling there."

His eyes were blue too, paler than mine, and narrowed just now. They looked me over for half-a-minute before he said anything more. Then, "Ve von't giff you information," he said, "but ve vill sell you some."

I suppose I looked miffed at that. Anyway he laughed. "Ve von't charge very much for it. It's chust a matter of principle; selling iss how ve earn our breadt. But you are a man on der road, far from home. You, ve charge a copper only."

The younger grinned at me. "Paid in advance. And hope you get your money's worth. You vere not very exact about vhat you vant. Vhat ve have may not be vhat you need."

I dug a penny out of my pocket. The profile on it belonged to Johannes II, King of Mizzoo. A good one for them. Johannes, when he talked, sounded a lot like these guys, especially the younger one, whose accent wasn't as thick. The older one examined the penny curiously, showed it to his partner, then tucked it in a vest pocket.

They gave me more than my penny's worth. Like most people, they enjoyed talking to someone who was ignorant about things they knew well. Allegheny, they told me, claimed all the land east of the Susky Hanna River, and under King Choi they'd made the claim stick. But Choi's wife had killed him—the rumor was she'd caught him in adultery with a chambermaid—and the Assembly of Counts had elected Armand Boileau their new king.

To make a long story short, Armand had been a reasonably just king, and Allegheny had prospered under him for a dozen years. But he'd let the defenses go slack. So the Lanksters had crossed the Susky Hanna, and the report was they'd gotten most of the way to South Mountain. Wherever that was.

"How would it work if I swung off north and went around the war?" I asked.

They looked at each other. "You vouldt probably neffer see de Ocean," the older one said.

"Why?"

He shrugged his shoulders. "About dat, iss not all right ve talk. It iss dancherous, in more vays den vun. Dat much I tell you, and you could der rest figure out for yourself. Better you go *sout'* und den east."

His accent had gotten thicker just thinking about it.

Back in Mizzoo they'd barely heard rumor of the devils, or Lizards, but in Ohio they'd been a topic of conversation in the inns. Not that anyone there claimed to have seen one. There were different versions of what they looked like.

Bhatti and Soong had only said that they didn't look a lot different than anyone else. "Lizards in human form," Soong had called them. Beyond that, they'd been closer-mouthed than I was used to: I'd been given no briefing at all, nor many questions answered. A troublous start for a mission, at least for my taste. They didn't even say why they were being that way, just gave me a map, a purse of coins, and a few instructions, mostly to do with secrecy on the road.

I thanked the two chapmen and went back to my table. The innkeeper's boy came around for my order, and I asked for bread, cheese, and boiled cabbage. It wasn't the sort of meal you have to wait long for. It came and I worked my way through it, sipping what was left of my beer as I ate, and ordering a refill. It occurred to me that if Father Hannery was going to be back in a couple of days, I might do well to wait around and see what he could tell me. Meanwhile, maybe I could help Finnigan for bed and board.

I became aware then that the room had gone quiet, conversations cutting off. I looked up. Someone had come in who looked like a woman in man's clothes—man's clothes with a difference. I stared; I'd never imagined such a thing. She *was* a woman, without a doubt; no man filled a shirt the way she did. But she was nearly as tall as me—taller than most of the men there—and wore a scabbarded sword at one hip and a pack on her back. And her clothes were black, fine leather, and the breeches covered long, strong-looking legs. Her skin was black, too, or darkish brown actually, and she was as good-looking as you'd hope to see. People were staring at her, maybe as much for her color and looks as for her clothes and sword.

She was used to being stared at, I had no doubt. She crossed the room as if she ate there every evening, and sat down at a little table in a corner, by an open window. The location wasn't likely to have been an accident; from there she could watch everything and get out quickly if she needed to. Looking nervous, the serving girl went over to her, took her order and left. The soldier's eyes were stuck on her as if she was a magnet and he was iron. Pig iron. I found myself on my feet, going over to her, telling myself she might have come from the east. As I crossed the room, she watched like a cat watches.

"Good evening, ma'am," I said. "You wouldn't happen to be from Mizzoo, would you? A county called Mbabane?"

I felt like an idiot.

"A county called what?"

"Mbabane. It's in Mizzoo," I added, then realized I'd already said that. Double idiot. Besides, I reminded myself, Mbabane was a county where no woman would dress like that, or go to faraway Allegheny. On top of that, she talked Merkan as if it was her main, or more likely only language, while in Mbabane they talked what they called Tswana. Their Merkan, when they spoke it, didn't sound like anyone else's.

"Mbabane. Hmh! Never heard of it," she said. "I'm from Shy Free Town."

She was looking at me as if I was some kind of interesting new bug. I opened my mouth to say excuse me and go back to my own table. Instead I found myself saying, "I've heard of Shy. On one of the Sweetwater Seas. That's a long way from here."

"On the Sea of Mishgun. Sit down," she said, and pointed at the stool across from her. It wasn't an invitation; it was an order. My knees bent and my hand reached back and pulled the stool under my rear.

"Did you eat?" she asked me. "Or was that plate on your table somebody else's?"

I nodded. "I've eaten." *Gentle Jesus!* I wondered if she could tell me who all, in the room, had an empty plate in front of them. From just walking through it once.

She got up and spoke quietly as if to keep our conversation private. "My name's Jamila," she said, pronouncing it Jah-MEE-lah. Then she reached across the table and we were shaking hands! "Jamila Smith. What's yours?"

For a minute I didn't know what to do. Ordinarily women don't shake hands with men, and when one does, she doesn't grip down, even if she splits the family firewood, wrings the family wash, helps shuck corn, and has a grip like a blacksmith. This Jamila, though, had shaken hands like a man. A real man. I couldn't believe how strong her grip was! Callused, too, like a farmer's. Or more likely a swordsman's.

"Mine's Luis," I told her. "Luis Raoul DenUyl." I followed her lead and spoke quietly. Besides, my mouth had gone dry.

"Luis." She smiled, white teeth flashing. "Nice name." Then: "Mizzoo's got to be as far from here as Shy is."

"Could be. It's pretty far." I said it as if nothing was wrong with me at all.

"Traveling through?" Her eyes pinned me down, or that's how it seemed to me.

"Uh, yes."

"And headed northeast, right? I've heard things aren't too good up that way."

"That's what I've heard too." How did she know, or guess, that I was headed northeast? I was nervous now, and she knew it, and thought it was funny.

"Might be a good idea not to travel alone," she said.

What in the world am I doing, I asked myself, *sitting here talking with this woman as if she were a man?* I was here because I'd shown I could handle bad situations, but this Jamila was something I wasn't prepared to deal with.

"I'll get by," I told her. "I'm used to traveling alone. I've traveled alone all the way from Mizzoo."

The serving girl brought her supper, and Jamila ordered a beer for me. I was pretty sure the stains on her right sleeve were blood, whether of deer, calf, human, or what have you. I wondered if she could actually use that sword—with any skill, that is. I suspected she could. I had no doubt at all that she was strong enough.

Then, pulling out a sheath knife from somewhere below the table top, she cut off a slice of bread and a slab of cheese, and broke down the sausage into about a dozen large bite-size chunks. It all took her maybe three quick seconds, the knife going zip! flick flick flick!

"From what I've heard," she murmured, "from Mizzoo to here is the easy part of the trip." She speared a bite of sausage with the stiletto, tucked it between strong white teeth, and chewed, the muscles in her brown cheeks and jaws working smoothly. "You need a traveling partner for mutual security," she went on, "and it so happens I'm going northeast too."

I got up from the table. "Ma'am," I told her, "I don't know when I'll be leaving Galway Town, or even for sure *if* I'm leaving." I turned my back on her, not wanting to risk those eyes again, and started toward my own table without waiting for the beer she'd ordered me. As I crossed the room, I noticed the soldier watching me. Two more had joined him, one chesty and strong-looking, one long and lean. The lean one looked the most dangerous of the three.

There seemed to be something going on beneath the surface here that I'd do well to stay clear of, and I decided to leave. But first I'd finish the beer I'd left at my own table; damned if I'd run off leaving something I'd paid for.

I'd sat down and lifted the mug, intending to drink what was left of it in a couple of swigs, when someone else came into the inn and caught my attention. It was a man—an overgrown farmer boy actually—my height and with thick beefy shoulders about a meter wide. And maybe a dozen whitish hairs on his chin; he was seventeen years at most. By his farmer clothes, reddish-brown hair and freckled pink face, he was local. His eyes reached the soldiers, stopped there for a brief moment, then dropped; he went over to the bar and ordered.

I turned my attention to the three soldiers again. None of them was looking at me now, or at Jamila. Their attention was all on the farmer boy. The first one said something to the other two and they all laughed, looking like three wolves that had picked out their calf for the evening.

"Hey! Glynn!" the first soldier shouted, and the farmer boy turned to look at him. The soldier said something in the local language then, and the boy, blushing furiously, left the bar, walking slowly, unarmed, toward the soldiers. I tasted bile. Something ugly, really ugly, was going on here.

The soldier stood waiting for him, leering, and drew his sword as the boy approached. The boy stopped, heavy fists at his sides, and the soldier said something more, maybe two or three short sentences. His buddies laughed; otherwise the room had gone dead quiet. A glance showed me the innkeeper's face grim and angry, but he was keeping clear of this.

The boy stopped a couple of meters from his tormentor. "Don't speak our tongue!" he shouted in Merkan. "Ye foul it with yer foreign accent and yer filthy mind!"

The soldier's smirk remained, but his eyes narrowed. His sword moved, found a button in the boy's shirt, and flick! The button flew. "All right. In Merkan then!" the soldier said. "Would you like me to undress you here the way we undressed your sister? You'll have to buy your own whiskey though." The other two soldiers hawhawed at that.

The boy paled. Another sword flick, another button flew.

"Well!" someone said loudly. "I never heard words come out of an asshole before!"

It was me that had said it! I was on my feet, my sword in my hand, and for that moment I was so mad I was shaking. But my voice seemed as even as could be. I began to walk over to them, calming with every step. "You use that sword pretty well for cutting buttons off an unarmed boy. I wonder if you've got the guts to step over to the dance floor and dance a round with me."

And suddenly there was enough hate in his face to fill Hell with. "Gladly!" His voice was hoarse with it. "And there'll be no quick death for you," he gritted. "I'll cut pieces off you like wolves do a cow, and listen to you sing! Starting with your balls!"

He half-backed his way to the dance floor then, keeping his eyes on me. I followed. When he got there, he waited, sword ready, near enough to where I'd enter that I'd have no chance to maneuver when I stepped out. So at the last moment I snatched an empty stool and slung it at him hard. He fended it off with his free arm, but it sent him back a couple of steps, putting him off his guard, and I was at him.

I had no intention of leaving him alive, but I wasn't in any hurry to finish him, either. Which was kind of stupid; Soong would have chewed me out good. Any-

one who's a bully with a sword is going to be at least
pretty good with it. He was, too, by most standards,
but not by the Order's. I parried and thrust, pinked
him a couple of times, then saw my chance and his belt
parted, dropping his pistols on the floor. He launched a
flurry of darts and slashes then, which I parried without
riposting, and then I let him back me around the floor
until he _knew!_ Knew I could do anything I wanted with
him. Basically I was a lot better than he was, and a lot
quicker, and on top of that, I could see he wasn't used
to lefties.

Panting and sweating, he stopped. "I'm a soldier of
the count," he husked. "Kill me and you'll be hunted
down like a dog."

"I'll be doing you a favor, killing you," I told him. "If
I leave you alive, they'll laugh you out of the county
and love every minute of it."

I'd hardly said it when I heard scuffling behind me
and gave a quick glance back, at the same time jumping
to my right, away from his sword-arm side. The farmer
boy had grabbed one of the other two soldiers from
behind: the husky one, who had his sword in his hand.
They were crashing around into things. I got only a
quick glimpse, though, because the one I'd been fighting was lunging for me. I threw myself out of his way,
landing on the floor and rolling, came up slashing, and
took him through the waist to the backbone. Blood
sprayed. He screamed and fell. At almost the same
instant there was another scream. I turned to look.
The thin soldier was doing a sort of spinning-in-place
dance with his right hand behind his back, and Jamila,
pack slung over one shoulder, was beckoning me to
follow her.

As I started in her direction, the farmer boy let go
the husky soldier, who dropped to the floor like a sack.
I grabbed the boy's shoulder as I passed, and pushed
him along in front of me; he was whiter than bread
dough. By that time the thin soldier had stopped his
dance and fallen too, on his face. I could see a knife

handle sticking out between his shoulder blades; I bent
and snatched it out, wiped it on his breeches, then left.

No one tried to stop any of us. I suppose they were
scared. But I'm also pretty sure that most of them
wanted us to get away. We'd just taken care of three
guys they were well rid of.

We paused outside the door and I handed Jamila
back her knife. "Thanks," she said. The farmer boy
didn't say anything, but I could see him shaking. Actually shaking. He'd killed his man too, I had no doubt;
probably crushed his rib cage.

"My pack's in a barn a little way from here," I said.
"We'll get it and then get out of town."

FOUR

After I got my pack, we left Galway Town, bypassing
the inn and the main street, slipping along behind
outbuildings and stone fences. The chances were that
someone had gone to the village constables by now, and
that they'd sent someone, or soon would, riding up the
ridge to the fortress with the news that three soldiers
had been killed. They might take their time about it,
but not so much that they'd get in trouble with the
count. And the count's people could find out at the
inn that I was traveling east.

Unless the innkeeper and the two chapmen kept it to
themselves. But others had probably overheard us
talking.

The count was almost sure to send mounted men
after us, but it wouldn't do him much good in the dark.
I wondered what kind of troops he had up there, and
how hard they'd work to catch us. The one I'd killed
hadn't been a Connemaran, but was he the odd exception, or were most of them mercenaries?

I'd thought of taking Finnigan's two nags—the farmer
boy could ride one and Jamila and I the other—but I
wouldn't pay back Finnigan's kindness that way. I have
to admit thinking, though, what it'd be like to have her
riding behind me with her arms around my waist and

her front against my back, men's clothes or not. I'd crossed myself against any more thoughts like that.

Once out of town, we traveled on the road to start with, at a trot. Glynn—his given name was Paddy—ran like a plowhorse: thud thud thud. Not that he was necessarily clumsy, or incurably clumsy; he just wasn't used to running. I suspected he'd tire out pretty easily at it, though he could probably walk all night if he had to.

On the other hand, Jamila loped like a wolf. I don't think I'd ever seen a grown woman run before, more than a few steps. I'd never seen a grown woman who could throw a knife before, either. Not and take some-one between the shoulder blades at five or six meters. And to the hilt!

About two kilometers above town, we slowed to a walk. The road was climbing fairly steadily now, and Paddy had fallen behind, staggering and wheezing like a wind-broken horse. Carrying a pack like I was, I was feeling that way myself a bit, but Jamila didn't seem to be having any trouble at all. Which irritated me for some stupid reason.

After Paddy'd gotten his breath back some, I led off up the ridge, not running, but at a hard, driving charge. The moon hadn't risen yet, but the night was clear. Livestock had long since browsed out all the under-growth, and the trees were scattered enough that we could see as well as we needed to. I kept expecting Jamila to ask me why we'd left the road, but she didn't say a word, so when we got to the top and stopped for a breather, I volunteered it. "They should be riding out of town after us about now," I said, "but they'll stay on the road."

Paddy was still sucking wind from the fast uphill climb, and his only answer was a weary nod. Jamila didn't even do that; she seemed to be listening to something. I listened too. For half a minute I didn't hear it, and then I did—hounds! I should have known.

"Let's go," I said, and started trotting again along the ridge crest. We'd head downhill of course, but not yet. I didn't want to cross the road until we were well beyond, and out of sight of, where we'd left it. Then we'd cross it and probably go on to the river. Hopefully something would come to me, or to Jamila, before we got there, about what to do next.

Running wasn't bad on the crest, with nothing but cropped down grass between the trees. When I was ready to start downhill, I glanced back. Paddy was with me, but not Jamila. I stopped but still didn't see a sign of her. "Jamila!" I called softly, and got no answer. I could still hear the hounds, though, and took off angling down the ridge side. I had no idea at all where she was or what she was doing, but this was no time to go hunting for her.

We pounded along pretty good, running downhill, and in Paddy's case it really was pounding! Stealth didn't come naturally to him, and he hadn't picked it up. As we crossed the road, I shot a glance both ways and saw nothing. We had to be close to two kilometers beyond where we'd left it.

The far side of the river was in heavy timber. On our side there was open pasture between the road and river, except for an irregular band of big old trees near the bank. When I came to them, I stopped and looked back again, hoping to see Jamila following, maybe at a little distance. There wasn't a sign of her, nor of the dogs yet, just a group of cattle lying in the grass farther up the narrow valley, probably chewing their cuds.

We went to the river's edge. The river was about twenty meters wide, the current strong and looking smooth enough that it was probably fairly deep. The bank was a meter or so high, and I slid down it into the water. It came up to my ass, even there at the edge.

"Oh, Mister Luis!" Paddy said. "Oi can hardly swim at all! Oi'll never make it across!"

"We're not crossing," I told him. "We're going to wade along the bank. Now get down here."

He did, and I led off wading upstream, bucking the current. The dogs were hot on our trail. I could pretty much guess what the searchers would do when they reached the river. Assuming they had men and dogs enough. They'd split up, half of them crossing. Then, on each side, half would go upstream and half down, the dogs sniffing for where we came out of the water. They'd see us of course, if we were wading, and if that happened, our chances were somewhere between zero and none.

What we needed was luck. Like finding some beaver stumps, which in a river like this would mean bank beavers. Their lodge would be dug up under the bank, with an underwater entry I might be able to find. Chances were good that I could fit through, and Paddy too, probably, if I could get him to try. A husky twenty-five-kilo beaver takes a pretty large tunnel, and they'd have dug it big enough to pull branches through with them for rations.

Of course, if the lodge was occupied, we might get in serious trouble. I wasn't sure how beaver would react to intruders, and we wouldn't be able to see anything.

We didn't find any beaver stumps though. What we found, here and there, were boulders in the river, and after wading a ways, we came to a big rock that stuck up a meter above the water, about a meter and a half from the bank. The water was up to my short ribs. "This is it," I told Paddy, and explained to him that when the dogs and soldiers came, we'd keep the rock between us and them so they couldn't see us.

"What if they come along both sides of the river at the same time?"

"Won't happen," I told him. "But if it does, then we hunker down as low as we can, close against the bank, and hope they don't see us. Dark as it is, our chances ought to be pretty good."

Then was when the dogs reached the river. And of course lost our trail. Their baying broke down to a yammer of yips and barking, and no doubt some whining we couldn't hear from where we were, while they cast about sniffing the ground. *Maybe we'll get really lucky,* I thought. *Maybe the troops'll decide to heck with it and go home.*

But I didn't really imagine they would, and they didn't. Before long we could hear an occasional bark as hounds came along the bank on our side, and we moved to put the rock between us and them. We could hear voices, too, calling in Merkan, which meant that at least one of them was a mercenary. We could also hear them coming along the far side, not far behind. I muttered to Paddy to keep low, then pushing him ahead of me, started back around the rock to the bank side.

Between boulder and bank, with the sound of rushing in my ears and my head barely above water, I glanced up. There, at the top of the bank and little more than two meters from me, was the lead hound, big, and looking right at me. I stopped dead where I was, and I'd almost swear we locked eyes for what seemed like half a minute.

We couldn't have though, because instead of sounding, or jumping in after me, he put his nose back to the ground and moved on. And the half minute probably wasn't longer than four or five heartbeats, I suppose. I'm sure he saw me, and just didn't know what I was, there in the dark. Maybe he thought I was a muskrat. In my almost twenty-one years, I'd only been that scared before maybe two or three times.

More hounds passed, and after a minute, men. I heard their voices, and a horse snort. Then they were gone, on up the river, a group on each side. Pretty soon all I could hear of them was the louder barks, and these picked up for a little on our side, as if the dogs had run across a trail that distracted them. Maybe a bear, I thought. Then I heard calls from the other side. Soon after that I heard a horse come back by, and then another, with no one saying anything. They sounded as if they were cantering. The dogs came trailing after them, hardly making any noise at all.

I had no idea what was going on.

We stayed where we were for a couple of minutes longer. And it's a good thing we did, because the next thing I knew, more men and dogs came along on our side, headed back downstream, the men swearing in what was probably the local language—not Merkan anyway. I decided it was the group from the far side, and they'd crossed over.

After they'd passed, it got quiet. Pretty soon I started wading upstream again, Paddy following, neither of us saying anything. I felt mean and ugly; everything in my pack was soaked and heavy—tinder, map, all of it. The map was linen, rolled up in oilcloth to protect it from rain, but that wouldn't mean a damn thing in the river. And I didn't know whether the ink was a kind that set when it dried, or whether I'd end up with a gray and pink blur. And while I remembered the approximate route, more or less, I wouldn't remember many of the place names, or the rivers and roads or what they were called, or where I was supposed to make turns.

We were passing along a stretch where the bank was almost sheer, a rock outcrop, when I stumbled on something. Something beneath the water, that gave. For whatever reason, I bent to see what it was. What I raised was a dead man in a hauberk. I had no idea what had killed him, but he seemed fresh, not long dead. We waded upstream another hundred meters till we came to a creek that entered it from our side of the river. We waded up the creek then, out into open pasture. The water was mostly only knee deep, and we moved in a crouch, my gaze aimed down the valley toward where the troopers ought to be. Pretty soon the creek crossed the road, and I paused to straighten.

"Well done."

I stiffened at the words, even as I realized that the voice was Jamila's. She was in the creek just ahead of us, in the darker darkness beneath a tree.

"Where in the name of Blessed Jesus did you go?" I demanded. That was the first time I realized I was mad at her for disappearing.

"Up a tree till they passed on by me. I grabbed a branch and pulled myself up. Climbed high enough that they wouldn't wind me." She said it as matter-of-factly as if she were talking about the weather. "As soon as they went by, I climbed down. Then I went on past where they turned down the ridge, angled down myself, and hid near the cows."

I began to get the picture. "And I suppose you've got a sling."

She grinned. "And some two-ounce lead slugs."

Paddy sounded awed. "And you hit them in the dark?"

"No problem," she said. "There were only two of them, and I wasn't more than about twenty meters away when I let fly. What little breeze there was came from across the river, and the hounds weren't seeing anything farther away than their noses. Then, when the others had crossed the river and headed back downstream, I went down to the water, jumped in, waded upstream and followed this creek. Just the way I knew you would."

So the first two horses I'd heard going back downstream hadn't had riders anymore. I joined Paddy in awe. I don't know which impressed me more: how damned-fool reckless she'd been, or that somehow she'd gotten away with it.

"The first one fell in the water," she went on, "and I don't think the other knew what had happened. He rode over to the first one's horse and I let fly at him. He fell in too."

At twenty meters in the dark. And they'd worn helmets! Yet she'd hit them so it laid them out. In the face or the back of the neck, probably—someplace where they wouldn't have yelled, just dropped.

If even one hound had been ranging around to the side, the whole pack would have been on her.

"Luis."

I never heard her say it. Or rather, I did but it didn't register right away. I was thinking that even though it had worked out, the odds had been so poor. . . .

"Luis!"

I came out of my fuddle enough to notice her eyes on me. She looked amused. "Ma'am," I said, "excuse me but *you are crazy!*"

She laughed. "No, I'm just very, very good."

"That too."

"Let's stay with the creek all the way to its head," she went on. "We can go east from there."

"That's what I intended to do." Suddenly I was angry. *Who does she think she's ordering around?* I asked myself as we waded. Sure she'd done well, unbelievably well, but I'd done pretty damn well too. Someone had had to head for the river and leave a trail for the hounds to follow. And someone had had to take care of Paddy.

I'd hardly thought it when Jamila looked back over her shoulder. "You've been honest-to-God wonderful tonight, Luis," she said. "I was really impressed with how you took charge of things. They'd probably have murdered Paddy, back at the inn."

I stopped. Paddy walked into me from behind. "And you did better than wonderful," I told her. "Paddy and I escaped them, but you gave them casualties. What's bothering me is— Hell, I don't know what's bothering me. I'll tell you, though: I can't see how you got away with it. Killing those two soldiers."

She laughed. "I'm lucky, Luis. I'm smart, I'm fast, and I'm very skilled. I had the best teacher in the world. But most of all, I'm lucky."

It could have been me talking; that's how I thought of myself.

We kept wading till the creek was hardly even a brook, less than a meter wide, gurgling down a ravine through dense forest. From there we pushed on over the ridge and headed northeast across hills. We hiked for more than an hour, slowly, hands in front of us to keep from walking into trees and to protect our faces from brush and branches in the dark. For these woods had been neither logged nor grazed. The moon came up—not much more than a half-moon tonight, but it made the going easier—for Jamila and me. Paddy was limping from sore feet, without complaining. My clothes had only half-dried on my body, and in spite of the hard hiking, they were cold against my skin.

Jamila had been leading. On a rocky overlook she stopped, and scanned the narrow, forested valley below us on our left. "No sign of anyone around here," she said. "No smell of smoke or livestock, no sign of axe." She turned to me. "Let's go down and build a fire. We can rest and dry our stuff."

It seemed like a good idea. We sure didn't want Paddy crippled up with blisters any worse than he already was. We stopped in the bottom of a cove in the ridge, and Jamila built the fire; her pack and tinder were dry. I cut a drying pole and tied it between two stout saplings, using clematis for cord, and Paddy and I hung our shirts up to dry, plus his shoes and Jamila's and my boots. He and I kept our breeches on out of modesty. Jamila had a dry shirt in her pack, and went off a ways to change into it. All she showed us bare were feet. Next I lashed up another drying pole and hung up most of the stuff from my pack, plus the pack itself.

Including the map. I'd have to wait a few hours, till daylight, to see what damage it had taken.

Jamila added green leafy twigs to the fire for smoke, and sat hunkered down across it from me, watching the flames. She was a really good-looking lady, and in spite of myself I wondered what her body looked like inside those black clothes. Paddy lay down on the ground with his bare back to the fire, and either went to sleep or seemed to. Jamila looked up at me. I couldn't guess what she was thinking about, but I could wonder.

After a minute or so, she said, "Good night, Luis," quietly, and lay down herself. The moon was halfway around to the south; the first dawnlight would be on us before too long. I stayed awake a little longer—long enough to turn the stuff on the drying poles. Then I freshened up the fire a bit, knelt for a minute or two of prayer, and lay down. It must have taken all of a minute before I was asleep.

FIVE

By morning's light, Paddy's feet looked worse than I'd expected. He didn't have stockings of course, a farmer boy like that, and he'd gotten river sand in his clodhoppers, so they'd rubbed his feet raw.

There was a brook in the draw below, and he wanted to go down and soak them. I told him he could go wash them but not soak them, that soaking would make them softer. Wash them, wipe them with his hands, and let the air dry them. Then I gave him a pair of thick stockings to put on when his feet were dry and he'd washed all the sand out of his shoes.

I don't normally wear stockings on a trek. They wear out too fast and they cost to replace. But I carry them. They're good to have in case you pull up lame.

After Paddy'd limped off toward the brook, I sat down on a log to see how my map had come through the night. Jamila had listened to Paddy and me talking. Now she came over and sat down beside me.

"Hi, daddy," she said. "I heard you taking care of your boy. Givin' up your socks like that!" Her voice was amused, but warm, too. It embarrassed me a little, but mostly it made me feel good. I didn't know what to say back, so I just held the map so she could see it better.

Until I forced myself to, it was a little hard to study it with her sitting so close and our arms touching.

The original map lines hadn't run at all. But what had been added later—a thin route line plus additional places and their names, all in red—those had run, leaving a wash of pink.

"What's the pink?" she asked, and I told her.

"You goin' to be able to find your way to Adirondack with that? To the right place in Adirondack?" She sounded dubious.

You could pretty much tell by where the pink was that I was heading for somewhere up there. I realized then that I shouldn't have shown her the map; most of our missions were secret, and Soong had especially stressed secrecy for this one. With my mind stuck on that, I didn't answer her right away.

"Maybe we'd better use mine," she said at last.

"Yours?"

"My map." She grinned, then got up and fetched it from her pack, which hadn't gotten soaked like mine. Wading, she'd carried her pack on her head till she'd gotten to the creek with its shallow water. Now she sat down by me again and unfolded a big linen rectangle. Her map.

The base map part looked the same as mine, which by itself would have been surprising. So far as I knew, or even suspected, no one outside the Order had maps anything like that. But what actually caught my eye, at once, was the route marked on it! From Ohio to Adirondack, the inked-on route looked the same as mine had. I quit staring at the map and stared at her.

"Who sent you?" I asked.

Her grin widened. "The Order. My masters, actually: Fedor and Freddy."

The Order! My eyes must have been out on stalks. She laughed, touching my arm with long fingers to take away any sting. "I should have told you sooner," she said. "As soon as I knew you were a Brother. But it was just too much fun keeping you in the dark." She leaned sideways then and kissed my cheek, just a peck. "I suspected when I first saw you: When you know what to look for, you can pretty much recognize someone that's done spiritual exercises. And when I saw you fight, I was ninety-five percent sure."

She paused, cocking an eyebrow. "I'd have been ninety-nine percent sure if you'd killed him right away instead of fooling around with him like you did. That was dangerous!

"But you didn't suspect me because the Order's not known to accept women. I'm an experiment, Fedor told me. To see if a woman can operate as a Brother in a world like this one. So far my grades have been excellent, on mission as well as in training."

My attention was partly stuck on what she'd said and implied, about my foolishness in not disposing of the soldier quickly, back at the inn. She peered into my face and misinterpreted what was bothering me. "It was a dirty trick," she said, "and I apologize. Are we still friends?"

I smiled ruefully, and nodded.

"Your muse knew, all along," she said. "Otherwise you wouldn't have let me see your map. Your muse knew, but it seemed so unlikely, you couldn't have it up front."

It was thoughtful of her to say that. It made me feel more comfortable. And besides, I told myself, she was right. We compared information then. Each of us had been told there'd be others sent from other places, not more than one from a place. And she hadn't gotten any more briefing than I had.

Then she told me a little about herself. She'd been a member of the Order for more than ten years, starting when she was eleven. I'd been one for just less than four; hadn't started till I was almost seventeen. When I told her that, she looked really interested.

"Not to put you down," she said, "but how come

they picked you to send? With only four years training and experience?"

I grinned at her, feeling proud and sheepish both. "That's what I asked. There are Brothers in our fellowship at Aarschot as good or better than me with just about any weapon you'd want to name, including hands and feet. And more experienced as missioners. And more advanced in knowledge of self; that's been my biggest weakness." I shrugged. "But Soong and Bhatti told me they both agreed: I was the one with the greatest survival power."

Survival power didn't mean muscle, although muscle was useful and I had a lot of it. In a situation—and they put us in plently of them in training—in a situation, I was the one who most often did the right thing. One thing Soong and Bhatti would do was have all the other students attack one of us with hickory-stick swords, hands and feet, whatever. But only one was assigned to make what would be the killing stroke if a real sword was used, or if the punch or kick wasn't controlled.

And of course, they never told you who the one was. That's what the test was about. But I never failed to go for the right one—the one most dangerous to me.

Another test was, Soong or Bhatti would try to take one of us by surprise, from ambush or when we were busy with something. It almost never worked on me.

Jamila knew exactly what I meant by survivability; her masters did the same things.

We agreed to use her map, at least till I had a chance to copy the route on mine. By that time I was over the worst of my self-consciousness with her. We knew more about each other, and we'd laughed together.

Paddy came back still limping pretty badly, but as ready as he'd get, barring a few days of barefooted rest. We ate a skimpy breakfast—johnnycake, cheese, a few berries left over that I'd picked one sunny noontime, a chew each of some jerky Jamila carried—then started out, taking it slow. Every little while, in a sunny spot, we'd stop to let Paddy take off his clodhoppers and socks, so the sun and air could get at his feet. I figured the sun would help them more than anything else we had available.

As sore as they looked, I wished I could carry him.

Obviously we didn't make very good time, but I didn't mind and neither did Jamila. The two of us walked together and talked about whatever struck us, anything except the mission we were on. Beyond remembering to take rest breaks, I mostly forgot about Paddy. And he was alert enough, and thoughtful enough, to leave Jamila and me to ourselves.

The day was the most beautiful I'd ever seen, the sky bluer than I ever remembered it, with absolutely pure white clouds that got more numerous as the morning went on. The temperature was just right, with a breeze that rustled the leaves, and made waves in the grass and flowers in an occasional meadow.

You don't run into many wild meadows in Allegheny, and seeing them made me wonder if maybe they were just there for that day—that maybe we'd made them by being there and feeling the way we felt, Jamila and me, and tomorrow they'd be gone. I never have known the names of many flowers, but there were lots of them there, lots of different kinds. I thought about picking some to give Jamila, but at first I couldn't quite bring myself to. She might think I was being foolish, because she could see them just like I did, live and moving. Then she picked some and gave them to me, and it was all I could do not to kiss her.

After a skimpy noon meal, we napped awhile in the sun, then trekked again. By early evening, the only sun came through gaps in the clouds. They were reddening above the hills to the west when we came out into a broad open valley. Up the valley to our left was Kings Town. The main part of town looked about two kilometers long and maybe one and a half wide, with a stone wall around it. Pretty impressive. The town had grown

some since the wall had been built, the newer parts
being outside it, with a field of fire kept clear between
the wall and the buildings outside. A ways to our right,
quite a bit south of the suburb, we could see an army
camped. I supposed it was getting ready to go fight the
invaders from Lankster.

In the suburb, on the main road, was a good-sized
inn, and we stopped there. By that time it was starting
to get dark, and they didn't have any rooms left. We
settled for buying supper, which cost more than we
were used to paying.

While we waited for our food, a man came over to us,
wearing a military uniform. He'd been eating with three
other guys in uniform, and they watched as he stopped
at our table.

"Can I sit down with you?"

"Sure," I told him.

He pulled up a stool from the next table. "You people look as if you've been on the road awhile."

"Awhile."

"You hungry?"

"We're taking care of that now. What is it you want?"

"I'm recruiting for the King's army. You look like
officer material. And your friend here"—he motioned at
Paddy—"looks like he'd make a fine soldier. The pay's
six bits a day for lieutenants, four for sergeants, and two
for common soldiers. Plus all you can eat and two
stoups of beer at the end of the day."

"I don't think so," I said. "Sounds good but . . ."

"You won't have to leave your lady, either. An officer's allowed to keep one with him." He looked her
over and smirked. I had this impulse to punch him
right on the nose. "If she wants," he added, "she can
turn a nice profit on the side."

I glanced at Jamila. Her smile looked a little thin,
and her eyes glinted.

It occurred to me that it might be best not to turn
this guy down flat. String him along and then slip away.

"Tell you what," I said. "Let me think about that and talk it over with my friends. I presume the King's officers play cards; I just might be able to turn six bits a day into something better."

He nodded, got up, shook my hand, and went back to his table. "How did you get so good with cards?" Jamila asked.

"I'm not. But I lie pretty good when trouble's on the line."

About that time our food arrived, and while we ate, I noticed the recruiter and his friends looking over at us a couple of times. I decided they weren't done with us yet. When we'd mostly finished our meal, the serving girl came over with three stoups of beer.

"From the gentleman over there," she said. I looked. The recruiter smiled and raised his mug. I waved acknowledgement to him as the serving girl walked away.

"Don't drink," I said quietly. "Unless you want to wake up in the King's army with a headache you'll remember forever."

We finished our stew, then pretended to drink. If it was what I thought, it would be plain soon enough that we'd faked it. So as soon as we'd set our mugs down, we shouldered our packs, then started for the door and whatever security we might find in the thickening twilight outside. We got all the way out, too, but the recruiter and his three buddies were only a few steps behind. They wore swords, but their hands were on their pistols.

"Fellow," the recruiter said, "you insulted me."

"How so?"

"I bought you drinks and you didn't drink them."

His friends had spread out enough that, between the four of them, they had us hemmed in. "What makes you think we didn't . . ." I began. My words were a feint, a cover. By the time I got the *didn't* out, my sword was free. It darted up under his ribs and out again before he had time to fall, then I slashed at his nearest buddy, taking his upper arm to the bone as he drew his gun. He screamed and fainted. Jamila had another down and dead by that time. The fourth turned and ran without drawing either sword or pistol, yelling for help.

We ran the other way.

Paddy surprised me in two ways. He got away a few steps behind us, but even on raw feet he kept pace, which took a toughness to pain that not many could match. And besides that, in the brief moment of fighting he'd had the presence of mind not only to grab the recruiter's sword, but his belt with its scabbard!

There was more to Paddy Glynn than muscles.

We slowed a step to let him catch up, and scuttled into a lane that ran between houses—frame cottages with thatched roofs, a strange combination. Glancing back, I saw someone on horseback turn in behind us, trotting his horse easily, not trying to close the gap. I turned down the next lane, ran a dozen meters, and stopped.

Jamila had her sling out of her belt pouch by then, with a two-ounce slug in place and ready. The horse and rider made the turn and halted. "Peace," he called quietly. He wore a wrapper wound round his head, like the people in a district I'd passed through in Hoozh. But he wasn't a Seek. The Seeks have big beards, and this guy didn't have any at all.

"What do you want?" I asked him.

He nudged his horse a few meters closer while raising his hands to the side, palms showing empty. "I saw what fighters you are, back there. I am traveling northeast to Adirondack, and from all reports, I would do well to have bodyguards. I would like to hire you."

I let my body relax. "What's the pay?"

"Six bits a day each. I will provide food, horses, and lodging for you. Upon our arrival at my destination, I will have my associates pay each of you an additional ten dollars in silver. And you may keep the horses."

"Adirondack? Hmh! That's a long way out of our way."

He shrugged, his eyes never leaving my face.

"When would we leave?" I asked.

"Considering what you did outside the inn, it will be best to leave tonight. We will go up the valley a few kilometers and pay some farmer to let us sleep in his barn. The constabulary may sweep the immediate vicinity here, but they will not mount a broad search for you. Since the army has been here, murders are common."

He sounded straight, though he talked funny—more high-class than even my mother—and his offer sounded good. But . . . It wasn't that I didn't trust him. I trusted him absolutely—to kill us or have us killed, if we let him. "Where'll we meet you?" I asked.

He seemed to think for a moment. Some of the yards there had low stone fences like those in Galway Town. "Take cover somewhere along the lane," he said. "Behind a fence. I will obtain horses and return as quickly as I can."

"Right," I said. "We'll be here."

He turned his horse and trotted off.

Poor Paddy. His face had turned absolutely joyous, listening to the hooded man and his offer. Now, when I said, "Let's get out of here," it fell like a puffball.

"But . . ." he objected.

"You can stay if you'd like," I told him, "but that was a Lizard. A devil."

It just blurted out, taking me by surprise. I don't lie just for the heck of it, and seldom to my friends. But unlikely as it sounded, even to me—especially to me—Paddy never questioned what I'd said. We started hiking, and turned east at the next lane as the first isolated raindrops fell. They took me by surprise. For the first time I noticed how low and heavy the clouds had gotten while we were eating.

We turned at a couple of cross-lanes, and in a few

minutes were out of the suburb, south of it, headed east through farmland toward the hills. Scattered raindrops kept falling without increasing much, but the sky, from which nearly all daylight had faded, threatened more and heavier. And there were Paddy's feet to consider.

Here by the city, the farms were large, their steadings separate. A hundred meters farther was a solitary farmhouse, set back from the road, with a good-sized barn and attached cowshed. As we got closer, I could smell the cowshit.

A large dog charged barking, to threaten us from beyond sword-reach. He quieted when I spoke to him, though his hackles stayed half-up and he growled a little, deep in his throat. I've always gotten along with dogs. I told Jamila and Paddy to stay back enough that she wouldn't be recognized as a woman, then we went to the farmhouse and I knocked at the door. A middle-aged man answered, short and stocky, with slanty eyes. He had an accent that reminded me of Chickwan County, back in Mizzoo, and quite a few other places I'd been. For two bits he agreed we could sleep in his barn, then spoke sharply to the dog and closed the door.

The rain was picking up a little as the three of us went to the barn, groped and found the ladder in the dark, and climbed into the hayloft. Faint light came in through the large hay door. Paddy spread some hay and took off his shoes, then flopped down without a word, still wearing my socks.

I sat down cross-legged a little back from the hay door, where I could watch the lane without being seen. It seemed unreasonable that our would-be employer could follow us here, yet somehow I felt a need to keep watch. For a while anyway.

The rain began to fall steadily but still lightly, muttering faintly on the roof. I hoped it would quit by morning—wet shoes would be a real problem for Paddy. I took my own off and wiggled my toes. Jamila came over and sat down beside me.

"You're doing a good job, Luis," she said, and put a hand on my arm. "I'm proud of you."

"Thanks." It occurred to me that with all those years of training and experience, she'd probably have done better than I had. But then I realized she might not have: Most people wouldn't want to deal with a woman except *as* a woman. Which could cause problems. In fact, I might have resisted accepting her as equal to a man, if I hadn't gotten to know her in a jam—three jams now—and seen how she operated.

"Not as good as I should have," I answered. "I blew an opportunity. If we'd jumped the guy that wanted to hire us, Paddy could have ridden his horse."

"Don't second-guess yourself," she said quietly. "Figure that what you did was probably right, however it looks."

She said that like Bhatti would have, or Soong. It was all that training. Only, Soong and Bhatti wouldn't have said "*probably* right." Maybe she'd thought I couldn't accept it without the *probably*.

"And we don't know how tough a Lizard would be in a fight," she added.

"A Lizard?"

"Sure. You said it yourself: he's a Lizard."

Huh! Why not? Although my eyes hadn't seen it. We'd been fairly close but it had been three-fourths dark out.

"My muse said it," I told her. "I guess I wasn't paying attention." Bhatti and Soong had told me more than once not to argue with my warrior muse. Ride with it. And I guess I do, but sometimes I don't believe it afterwards.

Jamila chuckled, a nice throaty sound. "What does your muse think about me?" she asked.

"I don't know. He hasn't said yet."

We sat there saying nothing then for a couple of minutes. Paddy started to snore. Not loudly, though, and I hoped it stayed that way. I was strongly aware of

Jamila now as a woman, and my muse, one of my muses, was sending me signals: my loins were stirring. I needed to squirm around a little and make adjustments, but I couldn't while she was there beside me.

So I got up, as if I could see out the door better on my feet. Nothing was moving in the lane. "Be nice to know," Jamila said, "if Lizards can see better in the dark than we can."

After I'd adjusted my breeches, I stayed on my feet, still watching, but back a little farther from the door. My warrior muse had nothing to tell me about how well Lizards saw at night, but it might pay to assume they saw pretty well.

Jamila got up too, and stood beside me. Tentatively I reached out and put an arm around her waist. We stood there like that for a minute or so, then she moved closer so we were touching hip and shoulder. It got a little hard to breathe. I had a big lump in my throat and another somewhere else. She was nothing at all like the occasional girl that'd come my way before. There'd only been two, actually, both before I'd joined the Order. Since then I'd avoided getting involved with women at all, on the theory that they'd distract me from training or missions. Besides, all the Orders have a low tolerance for womanizing, and unlike some Orders, the Order of Saint Higuchi forbids its members to marry.

So I removed my arm and took refuge in talk. "Tell me about yourself," I said, "and Shy Town. How did you get in the Order?"

"Well," she said, "Shy Town's on the Plains River, a few kilometers inland from the Sea of Mishgun. The townsite is sandy, and where it's not built on, it's old dunes partly overgrown with oaks. But there's a lot of wet prairie around, and people graze a lot of cattle. When I was ten, cattle raiders killed my daddy. And my mama, though not quickly enough. You know."

I did know. My Kansas mission had been to eliminate a gang something like that.

"Mama had hid me in the loft of the house, and while I couldn't see from up there, I could hear. So as soon as the raiders left, I came down.

"I wanted to kill them, so I got my dad's butchering knife and followed their trail." She paused, shaking her head and cluckling ruefully like a guy might have. "Their herd dogs spotted me, and I climbed a bur oak tree to keep from getting torn up. The raiders thought that was pretty funny. They gathered round and told me to come down or they'd send someone up to drag me down. I wasn't about to, though. I knew what would happen. So their honcho sent one of them up after me.

"While they were watching him climb around trying to catch me, a Higuchi team, Alexei and Victorio, took them by surprise and killed them all. All but the one in the tree: I slashed his face and then his hand, and he fell out. After Vic and Alec had run the dogs off—they had to shoot two of them to do it—I jumped down and cut his throat. Then Vic and Alex took me with them to the Brother House—after they convinced me they weren't like the raiders. And Fedor and Freddy let me stay and help the cook for a while. . . ."

The dog began to bark, alerting me. Someone was walking along the lane, leading a horse, moving something back and forth ahead of him, almost as if sweeping with it like a blind man with a stick.

The dog was going berserk now, three times as upset as he'd been with us. *Lizard*, I thought. A hound would know. He was right out by the edge of the lane, raging. Whoever it was took something out from under his cloak, something that might have been a short saddle musket, and pointed it one-handed at the dog. But there wasn't any bang, just a thin brief line of light that found the dog and silenced it instantly.

Then the horseman scanned around, taking in house, barn, fields. Finally he started on again, still sweeping the lane with whatever it was, and passed the barn.

When he'd gone thirty meters past, I turned and headed for the ladder, Jamila half a step behind.

"Where are you going?" she whispered.

"To get Paddy a horse. And get my hands on whatever the Lizard used on the dog."

She didn't say anything, just followed me down the ladder. There was a worm fence on our side of the lane and a low stone fence on the other. She slipped across the lane, black in the night and with no more noise than a shadow, and went over the fence without dislodging a stone. I moved along after the Lizard, or whatever he was, crouching low behind the fence on my side, certain that Jamila was keeping pace. The ground was wet beneath my bare feet, the stones hard, the rain a soft murmur on the land.

About sixty or seventy meters down the lane, the Lizard stopped again, and I stopped too. He stood there for a moment, staring back at the barn, then swung up into the saddle and, turning the horse around, touched spurs to it. I could see his saddle gun in one hand, and I held very still. When he was about even with me, I made a grunting noise, a bit like an old sow, loud enough to hear easily. I did it just once, so it would be hard to locate, but he could tell which side of the road it came from.

He stopped. I heard a nasty thud, and with a cry he pitched foward off the horse. He wasn't dead or even unconscious, but scrambled to his feet, stumbling, and peered under the horse's neck, gun ready. There was another thud, and the horse reared, making the Lizard scrabble backward. I was over the fence then, sword in hand, and on the guy, striking. He never knew what hit him.

The horse had started off up the road, but I didn't worry about that. I got the gun, which had a shoulder sling, and cross-slung it over my back. Then I examined the whatever-it-was; what I'd been thinking of as the Lizard. I'd just about cut its head off, but there hadn't been any great spray of blood. Now I cut it off the rest of the way. Something liquid was oozing out of the neck, but not in any big quantity. It wasn't dark, either, and it didn't feel or smell like blood. I picked the head up and pulled the wrapping off it. I couldn't see any hair, only a crest kind of like a chicken's comb, but stiffer and maybe six or seven centimeters tall.

Jamila had caught and mounted the horse, and it was circling in the road, kind of half bucking, while she talked to it, calming it. I walked toward them, then waited a little ways off till it was standing quietly.

"Sorry," she said to me. "I was too far back when you made your noise, and I seem to have missed his head. That stone fence is so low, I needed to go on all fours to keep under cover."

"It's all right," I said. "That way you were back where you could catch the horse." I held the head up by the crest. "Let's go knock on the farmer's door again. I want to see what this looks like in the light."

When we got to the farmhouse, I gave Jamila the Lizard gun. Taking it, she led the horse toward the barn. I knocked at the door. The farmer opened it enough to peer out at me.

"Did you hear your dog a few minutes ago?" I asked. He nodded.

"Somebody was snooping around. I saw him do something and your dog fell dead. So I snuck out and killed whoever it was; I think it was a Lizard."

The farmer hissed, a sharp intake of breath.

"But it's too dark out here to see what he looks like. Can I bring the head in by the fire?"

He didn't say anything for a minute, then nodded and stepped back from the door. I went in. There was a kid inside, a boy maybe fifteen years old, with a musket in his hands, watching with scared eyes. I went over by the fireplace and kneeling, laid the head on the hearth.

The crest was blue, and not only was there no scalp, there was no hair at all—no whiskers, no eyebrows, not even lashes. But the strangest thing was the eyes. A little bigger than a normal person's, the white of the one was purest white, while the other was amber red! Not bloodshot—red was its color! There was something obscene about it, the two being so much different.

The nose, though, wasn't really different from ours. And the face was tan and pink; the skin could have passed for human. Except—it didn't quite look natural. When I rubbed it with a firm finger, the tan and pink came off, leaving a streak of golden yellow and showing smooth dry scales, finer than any fish I knew about, or any grass snake's. Even so, if it hadn't been for the eyes, it wouldn't have been bad looking, alive.

The blood from the neck was nearly colorless.

The farmer was kneeling beside me, staring harder than I was. When we got up, he started talking in whatever his lingo was to his wife and son, talking fast but not loud. The kid swung the muzzle of his musket toward me and I grabbed the farmer around the neck for a shield, drawing my knife.

"Boy," I said, "point that musket at the roof, or your father dies."

He raised it a little, enough that I wasn't looking down the barrel. "At the *roof!*" I snarled, and the barrel tilted upward.

"Why'd he point that thing at me?" I asked.

"If you have killed a Lizard," the farmer said, "surely the devils will come out of Hell to get you. I do not want them to think we had anything to do with it."

"I see." And I did. "What's your son's name?"

"Ezekial."

Ezekial. At least they were Christians. "Ezekial," I said, "lower that hammer very carefully, or I'll run this knife into your daddy's heart."

Very soberly he lowered the hammer. From the corner of my eye I saw movement at the open door; Jamila was there with her sword in her hand.

"Now," I continued, "put the gun on the floor where you are and go stand with your face to the wall."

I watched him do it. The farmer's wife had a meat knife in her hand. I met her eyes and she laid it aside, putting it down as if the handle were hot. Jamila came in then, picked the musket up, and recocked it.

"Okay, farmer," I said, "you don't need to worry. We'll leave before daylight. And the Lizard—you can bury it in the morning or stuff it down the privy. Or bury it in the manure pile; that's a good place for it. Nobody'll ever know. It ought to cook down pretty good in sour cowshit."

He nodded.

"We could easily kill all three of you," I added, "but we won't. We are good people, not bad. But we are very, very deadly, so deadly we can kill Lizards. We'll take your musket now, so you won't do anything foolish with it, but we'll leave it in your barn when we go, because we are not thieves."

I let the man loose then, turned my back on them, and walked to the door, carrying the head. Jamila covered me with the musket. Outside, the light rain had just about quit. I took the Lizard head down the backyard path and dropped it on the ground outside the privy. Then I trotted down the road to the body, hoisted it over my shoulder, and carried it to the privy too, flopping it down beside the head. Going through its pockets and belt pouch, I found a little bag full of coins, and took them.

While I was doing all this, Jamila had gone into the barn. Now she came out with a rod-like thing, metallic-looking, with little things sticking out of it. It seemed to be what the Lizard had used to track us. She laid it down by the body.

"You throwing that away?" I asked.

She nodded. "I've got a feeling—" she began, then didn't finish.

I picked it up, hefting it. Surprisingly light. "Maybe we can learn how to use it," I told her. "I don't mind carrying it. For a while, anyway."

She shook her head. "Leave it," she said, and changed the subject. "We need to take care of the horse. Then we can go upstairs and sleep."

I tossed it down, shrugging—my warrior muse wasn't saying anything on the subject—and we started for the barn. "Suppose the farmer sneaks out tonight and goes to the constabulary," I said.

"He won't," she answered. I didn't ask why. We went in and walked over to where she'd tied the Lizard's horse; she unbuckled the bellyband and hoisted off the saddle. In the dark I didn't know where the farmer kept stuff, so after taking the bit out of his mouth, I used the bridle as a halter, tying it to a post by the reins. While we worked, she started to explain her muse. "I doubt these people trust the constabulary. And anyway they look at this as a matter of Lizards and Lizard magic. If they go to anyone about it, it'll be the priest."

I'd never thought much about magic. Never considered that I'd seen any. But now . . . Was the thin beam of light, the beam that had killed the watchdog, a magic of some kind? I remembered something Bhatti'd said once: that magic was just a word, a word for anything that was strange enough and you didn't understand.

"Do you think it's magic?" I asked her.

It was too dark down there to see a grin, but I was sure she wore one. "I believe in what I see. I saw the Lizard kill the dog with a gun that shoots light. The farmer would call it magic. I don't feel like I need to call it anything."

I went up in the loft, threw down some hay, and we used some of it to rub the horse down with. Most we put in front of him to eat, and on the floor as bedding for him. Then Jamila went back to the ladder and I followed her. The rain had taken on new strength while we'd worked, and the hayloft was filled with the soft drumming of it on the shingled roof. An easy sound to go to sleep by. But somehow we started kissing, then I started exploring Jamila's shirt. After that . . .

It wasn't like laying with the other girls I'd laid with. With Jamila there was a feeling that I don't know any other name for than love. It was an hour before we got dressed again and went to sleep.

I woke up to a deep humming outside that wasn't like anything I'd ever heard before. It was still night. Both of us went to the hay door to look out, but whatever it was, we couldn't see it from there, so we buckled on our swords and went back down the ladder to peer out the door.

Some fifty or sixty meters above the privy, a *thing* was floating, in the air, settling downward. "What the Hell!" I whispered, and hoped that wasn't where it came from. At a guess, it was eight or ten meters long, three or four wide, and—I don't know, maybe three high. I could see dim light coming out of it through windows. My hair stood up like the watchdog's hackles; there had to be Lizards inside.

As it lowered, a broad beam of light, pale violet, came out the bottom of it, and when it got down to a meter or so from the ground, the thing sprouted arms. We watched it lift the dead Lizard's body up into itself, then the head, and the tracking tool. Gooseflesh washed over me in waves. Now I'd seen magic!

Nothing more happened for a minute or so. Then the thing, the airboat, rose up to fifty or sixty meters again. Suddenly a different beam of light shot out of it, bright hard green, looking as if you couldn't cut it with an axe. It struck the farmhouse and played over it. The house burst into flame, almost as if the whole thing had caught at once—roof, timbers, floor, furniture. . . . people. It only burned for a few minutes, four or five maybe, before it was down to a heap of glowing rubbish smoking in the rain.

By the time I thought to look up at the airboat again, it was gone.

When we got back up in the loft, Paddy was still

asleep. He'd missed the whole thing. We hardly talked at all about how the airboat, or the Lizards in it, could have known where the dead Lizard was. If they knew that, what else did they know? Apparently not that the Lizard's killers were in the barn, or they'd have roasted us instead of the farmer and his family.

Mostly we talked about what we'd do next, keeping it short and simple. We'd stay the night where we were, and leave at dawn.

Then we settled down and went back to sleep.

SIX

I woke up to Paddy tugging on my sleeve. "Luis! Luis! My God! The house has burned down! Burned to the ground! And the people in it—if anyone had got out alive, they'd have come to the barn, but there's no one! No one but us!"

I sat up, thick-witted.

"Oi went out to take a piss and—it was gone." He was waving his hands like he was trying to dry them. "You can smell it. Like a great lunch-fire that's been rained on."

The loft was lighter than it had been. I got up and stuck my head out the hay door. The clouds were breaking up, and while there wasn't a trace of dawn yet, it wouldn't be long; the waning half-moon was peeking at me from well up the sky.

Jamila had stepped up beside me, looking too. "We might as well start," she said.

"Right." I could detect pigshit through the smell of horse and cow manure. But to butcher a piglet and roast some meat would take time, and just now it seemed like right away was the best time to leave.

We climbed down. I could see a little now, by the moonlight that filtered in. The farmer had a team, though no saddle we could find. Hopefully one was broken for riding; we'd find out soon enough. Jamila put a bridle on one of them and cut off the reins to riding length, while I saddled the Lizard's horse—I dubbed him "Luck," because for us he was. By the time we were ready, Paddy had milked half-a-bucket of milk, warm and sweet, which we swilled down for breakfast, all we could hold. Then, while I held off the sow with a pitchfork, he caught a weanling pig. He tied one of the cutoff reins around it, behind the forelegs, with a loop flipped around its neck.

With that we left, Jamila and I riding Luck, and Paddy on the farmer's horse, with the pig first dragging and finally trotting behind on its tether. We left the farmer's musket behind, but carried the Lizard's strange short gun in its saddle sheath. There still wasn't a trace of dawnlight, but we left feeling good.

We bypassed Kings Town on the south, and again on the east. While we rode, we told Paddy about the Lizard, and how the airboat torched the house, and showed him the Lizard gun. In the east, the sky began to pale. After a couple kilometers, the poor darned pig was about used up, so I hog-tied it with its tether and let the mare carry it, running the tether under the mare's belly behind Paddy. The pig squealed bloody murder for a while, but finally quieted.

Before we got to the high road, I stopped by a big cottonwood tree, took the Lizard's gun from its boot, and tried it out. It was easy to use, and noiseless. And it not only zapped off a piece of bark as big as my palm; it also burned a two-inch-deep hole in the wood beneath. Paddy swore and crossed himself; I was pretty darned impressed too.

When we reached the east-west high road, there was already a trickle of travelers heading east. The sky was silver ahead of us, and only a few bright stars could still be seen. We'd only gone a little way before we saw a cluster of people stopped at a bridge ahead. A squad of the king's soldiers was out early, and seemed to be questioning them. I made sure I could get the Lizard gun out of its boot quick and slick and ready to fire.

As we approached, five of the soldiers came over to us. " 'Ey dere," a grinning sergeant called, " 'ere's some look just right to go fight de Lanksters. And you, cher," he said to Jamila, "I never see one like you before! You look just right to go 'long de army and 'elp keep it 'appy, 'ey?" He turned his attention to me then. "You got a warrant of exemption, mon ami?"

They weren't looking for murderers; they were an impressment section looking for battle fodder. Several travelers were squatting off to one side with a guard over them. I saw now that they were chained together by wrist irons. Our sergeant had the hammer back on his pistol; at least one other had his musket cocked. They were the ones I cut down with the Lizard gun. The sergeant's pistol went off as I hit him; we were lucky he didn't hit one of us. The others fell back in dismay; two dropped their muskets and raised their hands before I even told them to. Jamila was off the horse in an instant, disarming them—swords, pistols, everything—then made them take off their boots and socks.

"Come down here," she said to Paddy, "and see if any of these fit you."

Besides the soldiers, about a dozen people, mostly chained, had watched the whole thing. They'd been as scared as the soldiers when I'd used the Lizard gun, but now, seeing their captors disarmed and barefoot, they brightened up. Jamila released the captives while Paddy sized up the boots and tried on a pair. I'm not sure he knew what a good fit was—whether he'd ever had one or not—but they were better than his harsh, stiff, coming-apart clodhoppers.

I trotted over to where the troops had picketed their horses and selected two, for Jamila and Paddy. I kept Luck. We gave the others to the travelers, along with the rest of the boots, kept the two pistols we found, and threw the other weapons in the river. Then we sent the soldiers hobbling barefoot back toward Kings Town, no doubt cursing us. Most of the civilians were still watching as Jamila and I pulled the corpses off onto the roadside, straightened their limbs, closed their eyes, and weighted the lids with pennies, then wished their souls well. The way the Brothers are taught to do when they have time. It helps ease the evicted souls, and reminds us, if we need reminding, that death is a personal thing to the people it claims.

There was a crossroad a hundred meters past the bridge, and I turned south on it. Paddy wasn't surprised; he didn't know any better. Jamila didn't seem surprised either. It was as if she knew what I had in mind, but it might be she just trusted my muse and me. People who'd seen what had happened at the bridge were sure to talk about it, so let them see us turn south. We went about two kilometers, then turned around and headed back north, the direction we needed to go. By the time we got back to the highway, the people along there hadn't seen us before and didn't pay us much attention. We crossed it and went on north up the valley.

The road kept near the east side of it. The ridges were timbered, but the bottomland was mostly cleared, the ground fertile and the crops good. Here and there along the road were woods though, and around midmorning we rode back into one of them, out of sight of any travelers. There, while Jamila and Paddy got a fire going, I butchered the pig, and we had roast pork for our first real food of the day.

I was ready for a nap then, but Paddy was looking at me as if he had a question. "What do you want to ask me?" I said.

"Well, sir, oi was hopin'—hopin' you'd take the time to start teachin' me the sword. Oi mean, us bein' companions now, ye know."

"How about this evening?" I said.

"I'll give him a lesson now," Jamila put in. "It'll do me good. Paddy, go cut a couple of saplings about like this." She made a ring of thumb and forefinger to show the size to get, and he went off, knife in hand. I looked her over.

"Don't be too hard on him," I said, then lay back down. I felt too full just then for sparring.

When they were ready, I sat up to watch. Her basic technique was flawless, but it was hard to judge how good she actually was because she was keeping it simple, and doing everything in slow motion so he could see. I was fairly impressed at how quickly he was getting the first principles. When they'd worked together for a quarter hour or so, she stopped and turned to me.

"You and I need to go a round, Luis, so Paddy can see what it looks like when someone's gotten really good. That slime gob back in Galway Town didn't give you half a workout."

I lay there looking pained. A demonstration for Paddy was at best a secondary reason for the invitation, I was sure. She wanted to test me. Which was fine. I got up and warmed up, then we faced off and started. I wasn't doing badly at all, and decided I was at least as good as she was. Then she opened up, and before long I'd been touched in enough places that I'd have been bleeding to death if our "swords" had been steel instead of chestnut.

She backed off and stopped. "You're good," she said. "Damn good."

Considering that she'd beaten me, I wasn't sure how sincere she was, but I settled for it. "Thanks," I said, and turned to Paddy. "You'll probably never see anyone better than Jamila with a sword. Protect her back and she could have killed that whole damn squad back there by herself, in a sword fight. And looked around for more."

She looked pleased. Paddy looked awed. We kicked

dirt on the fire then, left the remains of the pig, and started up the valley again. That afternoon Jamila bought a loaf, a big sausage, and a slab of cheese from a farmwife, and we swigged down some buttermilk at the springhouse. Later we paused where a good-sized creek came down out of the hills to cross the road, and rode up it into the woods a way, to bathe. Jamila borrowed a gob of my soap and rode up a little farther than we did, to save Paddy's nerves, I suppose, or keep him from embarrassing himself with a hard-on. There was moss on rocks along the bank, and when we'd stripped, he and I scrubbed one another with it to save soap. While I dressed, I thought how I'd rather have washed Jamila, and my conscience started bothering me. I'd have to stop in a village somewhere and confess myself for what happened the night before.

By then, thunderclouds were building. After drought all across Hoozh and Ohio, it seemed as if it wanted to rain at least once a day now. Once, looking up, I saw what had to be an airboat, a little spot moving against the blue. High as it was, I'd never have noticed it, except that what we'd seen the night before had made me aware of them.

"Look!" I said pointing, and they both looked. It disappeared into a cloud.

"What?" Paddy asked. "Oi don't see anything."

Jamila had, though; her face looked troubled. "An eagle, Paddy," I told him. "It's moved out of sight now." I'm not sure why I lied. Maybe because, not having seen it, Paddy might wonder if I was trying to play a joke on him. Or maybe I just didn't want to worry him.

The sun was shining right then, but somehow things seemed a little darker.

We passed through several villages during the day, but I didn't take the time to see a priest. By hindsight, I didn't really feel remorse. In early evening we came to a village called Bergerac. It had an inn at the near edge, and we decided to spend the night there. The weather looked too threatening to sleep in the woods if we didn't have to, and Jamila and I agreed that we might as well spend some of the Lizard's silver.

The inn had its own stable. We left our horses there, paid the stableboy, and went into the inn. I carried my Lizard gun with me, in my pack with the business end sticking out. That way it didn't look at all like a gun, what you could see of it. For one thing, there wasn't any hole in what I'd have otherwise called a barrel.

The food was the best I'd ever eaten in a village inn, and we had wine instead of beer. We didn't spend any more time in the taproom than we had to, though, just enough to finish supper and a second drink. We didn't feel comfortable now, with so many people around; at least Jamila and I didn't. Our last two inns, at Galway Town and Kings Town, had proven dangerous. Get up to our room and out of sight, that was my thought, and by the way Jamila knocked back the last of her wine and got up from the table, she felt the same way.

I'd actually considered taking two rooms, one for her and me and one for Paddy, but somehow it didn't seem all right to split up like that. Not for the reason I had. And I wasn't sure what Jamila would think; it might be taking too much for granted. Anyway a hired boy took the three of us up the stairs and showed us the room that was ours. It had one wide bed—the usual thing in inns—wide enough for three to sleep longways or five crossways.

With the sun down it was getting dark out, so we took off our boots, took the pistols out of our belts, and arranged ourselves in bed with Jamila in the middle. I'd have to be chaste tonight, which I wouldn't have minded if I'd been sleepy in the first place, but I wasn't.

I don't think any of us was asleep yet when Jamila sat bolt upright. "We need to get out of here," she hissed, and clambered over me to the floor.

"What is it?" I murmured.

She just shook her head, pulled on her boots and

started lacing them. Paddy and I piled out then, too. Paddy looked worried and unhappy; I suspect he'd never slept in a real bed before, and now he was losing out on the experience. He took longer than Jamila and I to get his boots laced and tied, but he hurried. Then we grabbed our packs. Jamila had shoved her pistol into her pack, so I put mine in my pack too, without asking why. She seemed to know what she was doing.

She was out the door first, and in the hall she turned not toward the stairway but toward the end that ended at a window. The shutters were open for air and light, and when we got there, she climbed out onto the roof of a built-on section, sliding down it to the edge, where she dropped her pack off and then jumped. I followed her to the edge and dropped my pack off too, Lizard gun and all.

Paddy looked worried; it was close to four meters down. I could hear commotion in the hall, and decided I'd better get him off first, or he might not do it, not quickly enough. "Jump," I hissed at him. He compromised. He went over the edge on his belly and clung for a moment.

"Here they are!" someone shouted from the window. He wasn't three meters from us. Paddy let go. I followed, landed rolling, and snatched up my pack. A pistol roared—Jamila's; she could see the window from where she stood. I pulled the Lizard gun out as I slung the pack on one shoulder, and we all took off for the stable while a body slid slowly down the roof and off the edge. There were two shots from the window, but they didn't hit any of us.

Our horses weren't saddled or bridled, of course, and in the darkening stable we couldn't have told which were ours anyway. The stableboy was just about to take the bit from the mouth of someone else's animal, and pausing, I boosted a surprised Paddy aboard. "Get!" I barked, and slapped the animal on the rump. It bolted for the back door, which was open for the light, and Jamila and I followed. I hoped Paddy could stay in the saddle—he wasn't much of a rider—but I didn't wait to watch. Jamila and I both sprinted in the other direction for the cover of a hedge, scrambled through a gap, ran behind a nearby house and across someone's kitchen garden into an apple orchard. From there we slowed to a trot, turning north into a lane lined on both sides with intermittent hedges.

There we stopped. "Now what?" I asked.

Her answer took me by surprise. "I don't know."

"Okay," I said. "Let's get behind a hedge and wait awhile. Then we'll go get our horses."

She shook her head. "We'll wait awhile, but forget the horses."

I shrugged. We went through a gap and hid till it was darker. I crouched there feeling bad about losing Paddy, but even with socks and better boots, his feet were in lousy shape for dashing around trying to dodge Lizards or whatever was after us. I'd done the right thing.

According to Bhatti and Soong, a warrior in close touch with his muse always does the right thing, even when it doesn't seem like it. And if you start second-guessing your muse, it may quit talking to you. Lots of people hardly ever hear from theirs.

Of course, a lot of that's from penalties.

Finally, when it was about three-fourths dark, Jamila got up and went back through the gap, with me close behind. She moved as if she had something definite in mind, and my muse told me to follow hers just now. We didn't backtrack, but I quickly realized she was taking us to the inn again. *Changed her mind*, I thought. *We're going to get our horses after all.* I'd hold the stableboy at knifepoint, I decided, while she saddled them.

But that wasn't what she'd had in mind. She remembered seeing a ladder lying behind the inn—I hadn't noticed it at all—and she leaned it against the wall below the window of our room. We went up it, then left it there in case we needed to run for it again. Our room seemed like the last place they'd look for us now, whoever "they" were.

After bolting the door, we went back to bed. This time we took off more than just our boots. Actually, she did, so I did. I felt a little nervous at first, being in bed with no clothes on and enemies around; it seemed reckless and irresponsible. If we'd been like that before, the Lizards or whoever they were would have gotten us for sure. But soon enough I forgot about worrying.

SEVEN

It was Jamila who awakened me. Judging by how dark it was, either the moon wasn't up yet or it was clouded over. I remembered what had happened earlier, and somehow didn't want to be awake. "Let's go," she murmured. I swung my feet out of the bed with a bad feeling, an unwillingness to face this day.

We'd put our clothes back on after making love, so all I had to do was grope for my boots, pull them on and lace them, buckle on my sword, and grab my pack— making sure the Lizard gun was in it. When I was ready, I looked at Jamila standing by the window.

Without a word she climbed out, and down the ladder. I followed, feeling grim. There were scattered clouds, with stars showing through the gaps, and the sky in the east told me that the sickle moon, nearly a half-moon, had risen, but not yet above the hills. Which made it somewhat after midnight, maybe two or three o'clock.

And the ground was dry; it hadn't rained after all. We could have slept in the woods, saved ourselves a lot of trouble, and still had Paddy with us.

Jamila surprised me; she led me to the stable. One thing about your warrior muse; it knows about things

you don't, and it'll change its mind as the situation
changes. You've got to be willing to go along with it.
We were going to take the horses after all. Inside the
stable it was too dark to see much. We found the stableman by his snores, and Jamila hoisted him to his feet
out of a sound sleep. I pressed the flat of my knife
against his face, and he was as helpful as you could
want. He lit a lamp, showed us which horses were ours,
and which gear, and gave us the lead rope Jamila asked
for.

Then I gripped his carotid, and when he went slack,
I lowered him to the floor. I used the lead rope to tie
him, while Jamila started bridling and saddling the
horses. I wadded a cut-off bit of saddle blanket in his
mouth and used his neckerchief to finish gagging him,
then stuffed one of the Lizard's silver coins in his pocket
for his trouble.

You might wonder why we didn't just kill him. Obviously it would have been simpler and a lot easier. For
one thing, though, it wouldn't have been Christian.
Also, a warrior's rules of conduct apply, and they're a
lot different toward bystanders than toward combatants.
That's one of the first things Soong teaches his novices.
The properly trained warrior always tries to avoid killing or damaging the accidental bystander, unless it
would clearly endanger his mission. Otherwise you get
into penalty situations with God, and it's easy to go
downhill from there. Even when you seriously harm a
bystander out of necessity, you make amends afterward
if you have a chance.

Unfortunately not many warriors and darn few soldiers know the rules. Which makes it hard on bystanders. It also limits the skill and satisfaction of the warrior,
who is likely to go criminal sooner or later.

When the horses were ready, I checked my saddle
girth and mounted. Jamila led off. We rode out through
the village without seeing a light, and hearing only a
few barking dogs. Once outside town, we nudged our

horses into an easy trot. Pretty quickly the moon was above the hills, lighting the forest along the ridge on our left, the one facing east.

We rode peacefully for about an hour. I still felt spooky about the coming day and what might happen, but being outside helped—outside and on the move.

Occasional creeks crossed the road, and we forded them. Then a sizable stream came down from the east, crossed by a bridge. Instead of riding over the bridge, Jamila rode her horse down the bank into the stream and we forded it. I wondered why. It occurred to me that whenever Jamila was in charge, my muse lay back and kept quiet. I told him silently that that was all right, as long as he let me know when he disagreed with hers.

On the other side of the river, we climbed back to the road again and jogged on. Minutes later I heard faintly a hollow booming in the night—horses' hooves on the bridge planks—and knew why we'd crossed the way we did. What a muse she had! Which is to say, what a warrior she was. Because your muses are really you, acting on another level; Bhatti'd said it more than once, and Soong too. When I'd ask how that could be, Bhatti'd laughed (he laughed a lot) and said we did it with mirrors.

Now my muse nudged me. Just ahead, forest crossed the road. I trotted my horse past Jamila's to establish first action, and rode into the woods. She followed without questioning. I doubled back a ways then, dismounted, and tied my reins to a stout sapling; she did the same.

"I'm going to ambush them with the Lizard gun," I told her, then jogged quietly to a positon beside a huge old white oak that gave me a view of the road. She'd moved off somewhere to my left. Closer to the road, I thought, to prevent anyone from flanking me.

We only had about a two-minute wait. It turned out there were seven of them, trotting their horses briskly, saddle guns in hand, ready to shoot on sight. They probably thought we were farther ahead than we'd been, because they hadn't heard us cross the bridge. At about twenty meters I fired the Lizard gun, adjusting my aim by the thin line of light, and cut down six of them by sweeping the gun across them. The seventh, who'd been bringing up the rear behind the remounts, I picked off as he tried to wheel his horse and run. I'd shot their mounts, too, and hit three of their remounts. Couldn't help it with the angle of fire I had.

Seven of the ten horses I'd shot were alive. After I'd put them out of their pain with my sword, I looked at the bodies of the riders, taking off their helmets, shaking my head. Not one of them was alive. It had been so quick and easy, I couldn't quite have it like that. What kind of fight was this, where they didn't have a chance to close with me or shoot back?

On the other hand, seven of them had come out to find and kill two. Although they'd probably expected three: they wouldn't have known we'd gotten separated from Paddy. Whatever; they were dead now. And none were Lizards, not one. All of them had hair and all of them had bled dark sticky blood.

Jamila just stood saying nothing, letting me go through whatever I was going through. Whatever had me silent. I glanced eastward and broke it. "It's starting to get light," I said.

She nodded without speaking. We didn't bother much with the bodies. Some were under their horses, and for the others, we just straightened their limbs. Then we prayed briefly, silently, for their souls. After that we walked back to our horses and hit the road again.

When it was pretty much daylight, Jamila turned her horse aside, into forest that came down to the road there. We were both fighting sleepiness by then, and it seemed unlikely that the Lizards would have another party chasing us. As far as that was concerned, it seemed to me they could hardly know yet that the first group hadn't killed us.

No, I told myself, *you're trying to talk yourself into something. They've got magic*, or whatever you want to call things like the airboat and Lizard gun. If the Lizards could find and pick up the body of the one I killed back at Kings Town, what was to keep them from finding this last seven? Or finding me in the woods?

I shrugged it off. I didn't know all their powers, but I didn't know their limitations either. And we had to sleep sometime. So if Jamila's muse told her to take to the woods and take a nap, and mine wasn't adamant against it, then I'd go along with it.

We ended up on the ridge crest, which was pretty wide. In places the trees were sparse, with lots of rock outcropping and lots of brush for the horses to pick their way through and around. But mostly the timber was too thick for much undergrowth. Meanwhile we seemed to have lost our sleepiness. The morning was getting hot fast, and that by itself gave an advantage to riding through shady forest instead of down a road through mostly open fields.

We kept riding north and east, coming upon an occasional cattle driveway crossing the ridge at some saddle. There was a kind of pine that was different than we had at home, with soft, fine, bluish needles. And something else a little like a pine but with tiny short needles that were dark green and flat. And leaf-trees with bark that was light blue-gray, hard and pebbly smooth. And more sugartrees than I'd ever seen, along with others that had smooth golden bark with little curly shreds. And some trees that, if they were black cherry the way they looked, ran bigger than cherry did back in Mizzoo. It seemed to me it'd be neat to know these Allegheny woods.

Among the blue-gray trees there were little pale stalks growing, with flowers but no leaves. And mushrooms that might be good to eat or might be poisonous; I'd never gotten to know mushrooms with any confidence. And . . .

I became aware that Jamila had gotten quite a bit

ahead of me, and had stopped to wait. When I looked at her, her mouth was a thin line, her eyes about three-fourths angry. At me.

"If I was a Lizard," she said, "I could have ridden up to you and you'd never have noticed till I'd cut your throat."

My flash of indignation died before it more than started, and a wave of chills ran over my hide. Jamila was right. My nature-boy muse, which should be standing by to assist my warrior muse, had taken over instead. And for that to happen, I'd first had to put my warrior muse on the shelf. I dusted him off and reinstated him. *Nature boy*, I thought, *this isn't the time or the place*.

"Thanks for the reminder," I said to Jamila.

About noon we came to a dense grove of the pine-like trees in a shallow saddle. They looked forty meters tall. Their shade was heavy, and we decided it was a good place for a nap. After picketing our horses in a little wind gap a couple dozen meters away, where they could browse on twig ends, we sat down on a log together, where the shade was darkest, and ate. We didn't talk much, but sat close enough that now and then our shoulders would touch, or our elbows. After gnawing on bread and cheese and some of the strong sausage we'd bought, we lay down a few meters apart and went to sleep with our boots on.

I'm not sure how long I slept; maybe the better part of an hour. And I'm not sure what woke me; maybe a stick snapped or a horse snorted. I'd barely had time to pick up my sword and get to my feet, when a net came spinning. I dodged and slashed, cutting it, sweeping it away from me. Someone jumped me from behind, pinning my arms. I hit him hard in the face with the back of my head, elbowed his ribs, stomped his foot, jabbed back with my fingers into his balls, and twisted, all in about a second, all without losing my sword. Doubled over and stumbling, he tried to get clear, and I slashed at him, feeling contact but nothing very solid. There was a pistol shot. I felt the ball strike the right side of my butt like a burning hammer, and I ran! Ran down the ridge with long desperate bounds, the sounds of two more pistol shots behind me.

I didn't stop for maybe a hundred and fifty meters—not until it struck me that I hadn't seen or heard Jamila. She was back there, or had been. Till then I hadn't been thinking, just acting, riding my muse the way I'd been trained. I pulled up gasping for breath, knelt behind a fallen tree I'd hurdled, and peered back over it where a stout branch jutted to hide my head. Nothing moved that I could see or hear.

Shit! No Lizard gun, no pack—and no swordbelt, which meant no purse or knife, or scabbard for my sword. And no horse. I was aware of warm blood sticky on my right leg, in my pants. Jamila could have been captured or killed, or she might, like me, have gotten away—maybe even unwounded. I hadn't heard her yell, but then, I hadn't yelled either, so far as I knew.

They'd thrown a net at me, and that poor dumb sucker had tried to rassle me down! That meant they wanted me alive if possible. But someone hadn't hesitated to shoot, either, though he may have been trying just to hobble me.

I looked around. I'd run down the east slope of the ridge, the side away from the road. Probably our attackers had come along the top, following us. I wondered if they had a tracker. It seemed likely, although horses are a lot easier to track than a man. I could track horses.

Even if they didn't have a tracker, somebody should have followed me down the ridge. I waited for a couple of minutes, for some sign of him. Nothing. I picked up a stick, a broken chunk of limb, flipped it off downhill and plainly heard it hit. No one moved or made a sound.

Well, shit! I stood up, ready to throw myself down again at the first sign of danger. Still nothing, so I started back up the ridge, circling a bit to my right. Climbing was harder on my wounded butt than running downhill had been, and it was starting to hurt pretty badly, but I was still mobile, about as mobile as before. Which seemed to mean that the ball hadn't hit bone, that it was a flesh wound.

I'd go back to where they'd jumped me, although it felt as if they'd be gone when I got there. If they were, they were a mighty sorry pack, with some feeble alibis to deliver when they got home. Maybe I could figure out whether they'd caught Jamila, or killed her, or what. And what direction they'd gone. Then I'd either follow them, or circle ahead and try to ambush them.

Maybe they were waiting to ambush me. It didn't feel like it, though. They'd figure I was a kilometer gone by now. But if there was an ambush . . . I had my sword, but they had pistols, surely swords as well, and probably a Lizard gun—mine at least. On the other hand, they wanted me alive, it seemed like—while I'd be happy to have them dead. I'd only seen one of them—the one who'd grabbed me—but I had a confused impression of at least two more. And at least three shots had been fired, which meant at least three pistols.

But if they hadn't bagged me before, when they'd taken me by surprise, and in my sleep at that, they weren't warriors at all. And while I was wounded, so was at least one of them. And I'd be surprised if Jamila hadn't killed, or at least injured, one or more of them.

I reminded myself too that guys who aren't real warriors tend to rely an awful lot on guns if they have them. They tend to shoot without maneuvering, without getting in close. And a pistol gets wildly inaccurate beyond twenty meters, unless it has a rifled barrel, which most don't. A lot of guys have a hard time hitting anything even at ten. Even an unrifled musket isn't accurate farther than thirty, forty meters, although rifled muskets are getting common in some districts.

That's the kind of stuff that ran through my mind while I snuck up the ridge. My warrior muse must have been blushing at all the internal monologue, the rationalizing. Or maybe not. Maybe just then I needed to do that.

No one was there when I got to where they'd jumped me—leaving blood behind, and no sign at all of Jamila, unless some of the blood was hers. I wondered again how they'd found us. Because tracking is slow. *And I wondered where they all came from!* I mean—there were the ones that came so close to getting us at the inn the evening before—Jamila had killed or wounded one of them. And I'd killed seven on the road earlier today. Now here were these! Where were they all from? And who was giving the orders? Lizards?

I took off, following their trail, trotting and listening, eyes peeled. No more stuff was running through my mind now. All eyes and ears; all business. After only a few minutes I saw movement ahead, heard someone swear at a horse. I moved faster, and at a break in the slope got a look. There were three of them in the saddle and two bodies tied over horses. None of them was Jamila. Two bodies! She must have killed them; I was pretty sure I hadn't, any of them. But I would! I fell away to my right then and took off downhill, keeping timber and ground breaks between us till I was sure I'd gotten past them. I was down on the toe of the slope now. Between trees I could glimpse an open field ahead.

I'd have to be careful. They'd be looking ahead, and there was a good risk I'd be seen, depending on how alert they were. I scuttled along till I saw them picking their way through a brushy blowdown opening, then waited behind a big old yellowbark, sword in hand.

Their security was nonexistent and their muses asleep. And they were talking as they rode, not in Merkan. The first was riding right past me when I jumped him—took his leg off above the knee—then leaped at the next while the first horse screamed and reared. The second man was slow! His horse was shying, but by the guy's expression, he hadn't even realized what was happening. I took his leg off too. The third was about ten meters behind, and I never had a chance at him. He put heels to his horse and took off galloping. He was bound to have had a pistol, but one arm just hung, and he was handling the reins with the other hand. Probably the guy my sword had bitten, up on the hill.

I watched him go, hoping he'd fall off, or get knocked off by a limb. At my best I wasn't up to running down horses, and I'd started to shake like a leaf, feeling suddenly weak. I realized I'd lost quite a lot of blood. The first two horses had taken off too; both would be more or less wounded by the strokes I'd given their riders.

When the shakes were past, I went over and looked at the men I'd delimbed; both were already dead. And I thought I'd lost blood! The ground where they lay was covered with it, soaked with it. The first had the Lizard gun cross-slung on his back, and I took it off. I could hardly believe they wouldn't have tried to track us down with a weapon like that. Unless something was wrong with it. Aiming at a tree, I pressed the stud. Nothing happened. I looked it over to see if there was some device on it, other than the trigger, that maybe had to be set some certain way before it would work. There was a sort of sliding button on the side; I moved it and tried again. Still nothing. Maybe it was out of whatever made it work, or maybe it was broken.

I tossed it aside and turned my attention to the two horses with bodies tied across them. They'd trotted off a little ways and stood watching me skittishly. There was no indication that either body they carried held life.

I considered hiking back up the ridge, to see if I

could track Jamila, but as weak as I felt now, I couldn't confront the climb. Instead I checked the two guys I'd killed, took the swordbelt from the bigger of them, and the purses from both. One guy had a scabbard my sword would fit in, so I took belt and scabbard, cleaned my blade on his shirt, and sheathed it. I also took his belt knife.

The one that seemed to have been the leader had something in a shirt pocket that I thought was probably a radio; it definitely resembled what my masters had shown us. I left it. I didn't see any good it could do me.

The horses were ambling down toward the clearing now, and I followed. They stopped at the field—it was planted with potatoes—to graze on the grassy margin, and one of them let me go up to her. I tied her reins to a sapling, cut the body loose, and took its purse. And my pack; its straps were fastened through rings in the saddle skirt.

The other horse, a gelding, let me cut its corpse loose, too. The only sign I found of Jamila was the men she'd killed, one dead by a sword blow, the other with a pistol! I didn't find her sword or even her pack, and I told myself she'd surely gotten away.

There was food in the saddlebags, and ponchos tied behind. I transferred the food to my pack and fastened the pack to the rings in the saddle skirt. Then I untied the mare and, gritting my teeth, pulled myself into the saddle. I didn't have the strength to walk much farther, and I couldn't stay where I was.

I nudged her with my heels and we started along the edge of the field, toward the road. The fact that I could sit in a saddle at all told me I didn't have a pistol ball in my buttock.

I had a choice ahead of me. I could ride to the next village, take a room at the inn, and lay over a few days, maybe find a medic there to clean the wound. But people would talk; word would spread. Or I could stop at the next hamlet and see if one of the farmers would put me up. Again people would talk, but word might not spread beyond the hamlet. In either case I could get hog-tied or murdered by someone hoping for a reward.

As I rode, it seemed to me I was holding up pretty well, so I decided to hang tough and see if I could reach the next county. They probably spoke a different language there, and there was a lot less traffic, sometimes a lot less trust, between counties.

About four kilometers farther I came to a village, PERIGUEUX according to the sign. It was on a crossroad that went over the side ridges, and in the center of the village, where the roads crossed, another sign had OTAVI TOWN 8 carved into it. Otavi Town. They were bound to talk a different language in a place named Otavi than in villages called Perigueux and Bergerac, and I told myself I had enough strength left to ride eight more kilometers.

So I turned east toward the next valley.

I made it over the ridge and saw a bigger one ahead between me and Otavi. Suddenly I felt weak and dizzy. I clung to the horse's neck for a minute, till my eyes focused again, then gritted my teeth and rode on. In the narrow bottom, between the two ridges, was a pretty little creek running through the forest. I knew I'd overreached, couldn't make it much farther, that if I tried, I'd pass out and fall off. So I turned the mare upstream at the ford and, hanging on to her neck again, waded her about a hundred meters through the hardwoods, till we came to a grove of the dark, pine-like trees with little on the ground but moss and dead needles.

Getting off without falling off was the hard part. I almost fainted from the pain when I swung my leg over the saddle. Feet on the ground, I had to cling to saddle and mane for a minute till my head stopped spinning, and when I let go, my knees gave way, sending me sprawling. I was lucky the mare was calm and patient.

It took me a minute to get up again, but I managed to gather some strength from somewhere and picketed the mare in a grassy glade close by, then hobbled her for insurance. Then I stumbled back into the grove, prayed briefly on my knees, lay down on my stomach and passed out.

EIGHT

I woke up hurting really badly. It was still daylight, unless it was daylight again, and I'd been having fever dreams. Looking back at it from here, I suppose I'd been less asleep than out of my head, maybe raving part of the time. I tried to get up, but my right leg wouldn't hold my weight, so I went sprawling back onto the moss and needles. Then I lay there sort of half-awake and slipped into fever dreams again.

The next time I woke up, it was to pain that made the earlier pain seem mild. Someone had pulled my breeches off and was doing something drastic to the wound. A few feet in front of me I could see a little fire. Whoever was with me took something or other out of it. Then a terrific pain knocked me out again.

I didn't know who it was doctoring me. The hand I'd seen was big, the wrist thick and downright furry.

The next time I was aware of anything, I was wrapped in a blanket so I couldn't move, and it was night. I was still lying on my stomach, and not likely to turn over. My butt hurt savagely. I must have moaned or something, because in a minute someone was next to me, feeling my forehead. Whoever it was rolled me onto my left side, raised my head a little, put the spout of a wineskin in my mouth, and squeezed once and then some more, till I shook my head that I'd had enough. It seemed to be about half wine and half water. In another minute there was a wet cloth cool on my forehead. That's all I remember from that time.

It was birds singing that woke me next. Dawn thinned the darkness. It had been midafternoon when I'd first lain down and gone to sleep. I was surprised at how much better I felt; better than I had any right to expect. I was weak and I hurt, but the pain wasn't nearly as bad as it had been.

Vaguely I remembered someone massaging my arms and legs and back while I was half-dreaming in the night. Another time there'd been a dream-like period of being touched lightly here and there, especially on both sides of my butt, while someone who wasn't Jamila recited a formula that Bhatti had taught us as novices, to help the hands take away pain.

I felt a sense of peace and went back to sleep.

I was still wrapped in the blanket when I woke up again. Beams of sunlight speared down through holes in the forest roof, their high angle telling me it was sometime around midday. A burly man squatted a few meters away, looking at me. He had close-cropped white hair that could have been flaxen-blond or prematurely white, and grew halfway down to his eyebrows. Definitely not a Lizard. But there was something strange about him.

My stomach growled and felt like it was puckering inside me. "You don't happen to have something to eat, do you?" I asked.

He tipped his head back and laughed. Then without saying anything, he opened a packsack and took out bread and cheese plus a handful of wild onions. I could hardly eat them lying on my stomach, but he couldn't simply unwrap me without rolling me over. He spared me that by raising me to my knees and sort of unpeeling me from the shoulders down. I felt weak, but stronger than I might have expected.

I ate breakfast like that, on my knees—dry bread and

cheese with onions, along with about half a liter of
water. When I'd finished, he gave me another good
swig of wine. I was tightly bandaged with something or
other, cloth or leather, around the hips and lower belly.
Even if it had been possible to sit, I wouldn't have
cared to try. And while I'd be able to take a leak like
that, I had my doubts about anything more.

Whoever he was, my benefactor had washed my torn
and bloody breeches and draped them to dry on a bush
at the edge of the glade.

When I'd eaten, I grabbed a stout sapling and tried
pulling myself to my feet. I made it, too, then almost
fell over. My white-haired friend propped me up till
the dizziness passed. Then, on my own, I hobbled
painfully a few meters off and peed. That taken care of,
it was time to find out some things.

"My name's Luis," I said. "Luis Raoul DenUyl. What's
yours?"

He grinned, not saying anything for half a minute. I
wondered if he was a mute; some places they don't
destroy mute babies. But it must have been him who'd
done the laying on of hands in the night and recited the
healing formula.

Then I became aware of his eyes. They were clear
and steady, but the colored part was a different blue
than any I'd ever seen, a strong violet blue, and the
black in the middle wasn't quite round, but kind of
oblong up and down. The sort of thing you could overlook, or tell yourself was an illusion.

"Mine's Tom," he said, "Tom Jones." His Merkan
was as good as anyone's, his voice deep and sort of
velvety, but clear enough, and as loud as it needed to
be in a quiet place.

"Glad to know you, Tom," I said, and we shook
hands. "Really glad. How the heck did you find me?
Back in here away from the road and with no path to
follow."

His grin widened. He had a wide mouth and big
strong teeth. Especially the corner teeth, the dog teeth,

and that's what they reminded me of, a little. "I was looking for a good place to lay over," he said, "and here was a nice creek for water." He paused. "Besides, I was looking for someone to travel northeast with."

So he was a member of the Order, had to be, on the same mission as mine. A Brother with a powerful muse. "Where did you come from?" I asked.

"West," he said. "Here. Have a swig." This time he handed me a small flask, not holding much more than a hundred millies by the feel of it.

I stared at it, uncertain for a minute, then drank, only a little swig. It tasted like wine but felt stronger than whiskey, with a spreading warmth that had nothing to do with how hot it was. It reached my knees and eyelids at the same time. Tom helped me down on my belly again, and as I drifted off, I felt his hands and heard the formula being spoken. I wanted to ask if he knew anything about Jamila, but I couldn't even get the first word out before I was asleep.

I must have been dreaming continuously till evening. Not fever dreams this time—I was over that—but wild and vivid nontheless. Jamila was in them. We kept killing guys, Lizards, and they kept killing us. We must have killed each other every way there was, till killing and being killed seemed like nothing at all, and we felt like old buddies.

Supper I ate by twilight and about half conscious, then had another swig of drugged wine.

You'd think I'd wake up with a real headache after that, but the next time I came to, in the cool of morning with the sun newly up, all I felt was starved. Enough to eat the ass out of a skunk, as they say in Mizzoo. Tom came up with the usual—dry bread, cheese, and wild onions—plus sausage and all the water I could drink. This time, though, he didn't bring out any wine, drugged or otherwise.

"You ready to go?" he asked me.

I wasn't ready to answer. I had a question of my own.

"Do you know anything about a lady named Jamila? I lost her. Day before yesterday, unless I lost track of a day in there somewhere. We were jumped by some people the Lizards must have sent after us."

He shook his head.

"She's a black lady. Darkish brown, actually," I went on. "Tall, about my height, wears black leather breeches and shirt and carries a sword. And strong! A warrior. Not like any other woman I've ever known."

"I never met the lady. Haven't seen her. And she doesn't sound like someone I'd forget."

"No, you wouldn't. Well, shit!"

Anyone who's in good shape as a warrior doesn't really cherish his life, even without the dreams I'd just finished having. It's not that you'd throw away your life, but you're willing to spend it—hopefully spend it smart. To be attached to life screws up your performance; the stronger the attachment, the poorer you do. That's true for anyone actually, and I had no trouble with it.

But I'd fallen in love with Jamila. Which was fine. It's all right for a warrior to be fond of someone, admire someone, like to be with someone—love someone—but *you need to have the same attitude toward their life as your own:* Be willing to lose it. Just then I wasn't managing that.

"Where'd you have in mind to go?" I asked.

"Adirondack."

Definitely a Brother. "Ah. I'll have to walk; it'd be a mistake for me to try riding."

He nodded. Carefully, gradually, I got up without help, and carefully went over to where my breeches still hung. They were dry, and awkwardly, very carefully and with Tom's help, I pulled them on. Bandaged like I was, I couldn't fasten them, but we got them on me so they'd stay up. I was going to sling my pack on my shoulders next, but he took it and started strapping it to my saddle skirt. Obviously he'd been taking care of the mare, too.

"I'm not sure we ought to take her," I told him. "I've

had nothing but trouble since I started to ride." Tom raised his eyebrows. "It made us too easy to follow," I said, at the same time thinking that riding hardly accounted for the things that had happened.

"We'll chance it," he answered. "She can carry your pack, and I'll lead her. That'll make it easier on you while you get your strength back. We can sell her down the road somewhere."

I shrugged. He started out, keeping the pace slow, leading the horse when he could have ridden. I followed, walking carefully, not taking what you'd call a stride, but not actually limping—a sort of half walk, half toddle. Either I hadn't been hurt as badly as I'd thought, or Tom was a very good healer. My bet was, he was a very good healer.

NINE

We didn't make more than fifteen kilometers the first day, walking slowly and resting a lot. I'd been averaging about fifty a day all the way from Mizzoo, judging from mileage signs and my map. Tom told me my wound had been messy, dirty, and infected. He'd actually trimmed it out with his knife and cauterized it with a hot pistol barrel! And here I was two days later, hiking up the road.

He didn't talk a lot. Off and on he whistled tunes I'd never heard before, and occasionally sang a little in a language that was new to me. Sometimes he even greeted people we passed as if he knew them. I noticed, though, that he picked people who looked like they could stand having a stranger greet them. Mostly they greeted back; at least they smiled a little.

We got to Otavi around midday. The county there was called Savo, and its people spoke a whirring language I'm sure I'd never heard before. Tom bought a feed of oats and barley for the mare. Never mind that the barley would make her fart and I'd be walking behind her. He also bought a gunny sack to rub her down with at the end of the day. He and I had a lunch of sausage and hot stew at the inn, eating at the bar, on our feet.

Lying on my left side by the campfire that evening, I told him all that had happened since I'd run into Jamila and Paddy at the inn in Galway. In that time I'd killed twelve men, thirteen including the Lizard, which sort of awed me when I thought about it. Tom didn't say what he'd been doing, but he told me some interesting things about Lizards. According to him, sometimes they had natural bodies, which bled blood when they were cut, and sometimes they had artificial bodies. The artificial bodies were a kind of machine, and the Lizard airboats probably had a thing that could find them. Talk about magic!

Natural or artificial, their eyes were always red, he said. The one I'd killed had probably worn something in its eyes to make them look like a person's—contact lenses, he called them—and one had popped out when I'd whacked him with my sword.

He thought that probably they'd been able to detect the tracking tool, too. And the Lizard gun. Which explained a lot, if it was true. But if it was, why hadn't they detected the Lizard gun in the barn when they were right next to it? Or hadn't they been looking for it then?

As Tom said, we had more questions than answers, but it didn't seem to bother him. Actually, it didn't bother me either, to amount to much. I just would have liked to know.

He didn't say how he knew the stuff he'd told me. And I didn't ask, although I've got a reputation for questions. I was having a hard enough time digesting what he'd already said.

The next day we made at least twenty kilometers. I could have done more, but Tom said it was plenty. It took us into a county called Bihar, where the people were dark and lively, and talked Merkan to each other, but too fast, with an accent like Bhatti's.

I was feeling a lot stronger.

No one looked crossways at us, in Savo or Bihar, even though we were walking while leading a perfectly good saddle mare. I got the feeling that no one was watching for me there, waiting to do me in. But it was more than that—as if we weren't quite as noticeable as we should have been.

The day after that we must have walked thirty kilometers. Walking gave me no particular pain, although my butt was still kind of sore. And while thirty kilometers made me as tired as fifty would have a week earlier, I wasn't used up by it. Tom was definitely a champion healer; I doubt that even Bhatti could have had me going that strong that soon. I was still bandaged, but not so tightly, and when I changed the bandage, I explored the wound with a careful finger. It was twenty centimeters long and maybe three wide, a deep groove with a helluva scab in it. A big hard scab that itched and was interesting to touch. I could sit now, carefully of course, which was welcome. Resting on your knees gets tiresome, and some places are too wet for lying down.

The next few days, things went pretty much routinely, and we got up to more than fifty kilometers per day, sometimes hiking north, sometimes east, sometimes in between, depending on the roads. And while we didn't question people, I saw no evidence that Lizards or anyone else was causing unusual trouble. What I'd heard in Connemara about dangers north and east had been imagination, I decided. For anyone who didn't have Lizards hunting him.

Sometimes I found myself daydreaming about Jamila: We were going to run into her around the next bend, or find her eating her supper in an inn. Daydreaming's a poor practice for a warrior, ordinarily. You need to be alert. I'd been depending on Tom to notice things for me.

Once about midday we met a slim wiry guy, fairly tall, sitting in the woods by the road, eating wild onions. He was interesting-looking. Dark, but not as dark as Jamila. His hair was straight, even straighter than the people's in Bihar, and his features and the brownness of his skin were different than theirs.

As soon as I saw him, I decided he was probably one of us. Tom had no doubt at all, and we stopped to talk to him. His name was Lemmi Tsinnajinni, and he came from a place called Dinnehville, in the Kingdom of Saint Croy. I'd never heard of Saint Croy. He said it was on one of the headwaters of the Mississipp. I got the impression that he was young—about my age—and old at the same time, and I was pretty sure he was a lot more advanced than me. His masters, he mentioned, were named Wong and Ara. Tom seemed to know them, which stuck in my mind like a bur. We talked a few minutes and then, to my surprise, Tom said good-bye and we left Lemmi sitting on the log with his onions.

When we'd walked on a few dozen meters, I looked at Tom. "Why didn't we join up with him?"

A white eyebrow raised at me. "What did your masters tell you before they sent you out?"

"They said an armed man traveling alone draws less notice than a group of armed men. But then, why are you and I traveling together now that I'm able-bodied again?"

He grinned. "Because I decided we should."

"Suppose I decide we shouldn't?"

His strange violet eyes looked shrewdly at me. "You can go by yourself any time. Whenever your muse tells you to; any one of your muses. Do you want to?"

"No."

"Why not?"

I found myself grinning. "Because I've decided not to."

He tipped his head back and laughed as if that really tickled him. "Good reason," he said.

Actually I'd had no notion of going on alone. I'd just reacted.

Where we were then, the hills were bigger—to my eyes they were mountains—and there was less cleared land, and fewer people. Fairly wild. We stopped a little early that evening. The sun wouldn't set for half an

hour, but the creek that crossed the road there was so
pretty, we couldn't resist, so we followed it back into
the woods. We didn't cook; seldom did. I cut some
bracken in a little glade and made two beds of it, one
by each of two fallen trees. Tom gathered dry wood and
some leafy twigs, for later when we'd want a smudge.
After that we ate. By the time we'd finished, the sun
was down. Daylight was starting to fade, and the mosquitoes were coming out in numbers.

I was getting ready to start the fire, when I thought I
heard voices—a murmur of them in the distance. I
glanced at Tom; he was listening too, intent. Without
saying anything, we got up and moved quietly the
seventy or eighty meters to the edge of the forest.

By the time we got there, we were crouched low,
keeping the border of saplings between ourselves and
the opening. There were about twenty people back in
the pasture across the road. They'd brought a wagon
and left the team hitched to it. And gotten a fire going,
a big stack of wood that was just starting to burn; they
must have hauled the wood in the wagon. A lot of it
looked like old fence rails cut in two.

The people formed a loose half circle on our side of
the fire, a crescent of pairs, threes, and fours, their
backs to us. I couldn't decide whether they were chant-
ing or arguing or what. It wasn't in unison or parts, like
a chant, but it had an emphatic feel to it. And it was
louder than regular conversation but didn't really sound
like argument. I wondered if they'd been drinking.

I crouched, watching, feeling no impulse to go over
and ask what was happening. Whatever it was, it wasn't
a picnic. For one thing, to roast a pig or calf, they'd
have had a fire going hours earlier, so they could cook
over a good bed of coals. And even as far off as they
were, close to a hundred meters, there was something
about the sound of their voices that was ugly. Bad-ugly.

The fire grew and the people moved back a bit from
it, their loose semicircle thinning more. When it really
got roaring, a guy with a big-crowned field hat took a

few steps toward it and turned facing outward in our direction. Everyone else stopped talking, and he began to preach, or orate.

It was more than just a few words. He rambled on while daylight slowly dimmed. Across the road and a bit to our left was a worm fence, with clumps of young thornapple here and there along it. It occurred to me that from the other side of it I'd be able to hear what he was saying. So I backed away into the woods to stay out of sight, then trotted to where the fence would shield me from the people by the fire. Tom followed, and there was no doubt at all that he knew what I had in mind. I glanced back to see how he was taking it. After all, it had nothing to do with our mission, and it could be dangerous.

He was grinning!

On the other side of the fence, instead of hay meadow, the field grew a mixed crop of barley and oats, nearly crotch-deep and growing almost to the fence. Crouching low, we scuttled across the road and along the fence. Closer to the people and the fire, we dropped to hands and knees and stayed back in the grain, crawling. Dusk was turning into twilight, but it didn't seem like a time for carelessness.

We crept out of the grain into an angle of the fence, where a clump of thornapple broke up the horizontals—a good place to peer between the fence rails. We were close enough that I could have followed what the leader was saying now, except it wasn't Merkan. Maybe I could have anyway, if my daddy's grandparents had taught us kids Vlaamsch, because it sounded a lot like it to me.

Not that his voice was like Grampa Max's. My great grandfather DenUyl, any time I'd heard him, had sounded easygoing, even when he was telling someone off. Like one time when I was about eight, I was running through the house and bumped into his smoking table, sending his tobacco fanning onto the floor. Then, in confusion, I'd managed to step on his pipe and break the stem. Dad, of course, had taken me out back of the woodshed and walloped me good.

No, this guy was delivering like the Methodist reverend in Colwyn Town. He was preaching, I was sure.

But he was about done. When we'd been settled by the fence for four or five minutes, he finally ended off, gave an order, and the semicircle opened up, almost forming an aisle. Three guys went to the wagon. While two let down the tailgate, another climbed on and seemed to pull something out from under the spring seat. He dragged it back to the tailgate, where they lifted it off the wagon and propped it up between them.

It was a young girl with her hands and feet tied. The guy on the wagon jumped down and cut the cords off her ankles, and they helped her walk to the preacher. She walked like she was drugged or drunk or something. As they got closer to the fire and we could see her better, she looked to be about thirteen or fourteen years old, and pretty. The third man followed along behind and a fourth had fallen in behind him.

Nobody was saying anything now. When they got her to the preacher, they stopped. That's when I noticed he'd taken off his field hat, and for a minute I thought he was a Lizard. Then I realized he had a kind of skullcap on, with a crest on it, made to look like a Lizard's. I saw dark eyebrows beneath it, and hair hung out at the sides. He reached out and tore the dress off her—it didn't seem to amount to much and she had nothing on beneath it—and for a minute I thought there was going to be a rape.

Instead, while the two guys held her upright, the third pulled her head back by the hair. The preacher held a knife up toward the sky and started to chant. That was the first Merkan I'd heard out of him: Something about offering this perfect virgin to Satan, and Satan should accept the offering and bless them all. Then quick as anything he cut her throat, and just as quickly they flipped her around, face down, and the fourth guy appeared to be catching the blood in a bowl.

They held her like that for half a minute, while the preacher stood aside. Then the two who'd been helping her walk grabbed the body by the knees and under the arms and threw it on the fire. The half-burnt-down fire collapsed when she landed on it, and sparks flew up six or eight meters.

My eyes must have bugged out like peeled eggs. I realized I'd been holding my breath, and my body was tight as a fiddlestring. I glanced at Tom; he looked as calm and alert as a warty toad watching a bluebottle.

The people at the sacrifice weren't saying any more than we were. They just watched the body burn. I understood now why they'd made the fire so long, two meters or so. After a minute, a couple of them threw more wood on top of the body, and a minute later someone handed the preacher a bowl, with the blood I suppose. He took a drink, then took it around to each of the others and they drank too. Several of them had to gather up their nerve to do it, but no one rushed them, and they did drink, or faked it. When the bowl had gone the rounds, the preacher threw the remaining blood on the fire.

Bit by bit the fire burnt down while we watched between the fence rails. Two guys with staffs poked at it now and then, or pushed burnt-off ends into the hot center. Someone went to the wagon and brought back a couple of jugs, and they started passing them around. There were some pretty big swigs taken, but not much talking. It seemed to me that if enough of them drank enough, we could go over the fence and carve them up. But the preacher said something and the jugs were put aside. He started a chant then, where he'd chant something and they'd chant a response together. I couldn't follow it. Basically it wasn't Merkan, though quite a few of the words were, and their unison was poor.

I dozed, probably for not longer than five minutes or so, before I ever realized I was sleepy. When I woke up, someone was on the wagon seat, turning the wagon around. We watched them leave, some riding in the box of the slow-moving wagon, the rest trailing behind.

I wondered what in Hell they thought they'd accomplished.

That's what I asked Tom back in the woods, after I'd gotten our little smudge fire burning: "What do they think they accomplished with that?"

I looked at his eyes while I asked it. They gleamed in the firelight, unreadable. All he answered was, "You'd have to ask them, Luis."

"I'd like to. One at a time, privately. And that preacher-type with the Lizard thing on his head. What did he think he was doing?"

Tom's eyes were steady on mine, but he said nothing, just shook his head slightly. I hadn't really been asking for an answer and didn't expect one. Tom was darned smart—or darned wise, another matter entirely—but I doubted he could tell me what had been going through the preacher's head.

I stared into the fire, remembering what he'd worn *on* his head. "They know what Lizards look like," I said. "Someone must have trafficked with them."

Tom didn't say anything back, but I could feel his eyes. And I remembered what he'd said about the Lizards sometimes using artificial bodies—that their natural bodies bled real blood. So I'd never seen an actual Lizard, a real one. I thought about that for a while: The one I'd "killed," if killed was the word, hadn't seemed like any clockwork. What I'd cut through, and what I'd looked at beheaded, had been kind of like meat. Gray meat. It just hadn't squirted blood, was all, though it had oozed pale gray pretty freely. How could something so unnatural be?

"Or maybe what he saw was an artificial Lizard," I went on. It was half question.

"They look about the same," Tom answered, "artificial or real."

"Why would one of them show itself to him? And

why did they do what they did over there?" I thumbed back toward the field. "What good did that do anyone?"

"It's a long story, Luis. To keep it simple—let's just say there's evil loose on Earth. A special kind, with reasons and intentions of its own that wouldn't make much sense to someone outside it."

I'd never given much thought to evil. To people who did bad things, yes. They were part of my job. But *evil?* What was evil, really? I decided that what I'd just seen in the pasture would qualify.

"How do you know these things?" I asked.

Tom smiled. "You'll know too, when the time comes."

We quit talking then and lay down against our logs on opposite sides of the fire. A few years earlier I'd have been irritated at an answer like his, or else all wrapped up in the mystery of it. But when you study under Bhatti, you get used to answers like Tom's. Or delayed answers, or no answers at all.

"Tom?"

"Unh?"

"Are you a master?"

"Nope."

"What are you then?"

"Good question. Sleep on it, and tomorrow you can tell me how it seems to you."

That was the last thing either of us said that night. But I couldn't help thinking about the angels who Bhatti and Soong mentioned occasionally, who had trained them. They also called them "monitors.' Angels had founded the order and trained its masters, and Tom had seemed to know the masters who had trained Lemmi Tsinnajinni. I wondered if Tom was an angel, and decided—decided there was no way I could tell yet. Maybe later.

TEN

The yelling of birds opened my eyes to faint dawn. It was chilly enough that if I'd just been starting this mission, I'd have had a hard time sleeping. As it was, we pulled on our boots, shouldered our packs, and left without eating or even saying much. Hiking would warm us.

I didn't bring up the question of what Tom was. Tom was Tom. That much was certain, and all I really needed to know.

The day's first village was in sight, a kilometer and a half ahead, when I saw what I felt pretty sure was the wagon of the evening before. It was parked by a barn in a large hamlet of about a dozen cabins. Although smoke from chimneys marked breakfast fires, no one was out and about yet—unusual for farmers in summer. Barn doors were still shut. A couple of hounds barked half-heartedly at us, keeping close to cover in case we drew pistol or slings. I had a notion to go look closer at the wagon, for evidence that it was the one from last night, with maybe twigs and bits of bark from branchwood, or an old fence rail left over. But if I found something, what then?

Tom glanced at me, as if to see whether I'd noticed

and how I was reacting. Our eyes met and he grinned. I didn't smile back.

We went on past the hamlet, and in a few minutes entered the village. People were out and about there, a few, and I wondered if they knew what some of their near neighbors were up to. There had to be rumors at least, and someone would be missing a daughter. *Or had she been the preacher's?* Somehow the thought gave me chills.

Two or three kilometers beyond, the sun came up and we stopped beside the road for breakfast. Then, as we hiked again beneath a climbing sun, the early morning chill left, and soon the day threatened to be as hot as any I'd seen that summer. Cows clustered in the oblong shade of pasture trees. Deerflies zipped and bit. We sweated.

In late morning we entered a village where the signs were in another alphabet, and passed a squad of soldiers in the square. They weren't the best-looking soldiers I'd ever seen, and people seemed to be avoiding them. Leaving town, the road curved round a smithy, and on the other side, beneath a pair of spreading sugartrees, were more soldiers, eight of them obviously foot soldiers. Two others stood holding the bridles of horses, probably of their officer and sergeant, while another two sat casually mounted as if ready to dash off momentarily. A lieutenant was in charge, and three civilians sat on the ground nearby with shackles on. It was the Kings Town bridge all over again, but this time I didn't have the Lizard gun.

A sergeant swung his pistol our way and raised the muzzle so I could look down it. Musketeers followed his example.

"Citizens!" the lieutenant called to us. We stopped, not wasting our energy explaining that we weren't. He walked over to us. "Do you have a warrant of exemption?"

"No," Tom said. "Are you accepting recruits?"

The lieutenant wasn't taking that at face value. Maybe we did want in, but he had us shackled with the other three anyway. He left us our packs and swords though, which surprised me. I suppose he assumed we wouldn't try anything serious chained together like that. And someone had to carry them; it might as well be us.

When the other three conscripts talked, it was in a language I thought I recognized from the Kingdom of Ozark as Osmanli, though it might have just sounded like it. A couple of the soldiers seemed to understand them; the others didn't.

Apparently by then the locals had people out warning other locals not to come down the road; at least no one else came along. Pretty soon though, the troops from the square arrived with four more conscripts. Then the soldiers ate and we didn't. After they ate, the lieutenant sent the sergeant out hunting with five other men, and an hour or so later they came back with three more victims, even surlier than the others. Afterward they rechained us so we were connected only by twos—a good idea if we were going to walk very far—and started us hiking down the road. It took a little getting used to, walking chained together like that, and it was slow, but we did better than you might expect.

After about three kilometers we turned off on a crossroad, barely a cart track. There weren't many wheel ruts. From the bare packed ground, and by browse sign along it, it was as much a livestock driveway as anything else. We climbed a ridge that must have stood a full two hundred and fifty meters above the narrow valley, then crossed some smaller hills until we topped one that overlooked a much broader valley.

In contrast with the rough country we'd just left, this was a major farming district. The forest above it had been heavily thinned by woodcutters and sheep, so we got some broad views of it. It was well-cleared and fenced, with big fields, some as large as ten or twelve hecters. In the distance, on the bank of a good-sized river, I could see a real town with a wall around it, looking big enough to have as many as four or five thousand people. We'd looked at the map earlier that day; this had to be Gotaborg. And it had to be where we were headed.

It was. There was a large stone fort a kilometer from town, and a big army camp just south of it with hundreds of tents in rows. The road took us past recruits, several thousand of them, drilling and sweating by companies in a cloud of tawny dust. I kept my eyes open, soaking up impressions; I intended to be out of there and on my way before breakfast the next day.

The impressment unit, the guys who had picked us up, took us to the fortress. Inside its walls, among the stone buildings, a linen canopy had been set up, strung from poles. In its shade, several men were working at tables with stacks of papers. I paid attention mainly to one, a tall and balding blond, an officer whose emblem of rank I didn't recognize but whose demeanor marked him as the man in charge. He sweltered and sweated in chain mail and a breastplate, symbols of responsibility, while not a quarter hour away we'd seen small, towheaded farmboys swimming naked in the river.

As we were brought in, he straightened in his chair and looked us over, hard-faced but not actually hostile.

"Colonel sir," the lieutenant said in Merkan, "these are our conscripts for today." He sounded as if we weren't a very good take and he was half-expecting to get chewed out on the spot. "There weren't many travelers," he alibied, "and almost all the local men we found had warrants of exemption."

The colonel's mouth was a thin slit. He didn't answer the lieutenant, just looked us over, his flinty blue eyes stopping on Tom and me, the only ones carrying swords.

"You know how to use dose swords?" he asked, gesturing at Tom. I thought I recognized his accent— Swenski. That or something close to it.

Tom smiled. "Yes, Colonel. And Colonel, I believe the duke will wish to see us."

The duke. That would be the Duke of North Allegheny, I thought, and wondered what Tom was cooking up.

The colonel's thin hard lips took flesh and pursed, but the eyes didn't change. "De duke knows you?"

"He doesn't know us personally, but he knows what we are."

The mouth became a slit again. "And vhat iss dat, dat you are?"

"It is not to be said in front of others."

The eyes lost some of their edge while the colonel thought about that, for about the time of two good breaths. Then he turned to one of his noncoms. "Sardyent," he said, still in Merkan, "take deir swords and lay dem on de table here. Den take dese two to de duke. And leave de shains on dem." He turned to Tom. "If the duke doesn't vish to talk vit' you, I vill have you flogged for vasting his time and mine."

Tom smiled and nodded. I wondered what it would feel like to get flogged. I'd seen a flogging; it didn't look like anything I'd care for. The sergeant called another man over and, with muskets uncocked but thumbs on their hammers, they prodded us across the trampled, dusty courtyard to the most imposing of the stone buildings. Inside, we climbed a stone staircase to the second floor, and went down a hall to a waiting room. It had its own armed guards. At a table, a liveried older man looked up from what seemed to be a Bible and listened to what our guards had to say. It wasn't in Merkan, but I supposed it was pretty much a translation of what Tom had said. It surprised the old man, and he looked about two-thirds insulted by it. For a minute he stared at us as if he could hardly believe it, then told our guards in Merkan that we'd have to wait.

I glanced around the room till a varnished plaque stopped my eye. Two plaques, actually, side by side, each with a motto, almost certainly the same in the two languages. The one in Merkan read: "Not by Works but by Faith."

These were Protestants. If Tom told the duke we were Higuchians, we seemed likelier than ever to taste the lash.

Meanwhile, there we waited, Tom and I. The chain that connected his right cuff with mine hung slack between us to our ankles; we looked like a couple of dangerous criminals. After a few minutes, a well-dressed man was ushered out of an adjacent room, an audience chamber, and the older man got up and went in. A minute later he was back, a tight, disapproving look on his face, and told our own guards to take us in.

Well, what the heck, I thought as we walked into the audience chamber. It occurred to me how unlikely it was that a tough case like the colonel would send a couple of dirty, road-worn guys like us to see the duke. Somehow Tom had talked us in. We'd see what else he could talk us into. Or out of.

The room was large enough for a pretty good crowd. Looking tired, the duke watched us cross it. He'd been sitting there listening to complaints and petitions for an hour or two, I supposed. That'd wear anyone out. One of his two bodyguards lowered his spear toward us and we stopped about three meters away.

Even sitting down, the duke was obviously a tough old soldier, lean and just now grim. Whatever Tom had in mind, it would have to be good. "So!" the duke said. "What made you think I'd want to see you?" *Another Swenski,* I thought, although his accent was slight.

"Your Lordship," Tom said, "I have a request and explanation that I can't give in front of these good men of yours. There is always the risk of someone mentioning it, perhaps where a spy could hear. But if they'd retreat to the limits of the room . . . with muskets aimed at myself and my companion of course."

The duke scowled, and for a minute I thought that was it. Instead he stood up, drew his sword with a large and muscley hand, and looked at Tom's and my guards. "Go stand by the windows," he ordered, gesturing with the blade. I watched them back reluctantly to one of the walls, their muskets pointing at us. He turned to his bodyguards. "And you. Go with them."

As his men moved away, he glowered at us. "If this is

some joke or game . . ." he said, and left the rest to our imagination.

When all four guards were standing some ten meters away, Tom spoke quietly, a murmur. "We are members of the Order of Saint Higuchi."

Oh shit! I thought, *here we go.* It seemed obvious that Tom thought the duke was Catholic. I'd never been good at extracorporeal drills; I'd probably yell when they flogged me.

"We're on our way to carry out a mission in the Saint Lawrence People's Democratic Republic," Tom went on. "Some of your soldiers impressed us for your army today, and we submitted. We understand your situation here, and preferred not to kill your impressment party. We felt confident you'd release us to continue our mission."

I hoped my eyes weren't bulging out too far. Even though the duke's attention was on Tom, he might notice. Without waiting for the duke to comment, Tom continued. "I presume the Lanksters are preparing a move against you here in the north."

The duke nodded slightly, narrow-eyed, listening.

"Until recently, Lankster hadn't troubled the north. They'd concentrated on the south. Now obviously that's changed, or it's expected to. They must be preparing a large force to attack you, considering your response, but I presume they're not ready yet, or it would be too late to conscript and train your own."

Listening, the duke had unslitted his eyes enough to show blue. Now he nodded, less in agreement, it seemed to me, than in decision. "So far," he said, "they have only modest forces in place, along the Lye Coaming." He kept his own voice as low as Tom's had been. "But our spies report a new army is being trained in the Lackawanna Valley, to hit us here. We don't know how near they are to ready, but we do what we can."

Tom nodded, his face more sober than I'd seen it before, to match the duke's mood. "And of course,

King Armand is in no position to send you help, even if you were willing to ask for it."

Again the duke nodded. "I was appointed to take care of things in the north, not to go whining to the king with my problems. I've sent couriers to him to let him know what the situation is, but I also know his situation. I'll hammer out an army here, that with God's help will not only stand them off but send them home with their tails between their legs."

"But Lankster isn't your only problem," Tom went on. "There are devil worshipers scattered through the wilder sections of the north."

The duke's jaw muscles bunched like walnuts, and his nod was a sharp head jerk. "Yes. By day pretending to be honest Christians or Moslems. But murdering; carrying out evil rites, enticing, trapping, defiling our youth. Recently they've begun to burn hamlets. And some of their rites are so obscene that those who take part are surely lost to God and man forever. Once in, they have no choice but to go on in Satan's evil and destructive ways.

"They frighten the people more than Lankster does."

The duke's face turned thoughtful then, his voice softer yet. "We suspect—no, we *know*—the source of this devil worship." He straightened. "What can the Order of Higuchi hope to accomplish in Saint Lawrence?"

Tom turned to me. "Luis," he said, "how many outlaws did you kill in the last ten days?"

"Uh, twelve. Thirteen if you count the Lizard." *And the two soldiers at the bridge north of Kings Town*, I thought. *Most of them with the Lizard gun I don't have any longer.* I was sure Tom didn't want me to go into all that, though.

The duke's eyes sharpened as he turned on me. "Lizard?" He almost hissed it. "You killed a Lizard?"

I nodded.

"Luis is a Brother from the Kingdom of Mizzoo," Tom said, "sent by the Order there as part of the mission. And more of us will be traveling through, mostly singly. I hope you'll let me look over your conscripts to find any of them your impressment parties may have picked up as they did us."

The duke looked thoughtfully at him. "You could be lying."

Tom grinned then, a flash of white teeth. "Of course. Do you think I am?"

The duke sheathed his sword and sat down. I could hardly believe what was happening. Tom had wrapped this tough old soldier around his finger. What powers did he have? *Was* he one of God's angels?

"You are creatures of the Pope," the duke muttered. He couldn't let himself be too easy.

"We are men of God," Tom replied, appropriately sober again. "That's the important thing, not what bishop we recognize or fail to recognize. We are men of God, and the rest of it is secondary."

His statement might have antagonized some men, but the duke seemed mainly curious now. "The men of your Order are said to be excellent fighting men," he said. "Perhaps better than any others. Show me your drills, and perhaps I'll believe you. I'll have you unchained for it."

"If we do that," Tom said, "we'll need to pretend we're something else—mercenaries from the Green Hills Republic—free lances you're considering sending behind Lankster lines. So there won't be speculation and rumors that may strike the truth."

The duke agreed and led us back into the courtyard, followed by his guards and ours. The lieutenant's mouth dropped open when he was ordered to unlock our chains, but the Swenski colonel didn't bat an eye. Obviously he knew his duke. They gave us back our swords, and I demonstrated my drill forms. Considering I hadn't practiced much since I left Mizzoo, I did really well. Actually I look even better than I am, because I'm so darned flexible and quick, and I've got a lot of spring in my body.

When I finished I saw the Swenski colonel and his

sergeant major looking impressed. The duke nodded approval.

Then Tom did his, and I could hardly believe it. I mean, he's not lean like me. He's burly and thick, built more like a docker or wrestler, or a bear, than a swordmaster. But he did things I'd never even seen Soong do! And quick! I'd swear he jumped a meter off the ground and came down a meter and a half to the side while hardly seeming to bend his knees. And without missing a stroke! The duke and the Swenski colonel both had their jaws resting on their breastbones.

With swords, I wouldn't have any more chance against Tom than Paddy would.

The duke gave orders then, and followed with the colonel as the lieutenant led us outside the fortress to the army camp. We waited on a reviewing platform for a few minutes, in the shade of a yellow-and-blue-striped awning. Then the recruits and their cadre began to file in from training.

And who do you suppose was with them? That's right, Jamila. Wearing sergeant's stripes, and ragging the poor recruits to beat the devil! With a tongue like a rasp and a grin like a wolf's. I had an impulse to yell and run down there, but I controlled it and didn't even say anything. She saw me, and gave me a big wink while she and the other noncoms lined up their raw platoons with cuffs and oaths.

She was the only woman in the whole army, and I saw a couple of conspicuously swollen, discolored faces among the other noncoms. I could imagine how they got them. And while maybe it shouldn't have, it tickled heck out of me.

"That one," I said pointing. "The tall black woman."

The duke's eyebrows jumped halfway up his forehead. Obviously he'd overlooked her when they'd marched in; a case of not seeing what couldn't possibly be there. Now he turned to the colonel. *"En kvinna i vår* . . . a woman in our army, Axelson?"

A slight smile actually touched the colonel's mouth.

"Yessir. It seemed de proper t'ing. An impressment section come in vit' a big strong young fella—red hair, pink face—and she come vit' him. She said she vass his mudder." Axelson chuckled. "T'ree of de troops had tried to—you know. She beat hell out of dem, and scared it out of de rest, and come in vit' dem. Vitout shains. She said if 'Paddy' had to be in de army, she vass going to be sure he got trained right, or hiss fader vould be very mad. And den—she did her sword drill for me." He gestured at me. "She iss as good as diss fellow.

"Dere iss no written regulation dat says ve can't have a vooman in de army. I don't t'ink it ever come up before. And she vass de best vit' a sword dat I ever seen. So I signed her up as a sardyent. On a provisional enlistment. Dat vay if dere vass problems, ve could offload her vit'out no hearing."

"We want the Connemaran, too," I said. "He's a novice in—our organization." I'd almost said "our Order" in front of the colonel. Strictly speaking, I'd lied, of course; Paddy wasn't in our organization. Though I'd meant what I said: The Holy Spirit in me considered him a Brother still uninitiated. He'd found us, brought himself to our attention, fought by us and fled with us. And managed to get found again by Jamila after he'd gotten separated from us.

The duke looked at Tom, who nodded absently; he was staring out across the assembled recruits, scanning. Feeling them over at a distance for Lemmi Tsinnajinni or anyone else that might catch his attention with something that said Brother to him. He didn't have to walk up and down the ranks.

But there were only Jamila and Paddy.

After supper they gave Paddy and me a small room in the Fortress for the night, and Jamila another. I'd missed her all right, but not as much as I might have expected. And I was willing to bet she'd missed me about zero.

Glad to see me, yes; missed me, no. She was more

advanced in spiritual exercises than me. The Order
trains you to live in present time, and you do, more and
more, as you do the spiritual drills. And sit with the
masters in Higuchi Communion. Mostly you don't notice the changes in yourself while they happen, but now
and then something comes up that makes you realize
how different your reactions have gotten, mentally, emotionally, and physically. It sort of sneaks up on you. I
hadn't changed as much mentally and spiritually in four
years as some do, but emotionally I'm a lot more calm,
and physically a lot tougher and more deadly. I don't
often get upset by things anymore, really, and when I
do, it's likely to be "flash" and then gone.

Actually I'd wondered, getting ready to leave Mizzoo,
if I'd lose some of that, being away from Bhatti and
Soong and the Brothers. But now, looking back at things,
it seemed to me I hadn't. Not even before I ran into
Jamila and Tom. What I'd had, I'd kept.

Tom spent the evening talking with the duke, while
Jamila and Paddy and I caught each other up on things.
After galloping out of Bergerac on the stolen horse, that
night that seemed so long ago, Paddy had taken a road
over the hills into the next valley, and followed it
northeastward. Late the next day he'd run into Jamila.

His feet had gotten quite a bit better, but he was still
riding the horse the day after that when they ran into a
press unit. Its lieutenant had figured to "conscript" the
horse too, and some of his men tried to get Jamila into a
handy shed. But after she'd punched and kicked the
snot out of three of them and overawed the others, the
horse stayed with her and the men let her be. The
horse was really hers, she said, not Paddy's, and she
was Paddy's mother, which looked ridiculous on two
counts. The lieutenant decided not to argue.

When they'd reached camp, he'd tried to have Jamila
run off, but the Swenski colonel decided the whole
thing was funny. And then she'd shown him her sword
drill. The Swenskis I'd known before—there'd only

been a couple of them—didn't laugh much. But they'd think it was pretty hilarious for a woman, especially a young good-looking one, to beat up three soldiers and lead their lieutenant around by the nose.

Here she'd been drilling recruits in use of the bayonet, both mounted on a musket for a short spear, and used as a half-meter-long shortsword. Most of their time, though, was spent drilling for discipline—moving as a unit, on command, and loading, aiming, and firing their muskets by the numbers. Hopefully they wouldn't panic and break when an army charged or fired at them.

She didn't think much of this army, but I suppose the Lanksters were little if any better, or hadn't been at this point in their training.

She also told me how they pronounced Gotaborg here. You wouldn't believe it: something like *yert*aboy. Till then I'd only seen it on a sign.

When finally she went to the little sleeping room the duke had had assigned to her, just across the hall, I hadn't seen any indication that she wanted me to sneak over later, so Paddy and I lay down on our pallets to sleep. We didn't see or hear Tom till morning; the duke had put him up somewhere else.

ELEVEN

We ate breakfast with the recruits—hot oat porridge, hot fresh bread and cheese. With this kind of food and plenty of drill, the fat ones would slim down fast and the farmer boys, herdsmen, woodcutters and the like would hold their own. After breakfast we hit the road. The duke had given Tom a safe conduct for all of us. Paddy's feet were sound now, so Tom sold the horse in town and we headed on foot up the valley.

There wasn't any need to climb hills or hike cross-country; we just stayed on a nice easy road for practically the whole day, which turned out beautiful. A cool pleasant breeze sent white clouds scudding across blue sky. We ate our noonmeal at a village inn where the serving woman talked with a strong Polski accent, and the bread, the cheese, the roast beef, all were about as good as you'll find, even if they lacked the condiments and sauces of the inn at Bergerac. We didn't see a lot of young men—I suppose impressment units had been through—but the people in general seemed good-natured, and the world felt good. The duke's gloomy words didn't seem to fit at all.

We made close to fifty kilometers in spite of a late start. Near the end of the day, we left the main road for a narrow track and struck off northward, to camp in open pastured woods on top of a broad ridge. The breeze still blew, keeping down the mosquitoes, so we built no fire. Before I lay down to sleep, I walked out on an outcrop and looked northward across timbered hills, and felt—felt as if things were different, not good, off there.

Sometime in the night it clouded over, and I woke up to raindrops pecking my face. I pulled my poncho out of my pack, spread it over me, and went back to sleep. After awhile it rained a little harder, a light but steady fall, and I was wakened by water trickling from my temple into my ear. I turned over and went back to sleep, but not deeply, staying more or less aware of the rain and the chill.

As usual, sleeping in the woods, we woke up with the dawn, although the birds were keeping quiet. We weren't saying much either. The rain and the sky were the kind that promises no letup for the day. If we'd had shelter, we might have holed up and had a day's rest, or at least a few hours. As it was, we got up stiff and cold, huddled briefly under our ponchos to eat rye bread and cheese and a dried apple each, drank some water, and hit the road by half-light. The track was already muddy underfoot.

Very soon we were out of the grazed woods into thick forest, with here and there the stumps of smaller white oaks near the road, no doubt cut for splitting into fence rails. White oak rails last a lifetime without rotting, and when it's not knotty, it's easy to split. Sometimes it even splits off the stump when you fell it; I learned that as a thirteen-year-old, when a woodseller I worked for was killed by one.

There were other stumps whose large naked logs lay moldering on the ground. Hemlock, Paddy told me; I'd never heard of hemlock in Mizzoo. There'd be a tannery not far off, he said, probably in the valley we'd left. Tanners felled hemlock trees, and peeled off and took away the bark. Usually they left the logs to rot, the lumber having a poor reputation. The bigger stumps we occasionally saw, flaring wide at the ground, he called white pine. The woodsmen cut the best of them for the wide clear boards they could saw out, leaving the smaller ones to grow. The trees with the curly golden bark he called yellow birch, and showed me how to peel off the papery outer layer to start fires with.

His voice, when he told me these things, reflected love of the land and the things that grew on it, and I wondered if I'd read my own desires into him when I imagined he wanted to become a Brother instead of a farmer or woodcutter.

"Why did you come with us?" I asked him.

"Ye stood up for me with the soldiers, back in Galway Town. You and Jamila. And anyway oi couldn't stay there any longer; oi'd have been arrested and hung."

"You could have stayed in Kings Town."

He shook his head, his loose, bowl-cut reddish hair flopping from side to side. "Oi knew no one there. And besides"—big shoulders shrugged—"oi'd never been with folk who treated me like you and Jamila did. As if oi was someone of worth. And afterward, fearless and strong ye showed yerselves, back at the river when the hounds were after us, and at the inn outside Kings Town, when those men might have killed us!

"Oi want to be like that. But oi can't be, without the trainin'; oi'd be carved up like a pig. And it seemed to me that if oi went on with ye, and escaped death long enough, someday oi'd become like you. Not just a great fightin' man, but a man kind and decent, and above any cowardice."

I didn't know what to say, so I only nodded as we trudged. I think pretty well of myself, but to have someone flatter my character like that was embarrassing. He hadn't gotten to know me well enough, seen all the warts and wens and weaknesses.

It wasn't that what he'd said about me and Jamila was false. It was that—I gnawed on it for a minute. It was *incomplete*. Besides which, we'd only acted like people ought to act; we'd been decent and self-respecting and competent. Maybe in Paddy's experience, I told myself, that was unusual. Then I remembered Shamus Finnigan, the wagoner of Galway Town, who was all those things—decent, self-respecting and competent. And as brave as his world would let him be. And all without the training we'd had.

Someone like the soldier I killed in the Galway Inn can warp a kid's view, I thought, then wondered what Paddy's father was like. I didn't bring the subject up; Bhatti hadn't trained me yet in the skills I needed to handle things like that in a way that helps. If I lived long enough, he might.

Meanwhile we hiked through forest and over hills, rain falling tirelessly on us from a dark and featureless sky. After a while we came to another valley, narrow and mostly wild, with here and there a few narrow fields along the bottom. The first hamlet we found was ashes and charred wood; the soot-blackened fieldstone foundations had been cracked by heat. There was a well, and we went over to it. The stench of putrefaction rose up from it, whether from animal or human we couldn't tell for sure.

But we could guess, because nearby, sodden in the mud, was the torn dress of a girl or small woman. Arson, rape, and murder were bad enough, but somehow, to me, throwing the bodies in the well and poisoning it made the raiders seem twice as foul.

We looked for tracks that might mean something to us, tracks showing something unusual that we might recognize along the way to help us know the raiders. There was nothing. The ground had no doubt been dry when they'd done it, and been rained upon since. I might have thought it was robbers, except for what the duke had said. And anyway, if I were a robber, I'd have been in the big valley, where the farms were prosperous, not up here in these wild, hardscrabble hills.

After a bit the road took us over a hill and into another small valley, and after a bit another. That's

what the day was like—uphill and down. It kept raining, too, never hard and never quite stopping. In places
the road was slick with wet clay so that our feet slipped,
especially on the grades. The hamlets all were poor,
and mostly widely separated. We came on another that
had been burned, perhaps a month past. At others,
people, warned by their dogs, eyed us sullenly, dis-
trustfully, from their doors. Generally two or three
would have muskets or shotguns in their hands.

With the sky a gray sameness, we could only guess
the time, but I felt sure it was after noon when we
finally reached a village. It was small, and in this out-of-
the-way district had no inn, but there was a tavern
where you could buy a scant meal. The tavernkeeper
waited on us himself. I could barely understand his
Merkan. No, there were no rooms to let; he and his
family lived in the few they had. No, there was no
livery stable where we might wait out the weather. No,
no one in Zaragosa had a room or shed to let to travelers.

The village looked so poor, you'd think they'd have
clamored for our silver. Rain or not, I wasn't unhappy to
leave it, and I'm sure they were glad to see us go. Not
even Tom smiled there.

Late in the day and deep in the hills, we came to a
tiny hamlet of four cabins, each with its barn and sheds.
The rain had finally stopped, though the trees dripped;
we couldn't tell whether it was over or taking a break.
Without asking, I turned off the road and headed for
the nearest cabin. Tom, Jamila, and Paddy followed. In
nicer weather the hamlet might almost have been pretty.
Sugartrees shaded the cabins. Patches of flowers had
been planted and tended, but just now they were drag-
gled and spattered with mud. Four hounds barked des-
perately at us from a dog pen, and I could almost feel
the tension from behind the cabin door I knocked on.

"Who is it?"

The words were Merkan! I wondered if that was the
local language here. You do run into places, like Aarschot,
where they have no other tongue.

"We're travelers," I answered. "Four of us, three men and a woman looking for shelter. We can pay you."

"We've no place for ye here. Go away."

I knocked again. "D'you think we're Satan worshipers?" I asked. "If we were, we wouldn't be knocking, we'd be torching and shooting. What we want is to sleep in your barn, and take a meal with you if we can. We can pay you. In silver."

I could hear murmuring from behind the split-plank door, and we stood off to the sides in case someone decided to shoot through it. After a minute it opened, and a man peered out with a shotgun in his hands. He looked us over, not missing our swords, then decided. "Coom in," he said grudgingly, and backed away, still holding his gun.

There were five of them inside—father, mother, and three children, the oldest a boy about fifteen who held a smallbore musket that I suspect was rifled, the kind used for squirrels and birds. Supper was cooking, a kettle of something fragrant hanging in the fireplace. The man asked to see our money, and we agreed to pay two bits each for our suppers and a place to sleep. We took our packs into their barn and left them in the hayloft, then went back to the house.

Their name was Whidby, and they were full of questions now: where we'd come from, what the news was. They'd barely heard of the war, and knew nothing of any conscription; they wouldn't have, so far from Gotaborg. Their Merkan was a dialect they called Inglish; their county was York, their hamlet Bedale. Their ancestors, they said, had brought Inglish with them from some far place during the Shuffling, back after God changed the world. From across the ocean, they thought; people are vague about the Shuffling, and almost nothing is known of what came before, except what Scripture tells. Some call the shuffling "the Forgetting"; it's seldom spoken of by either name.

The stew was pretty good. And hot; that was more

than welcome. The corn cakes were hot too, with butter melted on them. When we'd done eating, we talked awhile. Then the four of us went back to the barn and lay around talking some more while it slowly got dark out. The rain didn't start again, and on my way to the privy I noticed stars showing through breaks in the clouds.

Once in the night, the hounds barked, waking me up. But they quieted after a minute, and I went back to sleep.

Sometime later, a flurry of yelling and shooting woke us all. We were on our feet in an instant, pulling on wet boots, knotting laces hastily around our ankles, dropping our packs down from the loft, scrambling down the ladder. There were raiders, a lot of them, in twos and threes around the hamlet, all or most with guns. Some carried torches and were trying to light off the rain-wet cabins, using birch bark set against the doors as kindling. Others stood back, covering doors and windows with their muskets or pistols. Men and boys would likely be shot coming out; women and girls might not be so lucky.

The only light was from raider torches and flaming birch bark. Tom muttered quick instructions to the rest of us, then Jamila and I slipped quietly out of the barn toward the rear of two musketeers, our swords free. The general laughter and whooping covered any sound we made, and we hit them before they knew we were there. The two had been waiting for anyone who came out the door of Whidby's cabin, and neither fired a shot.

In the moment of killing, I smelled whiskey on their breath.

With one of their pistols, I killed the torcher who stood near the flames that licked Whidby's door. His own pistol in hand, he'd been waiting for a shutter to open and someone to poke a gun barrel out the front window. Grab the barrel and shove it up, I suppose, then shoot in through the window. But it hadn't worked that way.

Jamila had slipped behind a big sugartree, a raider musket in her hands, and I saw Paddy run out the barn door with our packs, heading for the road and the woods on the other side. Apparently no one had noticed us yet, or realized we weren't some of them. They assumed that everyone but them was trapped inside the cabins.

I turned and looked for Tom. The fires weren't big enough to light things much, but I could see him crouched over two bodies. Without waiting further I ran to the Whidbys' front door, kicked the flaming birch bark away from it, then slipped around the side of the cabin to see what was in back. A man with both sword and pistol drawn stood by the rear window, his back to the wall, waiting for anyone who tried to climb out of it. And grinning, no doubt. I slipped up to him from behind and cut his head mostly off, then took his pistol.

I heard another shot, then a yell of alarm and two more shots, and slipped quickly around to where I could see. Some of the raiders were taking shelter behind one of the other cabins; they'd finally awakened, were aware that someone was killing them. Others crouched, looking around. Things were getting dangerous. And one of the dangers was that some farmers would come busting out with fingers on triggers and shoot at us while we were trying to deal with the raiders.

I crouched, and slipped around in the darkness till I was behind some raiders, then moved in quickly, sword in my right hand, pistol in my left, and hit them before they saw me. I killed two with my blade in the time it takes to say it, then their two buddies turned. I pointed the pistol at the nearest and pulled the trigger, and to my relief it flashed and roared. The other of them had been reloading his musket and swung it clumsily at me like a club, but I dropped to my knees as he swung, and cut his thigh to the bone. He screamed, staggering backward, and I lunged, striking upward beneath his ribs. I heard more gunshots and screaming, and took off for the road.

There was a miniature stampede, raiders and Brothers, the difference being that we were warriors, hadn't been drinking, and knew who was who. I killed another from behind, and saw someone too slim to be Tom kill two more. Those who reached the road looked around for just a moment, swearing frantically, then ran off on foot. A moment later Tom came trotting up from the hamlet with a bloody sword and a wide grin.

While we'd been killing raiders, Paddy'd cut loose their horses where they'd been tied to saplings along the road, and had whipped them back into the woods. As nearly as we could figure, counting up there in the road, we'd killed at least a dozen raiders, and five or more had gotten away. Paddy thought there'd been ten or twelve horses; apparently some of the raiders had ridden two on a horse.

I glanced northward up the road at a star-picked sky. The Big Dipper lay nearly level across it, low and to the left of the North Star. I wasn't as good as some at telling time by the stars, but it seemed to me that at this season, that made it somewhere around midnight. Too early to hit the road again.

"Whidby!" I shouted. "It's all right! We've killed most of them, and the rest have run off south!"

We stood watching the cabins from the road. For a minute nothing happened, then I saw a door open, not Whidby's. A minute later, Whidby's opened too. "Don't fall over the bodies!" I yelled.

A minute later I heard someone shout. "Love of Jesus! Theer's two of 'em dead almost on me doorstoop. Wot happened, Whidby?"

I couldn't make out what Whidby answered. Other doors opened. A man came out with a torch in one hand and a gun in the other, and began to walk around, peering. "God be praised!" he called. "The boogers be layin' dead all over the place!"

"Whidby!" I called again. "We're out here by the road. We killed at least a dozen, and the rest ran off! On foot. Paddy cut their horses loose and ran 'em into the woods."

Every man and well-grown boy in the hamlet was out now, about ten all told, with every gun they had. Whidby and the man with the torch were walking slowly toward us, talking. Whidby was telling him about the strangers he'd put up, I suppose. We met them grinning, our hands held wide and empty. Inside of ten minutes the people of Bedale had made a full body count—fourteen. The men dragged them into a pile beside the road; they'd cart them off when daylight came, and meanwhile they'd serve to warn off any return.

All four hounds were dead, tongues out and swollen. I remembered the barking I'd heard, sometime earlier, and realized what had happened: One or two raiders had come up ahead of time, thrown poisoned meat to them, and left.

Nobody went back to bed just yet. A man named Big Little set out sentries. Children stared at us, especially at Jamila. A young girl sent coy glances at Paddy and me. Women poked up fires in fireplaces, added wood, began to cook. Earthen jugs were brought out from cool holes under floors, corncob stoppers were drawn and sour beer passed around. I suspect they had whiskey too, but wanted to stay sober.

We had to eat again, of course, tell them what had happened, and lie about who we were and where we were going. And no, we didn't want the raiders' horses. We traveled afoot; the horses were theirs now. When we came to a town, we'd tell the authorities what had happened. Maybe they could find out what place, a village most likely, had come up missing fourteen men and ten or so horses.

It took an hour or more before we made it back into

the hayloft. We talked about taking turns on sentry go, but decided the farmers were taking good enough care of that. And anyway the raiders would be steering clear of Bedale, at least for a while.

We even slept till near sunup, and ate breakfast with the Whidbys. A festive breakfast: They brought out a comb of honey to sweeten our porridge with, and fried bacon to add savor. As we swung northward up the road, the whole hamlet was out to bid us farewell, and it seemed to me that if we ever needed to hole up somewhere, this could be the place.

TWELVE

About noon that day we came to a good-sized village called York Town, told the chief constable there what had happened at Bedale (crediting unknown others with our part in it), ate noonmeal at the inn, and got back on the road. A dozen kilometers north of York Town, the country got less rugged, and the hilltops were wide enough that here and there, fields had been cleared on them.

It clouded up some that afternoon, tall thunderheads rumbling and flashing in the distance, and from a couple of points where the view was right, we saw dark rain curtains. But all we got was a few fat drops once, making spots on the dirt.

In spite of our late getaway, we made better than forty kilometers that day, judging by the map. Forty kilometers and three more burned-out hamlets—only three out of numerous, but how many more would burn by winter? Probably the farmers would set up a sentry system if it kept up; probably had in some hamlets already.

When we stopped to rest, it was at hamlets, where we told the people about Bedale as if we'd heard about it instead of being part of it. And made sure to tell them about the hounds getting poisoned. Within days the

moral should be all over the country around there:
Don't depend on your dogs to warn you.

It occurred to me that the Lizard worshipers might
switch to some other evil when they learned what had
happened to their raiders at Bedale. My guess was,
most of them were cowards, substituting liquor, numbers, and surprise for courage.

We spent the night at a village called Look Bahn,
where the people were smallish and wiry, nearly as
dark as Jamila but pretty much straight-haired. They
seemed to speak only Merkan, like the people of Bihar,
but they didn't look like them. Their faces were different, and the men tended to be more muscular.

The supper we got at Look Bahn tasted pretty good
until I found out the stew was made with dog meat.
Logically it shouldn't have bothered me. Meat is meat,
right? And it tasted good enough. But when I found
out, I felt like a cannibal.

We decided to stay at Look Bahn overnight and clean
up in the washroom at the inn. Whenever I saw Tom
naked, it troubled me. I mean, I'd seen some hairy
guys before, but Tom wasn't hairy—he was furry! If you
skinned him you could sell the pelt, honest to God!

I decided someone that hairy couldn't be an angel.

One drawback to staying in inns in summer is that
indoors it doesn't cool off as quickly after sundown. So
sometimes, in a room, it's too hot to go to sleep for a
while. I never had that trouble in the woods. (The
other side of the coin, of course, is that on toward
morning, indoors, you don't sleep cold.) So when I
stayed at an inn, I might sit around outdoors awhile
after supper, usually with a mug of beer, waiting for my
room to cool off. The inn at Look Bahn had an awning
out front, and sitting there with the others while the
dusk thickened, I started to look at some things. And to
ask some questions, keeping my voice low for privacy.

"Tom, how did that Lizard recognize us at Kings
Town? How did he even run into us? He wasn't looking

for bodyguards; I knew that then. How did he know what we are?"

"Presumably he was watching for Brothers of the Order. We know the Lizards have agents and spies in the government there. Probably it's more or less riddled with them. The Lizards have . . . substances they can give people that make them somewhat their slaves. Pleasure substances, let's call them. Money's just one of them, the simplest but least reliable.

"As for how they knew there'd be people like you to watch for—I suspect they may have picked up a Brother more or less by chance, and learned from him that others were being sent. We recognized early that this could happen. It's one reason you were told so little about the mission."

I bridled at that, though I didn't say anything. No Brother would tell about his mission, under any pain. Tom's violet eyes read mine, and answered my thought. "You're facing an enemy," he said, "who has ways of finding things out—ways you've never heard of before—and they may have been looking for someone more to question.

"The man in the inn may have been more than a recruiter. And he may have sent someone to the Lizard with word of you, while you were eating."

Jamila got into the conversation then. "How were they able to find us after the Lizard was dead?"

"The Lizard's body would have contained a transducer, a thing that told Lizard headquarters where he was and what condition he was in—in this case dead. The Lizards in the scout, in their airboat that is, probably located the body that way; the transducer would keep working long enough for that. They could have looked for him by tracing his gun, too, but obviously they didn't, or they'd have found you. The way they did later."

Soong had told me the Lizards were more dangerous than anyone I'd run into before, and I'd believed him. Now that I had some details, the danger seemed more real, more personal, more *dangerous*. I wasn't feeling good about things when we went in to bed, but I knew I'd be okay again with a night's sleep.

We got an early start in the morning, and by the next evening we'd seen a weathered sign with rough carved runes that read COMMONWEALTH OF THE LAKES 15. I didn't know what the Commonwealth of the Lakes would be like, except apparently it wasn't a kingdom. And my experience had been that if a country wasn't a kingdom, things were apt to be strange and unpredictable there.

THIRTEEN

As usual, we broke camp soon after dawn, reaching the border an hour or so after sunup. It was a clear, bright morning, still cool but not as cool as most, and I could imagine it getting hot before midday.

On the Allegheny side, the armed men at the border station ignored us, four road-worn travelers leaving the country on foot. They were interested in incoming goods they could collect a tariff on.

On the Commonwealth side there were changes right away. Instead of a cabin, their border station was a two-story frame building shaded on the south and west by big sugartrees. A sign ordered everyone to stop there. As we approached, a uniformed man stepped out, eyed our swords, and said something back through the door. Several more came out then, one of them an officer.

"Where are you people from?" the officer asked when we walked up.

"Allegheny," Tom said.

"Let me see your passes."

Tom took out the safe conduct the duke had given him. The officer said it had no authority on this side of the border, but he didn't look as hard-eyed as he had. Maybe the duke had a good reputation here.

"What's your purpose in coming to Lakes?"

"We're passing through. On our way to Adirondack. Is there a problem?"

The officer's eyebrows raised at mention of Adirondack, and he gestured at Tom's sword. "The problem's with those. You're not citizens, so you can't carry them here without a permit. Which I can't give you, and wouldn't if I could. You won't need them in Lakes anyway, but you'll want them when you get to Adirondack."

He stopped to rub his chin thoughtfully, then called back through the door again, and a minute later two more guys came out.

"Jennings," he said, "I want you and Nelson to take these people to Major Chakri in New Heber. Take Jones as your driver." He turned to us. "You'll need to give up your weapons to Corporal Jennings here. He'll keep them for you. If the major gives you a permit, Jennings will let you have them back and you can be on your way. If he doesn't, Jennings will bring you back here and you can have your weapons to take back with you to Allegheny." He raised an eyebrow. "Unless you'd rather just go back now?"

Tom grinned. "No. We'll be glad to accept your offer."

"I can't speak for Major Chakri," the officer said, "but I'll tell you honestly, I doubt he'll let you continue armed as you are."

"In that case we'll see you later, lieutenant. And our thanks for your courtesy."

The lieutenant nodded, a nod that carried a sense of shrugging, and went back in. I'd been impressed with his decency, but I couldn't help thinking that people tended to be agreeable toward Tom.

Corporal Jennings had us wait with Constable Nelson on a bench beneath one of the sugartrees. About ten minutes later, a man who had to be Jones came driving a light wagon around the corner of the building. Jennings collected our swords and put them in a luggage box beneath the driver's feet. Then we climbed in back with Nelson, Jennings climbed up beside Jones on the spring seat, and we started off.

Nobody examined our packs, so we kept our pistols! I suppose they assumed that anyone who had a pistol would carry it in his belt. But even so . . . I wondered if an angel could make people overlook things. But at least on the surface, Tom, if he *was* an angel, seemed to operate like anyone else, only more shrewdly.

Riding a wagon isn't the greatest way in the world to travel, especially sitting on the bed, but the road was as good as any you'll ever find. Not only were the low places graveled, but buried in the roadbed here and there were big tile pipes, half a meter to a meter in diameter, to drain the water from the upslope side of the road to the downslope side! I'd never seen anything like it.

Some ten or twelve kilometers brought us to New Heber, on a main east-west crossroad. New Heber was a good-sized town, with maybe two thousand people, and I'd never seen one so clean, or better laid out. And prosperous-looking, with the widest main street I'd ever seen, pretty much lined with sugartrees. People moved as if they had someplace to go and something to do.

The signs were all in Merkan, and I got the idea they didn't use any other language there, or not much anyway. At the far edge of town, Jones pulled the wagon up in front of a shaded brick building with a sign that said LAKES CONSTABULARY, WASATCH–DUCHESNE–UINTAH DISTRICT. We were led to a waiting room inside and told to sit. Jennings went to report, and was back in a couple of minutes.

"Come with me," he said. "Major Chakri will see you now."

The major's door had two small signs on it. The upper said COMMANDANT; the lower, *Major Brigham Chakri*. Jennings opened it and gestured us through. The office was a corner room, with broad windowed doors on the north and east walls, open to let what breeze there might be blow through. Outside was a green lawn, and flower beds of yellow and red, violet and white. I smelled roses.

Major Chakri kept his seat when we came in. He was big-chested and round-faced, kind of fat but not flabby-looking, with skin the brown of tree sugar. He kept us standing while he looked us over.

"The corporal tells me you're Alleghenians traveling to Adirondack. And that you have weapons you want to take with you. Is that correct?"

Tom answered. "Not entirely, major. We have just come from Allegheny, but only one of us was resident there."

The eyebrows raised a trifle. "Where are you from then? What is your homeland?"

"We're from different places, and subjects of no king but God. We are Brothers of the Order of Saint Higuchi."

Chakri didn't say anything for a minute. His scowl was enough. "The Church of Rome," he said at last.

People—Protestants mainly—sometimes call it that. The Holy See has been in Norlins since the Great Shuffling of course, but Church legend has it that it used to be in a great city called Rome, back before the Change. Some people even call Norlins "New Rome."

Tom nodded. "The Church of Rome," he said.

"And you're going to Adirondack? They're Buddhist there, most of them."

"We will travel *through* Adirondack," Tom answered. "You know of the Israelis."

The major's eyes sharpened. "Israelites you mean? What have you to do with the Israelites?"

"We will ally ourselves with them."

"Against whom?"

"Their enemies are our enemies. I can say no more."

"The Israelites are God's chosen," Chakri said, "and a people of great effectiveness. So far as I know, they don't seek allies. And I believe they do not permit your Church within their borders."

"Our God is the same God. And anyone can use allies, if the allies are effective enough, and honorable."

Chakri's wide mouth pursed. "Adirondack is a place of lawlessness and disorder, and in almost any locale there, you'll be noticed as strangers. You're well-advised to pass it by—Adirondack and the Saint Lawrence People's Republic as well. You can reach Israel by boat, from the Commonwealth. I suggest the port of Us-We-Go."

"You're advice is appreciated," Tom replied. "But our instructions are to travel through Adirondack and join with certain fighting men there." He changed the subject then. "I believe your men's muskets are rifled?"

Major Chakri frowned. I got the impression that the Commonwealth government didn't want foreigners to think, or know, that their constabulary's muskets were rifled. "Selected sharpshooters carry rifled muskets," he said. "That's true of many constabularies."

Tom nodded. "I'd like to shoot a target in competition with your best sharpshooter."

Chakri went for it. If nothing else, Tom had him curious now. We walked together to a shooting range half a kilometer behind the building, and from an off-hand position at 100 meters, a constable shot five rounds at a target. Three hit inside the twenty-centimeter bull's-eye, the other two close below it; darn good shooting. After three rounds to get used to the gun, Tom fired five for score and put them all in center bull, in a pattern not more than eight centimeters across. I was impressed but not surprised; the major was purse-mouthed.

"And may we show you something on your pistol range?" Tom asked. "I'd like you to see what can be done almost without sound."

Puzzled now, the major walked us to the pistol range. The targets there were sandbags roughly in the shape of a human torso and head, and a quiltwork of bullet-hole patches. "Jamila," Tom invited, "demonstrate your sling for the major."

She opened the pouch that hung from her waist, took her sling out, and hurled a slug. At twenty-five meters it struck the dummy in the face, burst the sackcloth, and buried itself in the sand. The major whistled silently.

After that, Tom had me do my sword drill. Then Chakri asked what Paddy Glynn did. "He's a novice," Tom answered, "newly joined with us, of unusual strength and greater promise. But more important to us in this, he is pure of heart."

Paddy blushed. I don't know whether he was embarrassed by the compliment or some impurities.

Then Tom invited Jamila and me to attack him—Tom, that is—hand to hand. At first we held back a bit, afraid we'd injure him. We ended up busting a gut trying to get to him, with no success. The major was impressed with all of us, but with Tom most of all. Back in his office he had us sit, and looked us over carefully.

"And you will not tell me to what enemies of Israel you will . . . do what you do?"

"I may not name them," Tom answered. "But they're the enemies of everyone who worships God, whatever church they worship in. Including those whose name for God is Allah or Brahma."

Chakri's gaze stayed on Tom for a long moment. It seemed to me he was deciding whether or not to be annoyed at Tom's including Moslems and Hindus with those who worship God. If so, he decided to let it be. Taking a piece of paper from a drawer, he stamped it with the constabulary stamp, then wrote on it, asking each of us our name. Jamila and Tom gave only their given names, as if they didn't have any others. I gave him all three of mine. Paddy beat that with four names: *Padraic Eamon Mac Gloinne*, spelling it out for the major, who shook his head over it. When he was done writing, Chakri gave the paper to Tom.

"I risk a reprimand for this," Chakri said dryly, "or worse, if you misbehave with your weapons. But these are ominous times. I see a common cause between us that outweighs our differences, and a force in you that outweighs the risk. There are some here who believe that the evil we see outside our borders can't threaten us as long as we . . ." Instead of finishing, he shook his head and changed the subject.

"While in the Commonwealth of the Lakes, do not identify your Church unless you must. There are those who would appeal my decision to the apostles, and I can't be sure they'd let it stand. They might imprison you for trespass."

Tom stood up. "We were not sent to disturb the order and peace of any people put on Earth by God," he said. "And with the assistance of His Angels, who are at the command of no Earthly church but answer only to God, I believe we shall prevail against our common enemy. If we don't, at least we will die in His service."

He offered Chakri his hand. The major shook it, looking really sober, gripping it hard as if wringing it.

"I suppose you have a map," Chakri said.

Tom nodded. "We do."

The major called Jennings in and told him to take us out and give us back our weapons; that we were free to go. When we had them, Tom asked Jennings to thank his lieutenant for his courtesy. Then we left town hiking northward.

According to Jamila's map, we walked something like forty kilometers that day in spite of the time spent at the border station and in New Heber. Add the wagon ride and we'd made about fifty, in spite of the heat and humidity which were as bad as any that summer. We stopped for the night at a village called Cluj. (In the commonwealth, all the villages have signs at the edge, so you never need to guess how their names are spelled.) Cluj didn't look much at all like New Heber. The streets were narrow and it wasn't laid out as well, though almost every yard had at least one sugartree shading the house on the south. Here too, Merkan was the language on the signs and from the people's mouths. And like the others, it had a common garden with trees and flower beds, which the locals called a *park*.

The supper was good, and the inn cleaner than most. They served no beer or wine, but there was fresh buttermilk, chilled. And sweet cider, in spite of it being out of season. I asked how they chilled them. They told me they cut ice blocks in winter and stored them, along with some cider barrels, in a shed full of sawdust, to use in summer.

There was a bathhouse, too, even a small one for women, with tubs, soap, paddles, and wringing posts for clothes. When our bellies were full and our clothes and bodies clean, I loaned Paddy my razor so he could shave the down he called whiskers.

And watching Paddy shave, something struck me about Tom that drove everything else out of my mind.

After we'd finished and put our wet clothes back on, we went outside to the park and sat in the twilight on a pair of facing benches. A sickle moon hung low and ruddy in the west.

No one was saying much, each of us alone with his thoughts or hers. Below the hairline, Tom's face was smooth except for eyebrows, *but he never shaved!* I shaved every time we stayed at an inn, but I'd never seen him shave! He had plenty of body hair, more than anyone I'd ever seen, and the white hair on his head came halfway down his forehead. But he had no whiskers. Which spooked me, not only because it made Tom seem stranger than ever, but because it was my business to notice things. And this I hadn't, till this evening.

I don't suppose angels have to shave, but I never heard that angels had furry bodies either, or got hungry and ate. And I'd seen Tom take a leak or a dump different times, too. Except for his eyes and his hairiness, he'd seemed to me like any man, only better at things than the rest of us.

My thoughts were interrupted by two claps of thunder, one right after the other, like "boom-boom!" There wasn't any rumbling or any lightning, and I couldn't see a cloud anywhere. Just "boom-boom!" I looked around, frowning. Jamila did too. Paddy looked worried. Tom looked slightly amused, as if he knew something we didn't.

"What was it?" Jamila asked him.

"Lizard," he said.

"Lizard what?" I asked. "Cannon?"

"No cannon," he answered. "Just a Lizard in a hurry, passing in the night."

And that's all he'd say about it.

I felt kind of . . . ill at ease, restless, and asked Jamila to take a walk with me. As we ambled down the street in the warm humid evening, I asked her if I could sneak into her room that night.

She stopped and took my hands in hers. "No, Luis. Not tonight; not tomorrow. Not anymore at all." Her face and voice were calm when she said it, not irritated with me for asking, not apologetic for turning me down. Just—this is how it is.

In spite of myself, I felt abused. "Care to tell me why?" I asked.

Now she did look annoyed. "Haven't you ever heard of pregnancy?"

I didn't feel abused anymore. I felt like a stupid ass. Which was just how I should have felt, because somehow I *hadn't* thought of pregnancy, not even once.

"We were lucky before," she told me. Her annoyance was gone now, her voice soft. I guess she'd read my face. "And it was my fault," she went on, "more than yours. I took the initiative before, not you. Since then I've had my period, thank God, and I'm not taking the risk again. It could affect carrying out my role in the mission, and it could get us both expelled from the Order."

"Right," I said. "And—sorry about before."

We walked to the edge of town without saying anything more, then turned and started back. When we were near the park, she stopped again. "Luis, about before. You don't need to be sorry. I'm not. I'm glad. It's just that we can't do it again."

"Thanks. For making it all right." We took each other's hands and squeezed, then dropped them.

That night, lying sweating on the bed beside Tom and Paddy, I ran alternate futures through my mind, like plays. Futures in which Jamila and I never touched one another again, and futures where we left the Order and got married. Until each kind of future seemed all right. It's a technique the Order teaches. It cut a lot of time off my sleep that night, but it was time well spent.

It also occurred to me that whatever else Tom might be, he was probably a confessor and counselor, and that I needed to talk with him about what I'd done.

When I finally went to sleep, it wasn't Jamila I had on my mind. It was Tom and his lack of beard.

FOURTEEN

The farm*land* in Lakes wasn't the best I'd ever seen, but the farms were, and there was more cleared land than anywhere I'd ever been. There weren't any hamlets; each family lived apart at its fields, and single farmhouses, shaded by trees, were scattered along every lane. Villages, mostly small, were closer together than usual, and all the main roads were ditched, their low stretches graveled against serious rutting.

Where it was hilly, the slopes were left timbered, and mainly the bottomlands were cleared. But where it was only gently rolling, upwards of half the land was cleared, more often than not, and it seemed as if each farm had its own woodlot for fuel: maybe half a dozen hecters fenced to keep out livestock, and thick with seedlings to fill the holes when older trees were cut.

So both the scenery and the hiking in the Commonwealth were different from anywhere else I'd been, from Ozark to Allegheny. Especially Ozark and Allegheny.

None of us talked much while we walked—but Jamila and I almost always walked beside each other, and sat together when we ate. I'd thought maybe, after our talk in Cluj, she'd want to keep more distance between us, and I was glad she didn't. She never invited me to lay with her though, and I never proposed it by as much as a hint, because she was right about the risks. But more and more it seemed to me that when the mission was over, I was going to propose marriage, even though marriage meant leaving the Order. And it seemed to me she'd say yes.

Considering what happened later, I was probably right about that.

All the way across the Commonwealth, we saw no signs of devil worship. Not one. What we did see one evening was militia drilling, and they looked a lot better—sharper and more disciplined—than the Allegheny Army units at Gotaborg. They'd probably been at it a lot longer, and a lot more willingly. To defend their homes, not because somebody dragged them there in chains.

We didn't see anyone carrying a musket or pistol, except the militia that evening and an occasional two-man mounted constabulary patrol. And I'm willing to bet that even in the militia, the muskets were rifled. No one wore a sword except constabulary and militia officers; we carried ours wrapped in our ponchos and tied to our packs.

As we got up toward the Tario Sea, hills gave way to flatlands that were more or less wet. There were more woods there, and where it was cleared, it was mostly pastures and hay meadows, green and springy. The mosquitoes were pretty bad, though the locals said they were tapering off. The cattle were some of the best I'd ever seen.

The river floodplains had been logged through—you could see the rotting stumps beneath the forest roof—but it looked as if just the best trees were taken. Most of the bridges had roofs, and sidewalls that came down partway to the planking! When I asked an innkeeper why they were covered, he looked surprised that anyone needed to ask. "To keep the snow and ice off in the winter," he told me. I wasn't used to snow being much of a problem. He told me it got waist-deep there sometimes—it could get shoulder-deep, even two meters deep—and that knee-deep was common. Usually, he said, the country would be well covered with it from before Christmas—sometimes a month before—till well into March, with maybe a thaw or two some years to remind people what the ground looked like. I'm not sure he wasn't exaggerating, but I think he intended to tell the truth. Maybe got carried away a little.

I decided I'd like to spend a winter there.

Late one afternoon, after a few days of hiking north and east, our road dropped down to the wider-than-usual floodplain of a good-sized river, the Us-We-Go, the border with Adirondack. There was a ferryboat of a sort, a big flat-bottomed rowboat tied to a short floating dock. She was four meters long or close to it—the boat, that is. Her stubby, square-framed boatman held out his left hand and pointed at each of us with his right, saying "two penny" each time. While Jamila was getting out his money, his wide grin showed big square yellowed teeth, and he ogled her with eyes that had a slant to them. He had a large head with a patchy beard, and someone or something had moved his nose a couple of centimeters off center. It had either been a fight, or a horse had kicked him.

He looked cheerfully crazy, as if he'd fight just for the fun of it. After we'd all gotten seated in his boat, he started rowing us across. There was a second set of thole pins forward of where he sat, and an extra set of oars in the bottom. I reached for the extras, but Paddy grabbed them first, seated them and began rowing too. The boatman looked back over his shoulder and grinned at him like a maniac.

I suppose if we'd had a horse, it would have had to swim across behind the boat, led by the reins. If we'd had a wagon, we'd have had to float it or go on to some other, larger ferry. I had a feeling that Adirondack was going to be different than any place I'd been before, even more than the Commonwealth was, but I really didn't have an inkling of what was in store for us there.

FIFTEEN

On the other side of the river, the road at first wasn't even a cart road, only a saddle trail and sometime cattle driveway, but we hit wheel ruts before long. It also lacked ditches—we'd gotten used to them in the Commonwealth—although some of the ruts would just about qualify.

I'd been told that Adirondack was mountainous, with mountains bigger than the Ozarks or anything we'd seen in Allegheny. But the first couple of days the country ranged from level to mildly rolling, with little roads and lanes going off everywhere. It was about half woods and half fields, an awful lot of cleared land by Allegheny standards and lots of others.

The thing that was most different from anywhere else I'd been, was that every county had a stone fort and every village a palisade. The people were different too. They carried themselves differently, their clothes were different, and no one seemed to speak Merkan.

There were two main races those first days, and that wouldn't change anywhere we went in Adirondack. One was like the ferryboat man: short with straight black hair and more or less slanty eyes. Japanese, Tom called them. The other was like ourselves—some with light hair, and mostly taller than the Japanese. There were also quite a few who seemed to be a mixture. Most of the hamlets were Japanese, though, as if God, in his wisdom, wanted a mostly Japanese kingdom here.

In spite of the fortresses and stockades, the people we saw working in the fields didn't look warlike at all. Most that we passed on the roads didn't look warlike either, but now and then we'd see someone carrying a sword, usually with a bow on one shoulder and sometimes a pistol or two stuck in his sash along with the sword. These armed guys never seemed to wear a belt; sashes were the thing. We also saw men I supposed were priests or monks. They wore simple robes, shaved their heads, and carried no visible weapon—or cross.

We wore our swords on our belts again.

I didn't see one musket in those two days. They seemed to prefer bows there, which makes sense if you're halfway good with a bow and the musket isn't rifled.

On the third and fourth days, the country got hillier and more wooded. We were on a main road, and a couple of times met patrols of eight mounted soldiers armed with swords, bows, and pistols. They never paid any attention to us. Twice we saw a convoy of half a dozen or more wagons, their drivers wearing pistols and with swords close at hand. Armed guards on horseback scouted ahead and rode behind, wearing their swords across their backs.

Once we heard an uproar ahead of us and took to the woods, moving to where we could see. There were five wagons stopped in the road, and it looked as if the people with them were tending their wounded. We didn't see who'd jumped them, but whoever they were had cut loose most of the wagon horses and driven them off.

I told Tom we ought to carry our pistols in our belts instead of in our packs. He just grinned and shook his head, and trusting him, I let the matter drop. I'd pretty much decided he was a master, whether he admitted it or not.

When I remembered to, I still felt a little spooked by his not having whiskers. But most of the time I didn't think of it.

On our fourth day in Adirondack, we passed a patrol that was two men short of the usual eight. A seventh horse had an empty saddle. The patrol guidon had a row of fresh scalps tied to his lance below the unit's pennant, while two uglies who seemed to be brigands were trotting behind on foot with their hands tied and a lead rope around their necks. They were trying to look defiant.

In some kingdoms they don't hold public executions, but I was willing to bet they did in Adirondack.

The weather was holding hot and muggy, and about once an hour we stopped for a short break, back a little in the woods. We'd just gotten up from one and were waiting by the road when eight guys on foot came round a nearby bend and saw all of us but Jamila. She'd stayed behind to take care of some business she preferred privacy for.

Eight guys, but not a road patrol; I had no doubt that they were bandits. Six of them belonged to the taller stock, but they were dressed like the other armed civilians we'd seen: barefoot, with breeches baggy in the ass and kind of snug below the knees; a loose shirt hanging out, with loose sleeves to the elbows; and the usual sash around the waist. Several of them had bows as long as they were, and quick as a wink they had big long arrows nocked and the bowstrings half drawn. Meanwhile they moved closer to us.

The biggest was the leader. He grinned a mean grin and talked at us in the Adirondack language. When that didn't take, he tried another language that I doubt I'd ever heard before.

"Try Merkan," I said. "None of us understand those lingos."

"Ah! Merkan! You guys give all you goods, us no kill."

"Us guys got no goods," I said, and held my arms out, palms open. "Nothing. Us guys poor people."

His grin broke long enough to laugh an artificial laugh; and he said something to the guys with him. They didn't laugh; they looked like they hated our guts. Then he spoke to me again, sounding downright friendly. "You guys got sword. You take you sword, put him on ground. We take 'em, let you go."

"I got good idea," I said. "Us guys join you guys, be friends. Help you rob rich guys. Get much goods."

At that he stopped grinning. I didn't know whether he didn't understand me, or didn't like the idea, or didn't like to change his mind, or what. I didn't much care which. I just wanted to give Jamila time enough to get around behind them before he gave the order to kill us. He could take as long as he wanted, deciding how to answer.

Once he'd decided, he was an effective speaker. "Take sword off *now*. Or us kill you."

We had an ace in the hole, of course: the loaded pistols in our packs. Thanks to Tom. In a dangerous country like this, *no* one would carry his pistol in his pack, right? The idea was stupid. What good would a pistol do in your pack? Well, for one thing, not even Major Chakri had thought to look. None of the Adirondack road patrols had stopped us. And these bad-face bandits would probably have shot us on sight if we'd worn pistols in our belts.

The bandits stood about a dozen meters from us—not too far. "Us guys no want die," I said, as slowly as I thought I could get away with. And instead of reaching for my belt buckle, I began to shrug out of my pack. Tom would know what I had in mind, and Paddy would follow our example. I hoped. The bandit leader just watched.

My biggest concern was Paddy. Tom would throw

himself on the ground as he drew. That went without
saying. But would Paddy know enough to do that?
I didn't want one of those long arrows through his
guts.

On the other hand, the bandits didn't seem to know
much Merkan. So as I laid my pack on the ground to
my left, and knelt to untie the thongs, I said cheerfully,
"Paddy, flat on your stomach before you fire."

I reached under the flap, thinking that if the bandits
had any connection at all with their warrior muses,
they'd know something fishy was happening and shoot
now. I could almost feel a long arrow slamming through
me. Then I heard this ugly "thwuck" sound, drew,
spinning, and heard a gunshot as I threw myself on the
ground. I cocked the hammer as I landed; pointed, and
pulled the trigger. (Not *aiming*, for God's sake!) Powder
boomed, the pistol jerking in my fist. At the same
moment there was another boom to my left rear and an
instant later another to my right.

I didn't take time to check results. I was on my feet,
sprinting, drawing my sword, trying to run a dozen
meters before the bandits could recover from surprise
and shock. The screaming and yelling hardly registered
on me.

And then there were none. I stood panting as if I'd
run a hundred meters. Jamila was standing in front of
me, her sword as red as mine. I looked around. Tom's
was bloody too. Paddy stood back almost at our packs,
sword newly drawn, looking stunned at how fast everything had happened.

Tom grinned at me, a different kind of grin than the
bandit chief's. "Jamila," he said, "this Luis is about five
times faster in a fight than he is in a drill. No wonder
Soong picked him to send."

She nodded. "Good thing I had a head start, or there
might not have been any left for me."

We looked the bodies over. The lead slug from Jamila's
sling had caved in the back of a bowman's head; her

pistol slug had taken another behind the ear. Three others had also been gunshot. That was pretty darn good; each of us had actually shot someone different! I thought I knew which had been Paddy's. One had taken a slug in the forehead and one in the middle of the chest. The other'd taken one in the knee, which had been just as effective for our purpose, but not the kind of shooting Tom or I would have done in this situation.

I pointed to the guy; he was on his side, starting to make keening sounds. "I think this one's yours, Paddy. What're you going to do about him?"

"Oh, Mr. Luis! Oi don't know what to do!"

"So far you've done pretty well. As I see it, you have two choices now. You can leave him like that, in which case the wolves might start eating him while he's still alive. Though more likely he'll lie there till he dies slowly or somebody else comes along and kills him. Or you can kill him now. Can you think of anything I've left out?"

Paddy's pale blue eyes begged me for some third alternative. I didn't have one. Then he drew his knife, and for a minute I thought he was going to put the guy out of his misery with it. Instead he cut off the guy's breeches above the knee, exposing the wound. That was some knee! Smashed! The ball had hit the kneecap dead center. The guy was passed out now, maybe at the sight of Paddy's knife.

Then Paddy pulled the shirt off a corpse we hadn't straightened yet. I watched for a minute without saying anything, while he cut the shirt and bandaged the knee with it, tight enough to pretty much stop the bleeding. Next he cut a crutch from a young sugartree and laid it by the guy.

I couldn't argue with that. Not that I would have anyway. If the guy had it in him, just maybe he'd make it to help somewhere.

While Paddy was cutting the crutch, I wiped my

blade on a dead bandit's breeches, sheathed it, and
helped Tom and Jamila straighten dead limbs and close
dead eyes, weighting the lids down with pebbles. When
that was done, we prayed for the souls. Then, Paddy
included, we picked up our pistols where we'd dropped
them, cleaned them as best we could with twigs, re-
loaded them, and put them back in our packs. It was
me who showed Paddy how to reload. After that we
started off down the road again.

SIXTEEN

After our fight with the bandits, the country got higher and steeper. We ran out of farms and villages. The forests were mostly thick and dark, the ravines deep and rugged. Some of the trees even Paddy didn't know, including a couple of the commonest, pointy-topped and looking almost black, with needles not two centimeters long.

The road didn't show a sign of wheel tracks anymore, or of cattle droving either. Along with human feet, saddle and pack animals were about the extent of the traffic. We saw no more patrols, almost none of the horses that'd helped trample the trail, and few people. In places it was too steep for carts anyway, showing quite a lot of bedrock. Streams brawled around boulders, and there were no bridges. If the season had been wet, we'd have been hard-pressed to ford some of them.

Occasionally there'd be a hut, usually abandoned but looking as if it had been used not too long before. I suspect they belonged to trappers and fur hunters who went somewhere else in summer, coming back in mid-fall like the trappers in Ozark, when the furs got prime again. But here, I suspected, the winters would be a lot longer than in Ozark.

With almost no people, we saw more wild game than back home. There were two kinds of deer, one of them the kind I was used to. The other was the darnedest-looking thing I'd ever seen, tall as a horse, or taller, with a fat nose, and a rear end too small for the front. We only saw a couple of them. When I saw the first one, I didn't even realize it was a kind of deer, but the second one had antlers I won't try to describe.

Once, in a little valley, we found a set of buildings that had been burned out—not a hamlet, but several small buildings built around a large one. We didn't see any bodies, but there were half a dozen recent graves nearby. There were about two hecters of garden, too, surrounded by the tallest post-and-rail fence I'd ever seen. To keep out the deer, I suppose. The garden was the biggest clearing we'd run across for a day and a half; weeds and crop plants struggled with each other for room.

I didn't think for a minute that the fire had been an accident. For one thing, sixty or seventy meters away at the end of a wide path, there'd been a smaller building that had also burned. And there weren't enough people within a day's hike to attack it the way Bedale had been attacked. The picture I got in my mind's eye was the Lizard airboat setting fire to this place like the farmhouse outside of Kings Town. Which is what I told Tom. He nodded.

The next morning it started to rain, cold and fairly hard, pouring straight down from a sky the color of shale. It kept coming as the day wore on, never letting up. The country was rugged, steep. It seemed as if the places fit for camping had water either standing or flowing, and crossing some of the creeks was tricky business. Finally daylight, such as it was, began to dim. When the last of it was gone, we'd almost have to stop, because even with the moon full, it promised to be darker than the grave when the sun was well down. The rain had eased a little, but it was still coming down pretty hard. Slipping and sliding at times, we reached the bottom of a valley, narrow and swampy, thick with brush and fallen trees. I couldn't think of a worse place to spend the night. The stream had swollen beyond fording, but we were lucky; beside the trail, a large pine had fallen across it, and we picked our way through the branches to the other side.

I told Tom I wanted to try for the top of the next ridge crest. It seemed to me we'd be better off camping up there. He nodded, even grinned.

It was approaching full night when we hit the last steep upgrade, and already as dark as some nights ever get. The trail was slick and greasy, so we trudged along beside it instead of on it, for better traction and for saplings to grab onto. I was cold through and through, my fingers like curved sticks. I couldn't see Tom's face, but I doubted he was grinning now—although with him I couldn't be sure. A couple of times I heard Jamila swear.

I was in the lead. When I finally reached the top, I peered around the best I could for ground that wasn't too rocky, where we could sleep. It could have been worse, but it was bad enough. The forest stand was thin on the crest, with more blowdowns than standing trees. I paused to look northward, down into the next valley. And—

"Look!" I called. Quietly, as if there might be someone to overhear. "Lights!"

The others came over. The lights were barely visible—if it hadn't been for a lull in the rain, we wouldn't have seen them—but they were real. There were several of them, like windows in a building, and surely not much more than a kilometer away as the crow flies.

"Let's go see what it is," I said. "It's downhill all the way from here, and it looks like heat and shelter."

"Yeah," said Jamila. "Let's do it." Paddy said nothing. I could hear his teeth clattering.

"Let's go," Tom said.

We started down. The trail on that side of the ridge was less steep than the one we'd just climbed, zigzagging down through the forest, and for a while we made decent time. But as we neared the bottom, we just couldn't see anymore. We were lucky the forest was as thick as it was, and the forest floor so spongy; it told us right away when we'd wandered off the trail, which we did a lot.

But if we couldn't see, we could hear. Rain was falling harder again, and over its steady muttering was the sound of a strong stream below. I began to wonder if I'd made a mistake, leaving the solid ridgetop for the light and warmth of someplace that suddenly, here in heavy forest, I wasn't sure we could find.

At last the slope toed out. On the flat, the timber nearly stopped, giving way to alder brush. With no forest roof overhead, I could see a little bit again, a few vague dark meters. We were in a swamp, but here, pole-sized logs had been laid down in pairs to walk on. Where the bark had worn off they were slippery, so we went on in a crouch.

A little ways farther, the trail disappeared, covered by water. Dark and cold, it soon reached my shins, and I hadn't even gotten to the stream proper yet. I paused, worried again.

Tom passed me. He was the heaviest of us, heavier than Paddy, and I suspected he'd be a good swimmer. We started after him. At the edge of the actual stream, he stopped, thigh-deep, and looked back at us. The current tugged at him. Two strides ahead, it was in full snarl and rush. He spoke loudly to be heard.

"Paddy," he said, "I'm going to let the current take me downstream. I'll go first and I want you to follow. Luis and Jamila will follow you. If you get in trouble, we'll help you. But you won't."

I couldn't see Paddy's face, but I imagined it: big-eyed, scared. Briefly I also imagined a fallen tree, one that ordinarily bridged the stream, submerged now.

And one of us, or more than one, getting tangled in its branches and drowning. "Yessir," Paddy said. Tom said nothing more. He went a couple of steps farther, then launched himself downstream, disappearing in the water and darkness. Paddy followed two steps behind, then me, the icy current grabbing me, sweeping me swiftly along. I had my pack on my back, and light as it was, I still had to fight to keep my head above water. *Get rid of it!* I told myself, then didn't.

After a little the current slowed, and I could see enough to realize I was in a small pond. My feet found ooze, and I started to kick, swimming instead of floating half-vertically, still moving downcurrent, still having difficulty with my pack, wondering why I didn't just get rid of it. In a couple of minutes I heard Tom say something ahead, Paddy answering. A moment later I joined them on a beaver dam, with knee-deep water pouring over it. Jamila arrived right after, her dark face and black clothing almost invisible.

"Okay," Tom said, "let's go," and plunged off the downstream side. Paddy followed, and then me. Even as I jumped, I told myself this was foolish, that we could have crossed on the dam and been done with it.

Here the current was less violent, though still swift. After a minute the stream emerged from brushy swamp into what seemed to be a clearing—and there were the lights again, not far away! Another minute and I saw Tom just ahead, pulling himself out of the stream onto a footbridge that cleared the flood by half a meter.

Then we were all standing on it, staring at the lights. "What are we waiting for?" Jamila said, and began striding toward them. The rest of us followed close behind.

The bridge was on a path that took us right to the building with the glowing yellow windows. The place was big and built of rock—big squared blocks of stone. I'd rarely seen anything as welcome to my eyes. It had a big heavy door with a big heavy frame. Tom lifted the massive knocker and struck twice, then we waited. All we could hear was the rain beating on the ground, and the sound of the stream a ways off.

A bar scraped, and the door opened. I saw a robed man against faint lamplight from some other room.

He asked us no question, just said, "Come in." As I entered, it occurred to me that we were going to make some big puddles on their floor. Stopping, I took off my pack, glad now that I hadn't offloaded it in the stream as I'd almost done. "We ought to leave our wet stuff out here," I said.

"By all means do," the robed man answered, and called to someone in the language we'd been hearing ever since the Us-We-Go: Japanese. He jabbered several sentences' worth, then turned to us again, switching back to Merkan as if there were no difference. "Towels and robes are being brought. Then we will see to your nourishment. Leave your wet things on the floor here; they will be dried in an oven to destroy any vermin."

His Merkan was as good as my mother's, though accented.

Hot food and getting rid of the cooties both sounded good to me. When we were down to the buff, or in Jamila's case the chocolate, a guy came with towels and robes stacked on his arms. Our host handed a towel to each of us while the second man laid the robes down on a bench nearby. My cold skin burned from the rush of blood as I toweled myself. No one said anything till we were dressed. Then our host gestured, and we followed him down a hall to a largish room with several tables, lit by its fireplace and a couple of bracketed oil lamps. A man was stirring a kettle on a pot hook.

"The stew is left over from supper," our host told us. "It is reheating." He gestured at a loaf of bread on the table, with a head of cheese beside it. "You may wish to begin."

We did. The cook had heated wine too, heavy strong wine, and the stew wasn't bad either, for having stood a couple of hours. The cheese was excellent. About the time I'd spooned in the last mouthful I wanted, my eyelids started to slide shut. Our host led us to a small room with four pallets on the floor, each with a woolen blanket folded on it and a weird little wooden pillow that fitted under the neck. I barely got lain down and the blanket over me before I was asleep.

SEVENTEEN

It was full daylight before Tom woke us up. Throwing
back my blanket, I rolled to my feet and looked out the
window. "Hey!" I said. "The sun's out!"

"Right. Cold fronts usually move through pretty fast.
You don't see many frontal storms like that in midsum-
mer, though."

Frontal storm? That was a new one on me; I'd have
called it a rainstorm.

"The washroom's down the stairs and to your right,"
he went on. "By where you go out to the latrine. You'll
see it. After that, it's last chance for breakfast."

We had the eating room to ourselves, Jamila and
Paddy and I. Tom must have eaten with the people
who lived there. Breakfast was oat porridge with a
wedge of cheese and a couple of plums. It reminded me
of breakfasts in the Brother house, back in Mizzoo.
Which was no surprise; this place was obviously a monastery. Had to be. In Adirondack, probably Buddhist.

After we'd eaten, we cut each other's hair right down
to stubble, and greased the stubble with stuff that Tom
gave us, stuff he got from the elderly robed man, who
was called Master Akihisa. It reeked like the stuff we
used back in Mizzoo when we'd come off a mission with
head lice.

153

I didn't know much about Buddhists, and wondered what they'd think here if they knew we were Catholic. Or did they already know? If Tom had eaten with them, he might have said something. Or—

Or had they been expecting us? I didn't know where that idea popped into my head from, but now it seemed to me that that's how it was.

When Soong had given me the map, he hadn't told me where, exactly, I was supposed to end up in Adirondack, or who I was to meet. Or anything. When I'd asked, he'd said I'd know when I got there. The red line on the map turned into a broken line a ways into Adirondack, where there wasn't any road anymore. That was after we got into the mountains. Then, after a ways even the broken red line quit, though the map showed the trail still going along.

Soong had told me if I couldn't end up at the right place with what I knew, then this mission wasn't for me, and I should come home. The map, he said, would get me close enough.

He never gave as much information as I'd like for a mission, but this had been the least yet. I supposed I'd get used to that kind of thing in time. I'd only completed my novitiate a little more than a year earlier, and on all but the last of my previous missions—I'd only been on four—I'd been a junior under a senior Brother. Most Brothers, by the time they'd completed their novitiate and juniorship, had attained greater spiritual certainty than I had. They could go off on something like this without any feeling at all that they needed to know more. God would provide through their warrior muse.

For me, though, I still wanted more information. "More data," Bhatti would say in his precise voice. "Always you want more data. When in fact what is needed is more faith! More spiritual certainty!"

I'd shrugged it off. Faith was nice when you had it, and in more and more things I did. But it's nothing you can force. And lacking enough faith, "more data" is nice. At least it would make me more comfortable, though I suppose, as Soong had said, it would keep me dependent on it.

Whatever. When I finished eating, I decided to find Tom and ask for more data. Not that I thought he'd give it to me, but I'd give it a try.

"Where are you headed?" Jamila asked as I got up from the table.

I told her, and without a word, she got up and followed me, Paddy in our wake. She looked curious. Not, it seemed to me, to hear whatever information I might get; she wanted to see what would happen, how Tom would handle me.

Paddy looked earnest. He had a lot of faith, but not in himself. He was green as grass. His faith was in any of us.

"More information, eh?" Tom said. And grinned. "Tell me what you already know, and I'll see if there's anything I know that you don't. What are we here for?"

"To do something about the Lizards. That's all I know. Eliminate them, I suppose. I don't have any idea how."

"Well, I have some ideas, but that's all they are. They're not information."

"I didn't even know what a Lizard looked like when I left Mizzoo."

"You know now, though."

"Yeah," I said, "but that was dumb luck."

Jamila interrupted. "Luck?!" she snapped. "Luck?! You already said he was a Lizard when all you'd seen was someone on horseback wearing a Seek wrapper around his head. In the dark yet! And nothing he'd said or done marked him as anything but human—a friendly one at that."

I was about to correct her: it hadn't been dark, only twilight. Then a realization struck me—*cognitions*, Bhatti called them. Chills flowed.

Tom's violet eyes don't miss much. "What was that?" he asked.

"About luck," I said. "And what it is. I've always been really lucky; luck could be my middle name. And it just came to me that luck is what I call it when I can't have what's really going on."

More chills. "What *is* really going on?" Tom asked.

"I don't know."

He laughed out loud. "Sounds good to me," he said, and grinning, pumped my hand. "So what else do you know?"

My grin matched his now; I could feel things starting to happen in me. "We were supposed to stop at the place we found burned out, a day and a half ago. That was the place the map route ended; the place we were supposed to go to. I just didn't realize it because the map didn't show it. This place we're at is a monastery, a Buddhist monastery, and that one was too. But the Lizards zapped it. Killed some of the monks there and . . . and the rest moved here! And . . ." Another wave of chills. "And more Brothers will be showing up here! Maybe some of them already have. This is now the gathering place."

Tom grinned even wider and looked at Jamila. "Makes sense to me. What do you think?"

She grinned back at him. "I'm convinced."

"Anything else?" Tom asked me.

"Yeah," I said. "Yes there is." The grin had slid off my face. "Why didn't they hit this place? Or will they? Tomorrow maybe."

"You've been doing a good job of answering questions," Tom said. "Answer that one."

"Well . . . The other place was made of wood . . . No, that's not it. They still could have gutted this place. Could the . . . Wait! They captured a Brother, or maybe killed one and got his map. And—could they follow the red line, the road I mean, and the trail, with an airboat?"

"I could," Tom answered.

"Okay, so they followed it and found the other monastery. Maybe they didn't know what it was; just a bunch of buildings in the forest. Maybe they didn't know what the Brother was. Anyway, they burned the place down."

I waited for the chills to come. They didn't.

"But you're not sure?"

I nodded, a little glum. "I didn't get chills."

"Ah. Do you need chills? To tell you whether you're right or not?"

"Hmh! No, I guess not. No, I don't." And there they were! Flowing over my body, tingling, making goose bumps.

Tom was grinning again. "You're right. You don't. They're nice to have, and they feel good, but you don't really need them." He paused. "Anything else to say?"

I looked. "Yeah. The master here, or masters." More chills, light this time, a touch. "The angels trained them. Just like they trained Bhatti and Soong." I turned to Jamila. "And Fedor and Freddy."

She grinned a mile wide, her teeth as white as Tom's.

I almost asked Tom then why he didn't have whiskers, why he never needed to shave. But Paddy was there, and I didn't want to spook him. So instead I said, "What do the angels who trained the masters look like?" Just then I felt sure that Tom was an angel, in spite of all his body hair, his fur. I didn't expect a straight answer, but I wanted to hear what he'd say.

Jamila entered in saucily. "Is it true that not all angels have wings, Tom?"

"They all have wings. But sometimes they travel without them." He grinned again and got up. "C'mon. I have some people for you to meet."

He led us into a yard, sort of a courtyard drill-ground, covered with sand. There were a dozen or so shave-headed Buddhist monks there doing martial drills. A dozen Buddhists and—Lemmi Tsinnajinni! He'd gotten there ahead of us, across the well-policed Commonwealth and up Adirondack's dangerous tracks, apparently the first Brother to make it.

After Tom had introduced us to the monks—using the Adirondack language to them!—Jamila and I went and got drill suits from the novice who issued goods, then returned to join the others. Their fighting drills were almost identical with those we did at the Brother house. The monks here had never known a female like Jamila before, a female Brother, and it tickled heck out of them when she'd beat one with a throw or death blow (deliberately held short of course, so no one got more than jarred or shaken up a bit). Whoever she beat (about half her opponents) would grin ruefully while the others laughed.

I didn't do badly either. Some of them, including Jamila, had more or less an edge on me in technique, but I won my share anyway, just like at home.

Everyone bowed and grinned at each other before and after every face-off. They were very good, but they didn't take things seriously. Just enjoyed being good.

We spent a week there, and it felt more and more like home. With certain differences: I never heard God mentioned, or Christ. Or Saint Higuchi, of course. And I never saw them pray. But they did spiritual drills, and lived a lot like we did in the Order. Outside of Adirondack, of course, their shaved heads would be a problem, if they did missions like we did. It wasn't all that uncommon for men to crop their hair to stubble like Brothers; the Church recommended it for hygiene. But a shaved head, actually shaved, would be conspicuous anywhere else I knew of.

It was on our second day there, in a little open-sided house at the edge of the forest, that I confessed to Tom about making love to Jamila in the hayloft and the inn.

Confession in the Order was a lot different than confessing as a parishioner—the way I did before I joined. Or during my first months as a novice, as far as that's concerned. But this confession to Tom went differently than *any* I'd made earlier. When I started confessing it, I felt no remorse. What I did feel was that something good was about to happen.

When I was done, Tom asked me what I thought was an appropriate penance. Just like Bhatti or Soong would have. It had always bothered me when they did that. I always felt they'd have given me a lighter penance than I ended up giving myself.

This time though, I told him I owed no penance.

"Okay," he said. "Tell me about that."

"Well—" I groped, trying to pin it down. "Because—" I felt a faint wash of goose bumps. "Because I don't feel it was a sin."

"All right. Was it a sin or wasn't it?"

"No," I said, "it wasn't." Stronger goose bumps. Tom could see something happening, and waited them out.

"Well then," he said when the goose bumps had settled, "if it wasn't a sin, did you need to confess it?"

"No."

"Good. Anything you do need to confess?"

I couldn't for the life of me come up with anything more than that I'd probably blasphemed a few times. I couldn't recall specifically.

"Okay, what penance for that?"

"Uh, supposing I help the cook tonight at supper?"

"Good. Your penance is to help the cook tonight at supper."

I felt like I was done then, so we got up and went back to the house of meditation, where we joined some of the monks in spiritual drills.

That evening, scrubbing tables and bowls and spoons, all of them wooden, and sweeping and mopping the eating room floor, I wondered why I was doing it. A blasphemy or two, unintended, unfelt, *unremembered*—maybe not even committed!—hardly seemed even a venial sin. And it hadn't bothered Tom that I'd exacted no penance of myself for fornication.

Enough of this equivocation, I told myself, irritated. I'd occasionally had trouble deciding whether I'd sinned or not, in this and that. Bhatti had told me once not to ask him again; that that was for novices and layfolk. A brother knew when he'd sinned and when he hadn't; all he had to do was be honest with himself.

And this penance I was doing was for something I maybe hadn't even done.

It hit me then, totally unexpected: There was a sin, but not what I'd thought. My sin was *treason to my own self in doing penance where I saw no sin!*

With the thought, a faint brief wave of chills flowed over me. I'd seen part of a truth, but only part of it. The rest would follow, sooner or later.

We stayed at the monastery for a week. On the third day, Jamila had come to breakfast quiet and preoccupied. I hadn't seen her like that before, and when I asked her about it, she said it was from a dream she'd had. A little later she went with Tom down the path to the little open-air house where I'd confessed myself. They were gone long enough that I'm pretty sure they went there for Higuchi Communion.

The next day she spent a lot of time in the House of Meditation, doing spiritual drills, but on the fifth day she seemed about like she always had. Except she stopped hanging around with me. She never told me what was going on with her, or even what the dream was; and if I'm right about what it was, she wouldn't have told me even if she'd wanted to.

That was also the week I got to know Lemmi—cheerful Lemmi, who always seemed to know more than he said. Among other things, we talked about where we came from. Dinneh County, he told me, was a pretty much level country of white pines, sugartrees (which he called "sugar maples"), and bitter winters.

He talked a little in the language of his people for me—the Dinneh, they called themselves. They use quite a few Merkan words in their language, he said, because there are so many things in Saint Croy that they didn't have where they lived before the Shuffling.

I got the idea that he knew more about "before the Shuffling" than I did. He said the holy men of the Dinneh could "see" before the Shuffling, but didn't tell other people what they saw. You had to "see it for yourself." In spiritual drills, I suppose.

It wasn't clear to me what the connection was between the Dinneh holy men and the Church. His father had been a holy man, and he'd been teaching Lemmi to be one, until Lemmi joined the Order when he was fifteen years old. I got the impression that they might be at least somewhat heathen.

I talked some with Tom again, too. One of the things I asked was, what do we do next? He said his plans were still loose, and that he'd talk about them pretty soon. I wasn't sure how long "pretty soon" was to Tom, because something old Master Akihisa said made me think that Tom might be even older than him!

Five more Higuchian Brothers arrived that week, each of them alone, and Tom decided not to wait any longer. We'd move on. Old Master Akihisa would send on any more who came in.

We left as a group: fourteen Buddhist monks, highly skilled and tough; eight Higuchian Brothers; plus Tom and Paddy. Master Keiji was our travel leader. Each man had his sword; each man plus Jamila. Each of us also had a shortbow, bone-backed and very stiff, whether his own or one provided by the monastery; I'd had some time on the butts to get used to mine. Finally, each of us carried a sack of dry beans and one of ground corn. Some had death stars; the monks called them *shuriken*. Jamila had her sling and a pouch of two-ounce lead slugs. And I was willing to bet that every one of us was on close terms with his warrior muse, which was more important than any weapon we carried.

We were twenty-three warriors plus Paddy. Paddy'd been practicing daily with bow and sword, part of the time with Tom instructing him, and he'd made good progress. He was already better with the sword than a

lot of people who carry one, and he had a natural talent
with the bow. But by comparison with the rest of us, he
was slow, clumsy, inaccurate, and too darned vulnerable.

And he knew it. But he had faith in Tom's decision to
take him with us, and I did too. If Tom felt Paddy had a
role to play, then it seemed to me he did. I'd prefer,
though, that he not get killed playing it.

EIGHTEEN

The foot trail we'd hiked and sweated and slipped on, on our way to the monastery, continued northward from it as a genuine cart road, and for a while the country was less rugged, though just as wild. Now and then we crossed streams, some quick and noisy in ravines, some sliding slowly, the color of tea, through swamps of alder, red maple, and evergreens. At midday break, two of the monks waded into one of them and caught trout under the bank with their hands. They ate them raw.

Every hour or two a footpath touched or crossed the road. Horses didn't seem to be used much in the mountains of Adirondack, and I could see why. On a warm sunny day like this one, there were so many horseflies and deerflies, they'd have driven a horse mad. The bottomlands of the Mississip can't compare when it comes to flies.

Halfway down a long easy slope, we met a warrior hiking up it—what Master Keiji called a *samurai*. He must have been a dozen centimeters taller than me, and wore his blond hair drawn up and tied in a topknot. His name was Bahvo Yohki, and he spoke Adirondack, or "Japanese," with an accent that even a foreigner like me could spot. I wished I knew what he was saying.

From what Master Keiji told us on a later break, Yohki had grown up in a backwoods district called Vahsen Lanni, and after his apprenticeship as a samurai, had been employed by a lord well off north. Then, three years ago, his lord had let him go, along with several other samurais. No one in the north had been hiring samurais then, so Yohki'd become a fur trapper and hunter, a winter profession he'd learned as a boy from his father. He'd been working as a field boss for the summer in a farming district off northwest when, a few days past, devil-led foreign soldiers had come there, burned the village and hamlets, and killed most of the people, including Yohki's wife and child.

No, he hadn't actually seen a devil leading them, but he'd seen a devil boat floating in the air nearby.

He himself had hidden, then slipped by night through the enemy camp, cutting throats. Now he was going south across the mountains to see if some southern lord was hiring samurais.

He showed us a string of human ears, right ears, the darnedest thing I'd ever seen. He hadn't taken tally of the last few foreigners he'd killed, though—in fact he'd killed them with his sword—because an uproar had begun and he'd felt rushed. I'd darn well bet there'd been an uproar!

He also said that the foreign soldiers must all have had rifled muskets, because their fire had been effective at distances of a hundred meters and more. No unrifled musket did anywhere near as well, and of course, swords had been useless except at close quarters.

When Yohki'd finished his story, Master Keiji invited him to join us, saying he couldn't pay him but he could offer him the fellowship of other warriors who were going to make war on the devils. So when we started hiking again, the tall samurai was with us.

I'd been impressed by those ears, and I could understand why he'd done it. But a Brother wouldn't cut off any ears, and I'll bet none of the monks would either.

It's a good way to earn penalties with God, penalties that catch up with you sooner or later.

The next morning we ran into a burly, top-knotted samurai standing straddle-legged and barefoot in the middle of the road. He called to Keiji aloud: "Sensei Keiji!" and drew his long curved sword. "Sensei Keiji" were the only two words he said then that I understood. But he seemed to be delivering a challenge to the lot of us!

Keiji smiled and made a fairly long reply, delivering it in a formal manner, following it with a slight bow. Then the samurai spoke again. The next thing I knew, they seemed to be having a poetry contest, exchanging verse after verse, till Master Keiji chuckled and shook his head, as if conceding defeat. The samurai laughed as if something was pretty funny, sheathed his sword, bowed, and embraced Keiji. When we started walking again, he was with us too.

His name was Zenichi Ogata, and he had his own story. The farms and villages two days ahead had been laid waste by devil-worshiping foreigners. It was a district farther east than Bahvo Yohki had told about. Ogata's lord, who'd ruled there for years, had come under the influence of a foreign advisor who obviously had been in league with the devils. By ones and twos, his lord had dismissed his samurais, replacing them with peasant soldiers who, all in all, were no cheaper because he'd hired nearly three times as many of them. He'd kept just four samurais, including Ogata, mainly to discipline the soldiers.

When the foreign army had come, his cheap soldiers, those who weren't quickly killed, ran away from the rifled muskets, and from fierce bats that attached themselves to the face. The four samurais had fought ferociously, and all but he had been killed. Their lord had been killed too, ending Ogata's covenant with him, and Ogata had hidden inside the castle in a storm sewer until it got dark. Then he'd escaped, killing two foreign soldiers he'd overheard talking in Merkan. They'd expected to conquer the whole world south to the southern sea.

Later that day we stopped where a spring trickled out of a mossy slope. Before anyone could drink, Master Keiji knelt in front of it and seemed to pray. A few meters away was a tiny, hemlock-shaded hut, its logs and low, split-shake roof green with moss. It didn't look big enough for even one person, and the door wouldn't have been taller than my armpits.

All of us, even Tom, Followed Keiji's example and got down on our knees in front of the spring. I offered a few silent Hail Marys. When Keiji got up, a little old hermit came out of the hut. He was so short, he hardly had to duck his head to come through the low door. Against the bloodthirsty flies and mosquitoes, all he had on was a loincloth and sash. And he didn't say a thing—no questions, no comments. In his sash he carried a sword, and small though he was, I suspected he was good with it. His small body was sinewy and tough-looking, despite his gray hair and the loose skin at elbows and knees.

Keiji bowed to him and the old man bowed back, but as far as I saw, nothing was said. When we left, a few minutes later, the old man came with us, carrying nothing but his sword and knife. I might have wondered how he'd survive the night, but I didn't. Because in spite of his bare hide, the flies wouldn't land on him or even buzz around his head, not even the deerflies. And he didn't stink, either. It seemed to me that heathen or not, the old hermit had to be pretty holy if the flies wouldn't harry him, and I suspected that the chill of night wouldn't trouble him either.

At the next break I asked Master Keiji about him, and why we'd knelt by the spring. Old Mitsuru was a sage, Keiji said, a holy man. He'd knelt because there was a spirit in the spring; old Mitsuru had installed it there. And no, he hadn't been worshiping it. A wise man did not pray to such a spirit, but communed with it and admired it.

Just before sundown on that second day, we crossed over a pass and went down the other side into a valley that had burned a few years earlier. Young seedling trees covered most of the ground with healing green, the snags of fire-killed pines standing pale gray and charcoal above them. A sinuous stream snaked along the valley bottom, and along it were numerous camp-fires, their smoke rising a dozen or two meters to spread out above the camp in the moist and cooling air.

The people there were refugees. Tom and Keiji, with some of us following, sought out their leaders, two samurai half-brothers. It was Tom who asked the questions, speaking Adirondack. Their people, the samurais told him, were survivors of a farm district overrun by foreigners. It lay two days' march northeast. The stream by the camp was rich in fish, and the burnt forest rich in rabbits three times as big as rabbits in Mizzoo. The people were fishing and trapping, smoking most of their catch, preparing food for a trek over the mountains.

Dusk was thickening, but pungent woodsmoke kept the mosquitoes at bay as Tom talked with them. Keiji translated for those of us who spoke no Adirondack. "There were not many samurais. Mostly there were only soldiers. They were willing to fight the foreigners, but turned cowards when the demons came."

"What demons were those?" Tom had asked.

"Two kinds. There were bats that went for the face, the eyes. They dove at men and horses. The horses went crazy and threw most of their riders off. I saw men with their eyes torn out."

The samurai paused, seemingly looking at his memory images. "The other demons were flying dragons breathing fire. Soldiers broke and ran screaming when they saw them coming. I decided I would kill one, and struck at it with my sword as it came at me. The sword went through it like smoke, and the flames of its breath had no heat. When it slashed at me with its great claws, they too were like smoke, not harming me at all."

Tom was frowning. "But the bats were real," he said thoughtfully.

The samurai nodded. "The bats were real. But not as quick as other bats. Not at all. I struck down three with my sword. That would not have been possible with any other bats I've seen."

"Did they bloody your sword?"

The samurai's face turned thoughtful. "I am not sure. It was already bloody. I believe, though—I do not think any blood splashed when I halved them. Not from any of them. But I was very busy at the time."

"Were there many of them? These bats?"

"Not a great number. Two dozen, perhaps three. About the size of a crow."

Tom nodded. "You did well to escape and bring these people away from that place."

The talk turned to the foreign soldiers then. They'd had rifled muskets, there was no doubt of it. But as soldiers, they were only pretty good—well disciplined, but no more aggressive in combat than they had to be.

The two samurai brothers talked privately then and decided. One of them spoke some Merkan. He would come with us. The other would continue to lead the refugees south; their sister and her surviving child were with the refugees.

We camped just upstream of the refugees and cooked beans for supper, along with trout they'd given us. We also baked large johnnycakes on a sheet of iron; we could eat them cold for breakfast and at midday.

When I wrapped myself in my poncho on the ground, Tom and Master Keiji were sitting a little ways off from the rest of us, talking. I tried to hear what they said, but I wasn't close enough. After a few minutes they wandered off up the river. I decided to stay awake till they got back, to talk with Tom, but after a few minutes I fell asleep.

NINETEEN

The next morning we were up with the birds, and it
didn't take us long to get started. A night on the ground
always left us stiff and chilled, and eating yesterday's
dry johnnycake didn't warm anyone. Hiking did.

We were a malodorous column of warriors; the beans
were doing their noisy, smelly worst.

It was my half-day to carry the bean pot, and I
wondered if the ugly thing was really necessary. What
would uncooked beans taste like? Raw field corn I'd
eaten more than once; hard and dry, it wears your jaws
out chewing.

A kilometer past the river, we got into unburned
timber again. A couple of hundred meters farther, we
came to where a well-used trail left the road eastward.
With his sword, Tom blazed a big pine there and we
turned off on the trail. That blaze was all the message
he left for any other Brothers who came along. If they
didn't read it, didn't follow, we'd do without them.

At the midday break, we ate dry johnnycake again
and washed it down with water. Then Tom and Keiji
stood up in front of us, side by side. "Brothers," Tom
said, "and samurai." He talked in Merkan, Keiji repeat-
ing after him for those who didn't understand. "Master
Keiji and I talked things over last night. We've learned
things the past two days that have changed our thinking.

169

"Our plan has been, and remains, to enter the Saint Lawrence People's Democratic Republic. The devils have their stronghold near the seat of government, Eisenbach, and we intend to destroy them there. But now there's an invading army between us and them, and it's needlessly dangerous to try slipping through it.

"So we'll bypass their army. We'll cross the big lake, Shampreinu-ko, and hike north through the Republic of V'mont. Keiji and I communed with angels last night, and they told us the enemy has no army at their border with V'mont.

"In V'mont we will travel at night to avoid causing rumors and confrontations. When we enter the enemy land, we will move with all possible stealth, avoiding contacts if we can, until we reach the devils' stronghold. All the foreign soldiers we might kill will mean little, if we do not reach and destroy the devils who control the government there. If we're discovered and attacked on the way, we will scatter by twos and continue to find our way to the devils' stronghold.

"Our purpose is to destroy as many of the devils as we can, *and cause as much destruction as we can inside their stronghold.* We are not interested in killing foreign invaders except as absolutely necessary. If we kill the devils, or cause enough damage inside their stronghold, the foreign invasion will soon collapse, and the foreign soldiers will go home."

He looked us over. "Are there any questions?"

There weren't among the eight of us in the Order, not even me, nor among the monks and samurais. Jamila and I had been squatting beside each other again for a change. "If we do get scattered," I told her, "I'd like us to stick together."

She nodded. "If that's how it works out," she said, "that's how I want it too."

Early that afternoon, two more Brothers caught up with us. They'd arrived at the monastery the evening after we'd left, and had pushed hard to catch us. Early that evening, while we were making camp, still another Brother caught up. I wondered how many others might be back down the road, headed for a Buddhist monastery they'd never heard of, which had been burned down. And how many would eventually find us.

It occurred to me then that some might have been sent to different places than the monastery—that we might be only one of several independent forces—but after I thought it, I somehow didn't think so. My muse talking to me, I suppose.

When we'd eaten supper, Tom told Jamila and Lemmi and me not to bed down yet. After that I saw him take something out of his pack, something small that he held in his hand. With the daylight fading, I couldn't see it clearly, but I decided it must be a radio, like Soong and Bhatti had. Suddenly there was a tiny red light on it, pure red, maybe the size of a ladybug. A weird light, bright and sharp and steady, that never came from any flame or spark.

If it was a radio, though, he didn't say anything into it, just put it back in his pack with the little light on. Then he took the new Brothers aside and talked to them for a little bit.

When he was done with them, he had the three of us pick up our gear and follow him. I had no idea what was going to happen, and it made me uneasy; Tom had something going on that he hadn't told about in the briefing, such as it was. Now he was going to tell the three of us, or show the three of us, and somehow I didn't want to know, as if there was something bad about it.

We were camped by a creek, and he led us along it through young forest. In the thickening dusk, we had to walk with our hands in front of us, to fend unseen twigs from our faces. After something more than a kilometer, we came to an old beaver meadow. Tom paused for just a moment, gazing up its length, then pushed on.

The meadow had been a big pond once, and had silted in long before. It was likely to be wet, so we skirted it to one end of a dam so old that its mud and sticks had become soil. A couple of big pines were actually growing on the dam near our end. Tom led us out on it and we squatted down near one of the pines.

The last twilight had faded. Stars bannered and glittered. I remembered what Bhatti had said about them—that they were distant suns, with worlds more or less like Earth circling them. I believed him, but they'd never seemed entirely real to me.

So far as I'd ever heard, distant worlds aren't a subject that priests talk about to their parishioners. I don't think the priests know about them.

"All right," Tom said, "here's the situation. I'm sending the three of you off to work with someone else, and there are things you need to know. But first some questions." He looked at me. "Luis, do you really think I'm an angel?"

For whatever reason, my nervousness, my foreboding, had disappeared as we'd walked. I felt clearheaded and calm. "I don't know," I answered. "There've been times I felt sure you were, and other times . . ." I let it trail out, which said as much as words.

"What is an angel?" he asked.

That was something I'd learned as a child. "An angel's a creation of God, higher than humans," I said. "Sometimes He'll send an angel to intermediate for Him with humans." Then I added something I'd been taught as a novice. "The masters were trained by angels. Yeah, I think you're an angel."

"All right. Lemmi, do angels come from Earth?"

I heard Lemmi chuckle in the darkness beside me. "No. Angels come from Heaven." Something about the chuckle, and the way he'd said it, made it sound as if he knew more than that, and I felt a jab of irritation because I didn't.

"Jamila, do angels fly?"

"They must," she said, "to get to Earth from Heaven."

"Lizards fly too," I pointed out. "Jamila and I saw what had to be Lizards, flying in a boat in the air. They picked up the Lizard I killed, or the Lizard-thing, and set fire to a farmhouse from up in the air, with something like a giant Lizard gun."

"Okay. But let's call them devils now instead of Lizards. You'll understand why later tonight."

Later tonight! The words sent goose bumps racing.

"Now, I'm sure you've been taught that Satan is a fallen angel, the chief of the fallen angels."

I'd learned that as a kid, long before I'd become a novice in the Order.

"Well, you may be relieved to know we're not up against Satan in this.

"Tonight you're going to meet some angels, other angels than me, who aren't fallen. They're going to take you to Israel in an airboat. You'll join with some Israelites to attack not the devils but the government of the PDR—the People's Democratic Republic. What you're going to do is assassinate the head of government there and as many of the men around him as you can. It may well disrupt the PDR's invasion of Adirondack, and more important, it'll be a major distraction for the devils.

"And no, I don't have any information on how you're to do it. The Israelites will brief you."

He didn't say anything more for a few seconds, but I doubt that any of us thought he was done. He was looking at what came next.

"By the time you've killed the PDR rulers, you'll have a sense of the place and its opportunities. At that point I'll want your help with the devils, any help that occurs to you.

"The devils' stronghold is actually a starship that flew here from deep in the sky. From another world like this one, out among the stars, a world where artisans are far more advanced then here in what they can make. We believe this starship of theirs is one that was reported damaged by an angel ship—a sort of angelic constabulary—in a fight near a distant star. And that it came here to hide. And our best guess is that it can't leave—that after it landed here, having been damaged, it couldn't rise again."

The chillbumps were running once more, this time not a good kind. My mouth had gone dry.

"Their starship sits on top of a small hill outside the town of Eisenbach," Tom went on. "There are no dwellings near it, and all the trees have been cut off the hill. The country around it is generally open. And the devils are sure to have set out alarms to warn them of anyone snooping around. They'll be prepared to defend it.

"Keiji and I will take our people—monks, Brothers, and samurais—and try to somehow get inside their ship. You three, with the Isrealites, will distract them seriously when you assassinate their puppets, the PDR rulers. And when you've done that, you'll be free to leave the Israelites and operate on your own."

I interrupted. "If you angels have airboats, why don't you attack it from the air? With something like the Lizards used to burn down the farmhouse." I paused than and asked what was really bothering me. "Why doesn't *God* do something?" I was feeling uneasy again.

"Three reasons at least," Tom said. "First of all we're limited in what we're allowed to do. Second, we've got only two airboats for this entire quarter of the world, neither of them with a heavy weapon, while we can assume that the starship can blow us out of the sky. It was dangerous for us just to fly over it. And third, angel bodies can be killed like anyone else's, and there aren't many of us on Earth, nor any prospect of getting replacements for a dozen years."

He paused. "You see, good doesn't automatically defeat evil. We, and that includes you, have to earn our victories.

"And God *is* doing something about it," he added. "He's sending us."

I sat looking at that, saying nothing. Of course the victory of good wasn't automatic. If it was, there'd be no need for the Order, and I'd be cutting wood back in

Mizzoo. But it still seemed to me that God could do something more than send us.

No one else was talking now either. The only sound was the occasional soft slap when someone harvested a batch of mosquitoes on their face. I wondered how many stars there were. The moon, what there'd be of it, was about new, and wouldn't come up till near dawn, so the Milky Way looked strong and white. Bhatti'd said it was a fog of stars you couldn't begin to count. Which meant there had to be billions of them.

After awhile, something dark and moving caught my eye, and I watched—an airboat settled near us at the edge of the beaver meadow! My eyes were glued to it. I didn't feel scared, but somehow my hair bristled. It was too dark to be sure, but when it stopped coming down, it looked to me as if it had stopped short of the ground instead of sitting on it.

Tom got up and we did too, walking back off the dam and over to the airboat. It was maybe five meters long and three high, including a little round cupola on top, and it floated a couple of decimeters off the ground. The whole thing looked like dark steel. I couldn't see anything that looked like wood. As we walked up to it, double doors opened in the side—slid open instead of swinging on hinges or straps. Inside it was dark, but I could make out, dimly, another angel waiting for us.

"Hop in," he said, "before the mosquitoes take over."

A little ramp had come out when the doors opened. We went in and they closed behind us. And suddenly there was light; the walls glowed without lamps. Beside me was a window I could see out of, see the grass on the meadow, the old dam with the two pines on it—but I couldn't see a sign of light from the boat. I mean, there should have been a patch of light shining on the ground from the window, but there wasn't. It was as if none of the light shone out through it, even though I could see out!

The Lizard airboat had shone light out the windows. Maybe ours was better.

I reached and touched; the window felt just like glass. Then turning to say something, I got a look at the guy who'd talked to us through the door. *He was a Lizard!* He had a crest on top of his head. Both of his eyes were red.

My own had to have been staring.

"You must be Luis," the Lizard said. He turned his strange eyes to the others. "And Lemmi and Jamila. My name's Ben and that's Dave." He gestured toward the front of the boat, and I managed to pull my eyes away from him. A guy sat up front in a seat that swiveled, and he'd turned in it to look grinning at us. He looked as human as anyone.

"Hi, people," he said. "Tom, if you and Ben will help these folks secure for flight, we'll be on our way."

I let myself be led to a seat that was curved and padded, and after I'd sat down, something I couldn't see snugged across me, not too tightly, from hips to chest. Sort of like a broad band. I could still shift around in my seat. Lemmi had sat down too, and I could see that the same thing had happened to him. He was shifting around a little, testing it, not looking spooked at all. Jamila looked calm as could be. Then Tom took a seat across from me. Obviously he was going with us, which took me by surprise.

The Lizard, Ben, stood looking at me. "You didn't expect to see someone like me," he said matter-of-factly.

I nodded. "The last one I saw like you, I cut his head off."

He laughed. "We heard about that. Well done. But don't judge all of us by him and his buddies." Then he went up front and sat down by the human called Dave.

"Take your time," Tom said after him. "The four of us back here need to talk." The light dimmed, leaving us in semidarkness. I felt the boat rise up, and looked out the window at the beaver meadow dropping away beneath us. Then we swung around, still rising, and moved off over the forest.

"You see now why I said to think of the enemy as

'devils,' not Lizards," Tom said. "There are angels and there are fallen angels."

"Why," I said slowly, "didn't you tell us this earlier?" I gestured at the Lizard, Ben.

"There's appropriate information and there's confusion. Information that doesn't apply to the problem at hand will sometimes distract and confuse. Does that make sense to you?"

I nodded slowly. Things seemed to come together a bit. Some things. A little. "You guys aren't like the angels in Scripture," I said.

It was Jamila who answered, her voice soft. "Luis, maybe it's more that the angels in Scripture aren't like Tom and the others."

I glanced at Lemmi. His black eyes were on me as quiet and steady, and as *neutral*, as could be. It seemed to me I was alone in whatever trouble I was having. He and Jamila were ahead of me spiritually; that was probably the difference.

I looked at what she'd said. Okay. Real is real. Bhatti had made the point more than once: "In cases of disagreement, what you see and hear and touch outranks rumors and reports." And I'd always, even as a little kid, taken Scripture with a grain of salt. A lot of it had felt real, but some had seemed like stories people tell to make a point, maybe get you to see things their way. And what felt real one time didn't always feel real later on. These three guys were definitely real. The question was, were they really angels? I looked at Tom again.

"What do you guys call yourselves when no one else is around?" I asked. "Not 'angels,' I'll bet."

He grinned, not too wide. His eyes were as calm and steady as when he'd been nursing me back to health—probably saving my life—back in Allegheny. "Right," he said. "We call ourselves *monitors*. We're special agents of a much larger group of people whose title would translate as *overseers* in Merkan."

Larger group of *people*. "Overseers?" I said. "What do they oversee?"

"They oversee—the worlds that mankind lives on. The human life form, of whatever kind."

"Humans," I said. "I suppose that includes Lizards and people like Jamila and Lemmi and me. And monitors like you, right? You're not a Lizard and you're not like us either. You're furry. Your eyes are different. And you don't grow whiskers."

"Good enough. You've got it."

"What about the devils?" I asked. "What do you call them, among yourselves?"

"They're part of a . . ." He paused, looking rueful. "Merkan doesn't have the words to talk about some of these things any longer. Not clearly or easily. The devils are a culture—a set of people we call . . ." Tom said something in another language. "That'd be 'sado-hedonists' in Old American; let's call them S-H. Sado-hedonism is almost like a church, a religion. It's as if the S-H worshiped Satan, tried to be like him. But actually they don't. It's just that they dedicate themselves to pleasure, and their senior pleasure is to cause other people fear, agony, grief . . . misery in general."

He'd said *people* again. "Angels" were people. "Devils" were people. "Where does God come into this?" I asked. "What do you call Him?"

Tom smiled slightly. "He's the Programmer. The Designer, the Creator. Generally we refer to him as 'the Proprietor.' "

Programmer didn't mean anything to me, but Designer and Creator did. And Proprietor. And they seemed to fit what I'd been taught. "What's He like?" I asked.

"He's pure soul, which has no substance and no location in time or space. So when he wants to communicate with someone directly, he—he puts out something for them to communicate with, that you could call an aspect of himself."

"You mean the Holy Spirit?"

"You could call it that. Yes."

Apparently I could call it that or I could call it something else. I'd had about enough of this subject for a while; I needed to let it settle out. But I took one final shot. "Be interesting to hear how you'd answer those questions for a Buddhist."

Tom laughed, a real "haw haw haw." I felt a kind of smile tug on my own cheeks, though I didn't know why. Then I thought of another question to ask. "You said the starship would be defended, and they might have a gun like they set the farmhouse on fire with. What else might they have?"

"We already know they have small beam guns, like you took from the one you killed. And they might use illusions of dragons and whatever else they might think of. Which can look as real as flesh and blood. They obviously have a holographic projector—excuse me, an illusion maker—on at least one of their scoutcraft. But illusions are nothing to worry about if you know what they are.

"They'd have to have a droid tank on board, too, maybe more than one. Droid tanks are what they'd have grown their droid bats in, and artificial bodies like the one you killed." He frowned thoughtfully for a minute. "They could even grow something so unlikely-looking that you might think it was an illusion. Keep that in mind. Something big and awful-looking could possibly be real. But they're more likely to use smallish things like bats. It takes a fair amount of time to grow things in a tank, and they can probably culture twenty bats at a time in a tank that might grow only a couple of human-sized bodies."

Tom cocked an eye at me, then looked around at Jamila and Lemmi. "Are you following all this?"

I was following it, but I wasn't very happy about it. These devils sounded like an awful lot to handle. They could send things out to kill us without putting themselves in danger. "How long have they been here?" I asked. "They could have been making these things for years and have a bunch of them stored up. They could have bushels of rattlesnakes and scorpions and poison spiders."

Tom shook his head. "They've been here three years at most. And there are limits to the number of droids they can have. You see, once these things are made, these artificial Lizards and bats, they have to be stored in stasis chambers—special lockers or cabinets—when they're not in use. And they can't keep them in use most of the time. Droids, whether bat or human, can't eat food, or get rested by sleeping. But they do tire and run out of energy, like real bodies, and they get re-energized—get nourished, recuperate, regain their strength—in stasis chambers. There'll be a stasis locker for each artificial Lizard body, and one or more for other droids. But their ship isn't very big, as starships go, and when you get down to it, in their situation, droids are gadgets. Useful gimmicks. They'll have only limited space for such things.

"Something else about droids. Most of them, but not all, will be stupid. Droids can be controlled in either of two ways: the devils can leave their own bodies, so to speak, and occupy the droids. *Be* the droids. A droid occupied like that is as intelligent as its operator. And it doesn't need to look human at all. But then if you kill the droid the way you did at Kings Town, it's a severe shock to whoever's occupying it. The Lizard operator will snap back into his own body and end up with what amounts to a severe case of the flu, with a crippling headache. Most people who've had that happen to them are ready for sedation and a dozen hours of sleep, and feel pretty rocky when they wake up.

"And there aren't a lot of devils here. Maybe thirty-five or forty.

"A droid can also be programmed, set, to operate on its own. In that case the droid is stupid. Single-mindedly dangerous but stupid. Droid insects can be made, but they don't have anything like the mobility of flies or bees, say. Droid bats do better, but they can crash into things and even trap themselves in corners sometimes.

"So while the devils may have some surprises for us, I don't expect . . ."

Suddenly the airboat jumped, swerved, stopping Tom in mid-sentence, jerking me against whatever it was that held me. My eyes snapped to the two angels, the two monitors, up front. I got the notion that Dave was driving the airboat. Ben was doing something with handles and little push-knobs, looking at a box that seemed to have a window into somewhere, with different kinds of lines and lights moving in it.

We swerved sharply, and my stomach lurched. It felt like we were careening all over the sky. Ben made a kind of "hah!" sound, and said something in a language I'm sure I'd never heard before. Then a hole burst through the window on his side, and I smelled burning meat as his head flopped sideways. Tom yelled, more like a roar, the boat spun and swerved again, and I felt myself pushed back against my seat as if a giant hand was pressing me.

After a few seconds it eased, and I looked around. The thigh of Tom's breeches on my side was ripped, soaked with blood that trickled onto the floor, and his eyes were closed as if he was praying, or maybe concentrating. If I'd ever wondered whether he bled like other men, my question was answered.

Ben was dead, without a doubt. Dave seemed to be all right, and Jamila and Lemmi. Dave got a small box from somewhere, turned in his seat, and tossed it to Tom, whose eyes had opened. Tom took a scissors out of the box and cut the leg of his breeches.

The fur on his thigh was matted with blood. Red blood. Along the side was a big rough gouge, almost like a deep ugly burn, like a Lizard gun might make. The blood wasn't pouring, it wasn't that kind of wound, but it was running out pretty good.

Next he took out a kind of container, a little cylinder, and sprayed white foamy stuff out of it onto the cut. The foam settled, seemed to disappear, and the blood quit flowing. Then he took another container and sprayed on some colorless stuff. After that he took a little tube and pressed it against his leg for a moment.

"How're you doing?" Dave said without turning around.

"Good enough. Were there two of them?"

"Yep. And *were's* the word. Ben knocked one of them down just before we were hit. The way it flared, I'm sure its crew was killed."

"That's something then. How do you suppose they found us?"

"There was a PDR army camp a few K's ahead of us, on the north shore of Shampreinu-ko. I suppose the aircraft were just arriving or departing there."

Tom didn't say anything for a minute, but I could see he was thinking about that. "What direction did your evasive maneuvers take us?"

"South. Let them think we were up here to observe, not that we were headed for Israel."

"Good. That's what I was worried about. Too bad we don't have a couple of light atmospheric fighters instead of armed utility craft.

"If there's no sign of the bogey again, when we've gotten well south of Shampreinu-ko, turn east through V'mont airspace. We might as well go all the way to Statamain before we turn north. Same objective."

"Right."

I pretty much understood what they'd been talking about, which gave me a certain amount of satisfaction. Tom had sounded as if nothing had happened to him, but now he did something that made his seat tilt back, and closed his eyes again.

Earlier, when I'd been questioning Tom, Lemmi hadn't said anything, and Jamila almost nothing. I wondered if I'd sounded like a dolt. Or whether they'd have asked questions if I hadn't.

Now no one said anything for a while, and I dozed. When I woke up, I could see the ground getting closer. This was farm country, with a lot of cleared land. Dave woke up Tom with a single calm word in their unfamiliar language. Nothing would wake up Ben. Ben the Lizard. Ben the angel of—what? Angel of God/Creator/

Programmer/ Proprietor? No, Ben the angel of—what had Tom called them? The Overseers. Whatever Overseers were.

I'd be glad to be outside again, on the ground with things to do.

Tom was looking at the three of us, looking as if his strength was wearing thin—paper thin. "We'll land soon," he said. "Jamila, as first in experience, you're in charge of the three of you. Lemmi is your first deputy. Until you've joined with Yosheh, the person in charge of the Israelites you'll work with.

"There should be some Israelites waiting for you where we land—where we come down to the ground. If they're not there when we get there, wait for them; they should be on their way. And if for any reason you have to leave without joining up with them, remember that the government of Israel does not approve of armed foreigners in their country. You could be imprisoned."

Dave broke in. "They're waiting there now," he said, "in the woods next to the meadow." I wondered how he knew. Could he see them in the dark, in the woods, from up in the air?

"Good," said Tom, and turned to us. "The government of Israel is a little like the government of the Commonwealth: they keep pretty good track of what's going on. Or try to anyway. And as I said, they do not tolerate armed foreigners. They'd be much more likely to jail you than throw you out. They might even execute you. But the people you'll work with know the ropes and the country."

He looked at me then. "Any questions?"

"Yes. If the Israelites already have a force going to Eisenbach, why add the three of us to it?"

His seriousness of a minute before was gone. He grinned, not as big as usual, but he grinned. "An intuition," he said. "A hunch." For a moment in the halflight, his eyes seemed to twinkle like Bhatti's so often did, and Soong's. Then he returned to the only briefing we'd get from him. "Our people among the Israelites,

Meirists they call themselves, are different than Brothers of the Order or the monks in Adirondack. They're good but they're different."

Then, instead of explaining, he shut up. It occurred to me that one reason for not explaining things was to make me observe and decide for myself. We were coming down. I could see the meadow not far below, bordered on my side by woods. After a minute or two we stopped near the woods, either on the ground or almost. Whatever had been holding me in my seat let go. The doors slid open and Dave got up, slipping past Ben's slumped corpse to stand by the open door. As I got up, I was wishing I'd gotten to know Ben beyond the few words we'd exchanged.

We shouldered our packs, Jamila and Lemmi and I, shook hands with both angels, and got out. As soon as we were clear of the ramp, the doors slid quietly closed again, and a minute later the airboat rose up smoothly to disappear into the night sky.

"Here comes our welcoming committee," Jamila murmured a minute later. I watched them come out of the woods, eight of them, it turned out, come close enough that I could see their guns, shotguns. Pointed at us.

"You're under arrest!" one of them said. "One move, devils, and we will kill you where you stand!"

TWENTY

The jail had four cells, about three by five meters each, but we were the only prisoners. They put Lemmi and me in one, and Jamila in the one next to it where we couldn't see her. It could have been worse; they could have separated Lemmi and me, too. The cell had two stools; two bunks, one above the other, with shuck mattresses; a walled-off corner for the pot and lime bucket; and a little table with a crockery washbasin, tin of soap, big water bucket, and a dipper. Not bad.

When we were locked in, one of the guys who'd arrested us told us to put our hands through the bars. Then he unlocked our wrist irons and took them off. That was the only Merkan we'd heard spoken after the arrest.

I wondered when the trial would be. Probably in the next day or two, if we got one.

After they'd taken off our wrist irons, the crew that arrested us left without telling us anything. They'd talked quite a bit among themselves while they hauled us to town, but we hadn't understood any of it.

We had two jailers. One was stationed in the room the cells opened on, sitting in front of the opposite cell where he could look into both of ours. He wore a holstered pistol and a short sword, and by the door was a rack with two shotguns that were probably loaded. He didn't carry the key ring; it hung on the gun rack too.

The other jailer was a woman with some insignia of rank on her sleeves. A sergeant, I guessed. After she'd looked us over in our cages, she'd said something in a tone of voice that reminded me of spitting, then walked back into the office in front, leaving the door open.

About the first thing Lemmi and I did, after she left, was go to the one small window and take turns standing on a stool to look out. The bars were about ten centimeters apart, and the stone wall about forty centimeters thick. All I could see outside was dark night, and a row of trees about five meters from the wall.

Our watchman, a dark, good-looking young guy, had picked up a book and started to read. Every little bit, though, it turned out—every time he turned a page— he'd look up at us. He looked up while Lemmi was having his turn at the window, and yelled angrily. Lemmi hopped down. In an irritated voice, the female sergeant called something through the doorway. The watchman rattled back, presumably telling her what we'd been up to. She said something brief and snappish, and I heard the door close.

The watchman sat back down, glaring angrily at us, not picking up his book right away. I looked at him and shrugged. It seemed to me his reaction had been a little extreme; there was no way we were going to escape through those bars. After a couple of minutes, he opened his book and began to read again.

I was about ninety-five percent sure he didn't speak Merkan, but what I wanted was a hundred percent certainty. The three of us needed to talk to each other about how we might break out. And we couldn't reach Jamila with whispers. So I decided to test the guy.

"Can we have something to eat?" I asked. Not that I was hungry. He looked up and scowled without saying anything, then turned back to his book. My certainty went up to ninety-eight percent. I went over by the wall between our cells. "Hey Jamila," I said. "That young jailer is a pretty good-looking guy, wouldn't you say?"

She started to answer and he came off of his chair yapping in Israelite, drawing his short sword and shaking it at me. Which seemed to mean we weren't supposed to talk to each other, or not between cells at least. That was a complication I hadn't foreseen. I tried to speak soothingly to him, apologizing, which made him rant all the worse, so I went and sat down on a stool. He was glaring at me when the female jailer came in. She scowled through the bars at us and then left again, this time slamming the door behind her. So it wasn't just the guy. Either the jail had a policy against talking, or we were considered dangerous, even locked up.

Lemmi's grin stretched clear across his face. We took our stools back by the outside wall, sat down next to each other, and started whispering, although we didn't have much to say yet. Our watchman looked up and snapped something at us. We tried to look innocent, and when he turned back to his book again, we whispered some more, keeping an eye on him, stopping whenever he looked. I hadn't done anything quite like that since I was twelve and graduated from Saint Francis Boys' School.

He must have known what we were doing, but apparently we were within the limits he'd put up with, so all he did was give us dirty looks. Like Sister Monika used to.

We were both tired, though—it'd been a long, hard, all-day hike—so after a little we quit and lay down; I took the upper bunk. The fluttering flame of our watchman's oil lamp put me to sleep within two or three minutes.

It seemed as if I'd been sleeping quite a while when voices woke me, sounding official as heck. I swung out of my bunk to see, and almost landed on Lemmi, who was rolling out of the lower. Two men in constabulary uniforms had come in and were talking with the watch-man, in Israelite of course. I watched him turn then as if to go to the office, maybe to check something with the sergeant. When his back was turned, one of the newcomers walloped him on the head with a blackjack. I winced as he fell. One of them strode quickly to the key ring, then hurried to our cell with a finger to his lips and unlocked our doors.

By the time all three of us were out, the unconscious watchman was on his belly with his hands already tied behind his back. Quickly his legs were doubled then, and the cord, a long leather thong, was looped three or four times around his ankles, then drawn up and tied around his neck; a technique Soong taught. That taken care of, they gagged him. Within a minute from the time I woke up, the whole thing was done.

With a finger to his lips again, one of the two mo-tioned us to stand behind the office door. He opened it and spoke to the sergeant. As she stepped through, she too got blackjacked, and the door was closed behind her. They tied her up and gagged her like the watchman.

One of our rescuers signaled our silence again. "Put hands please behind your back," he hissed, and when we did, he put wrist irons on us again. I wasn't entirely happy about that: Then, manacled, we were taken into the office.

In the office, a third man was trying keys in a closet door. Him I knew: he'd been one of the crew that arrested us and brought us in—the one that had spoken to us in Merkan. He flashed us a grin as the closet door opened for him.

If anyone had looked in the office window, he'd have seen us and maybe wondered. I remembered two men standing guard in the darkness outside the door, and decided they'd already been taken care of.

One of our rescuers picked up a short shotgun and held it to our backs. His partner opened the outside door, picked up another shotgun, and motioned us through. Then the two of them followed us out into the night, leaving the other still rummaging in the closet. A fourth, with yet another shotgun, was standing there talking quietly with the door guards. He led off to an enclosed wagon a dozen meters away, the guards watching. It could have been the same wagon we'd been hauled *to* jail with; it had the same strange-looking writing on the side. We were prodded up into it and made to move all the way to the front. Then two of the Israelites, shotguns ready, got in with us.

In broken Merkan, we were ordered roughly to sit down. We did as we were told, and waited. It occurred to me to wonder if, instead of being rescued, we were being captured by some sort of rival faction. A minute later we heard someone get onto the driver's seat up front and speak to the horses. The wagon began to roll, and one of our rescuers removed our manacles again.

I could hardly believe they'd left the door guards standing outside the jail. All that would have to happen, to have the alarm raised, would be for one of them to go in and find the jailers bound and gagged. Probably, I decided, our rescuers, or whatever they were, felt it was riskier to have them absent from their posts.

The horses were trotting briskly. The only window in the wagon was in the back door, and one of the Israelites was squatting in front of it, shotgun ready. We stayed on a graveled road for about a quarter hour, I'd guess, then turned right on a rutted dirt road. It seemed to me the wagon had been pointed west to start with; that meant we were going north now, unless the gravel road had curved. Meanwhile I had a nervous stomach thinking about a door guard going into the jail—for a drink of water, maybe. It seemed to me that if we were recaptured, we might well be executed, maybe shot on the spot.

We jounced over the rutted road for about another quarter hour. Finally the wagon stopped, but no one opened the door. I heard talking outside in the Israelite language, and rusty hinges squeaked. The wagon rolled again, was jockeyed around and backed up a few meters, then stopped. In a minute the wagon door was opened and we were let out.

We were in a barn, and were gestured out, three of the four Israelites leaving with us. The fourth stayed behind, unhitching the horses. No one had said anything yet, not even in Israelite.

The one who'd led the original arrest party had ridden up front on the driver's seat. Outside, he gave us our packs and swords, which I suppose he'd gotten from the closet. He had a pack and sword of his own. It occurred to me that four people had put themselves at serious risk to free us. And done it with restraint and high skill.

"My name is Yakov," the Israelite said, "and I am going with you. We must go from here quickly. There will surely be a search. It may already be starting."

Yakov turned then and led through thigh-deep grass and weeds toward a tall fence, a horse fence, the rest of us following.

"I understood there'd be more of us," Jamila said.

"The plan was that there would be three others, but apparently Yosheh, Ophra, and Dru are under arrest somewhere. I will be your guide and only fellow warrior."

"You're a member of the constabulary, aren't you?" she asked.

"For more than a year, as a Meirist spy, ever since the government began to harass the Meirist Brotherhood as a forbidden secret society. But now"—Yakov stopped beside the fence and shrugged—"I have this new assignment."

We went over the fence on a stile, and started at an easy trot across a field of half-grown-out hay stubble. Westward; the Pole Star was on our right. I thought of telling him we'd hiked fifty or sixty kilometers already that day, but decided that as long as I could keep his pace, I'd do it and keep my mouth shut.

"What happened that we got arrested?" Jamila asked.

"We're not sure. Apparently we have a spy or a traitor who informed the constabulary that you would be landed where you were. I should have been told of your coming by Yosheh; that I wasn't—that I only learned of it when I was assigned to lead an arrest team—was my first indication that anything was wrong. After we had you in jail, I contacted some friends and we mounted this hasty rescue.

"Of course, this act destroys my value as a spy, but . . ." He shrugged. "If Yosheh or any of the others have been exposed, then my own effectiveness and safety were compromised anyway."

We paused to climb another fence, then jogged again, across a pasture. Cattle lay in the starlight, heads and ears raised to look as we passed at a little distance. I hoped there wasn't a mean bull among them.

None of us said anything more for a bit, saving our breath for jogging. Then Yakov spoke again. "This situation may be puzzling to a foreigner. I will try to explain. In Israel, for nine years, the National Party has ruled. And though it despises the—I believe in Merkan you call it the PDR—our government is absolutely against any intrusion, even covert, in foreign affairs. And the Party's discipline, and its majority in the Knesset, are strong enough that it need not compromise its convictions.

"On the other hand, the Herut, the principal opposition party, is weak enough that certain extremist elements, in it and in other minority parties, have performed kidnappings, burned barns, even assassinated officials in frustration with various government policies. Thus there are spy networks on every side, and distrust throughout the nation's political structure."

Again we trotted without talking for a while. Then we came to an uphill stretch that left no breath at all for talk. Tom had said that the organization here was different than the Order in some respects. I could sure enough see one difference: they were hunted, persecuted, in their own country. When we started downhill again, Yakov picked up where he'd left off.

"It is not as bad as it may sound," he went on when he could. "In the everyday life of the everyday citizen, all this is mainly a source of interesting rumors and conversation."

He changed the subject. "About the PDR: It does not presently threaten Israel. It is a much more populous state, and much wealthier, and its army is not to be deprecated. But Israel can be fierce, and the PDR is careful and correct in its policies toward us. It is also our principal trading partner; our other neighbors, V'mont, Brunswick, and Statamain, are poor nations, with little to trade but furs.

"But it is appropriate to be concerned with what PDR policies will be toward Israel if the PDR grows richer and more powerful through conquest. Especially under the influence of the devils."

We were coming to woods now, a bottomland forest along a river. We trotted along its edge for a couple of kilometers till we came to a well-used path, which we followed into the woods. It was dark enough among the trees that we slowed to a careful walk, feeling our way by the hardness of the path till we reached the river.

There were several overturned boats on the shore, and a couple in the water tied to saplings. Crouching, Yakov examined several, as if looking for one he knew. "Ah! Here!" He muttered.

We righted the one he'd chosen. There were no oars beneath it, but there was a pair of paddles. Pushing it in the water, we got in and started northwest down the river, keeping close to the bank where we'd be hard to see, paddling quietly and avoiding talk for five or six kilometers. Sound carries well over water.

When we got out, it was on the west side of the river at another place where boats were landed. Then it was hike again, but this time we only walked. We didn't stop till the first light of dawn, with the moon climbing the sky behind us like a fingernail paring. Just above a creek was a narrow gully we could hole up in, roofed over with an interlaced growth of heavy brush. We drank at the creek, then Yakov dug bread and cheese

from his pack and we ate. I wasn't as used up as I might
have expected.

"How far to Eisenbach?" I asked.

"About a hundred and fifty kilometers. But it will go
much slower soon. We will cross the border at about
midnight. After that we must travel very carefully. In
the PDR, every person is apt to report suspicious people. So far as possible we must be either unseen or not
worth noticing. And it is against the law, in the PDR,
for anyone but soldiers, the constabulary, and local
police to carry weapons."

When we finished eating, we crawled into the gully
and lay down. As tired as I was, though, I didn't go to
sleep until bird clamor was greeting the spread of
dawnlight. Too much was running through my mind.

TWENTY-ONE

It felt kind of strange, sleeping outdoors in daylight. Not that any sunshine got through the thickness of leafy brush above us, but I was more wakeful than at night. I'd sleep and wake up, maybe doze for a while and wake again.

The mosquitoes didn't help any. They never did. I'd have built a smudge, but someone might have seen the smoke and come looking.

A small bird woke me once, standing in the mouth of our hidey hole saying, "Chip! Chip!" Another time a mink looked in on us. I was about half-asleep and maybe he made a sound. Anyway, my eyes popped open and there he was, for about as long as it takes to blink; then he disappeared.

Once I needed to take a leak. I crawled to the mouth of our gully, listened hard, then slowly stuck out my head and looked around. I didn't see or hear anyone, so after a minute I went out and did it.

Somewhere about midday we were all four awake at the same time, so Yakov got out some grub again: bread and cheese. Then we lay around some more. I looked at Jamila and she looked at me, and I couldn't help but wish. When we finished this mission, I told myself again, I was definitely going to propose to her.

The rest of the day was mostly spent napping, although we did eat again. That's right: bread and cheese. When it started to get dusk, we all got out and stretched our legs. Yakov knew where we were, close enough, and he led off. Pretty quickly we came to a country lane and followed it toward the sunset—a sight worth seeing, first gold, then vivid rose, dusky rose, and finally purple.

We made good time. It was late enough that everyone was out of the fields, home eating supper. After that they'd probably sit around awhile before going to bed, whetting a scythe, whittling rake teeth, spinning flax, mending shoes, maybe knitting a cap. We'd not likely be noticed, even by someone going to the privy or the well.

Night replaced twilight, and we came to a main east-west road, ditched like the roads in the Commonwealth. The country was mostly farm fields and pastures; woods covered only about a third of it at most. When we approached a village, we bypassed it cross-country, climbing occasional fences.

Stars wheeled slowly, circling the Pole Star; the Milky Way was a pale swath sweeping the sky. After a few hours, Yakov stopped where a country lane crossed our road. Another village lay a kilometer ahead, its buildings shadowed humps in the moonless night.

"It's time to eat something," Yakov said. I was willing, but there wasn't very much. He cut what was left of the cheese into four, along with the remains of the last loaf, and passed them out. We chewed and swallowed without talking.

"This village is called Yafo," he told us when we'd finished. "It is on a river which is also the PDR border. I will sleep here behind the hedge, and when daylight comes I will go in and buy certain things, then cross the bridge, the border." He unbelted his sword and handed it to me. "Carry this for me," he said. "I won't be able to cross with it." Then he shrugged out of his pack, took

the pistol from it, and gave the weapon to Lemmi;
Jamila put it in Lemmi's pack for him.

"You three," Yakov went on, "go south from here, far
enough to pass the village. Then walk west and cross
the river into the PDR. When you're across, find a
hiding place and sleep till daylight."

"You're sure you don't want someone along to help
you?" Jamila asked.

He shook his head. "No. It is necessary to clear both
border stations, and I'm the only one with official-
looking identification. The PDR is not a trusting country, and Israel . . . is not trusting either.

"There's a village on the PDR side too: Wodz. Stay
clear of it and don't be seen. Walk west, then north
again, and hide where you can watch the road. I'll come
along sometime about midday, with a handcart if I can
get one. One of you be awake to see me, because I
won't know where to look for you. If I haven't come
along by evening, go on without me."

Ah, I thought. *So there's a chance he'll get picked up.*
I considered staying behind and following him, in case
he had trouble; after all, he'd saved our skins. And we
needed him. But he was in charge and knew the situation, so I simply shook his hand. The others did too.
Then we turned south on the country lane and left. I
looked back after a dozen meters. He was watching
us go.

We stayed on the lane for maybe two kilometers,
then climbed a fence and started cross-country over
stubble fields. A woods bordered the river, and we
entered it. It was so dark beneath the forest roof that I
literally could not see my hand before my face. Jamila
was leading, groping her way with feet and hands,
murmuring to us so we wouldn't get separated from her
in the blackness.

"Stop," she said, and we did. "I've run into something. Wood." I pictured her crouching, her hands
exploring. "Poles about ten or twelve centimeters thick.
Firewood poles or maybe fence rails that somebody

piled here for hauling. They're about . . . three meters long."

The upshot of it was that she and Lemmi each grabbed one and went on to the river, dragging them. I stayed by the pile so they could find it again. Guiding on my voice, they came back one at a time for seconds, thirds, and fourths. Finally I went to them, dragging another. Maybe cottonwood, by the heft of it. The bark had been peeled off so they'd dry fast, and the wood was light. They'd make a high-riding raft for our clothes, packs, and weapons.

At the riverbank we could see considerably better, but not well enough to tell poison ivy vines from any others. I'd always been immune to poison ivy, so I was the one who cut vines from riverside trees, for tying the poles together. When the raft was ready, we took off our clothes, bagged shirts and boots inside our breeches, and put them on the raft with our packs, swords on top. Then we launched the raft and, wading and swimming alongside, crossed to the far bank.

After that it was simply a matter of wiping as much of the water from our bodies as possible with our hands. I thought about what it would be like to wipe Jamila off, and what it would lead to. Could lead to. But she'd long since made clear to me that she was off-limits, and for good reason. Besides which Lemmi was with us. After that we stood around shivering for a few minutes, air-drying some, and put our stuff back on.

We were in the People's Democratic Republic! After all those weeks on the way. It seemed to me that it couldn't be a whole lot more dangerous to us than Israel had been.

Lemmi leading now, we groped our way through the woods to another stubble field, trotted across it and, not wanting to leave tracks, skirted a part that had already been plowed. Then we crossed a lane and another stubble field, and a cornfield beyond that. There was a north-south lane there, too, bordered a little farther north by open woods.

We reached the woods and Lemmi led us into them. They were open enough that we could see a little, dimly. Almost at once we came to a sugar house, with its big caldron for boiling down sap. Inside it smelled of char and ashes and the mustiness of old dry animal shit, so we bedded down outside beneath the forest roof. If it blew up a rain, *then* we'd move inside.

TWENTY-TWO

We were up with the birds again, hungry and with nothing we could do about it. We just got up, scattered for a minute to take a leak, then started out with just enough light to see a bit. By sunrise we'd lain up in the narrow strip of tall grass and weeds between a cornfield and a hedge-apple hedge, to wait for Yakov. By mid-morning we'd run out of water. By midday we were feeling pretty dry. By midafternoon we'd have paid a silver piece for a liter.

There was a hole in the hedge big enough to crawl through, and being the most impatient, I was the one who, whenever no traveler was near, lay with my head sticking through to watch up the road. There'd been quite a bit of traffic, sometimes four or five wagons or carts, horsemen or foot travelers, in sight at the same time. But no Yakov. Just now, though, I could see a big handcart—the two-wheeled kind that you push—and I actually hoped it *wasn't* Yakov. Because I sure as heck didn't want to take my turns pushing that monster all the way to Eisenbach. I told Jamila and Lemmi what was coming, and at sixty meters pulled my head back; like them, I'd peer through the base of the hedge as he went by.

All three of us recognized him at the same time.

199

"S-s-s-st!" Lemmi hissed, and "Yakov!" Jamila called softly. I pushed my pack through the hedge ahead of me. Yakov stopped the cart and set the brake ratchet, a big grin on his face.

He'd bought the handcart in Yafo that morning. There was a guy there who made them, for peddlers about to set out into the PDR. He'd also bought a load of iron pots and pans. I don't know whether he'd had that much money, or whether it was something some Meirist or Meirist sympathizer in Yafo set him up with. Finally he'd taken the time to get a false floor built in the cart, for a place to stash our weapons, with a sliding half-door in the back, between the cart handles, where we could get them out without unloading the cargo. Then, in Wodz, he'd paid duty and bribes to the PDR border guards. Now we were wandering peddlers, with about a hundred and thirty kilometers between us and Eisenbach.

The PDR had problems, Yakov explained. Their government had been building up and paying a large standing army the last couple of years, and getting rifled muskets made for all its troops. It had already been big on spending for government buildings and palaces, things like that. So even basic things like pots and pans were scarce and expensive there. It wasn't unusual for an Israelite to buy a load of something on his side of the border and cart it into the PDR to sell at a good profit.

Formally, he told us, the PDR government put restrictions on that kind of trade, but in fact they usually looked the other way. We might have to bribe the constabulary now and then, but usually they weren't too greedy. They knew if they started to hit Isreaelite peddlers too hard, the peddlers would quit coming and the bribes would dry up.

For the next few days, that's what we were: peddlers. We only paused to sell when people came out and stopped us. We didn't want to sell out; our cargo had to last to Eisenbach.

I was glad to see it shrink, though, because that was one heavy cargo, a brute on the hills. At first, there'd been more pots and pans in it, nested, than I'd have thought one cart could hold.

In one village a constabulary patrol stopped us and began to threaten. A small crowd gathered then, a small *angry* crowd. The result was that we were allowed to sell and move on with only a token bribe. In fact, a bunch of surly young guys went along with us a ways, in case the constabulary followed us to revenge their embarrassment.

And although we heard others, the general language was Merkan, not Israelite like in Israel or Japanese like in Adirondack.

We stayed at inns when we hit a village at a reasonable hour. There was always a walled or fenced courtyard where traveling merchants could leave their wagons and carts overnight, and two of us would sleep beneath our cart as guards. The other two would share a bed. The third night it was Jamila's and my turn together in the room, and I really, really wanted to at least kiss her, even though I knew it was a bad idea; it would be hard to stop with a kiss after two nights of love-making back in Allegheny.

But I knew how she felt about it, so we sat at opposite ends of the little bench in our room and talked for a while. "Jamila," I said, "I almost asked Yakov to let me take his place under the cart tonight. It's awfully hard to be here with you like this and . . . not do anything."

"I know," she said, nodding. "I know." Her half-smile was sad.

"But it would have seemed peculiar to him."

She nodded again in the twilight. "I know." This time her smile, still small, held a certain amusement. "And it would have been worse if *I'd* offered to sleep outside. He'd really have wondered about you." She laughed then, softly. I did too; couldn't help it. She laid her hand on the bench between us, palm up, and I put mine on top of it. "You are a nice man, Luis," she said, very soberly, and I asked myself if it could do any harm to make love again, just this once. The answer, of course, was yes. I shook my head ruefully.

Then she disengaged her hand and touched my arm. I turned half toward her, melting inside, and she leaned to kiss me, a kiss that lingered, then strengthened until we were embracing awkwardly on the little bench, her sudden fervor startling me. In a minute we were out of our clothes and in bed. I wondered once, for just a moment, why she'd done what she'd done, but I asked no question. My attention locked onto the moment, and Jamila, and our love.

Later I lay staring at the ceiling. "When this mission is over," I said, "I want to marry you. Even if it does mean leaving the Order. Would you?"

Her hand found mine. "Have you thought it through?" she asked. "What would you do besides be married to me? To make our living? Would you be happy doing something else?"

"Um-hm. I'd be a good constable for some village, maybe Aarschot. Or in Illinoi if you'd rather. Or I could teach writing and reading. I'm good at them; my mother saw to that. Or I could go into the timbering business—cut logs and poles and firewood. I'm good at that, too; it's what my uncles do, and I worked for them when I was a kid." I turned to her. "Or I could herd cattle on the Plains River, if you'd rather."

She squeezed my hand. "Luis, you're not the first person to ask me. But you're the only one I'd even think of saying yes to, and I'd like to say it here and now. But let me think about it—not that I haven't already, lots of times. But those other times don't count, because you hadn't asked me yet."

Her eyes were on mine in the near dark.

She went on. "What I'm saying is, I don't want to answer you now. It wouldn't—wouldn't be fair to you. When this is all over, and if somehow I'm still alive, ask me again and I'll give you a straight answer. Because I do love you."

I nodded and swallowed. We didn't talk after that,

and after a few minutes got dressed and went back to bed. *"If somehow I'm still alive."* A strange thing to have said, as if she expected to die on this mission. I didn't. I knew I *could* die, here in the PDR, but I expected not to. Why would she feel differently?

I turned my head slightly, enough to look at her; her eyes were open too, gazing upward. At what? I wondered.

My dreams that night were troubled.

TWENTY-THREE

It took us five days to get to Erfurt, twenty kilometers short of Eisenbach, pushing the cart and selling pots and pans from time to time. The hills hadn't helped any. We still had half a cartful of pots and pans, plus two live chickens in a basket and a twenty-five-kilo shoat trussed up in the cart. We'd taken them in trade. What constable would imagine that a pushcart outfit like us planned to assassinate the Chairman of the PDR?

Five days to barely reach Erfurt.

Erfurt was no mere village. We came over a hill and there it was, a kilometer away, by its looks a town of four or five thousand, or maybe a little more. It was my turn between the handles, and even with help I'd worked up a heavy sweat pushing the cart uphill. Now I strode easily down the other side, holding onto the brake handle to keep from going too fast, feeling the brake shoe rub the iron wheel rim. The sun had gone down when we entered the outskirts. The sunset was fading toward dusky rose.

Four mounted constabulary were trotting their horses in our direction. I hoped they intended to trot on past, but somehow I didn't think they would.

Right in front of us they stopped, leaving me no real

choice; I set the brake ratchet and looked up into the muzzles of three short-barreled saddle muskets and one pistol. They'd be rifled, I knew. A man with four stripes on his lower sleeve leaned slightly down and glared at me. "Peddler! Show me your permit to sell in Thuringen County!"

I looked at Yakov. This was a situation we hadn't run into before. If any of us had such a permit, which I very much doubted, it was him.

He stepped forward, shrugging. "I'm sorry, sergeant," he said. "I didn't know we needed a permit to sell in Thuringen County. Where is the county line?"

The sergeant looked at him with all the warm friendliness of a snapping turtle. "Back the vay you came from. Eight kilometers."

Yakov blew a sigh of relief. "Thank God! We haven't sold anything in the last eight kilometers. Where can we get a permit? And how much does it cost? If it's expensive, maybe we should turn around and go back."

I felt the sergeant's flash of fury, contained but intense, at what he must have considered impertinence. "Vhat iss your name?"

"Yakov Duker." Yakov took a paper out of his pocket and handed it to the sergeant, who glanced at it, crumpled it, and threw it on the ground. Yakov picked it up, doing a good job of looking abused as he smoothed it on his thigh.

"That iss vorth nothing," the sergeant snapped. "You are under arrest for selling vithout a license." His glance took in the four of us. "All of you, come vith me!" He turned his horse and led off; I released the brake ratchet and started downhill behind him. His three men let us pass, then fell in behind us.

This, it seemed to me, was the worst trouble I'd been in. I could easily imagine the cart being impounded and us in jail. Then when they examined the cart, they'd find the weapons, and we'd end up on the ends of four ropes, swinging in the summer breeze while the flies gathered. Yakov's eyes flicked my way, his expression grim, and he nodded toward the cart, just a slight nod. It seemed to me he was actually nodding toward the weapons—that he wanted me to get them out somehow.

The clopping of numerous hooves and an oath in Deutsch pulled my attention rearward. A small but massively built wagon, behind a six-horse team, was moving briskly after us down the hill, its brakeman bending the brake handle to control it. I could see its load of rough-squared stone from some quarry, and moved hard right, as if to give it more room to pass. Then, taking even myself by surprise, I swerved left in front of the horses. The lead pair tried to avoid the cart while I sprang out of the way. The left-hand lead horse hit the cart with his shoulder, knocking it over, sending a clatter of pots and pans and a squealing shoat across the cobblestones.

Even as the wagon leaned, I dove for the cart again, as if to set it back up. The wagon tipped beyond recovery and went over. Horses screamed, and the wheel pair went down. Great blocks of stone rumbled out onto the pavement, knocking down one of the constabulary horses with its rider, sending another bucking and jumping. Sliding open the door to the hidden compartment, I pulled out a swordbelt, drawing the blade as I did.

It was all I had time for. The sergeant had turned his horse. His arm straightened, pistol pointing, and I jumped, rolled, slashed at the horse's shoulder, felt my sword bite. The animal squealed, iron-shod hooves pawing, the sergeant swearing. I heard a gunshot, a musket, felt something sting my cheek, sprinted low across cobblestones and down a side street. There was another shot, and another, and somehow I found more speed. I didn't hear anyone following, didn't take time to look back. I turned the first corner, saw a chest-high board fence ahead on my right, and somehow vaulted over it, belt in one hand and sword in the other. Then I crouched behind it, panting. I couldn't hear anyone coming, no hooves, no pounding feet, no gasping but my own. In the distance I could hear shouting, then another gunshot.

I had this terrible urge to run back there and do something, without any notion what, but somehow I didn't, as if my legs were disconnected from my mind. Or as if underneath I knew it was too late to change anything back there. I could only hope the others had gotten away.

I buckled on the sword belt, wiped the blood from my blade with handfuls of weeds and grass, and sheathed it. Aware again of pain in my cheek, and a slight trickle of blood, I reached up. A splinter of coarse wood was stuck there. With one hand I pulled it out, with the other pressed the small wound with a finger. A splinter from the handcart, I decided, torn loose and sent flying by a bullet.

Looking around, I found myself in a stonecutter's yard. It was littered with blocks, large and small. Farther back from the street was a long shed and a barn. Shards and chips of stone almost carpeted much of the yard, with little mounds of them here and there. The place seemed deserted, as if everyone had gone home for the day. Then a man came out of the barn, a stableman I supposed, and I froze where I was. He wasn't looking directly toward me, but off at an angle toward where the shooting had sounded from.

Very slowly I settled to the ground. Dusk and the coarse grass and weeds near the fence would make me hard to notice. After a minute the man went back in. It occurred to me that constables might be along shortly, looking for me; I needed either to find a better hiding place or run on farther.

The neighborhood looked to be mainly businesses like the stonecutter's, but there were numerous huts where presumably workers lived. It was probably supper time; that would explain why no one seemed to have seen me. But the repeated shooting would have brought at least a few people outside by now, the way it had the stableman; it seemed best just to hide for a bit.

Crouching low, I slipped over to the shed, listened outside for a minute, then went in. It was obviously a place where the stonecutters worked when the weather was cold or stormy; there were three stone fireplaces where men could warm themselves, to take the edge off of winter. There were dirty glazed windows for light. Blocks of stone lay about, the larger ones on stoneboats, sledges.

I went to one of the fireplaces, knelt, and looked up its sooty chimney. It was wide enough to climb into if it came to that. Then I posted myself by the side of a front window, to watch. A few minutes later I saw four horses coming, work horses, with the teamster walking behind. He turned them through the gate into the stoneyard, and now I could see how badly he was limping. Two of the horses were limping, too. This was the team, what was left of it, that had been pulling the stone wagon. Now all they dragged behind them was the evener, the double-tree. Everything else, I supposed, was wreckage. I watched them out of view toward the barn.

Earlier I'd felt worried, troubled. Now I was hit by a terrible depression. I felt sure that at least one of us was dead; maybe all but myself. And if any of the others still were free, we'd have trouble finding each other.

As novices we'd been trained to deal with emotions like this one—to kneel erect, attention focused on the Christ, and let the mind quiet. It took skill, a skill developed by much drilling, and it had worked for me before. Now I couldn't even try. As if nothing would do any good. All I could do was stare numbly out the window.

I lost my sense of time, and if a troop of constables

had ridden into the yard, I'm not sure I'd have noticed. After awhile though, hunger got through to me, and I became aware that dusk had thickened to twilight. Without making any conscious decision, I left the shed and the yard and began trotting south down the street, which quickly became a country lane. Woods, I'd noticed earlier, covered a long ridge south of town. I'd go there and follow it westward. I still had a mission at Eisenbach, even if it was impossible.

TWENTY-FOUR

I trotted two or three kilometers, till the lane ended at another one running parallel to the ridge. From there I jogged across a stubble field to the woods. I didn't climb the ridge right away though. I was as thirsty as I was hungry, and there was likely to be a spring somewhere along this north-facing slope. If there was, and it had a decent flow, there'd be a rivulet trickling down from it. So I turned west and trotted along the foot, the edge of the trees, hoping to find water. At length I did, and drank myself full.

Then I climbed the ridge. The woods were grazed and open, and a horned moon stood well up in the west, so the visibility wasn't too poor. Running and hiking had dulled my hunger pangs for the time being, and might well hold them off for hours, but I knew from experience that if I didn't eat by morning, I'd feel weak. And that while I could override the feeling and keep going, it would slow me.

There were a few saddles and breaks in the ridge, most with a road passing through. But mainly it ran on for about fifteen kilometers, and when I came to the end of it, the moon was low. By that time my stomach was complaining in earnest and my feet were starting to drag. To the northwest, a few kilometers off, I could see Eisenbach, a darker darkness in the night, and as late as it was, and as far, I could see scattered lights there—

—While off southwest of Eisenbach, I saw on a hill what looked like a dome of bluish light, flickering. My skin crawled, my hair bristled. The place of the Lizards; it couldn't be anything else. Silently I wished Tom and Keiji luck in capturing it. They could use all the luck they could get.

Tired as I was, I was tempted to stop and sleep. Thin broken clouds had moved in, and it wasn't as chilly as it sometimes got by midnight. But when I woke up I'd be even hungrier, so I decided to keep going, and started down the end of the ridge toward the road I could make out aimed at Eisenbach.

I was most of the way down the slope when I saw a group of cattle ahead; saw them when one of them got up. I stopped. I'd seen cattle earlier that night, a couple of times; they'd gotten up and trotted out of my way. This time I decided it was time to kill one if I could. After the one had gotten up, the others had done the same, but I stood still, and after a bit, some of them lay back down. Others stayed on their feet, grazing.

As quietly as I could, I drew my sword, the sound a barely audible hiss. None of them spooked; I doubt they heard it. I stood still for several more minutes, five or ten, long enough to let them forget about me. Then very, very slowly, inching along, I moved toward them. As I got closer, I saw that one of the nearer was a late calf, small, lying near its mother. I chose it as my target; it'd be easier to kill, and less loss to the farmer. If the cow decided to go for me . . . I'd worry about that when it happened.

At thirty meters I rushed, sword half raised. Cattle began to rise in alarm. The calf was on its feet by the time I reached it, but confused, uncertain, starting first left, then right. I struck and it went down. Hooves thudding, most of the animals had broken downhill or along the slope. The cow hesitated for just a moment, then followed the others.

After I'd cleaned my sword on the calf's hip and sheathed it, I opened the paunch with my knife, felt for the liver, and wrenched it out crudely in the dark. I'd always liked beef rare, but raw . . . The best I can say is, it cured my hunger. When I'd finished the liver, I cut a narrow strip out of the flank and ate a few bites of that. If it'd been roasted, I could have eaten twice as much.

Then I continued down off the hill. The cattle were spooky now, trotting or galloping off before I got anywhere near them. I climbed the rail fence that ran beside the road, washed the calf blood off my hands and face with ditch water and grass, and started hiking north, carrying my scabbarded sword over my shoulder. The grass on the roadside was thick and long. If I saw anyone coming, I could toss my sword into it.

Before long I passed a hamlet. Like all the other hamlets I'd seen in the PDR, it was strangely quiet: no dogs barked as I passed. It had one big fancy house with a high fence, a dozen or so small cabins, and various sheds. But only one barn, big enough for all. About a kilometer short of Eisenbach, I crossed the ditch, flanked a hedge that ran there, and lay down in the tall grass behind it. There were mosquitoes, but tired as I was, and as used to them as I was, they didn't keep me awake any time at all.

TWENTY-FIVE

It was the sun in my eyes that woke me up; I'd
overslept. The field was a potato field, and people were
already out in it, hoeing; four of them. Without raising
up, I hid my scabbarded sword in the heart of the
hedge and covered it with dead leaves. Two of the farm
hands saw me when I got up, and paused to watch, but
I didn't hear anyone call out.

My sword was six steps from the end of the hedge.

I was thirsty again, but not enough to send me off to
the stream I could see now, half a kilometer the other
side of the road. I had some coins in my pocket, in a
drawstring purse: mostly silver, one gold. Coin of the
realm, from the sale of good Israelite pots and pans and
PDR poultry. I'd eat a proper breakfast in an inn.

Rolling up my sleeves hid the calf's blood on them.
There were only a few small drops on my breeches and
shirtfront.

I stopped at the first inn I came to. It was clean, with
respectable-looking customers who seemed to be trades-
men, while I was grubby and unkempt enough that people
looked. So instead of ordering food, I bought access to
the washroom for two coppers. I stripped, and with one
of the common rags hanging on pegs—the boy who
led me there said they were boiled each night—scrubbed

myself down at the pump with soap and cold water, hair and all. When I'd rinsed off, I used one of the tubs and paddles to wash and rinse both shirt and breeches, then wrung them out and put them on wet.

From somewhere in town, a big bell tolled eight times, telling me the hour.

I told the innkeeper I'd be back when the sun had dried my clothes. Actually I'd been too noticed there, and wouldn't be back at all. I walked the streets, staying on the sunny side, and found the palace of government. It wasn't hard. There was a big stone fortress in a square near one end of town, a lot bigger, and with taller, stronger walls, than the fortress in Gotaborg. The palace was inside it, along with other buildings; their towers showed from behind the wall, a couple of them twenty meters tall or more. The open outer gates were thick and faced with iron. Behind them was a portcullis that, when lowered, fitted into holes in the pavement. The gate guards numbered eight, all somewhat bigger than me and well-armed, with weapons they looked like they could use. With my sword I could probably take two of them, maybe three, four at most. After that I'd be dead meat.

I stood back and gawped like a herdboy from the backcountry, trying to look as dull-witted as possible without being arrested as an imbecile. Harmless. Some people were let in after showing a paper. Others went in unquestioned, people the guards obviously recognized and knew were all right. A couple of carriages stopped before the gate. Guards opened the doors and looked inside, checking the passengers before letting them through. A goods wagon stopped, and two guards dug around in it till they were satisfied no one was concealed. It hadn't occurred to me that their government was so afraid of people; I don't think even Yakov had realized it.

I circled the fortress. There was a gate on each side, all alike. Inside, in one of the towers, the bell tolled nine. My number one target, the Chairman of the

PDR, was somewhere inside, if not just now, at least a lot of the time. I was sure of it.

And somehow I began to feel better! It was starting to seem like a game again, one I could win. I even told myself that Jamila had escaped, and maybe Lemmi. Maybe Yakov. Maybe all three. Why not? I had! Each was a survivor, Jamila most of all. Look at her history. The last shots I'd heard, a couple of minutes after the wreck, had been to kill the crippled horses, that was all.

The survivors would do what I'd done, find their way to Eisenbach, and our warrior muses would bring us together. We'd work out a plan and carry out our mission.

With that decided, I explored the streets and alleys all around till my clothes were hardly damp. Then I found a different inn and had the breakfast—noonmeal— I'd postponed earlier.

One of the problems I had—the biggest one right then, it seemed to me—was ignorance. Of the dangerous sort. (It wasn't that Bhatti thought ignorance was good. But the best information was observation, at the site, by the user. And the best action grew out of what your muse made of it. Sometimes, of course, you needed certain information you couldn't get that way. Also, as Tom had reminded me, there was necessary information, and information to satisfy an appetite for information.) Yakov had told us that the PDR had more laws and rules than anywhere else, and most of them I didn't know.

I wasn't anxious about the whole body of PDR law. But I did want to know enough to get a sense of how to operate there.

Asking questions, though, could be dangerous; I also remembered Yakov saying that anyone in the PDR could be an informer. Questions would mark me as a foreigner, and in the PDR, foreigners without permits could be jailed. As Israelite peddlers, we'd been foreigners without permits, but of a familiar harmless sort, generally tolerated. And finally that had failed us.

But it seemed to me that in a country like that, there were bound to be people who didn't like their rulers, their officials, their government. People on the fringe of the law or outside it. They'd know what I needed to know, if I could identify one of them and talk to him.

So I walked down a dingy side street till I found a saloon. I didn't recognize it by the sign, which said *Bierstube.* It just felt like a saloon. Not the best place in the world, judging from its front and its neighborhood, but it could be the place to start learning how things worked here.

I went in. The saloonkeeper stood like a big expressionless heap, watching me every step from the door to the bar. It was maybe half-past ten in the morning, and he seemed to be the only other person there.

"Was willst Du haben?" he asked. Louder than necessary, as if I was hard-of-hearing or he was.

I didn't know the words, but I knew what he was asking. "Beer," I told him.

He grunted and turned to a keg on a heavy plank backbar. *"Ein Bier,"* he said, again a lot louder than necessary, and drew off a half-liter mug for me. I paid him, went to a corner table, and sat down. I could take a lot longer drinking it if I wasn't standing right in front of him. He let his eyes leave me and sat down so that only his head showed, gazing at nothing.

The beer tasted better than I'd expected.

I wasn't surprised, a couple of minutes later, when a young woman entered from an inside door. She was pink and blonde and well-filled-out, maybe seventeen or eighteen. The saloonkeeper hadn't talked so loud just to hear his own voice; he'd been alerting her. She came over, her hips swaying as she walked, and sat down across from me. A whore, I decided, but a fairly good-looking one.

"Guten Morgen," she said cheerfully. *"Ich heisse Lise-Lotte. Du bist neu hier?"*

I thought I knew what the first part meant: good morning. "Good morning," I said back to her. Quietly, in little more than a murmur. "I'm Luis. I speak only Merkan, and a couple dozen words of Vlaamsch."

I was stretching it about my Vlaamsch, not that Vlaamsch would mean anything to her. I'd only ever heard of one county, supposed to be somewhere in Hoozh, where it was spoken, though I suppose there are others. But in the PDR, my exaggeration might make me more acceptable than if I spoke only Merkan. I'd run into places and people like that.

She followed my lead in speaking quietly. "I am named Lise-Lotte, and I speak goot Merkan, Luis. Vhat you do here?"

I looked around carefully before I spoke, as if not wanting to be overheard. "Looking for a job," I said. I turned my eyes back to her then. "And a friend. I don't have a friend in your city yet."

She smiled, showing dimples. "I don't know any chobs now. But maybe I vill be your friend." She raised an eyebrow. "Vill you buy for your friend a beer?"

I took out my purse and gave her the price of one. Her grin showed teeth that, in their white neatness, seemed too small; then she took the coins to the bar, where the man drew a mug for her. She sipped some off the top before coming back and sitting down again.

"From vhat place are you?" she asked, pleasantly but still quietly.

"Far Mizzoo," I said. She'd obviously never heard of it. I'd have been amazed if she had.

"Vhy you come to our country here?"

"I'm a wanderer. Last spring I went to the Commonwealth of the Lakes. Heard there was lots of work there, for good pay. You've heard of the Commonwealth?"

She raised her face from her mug and nodded.

"Anyway I went there. From Shunango." I made a face. "And ended up in a Commonwealth jail for getting in a fight."

She arched an eyebrow. "In chail!" We were both

still talking in an undertone, not much more than a whisper.

"For two months. Then I took a riverboat down the Saint Lawrence to the People's Republic. Now I need to get a job before I run out of money."

Her look was calculating. "How much money you haff?"

"Enough for a few days. A week if I'm careful."

"Goot. Maybe I vill be your friend. Maybe I talk to people I know."

So her friendship was still at maybe.

"First you come vith me," she went on. "Ve talk better vhere iss more—" She didn't know the word. "Vhere no vun else can hear." Getting up, she took my hand. I got up too, and followed her out of the tap-room. Not into the street, but through the inside door, to a stairwell. We went upstairs, down a short hall, and into a bedroom. After bolting the door, she set her beer down on a little table and proceeded to take off her blouse, exposing her breasts, cupping them with her hands and pointing them at me. She was round and firm, and cocked an eye at me again.

"You like them?"

Instead of saying anything, I put my beer next to hers and shucked out of my breeches. She raised both eyebrows at what she saw, and got out of her skirt while I pulled off my shirt.

"For other men," she said, "fife schilling. For you, only two. Because I am your friend."

And because there isn't much business this time of day, I added silently. I bent, took the purse out of my pocket, and gave her two schillings. There was a bench by the wall, and she sat down on it, setting her beer beside her, and patted the seat on the other side for me to sit. I sat, and we both took another swig.

"What sort of job do you think I might be able to get?" I asked.

She reached down to my lap and began to fondle me. "Vhat vork do you do?"

Her hand made it hard to think, but I answered.
"Well, I've been a policeman, a woodcutter—different
things. I'm a good fighting man, but I don't much like
soldiering."

She leaned against me and blew in my ear, then
started licking my shoulder, working south across my
chest. I was starting to have trouble breathing. "Ve talk
about vork later," she said. "Ve take chust now our
pleasure."

We did, too, for about an hour. I'd heard that whores
were always in a hurry to get you done and get you out,
and that they took no pleasure in it. She was a panting,
grunting, moaning exception, at least this time. And
she knew things to keep me going that I'd never heard
of. When I was totally used up, she patted my leg and
said I was her *"lieber freund,"* and that if I'd come
back when the tower clock struck four, she'd have
someone in the saloon for me to talk with.

When I walked out through the taproom, the saloonkeeper was staring at the far wall, just like he'd been
earlier.

I didn't have anything better to do between noon and
four, so I explored some more. I must have walked
about every street in Eisenbach. At the southeast edge
of town I came to a field with a little crescent-shaped
hill that half encircled a depression. The depression,
maybe a quarter hecter across the bottom, looked as if
it had been a little swale once, or a marsh. If so, dirt
had been hauled in, and covered over with sand. The
slopes around it had been terraced, the terraces no
wider than steps and paved with rock slabs, so people
could stand there better. There was room for thousands, maybe twelve or fifteen thousand, to watch what
went on in the bottom.

It was almost as big as the arena in Norlins where the
Pope holds special masses. More than big enough for
the people of Eisenbach, I thought. People probably
came in from the countryside too.

When I got there, there was a wagon parked on the sand, and three guys had just set down a big squared-off wooden block, taking care to make it level. Chopping block, I thought. It was just about the right height to kneel by and lay your chest and head on it. There were three other blocks on the wagon, and I watched those get set out too, in a neatly spaced row of four.

I'd been feeling pretty good till then. Now I felt damn near as bad as I had in Erfurt the evening before, at the stone yard. There are places where they execute criminals by chopping off their heads, and that's what these were for, I had no doubt of it. I couldn't help but wonder if I knew any of the victims.

I walked over to the wagon. My feet didn't want to go—it felt like walking through glue—but I seemed to get there in ordinary time. "How many?" I asked.

The boss, a powerful heavy-set man, grinned. "Eight. And vun uff dem dey say iss a voman! Vhat you t'ink uff dat?"

"When?" I asked.

"Two nights from tonight, at six uff de clock. But better you come early, if you vant to see goot. Maybe at four. This place be crowded."

I seem to remember thanking him. Then I turned and walked back into town. I would be there in two days, at four. I had to know for sure. But I didn't have to watch.

TWENTY-SIX

What I'd learned at the arena made everything else seem unimportant. My optimism had burst and disappeared, and I couldn't imagine getting at the PDR chairman to kill him.

But for whatever reason, with the bell in the clocktower still buzzing after ringing four o'clock, I walked into the saloon to keep my appointment with Lise-Lotte and whoever she brought with her. After the bright sunlight outside, I stopped for a moment just inside the door, letting my eyes adjust. The same heaped-up saloonkeeper stood at the bar, but he had half a dozen customers now. Lise-Lotte was sitting at a table with a small man and two mugs of beer. Actually they were getting up when my eyes found them. She didn't wave, didn't even let her eyes stop on me, as if I wasn't there. They crossed the room and walked past me out the door, into the street. As if they didn't want anyone to know they were meeting with me.

I stood and scanned the other customers for a minute, pretending I was looking for someone and not finding him. Then I left too. Lise-Lotte and the guy with her were walking casually along, talking. I followed, gaining on them at first, then holding at a distance of eight or ten meters. If they knew I was there, they were ignoring me.

I was feeling better already; I was doing something.

They turned left at the second corner, and so did I. A few doors down, they went into a two-story brick building, what they call an "apartment building," that has several or more different living places in it. I stopped outside the entrance and leaned against the wall, looking up and down the street as if I was waiting for someone. After a couple of minutes I went in.

What I'd really been doing was listening, not looking. I'd heard their feet go up a number of stair-steps inside, so I went up too, and down a hall. One of the doors wasn't quite closed; I stopped, heard Lise-Lotte's voice murmuring inside, and rapped quietly on the doorpost. *"Kommen Sie, bitte."* I didn't need to know Deutsch to understand what she'd said, or meant. I stepped in and closed the door behind me. The man had gotten up, holding a small pistol in his hand. He motioned me to another chair and sat back down again, the gun still pointed at me.

"Luis," said Lise-Lotte, "this iss Dietrich. He hass often need for men who are—experienced in certain things. If your experience iss right, he vill giff you maybe a chob."

Dietrich had been looking me over with narrow green eyes. Now he went into a short speech in Deutsch while watching me intently. I waited for Lise-Lotte to interpret for me, but she didn't say a thing. After a few seconds he spoke in Merkan. I was surprised at how well; he hardly had any accent except for forming the words farther back in his mouth. I suspect he'd spent a lot of time outside the PDR.

"Lise-Lotte says you were in jail in the Commonwealth for fighting. And that you said you are a fighting man. Is that so?"

"That's right."

"Where in the Commonwealth?"

"New Heber."

"New Heber?" His eyes were intent, and so was his trigger finger, I was sure.

"The seat of Wasatch County. Down by the Allegheny border."

I felt him relax just a little, and he nodded slightly. At least I knew something about the Commonwealth. "There are a lot of men who think they are fighters," he said. "Are you willing to be tested?"

I wondered if he was going to be my test. He was a lot smaller than me, but then, so was Soong. And there was a special energy about this Dietrich. Also, his nose had been broken at least once, and out of his thinning, short-cropped hair, a diagonal knife scar crossed his forehead almost to the left eye.

"Yeah, I'm willing," I told him. "How're you going to test me?"

"I have someone who will test you with empty hands. I can tell a lot about how a man handles himself in danger and with weapons by how he fights with his hands."

"And feet," I said.

His eyebrows raised about a millimeter. "And feet if you wish."

"Where do I take this test?"

He looked me over again, then went to the table, took a chalk and an irregular piece of slate, and quickly sketched a map. "Be here at six," he said, pointing to an X he'd drawn. "And I suggest you eat very soon or not at all. You will not want food on your stomach for the test."

I nodded. "You talked a string of Deutsch at me when I came in, and I didn't pass the test. Are you sure I won't need to speak it?"

"You *passed* the test," he answered. "If you were what I suspected, you would have understood. And *reacted*. And if you had, you could not have hidden it from me. I watched your eyes very carefully." He smiled without humor. "If you pass the fighting test, I'll be content whether you speak Deutsch or not."

He turned to Lise-Lotte. "Go now, my dear, and do not wait outside." She left without saying anything, and he didn't say anything either for a couple of minutes. Then he gestured at the door. "Now you. I will see you this evening."

I nodded, got up and left. I didn't have any idea what this would lead to or where, but at least I was doing something. As for six o'clock—I didn't have any doubt at all that I would pass his fighting test.

TWENTY-SEVEN

I had no trouble finding the meeting place, which was another saloon. A guy was standing out front, holding the wall up with his back. As I walked toward him, he gave me a look and I met his eyes. He straightened and walked away, turning into a narrow alleyway between two buildings. I walked into the saloon, pretended to look around, then stepped back out and went into the same alleyway. The guy was waiting.

"Come," he said quietly. "I vill take you to Dietrich."

We went on down the alleyway to an alley behind the buildings. A light carriage was waiting there, and he motioned me in. There was another guy inside it, who took out a black cloth. "I must wrap this around your eyes," he told me, "so you vill not know vhere ve go. If you fail the tests, ve vill bring you back here and you vill not know vhere you haff been. If you pass them, it vill be all right for you to know."

I shrugged and let him blindfold me. Actually it was reassuring. If they disposed of people who failed, then there wasn't any *need* to blindfold me. These people might be more ethical than I'd expected.

"Now," he said when my eyes were covered, "you vill need to get down on the floor so you can't be seen through the vindows."

I did that too. We went quite a ways behind the clop-clopping of the horses, around corners, then off cobblestones onto gravelled road, and finally onto dirt. Wherever they were taking me, it was out in the country. At last we stopped. My caretaker helped me out of the carriage and led me a short distance, still blindfolded. It seemed to me we'd gone into a building, though I could feel a breeze and there was dirt—sand—instead of floor underfoot. I heard and sensed other men, too. We stopped, and it was Dietrich's voice that spoke.

"You are here, Luis. Martin, take off his blindfold."

Martin did, and I looked around. The place was roofed, but open to the breeze and fading daylight, reminding me of a tobacco shed, except there was no tobacco curing, or even the faded smell of it. Half a dozen men stood waiting, not including Dietrich and Martin, ranging in size from taller than me and huskier, to about Dietrich's size.

"Luis," Dietrich said, "meet Karl. Karl is a very clever fighter with his hands, and very strong."

The others stood in a loose circle, seven or eight meters across, with me in the middle. A shirtless Karl stepped forward a couple of meters, then stopped and bowed slightly. I bowed back. He was about my height but heavier, with long muscular arms.

"I have taken the liberty of telling him what you said about your feet," Dietrich commented drily, "that he should not be taken by surprise."

I nodded. I had other surprises for him, and wondered if he had any major ones for me. We stood about two meters apart. "If you are both ready," Dietrich said, "you may start."

I nodded. Karl nodded. I took an opening stance. Karl stood with arms up and bent, fists raised to strike. He looked at me, uncertain. My arms were raised but loose, my hands open, and it seemed to him I wasn't ready to start yet. When I didn't change, he came at me. He was left-handed too, and shot a quick right jab at my face. My left forearm block parried it upward, rotating his trunk to the left, which threw his balance off slightly. He threw a left then, but with his trunk twisted a bit to the left, it lacked speed and force. I grasped his left wrist with my right hand and jerked, landed a left backfist strike to the bridge of his nose, then drove my left elbow against his temple with less force than I might have. As he started to fall sideways, I delivered a snap kick to his ribs.

At least that's what I think I did. It was as natural as walking, and the whole fight lasted maybe three or four seconds. To tell it, I've had to reconstruct it in my mind, and it may not have happened just that way. However it happened, Karl lay on the ground, stunned and gasping for air.

I looked at Dietrich. "I don't suppose you want me to do anything more."

He stared first at Karl, then at me, and shook his head. "No, that was enough. We came here for a test, not an exhibition." His look became thoughtful, and by hindsight perhaps calculating. "But I had not expected it to be over so quickly."

It seemed like a good time to be political, if not with Dietrich, then with Karl. "It needed to be fast," I said. "When you fight someone as strong and hard as Karl, you don't expose yourself to his fists any longer than you need to. He could knock your head off."

Dietrich shook his, a small twitch of a movement as if dismissing what I'd said. "I suppose you also fight with the knife?" he asked.

I nodded. "Do you have one I can borrow?"

"I did not intend that anyone here fight each other with steel."

"I don't intend to fight with it," I told him. "I want to throw it."

One of his men drew a knife from a sheath in his boot, and at Dietrich's nod he handed it to me. It wasn't a throwing knife. I hefted it, tossed it up and caught it, and got the feel of its weight and balance, or lack of balance. Posts about fifteen centimeters thick supported the tie beams overhead. I turned toward a post just outside the circle, and threw, hard. The blade socked into it some four or five centimeters.

"And the sword?" Dietrich asked.

I suppose my eyes brightened. "My favorite weapon," I told him.

His face hardened. "You are not what you claimed. You are a Meirist."

I pretended not to understand. "Meirist? I don't even know where Meir is. Never heard of the place. I'm from Mizzoo, like I told you."

He wasn't accepting that for a minute. I'd outsmarted myself; shown off; been too good. And around the circle, pistols had appeared. "If not a Meirist," Dietrich insisted, "then you are from Adirondack. A samurai."

I bowed. "You've found me out," I said. "I am from Mizzoo originally, though; it's my home country. More recently I'm from Adirondack."

"What are you doing in the People's Republic?"

As dangerous as it seemed, I told him the truth, or a major part of it. It seemed to me I was already in serious danger, and the truth's what came to me. "Your chairman here is a tool of the Lizards," I answered quietly. "A puppet. And lacking any way to destroy the Lizards, I decided to destroy him. But I'm new here. I haven't figured out how to get at him yet."

A few of them took their eyes off me long enough to glance at each other, but not enough of them to let me break for it. "Sit down on the floor please, Luis," Dietrich said. "Or the ground in this case. My comrades and I need to make a decision."

I sat. They started talking Deutsch to each other; I understood none of it. After three or four minutes, Dietrich turned to me again. "The major purpose of this group is to destroy the chairman and certain principal people in his apparatus. We are interested in the skills you have; we have certain, ah, resources. I will say no more about it now, but within a few days we hope to have access to the palace.

"You have lied to us, and while that is understandable, we are not entirely able to trust you. So we will not set you free yet. But when our plans mature, as they promise to do, and when we are ready to act, you will be part of them. When we have fulfilled our goal, we will all be Heroes of the Republic, yourself included.

"I regret that this is necessary, but we must shackle you. Your wrists just now, but when we have taken you to where we will keep you, we'll free your hands and shackle your ankles."

He raised his hand to stop whatever I might say. Actually I hadn't been going to say anything. "You'll be well fed," he said. "And well treated except for the shackles."

They bolted wrist-irons on me then, and after a short discussion in Deutsch, they put my blindfold back on. I was loaded into the carriage again and driven into town. The room I was put in had the windows shuttered, but I had a decent mattress, stuffed with fresh bracken by the smell, and the shutters were louvered to let air in. There was a guard outside the door, but he wasn't hostile, and I decided I was doing all right. We had the same central mission, these guys and I—kill the chairman. And it seemed to me that we might actually get it done.

Kill the chairman! The thought reminded me of the arena and the headsman's blocks. And that a woman was scheduled to be one of the people beheaded. *How could I have let that slip my mind, even for a minute?* The day after tomorrow! It was like a blow to the gut. I called to my jailer.

"Herman! I need your help!"

Herman wasn't careless; he'd seen me fight. So he looked through a little grille first, and when he opened the door, he had a pistol in his fist. "Vhat iss it you vant?" he asked.

"Dietrich," I said urgently. "I need to talk to Dietrich."

"Dietrich iss not here. Probably he vill be back tomorrow."

Tomorrow. Of course! What was the matter with me? I didn't need to talk to Dietrich now. I had nearly forty-eight hours—about forty-four—before I needed to be at the arena. "Thanks," I said. "If you see him, would you tell him I need to talk with him?"

Herman looked at me, a bit puzzled that my urgency had died so quickly. "I vill tell him. Now go to sleep. Because I am going to, and I don't vant you to vake me up."

He closed the door again, and I heard the lock turn. Then a bar slid into place. I lay awake for a long time, trying to think of what I could say to Dietrich. To talk him into letting me go to the executions.

Not that there was anything I could do about them. But I needed to *know*. Know whether the woman was Jamila or not.

TWENTY-EIGHT

When I did fall asleep, I dreamed long involved dreams with Jamila in them, and Tom, and others who were supposed to be Jamila's masters, Fedor and Freddie. Jamila and I had something important to do. Just what, I'm not sure I knew even in the dream. Whatever it was, it seemed as if everything was conspiring to keep us from getting it done.

Jamila didn't seem worried about it, though. Finally she came up to me with her packsack over one shoulder and told me good-bye. I asked her where she was going, and she said to get her head cut off. She seemed as cheerful as could be. I wanted to go with her, but Dietrich was there then from somewhere, and he said I couldn't, that I had work to do. I said he should do it himself, that I had to go with Jamila. But then he was Yakov instead of Dietrich, and he said he couldn't because he was dead. That it was up to me.

I turned around then and Jamila was gone, and I was sure I'd never see her again. I seemed to be less than a meter tall, a little boy, and no one was there but me; Dietrich/Yakov was gone too. Crying, I ran to catch Jamila, but there was a big crowd of people, and I couldn't find her. They were all yelling.

I woke up with a start. None of it had been real

231

except the tears; my face was wet with them. I went back to sleep pretty quickly, and as far as I know, I didn't dream anymore.

My morning guard was Herbert, Herman's brother. He volunteered that Herman had told him to give Dietrich my message. He didn't know when Dietrich would show up—probably sometime during the day.

Someone called down the hall, and Herbert left. When he came back, a couple of minutes later, he brought my breakfast. It was better than most I'd eaten that summer—eggs and bacon, and a dark smelly rye bread with butter. And a mug of fresh buttermilk; I wondered where they'd gotten that.

I didn't feel as bad as I might have expected, though there was plenty of time for that yet. Sixteen o'clock on execution day was thirty-two hours away; the tower clock had just rung eight. My real problem would be to pass the time, so I asked Herbert to teach me some Deutsch. He was getting bored, too, so he taught me the names of just about everything in the room, plus the parts of the body—had me repeat them time after time till I had them down sure. (Herbert seemed straight enough, but I didn't entirely trust him not to teach me some dirty words and say they meant something else. I'd check them with my next guard.) It was ten o'clock before we got tired of that.

Next I decided to exercise. My ankles were shackled, but the chain between them was about 800 centimeters long, so I could do quite a bit. Afterward I'd do some drills to quiet myself spiritually and gain perspective. I hadn't done any exercises since I'd left Mizzoo, except at the monastery in Adirondack and a little sword drill on the trek after that.

I started with stretching, and wasn't surprised that I'd lost some flexibility, but I took it easy enough that I wouldn't hurt myself. I was only good for twelve and fifteen one-armed pushups—right and left arms respectively—but I did what I could and switched arms until I couldn't do any any more. Then I did all I could with both arms together, went on from there to work my belly with sit-ups and leg raises, and finished off with all the squats I could do. At the Brother house I'd do a thousand squats at a time; here I couldn't squeeze out a hundred! Surprised heck out of me, considering I'd probably walked more than two thousand kilometers since late May. And pushed an overloaded peddler's cart up more than enough hills.

Herbert heard me breathing hard, looked in on me and watched for a while, then said something in Deutsch, shaking his head.

After that I did my spiritual drills. They didn't work as well as usual, but when I was done, I felt pretty good. Then I did my Deutsch drills, pointing and naming.

A guy named Ginter, or something like that, took over for Herbert, bringing my lunch with him. After I'd eaten, I asked him to help me with my Deutsch. He gave me this hostile sneer and said he didn't feel like it. Herbert had given me a book, in Deutsch with pictures. I started reading it out loud now, and I mean loud, sounding it out the best I could and understanding none of it. I must have butchered it. After a couple of minutes, Ginter came to the door and told me to stop. I invited him to come in and take it away from me. He swore at me in Deutsch and disappeared, and when I went to the little window to see what he was doing, he wasn't there.

A few minutes later, Karl came and asked me what I was doing. I told him Ginter had been an asshole, and how I'd run him off. He told me Ginter was an asshole sometimes—they all knew that—but that he'd paid two schillings for Karl to stand his watch for him. Karl worked with me on Deutsch for a while, I learned: *ich bin; du bist; er, sie, es ist; wir sind; ihr seid; sie sind.* Stuff like that. We did *der, die, das,* too—with all the modifier endings that went with them, so many it seemed hopeless. After a little while Karl told me not to worry

about them—to just say *duh* for *the*, and worry about
the fine points later.

It seemed to me I'd made a fair one-day's start on
learning Deutsch. Not that I'd learn enough here to do
me any good; I wouldn't be here that long. But it did
pass the time.

I also learned that I'd overdone my exercises. My
shoulders, chest, and arms were starting to get sore,
and my legs too. So when we got tired of the Deutsch
lessons, I did stretching exercises again for the sorest
parts, to keep them from getting too stiff.

After supper, Lise-Lotte showed up to see how I was
doing. I told her how sore I was, and Karl let her in to
massage me. You can guess what that led to, but not
before I'd moved my mattress against the inside wall,
where Karl couldn't watch us through the little window. She was still there when Herman came on watch.

Dietrich never did show up that day.

I woke up that night to use my chamber pot, and
found I was sorer than heck, so I did about half an hour
of stretching again. I decided that soreness was better
than the dream I'd had the night before.

Dietrich came in a little after breakfast. Herbert was
on watch again and teaching me Deutsch verbs.

"I hear you wanted to see me," Dietrich said.

"Right. There are going to be some executions this
evening."

His face hardened, and I realized I wasn't the only
one who might have friends scheduled for the block
there. "I know," was all he said

"I didn't come to this country alone," I told him. "I
came with three friends, and we were stopped by constabulary. I caused an accident to happen, and we ran
different ways. I don't know if we all escaped, or if I
was the only one. There was shooting, and maybe
captives."

He looked at me for a minute. Then he was looking
at something in his mind, although his face was still

aimed at me. Finally he spoke: "And you want to see if any of them are going to have their heads chopped off."

"That's right."

Again he didn't say anything right away, so I tried something else. "Maybe you'd like to see if any of your friends . . ." I said, and left it at that.

"I *know* some of my friends will," he said.

I felt embarrassed. He knew he was going to lose friends; I was only worried that I might. Of course, probably none of his was the woman he loved, but I couldn't be sure of that. After a long minute he said, "What good would it do you to go?"

"I'd know then, for better or worse. I'd know whether to hope."

"Hmm. Do the authorities know what you look like?"

I shook my head. "They don't know me. Not here. They may not even know I exist. It was at Erfurt we were stopped, and even there I doubt anyone would recognize my face."

"Erfurt!" His eyebrows had jumped. "Was there a wagonload of stone?"

Judas Priest! The story had spread! "That's right," I said. "And a pushcart full of pots and pans, and a pig. I turned it in front of the wagon, in front of the team actually, and the horses swerved so that the wagon dumped over into the constabulary."

His eyes found mine. "The story is known here. And I have heard that one they took prisoner will die tonight."

I could hardly ask the next question. "Do you know— which one?"

"I have not heard anything about that. But the person is a Meirist, I have heard. You said you were not."

"I'm not. But they might think I am."

Dietrich looked at me a few seconds without saying anything, as if making up his mind. Then he stood up. "You can go. With me. I don't know why I am doing this for you, but we will go."

I thought I knew why. He was a decent man. A decent man who wasn't too afraid of risks.

"For safety," he said, "I will have Karl loan you some clothes. Something more ordinary here than yours are." He paused and stared hard at me. "But first you must promise me two things."

"Yeah?"

"You must promise to make no outcry. And you must promise . . . to watch. The whole thing."

I stared back. "Why? Why must I promise to watch the whole thing?"

His voice was as dry and harsh as blowing sand. "So you will hate. The way I hate."

I nodded. "I'll watch. The whole thing." *But I may not hate,* I added silently, and the thought took me by surprise. I expected to hate, but for some reason I hoped I wouldn't. We'd see.

TWENTY-NINE

We arrived at the arena at sixteen hours—4 P.M.—
two hours early. There were at least a thousand ahead
of us, mostly in front, around the edge of the sand.
Some were lunching from baskets and flasks. Dietrich
said we'd do better to stand a little way up on the slope,
so we did. Down front there'd be a lot of crowding and
shoving, and if anyone pushed in front of us, he said,
we could have trouble seeing over them. I probably
wouldn't, I was taller than most, but Dietrich might.

Someone was guaranteed a view. At the opposite end
of the arena, the U-shaped bowl was open toward town.
At that end, in a raised box, there were three high seats
flanked on each side by half a dozen not so high. I
nudged Dietrich. We were standing fifteen or twenty
meters from anyone else, and it was safe to talk quietly.

"Those seats," I murmured. "They must be for the
chairman and some deputies. Why didn't we bring guns
with us? We could have killed them right here. Tonight."

He shook his head. "They do not often come to such
events. Sometimes, but not usually. When they do,
they wear armor beneath their robes, and guards stand
by them, watching. The seats will be occupied, but by
minor functionaries."

By the time the clock had tolled seventeen, things

were getting crowded. There were men, women, and children, some of the smaller children sitting on the shoulders of fathers, uncles, or big brothers.

Before six o'clock the place was jammed with people, all but the arena. There the victims, criminals, whatever you want to call them, were standing isolated in a tight group, surrounded by guards. We could sort of see them, but not really; the guards hemmed them in too closely. The box seats were empty, but the area around and behind them was roped off and free of spectators, the ropes lined with soldiers, bayonets fixed. Then a couple hundred cavalry rode into view from town, leading, flanking, and following several carriages. They halted not far behind the box seats. The crowd had gone still. Figures emerged from the carriages, at first men in uniform, then figures robed. They filed to the seats. A cheer arose, and if less than a roar of enthusiasm, it was at least fairly loud.

Dietrich looked at me and shrugged, as if to say, this time they came after all. Then we began to yell too; it seemed like the wise thing to do. Dietrich was right about one thing. They were well guarded, and in this pack of people, it would be nearly impossible to get off a decent shot.

We could hear the clock toll six as they were being seated. Almost immediately afterward, the headsman, masked, strode out through another roar of cheers. It was easy to see who the star was at this entertainment. He was huge, caped, dressed in red and black. He posted himself at one end of the row of blocks and stood immobile, leaning on his great ax. Then, dressed in gray robes that left their legs mostly bare, three of the condemned were marched to the blocks. They were hardly noticed, though, because a fourth had thrown himself onto the sand, screaming. Guards jumped, grabbed thrashing legs and arms, and carried him to a block while he shrieked his throat raw. When they got him there, the crowd cheered again.

None of these first four were Jamila or Yakov or Lemmi. That was a definite.

A man in fancy uniform walked to one of the condemned and read several sentences aloud in Merkan. The crowd had stilled, and the man had a big voice. I could hear every word: the man's name and his crimes— or at least what he'd been accused of—conspiracy, treason, and terrorism. Then a guard, a huge man, grabbed the condemned and shoved him to his knees. The crowd cheered wildly now. Unforced, the gray-robed man laid his uncovered head on the block, cheek down. I wondered if he'd closed his eyes. He must have. The headsman stepped up, took his stance, raised his huge-bladed ax and swung. The crowd roared! We must have been fifty meters away, but I could see the head hop off the block from the impact, or maybe partly from the spewing blood.

It was repeated twice, and the people around us were so caught up in it that apparently no one noticed that we didn't join in the cheering any longer. The screamer was last, screaming again and struggling. Once more guards had to hold him, by wrists and legs. Even then he flopped around enough that the headsman's stroke missed the neck and chunked into his shoulder. At that the body went limp. The next stroke did what the first should have.

With each death, the head and the body were thrown in a handcart and taken away. Finally two men came, each with a wheelbarrow and shovel, and strewed fresh sand to cover the blood. Another appeared with a large pail, brush, and water presumably soapy, to briefly, energetically, scrub the blocks, one after another.

My gut knotted. The four remaining condemned were brought up. None were left behind, and none was Jamila or Lemmi or Yakov. I would have joined the crowd in cheering now, but Dietrich's grim face kept me still.

I was hardly aware of the final four beheadings. I felt lightheaded, as if I might pass out. Then it was over, and Dietrich and I moved slowly with the pack until it dispersed. An hour later we were back at the building I'd been held at, a house at the edge of town. I suspect it had been the big central house of a hamlet the growing town had engulfed.

Apparently Dietrich and I were the only ones of his group who'd gone to the execution, but the others seemed to have it on their minds. No one was talking or playing cards that night. There was some silent drinking. Lise-Lotte didn't come round to massage my sore muscles or anything else, but I did some stretching and got Herman to give my arms and shoulders a rubdown. The soreness was starting to ease off a little.

They didn't shackle me or lock me up that night. I was accepted now, if not as one of them, at least as an ally.

No one had told me yet what their plan was, though, or what my part might be in it. And tonight didn't seem like the time to ask. Maybe tomorrow morning, if Dietrich stayed around long enough.

THIRTY

Tomorrow morning became today. Dietrich had left before the rest of us ate breakfast. No one else would answer my questions about plans, I suppose because they weren't sure Dietrich would want them to. Which really meant that while they trusted me, they didn't trust me all the way.

At the Brother house there'd be weeks at a time when you wouldn't have a mission. At any particular time there were always some who didn't. The Order had a policy that during a year, each Brother would spend half or more of his time at the Brother house. But we never lacked things to do there. We were busier, on the average, than when we were gone on mission. We drilled: physical exercises, weapons exercises, spiritual exercises, lessons in geography, history, and what have you.

These guys weren't into that sort of thing. From a few questions, I gathered that Dietrich hadn't given them much to do so far. He'd send some of them out to get information—talk to this one or that, find out who knew what—carry messages, that sort of thing. Maybe clean the kitchen. Dietrich had only been recruiting and assembling them for a few weeks. Most of them weren't really warriors, but they were probably as close to warriors as you'd find in the PDR, where soldiers were the thing. When I asked who paid the bills, they told me to ask Dietrich.

Karl was Dietrich's second in command, and when Dietrich wasn't around, Karl could assign household duties. But today most of the guys were at the house, and no one was doing much except playing cards. It wasn't the sort of situation I'd want to be around for long.

I got Karl to work with me on Deutsch again. We did things like *Ich habe hunger, Ich habe durst, Wo sind die gewehre?*, and *Kannst du gerade schiessen?* When I'd learned one, Karl showed me how it was written and I'd write it down, then write it some more. I was a little surprised at how some of them were spelled.

Karl never seemed to mind that I'd whipped him so easily when Dietrich was testing me. We were getting to be friends.

Dietrich came back after supper, and had all of us meet with him in the common room. He'd found out, he said, the name of the man they'd been hoping to find. Then he assigned a team of two to learn where the man lived; he'd brief them in half an hour.

The news started a real buzz among the guys.

Then Dietrich called me over to him and we sat down together. "You wonder what this is all about," he said. "I will tell you. When the Fortress was built, pipes were laid in the ground to take its sewage to a stream below town, and others to bring water from the river. Not long ago a story came to my ears, one which might easily have been a lie—that a tunnel was dug at that time which was not for pipes. Through it, one could escape from the Fortress in an emergency. And supposedly all of the workmen who made the tunnel were killed when it was done. But one young man, the story tells, had broken his arm a few days earlier, and was staying home, and the people who did the killing didn't know about him. They thought they'd killed them all."

Dietrich's quiet green eyes were watching to see how I was receiving all this.

"That was thirty-eight years ago," he went on. "Much of Eisenbach has been built since that time. I have been trying to trace the story to its roots, if it had any. Without stirring up interest in it, without starting talk that would find its way to officials. It has not been easy.

"Last week I learned the name of a man who supposedly knew that workman—had been his friend and knew the place he had fled to when he heard about the murders of the others. The day before yesterday I learned where that friend supposedly lived. Today I talked to him, and with the help of a little pain I found out what we need to know: the name the workman had taken and the place he ran away to, so long ago. Though we can assume he has moved since then."

Dietrich shrugged. "*If* he is still alive, and *if* we can find him, we should have a way of getting into the Fortress." He looked hard at me. "And with you among the men we send in, I believe we have a very good chance of killing our beloved Chairman Hiffenstahl and those around him, who are giving our country to the Lizards."

"Who'll take his place when we've killed him?" I asked.

"You would not know the name. And there is no reason you should."

"What kind of man is he?"

The thin lips smiled but the eyes were cold. "Much better than Hiffenstahl. A hard man, harder than he needs to be, but he will pay attention to his responsibilities, he hates Lizards, and he does not sleep with his valet."

Whoever he was, he'd be the one who was financing these guys. Not that it made any difference to me.

The next day I got four of them interested in sword training. In the PDR, sword training was pretty much reserved for the aristocrats, which was something you got to be mainly by being born into the right family. Police and the constabulary got some sword training, but not to any degree of expertness. That was obvious to me because two of my volunteers had been in the constabulary. They had skill enough to keep from cutting themselves, and to kill or intimidate common citizens, but not much more.

That afternoon Karl gave me my Deutsch lesson again. Herbert was one of the two whom Dietrich had sent to find the old man, the one whose arm had been broken thirty-eight years ago. We were wetting our throats with a beer when Ginter came in. He'd been downtown. Teams of government men, he said, were out posting and handing out notices that all male citizens were to be at the arena that evening at nine o'clock. The Lizards were going to have a ceremony, and sacrifice to their god.

Ginter's semi-permanent sneer was bigger than usual. At least it was for the right people this time.

I asked if any of our guys were going, and no one was. They'd stay inside where the street patrols wouldn't hassle them to go. Me, I *wanted* to go; I wanted to see the Lizards in action. But Karl was in charge and told me no.

It was no big deal to me. I shrugged it off and took a nap till supper.

I don't know whether it was something I dreamed or not; I don't remember dreaming. But when I woke up for supper at six, I knew I had to see that Lizard ceremony. Which meant I'd need to sneak out; Karl was a good guy, but a hardhead. At supper he named the lucky guy who had cleanup, and this time it was me. I scrubbed the table, washed the dishes, scrubbed the pots, scrubbed the stove, and scrubbed the floor, probably faster than anyone there had done it before. Unfortunately, cleanup also got stuck with any potatoes that needed peeling, and that took some time too.

It was close to 8:30, and dark, before I got a chance

to sneak off. The house had a yard with a stone wall around it, two meters high. Someone always stood guard inside the gate at night. I commented that I was going to the privy, and once in the backyard I went over the wall. I had half an hour to get to the arena, time enough if I jogged, though I probably wouldn't have a good place to watch from.

I'd trotted about half a kilometer when three police-man appeared around a corner—I almost bumped into them—and ordered me in Merkan to stop. I guess adults in Eisenbach just don't run unless they're run-ning away from something. I didn't try to get away from them. For one thing, they were close and had pistols, and anyway, I thought all they wanted was for me to go to the arena.

In Eisenbach they like their policemen big. The ser-geant stood half a head taller than me and must have outweighed me by fifteen kilos.

"Let me see your vork card!" he said accusingly, and held out his hand. Work card? I grabbed hand and elbow and bent the wrong way, jamming upward and twisting, felt the joint go as he screamed, lurching sideways into a second guy. My right foot drove into the third guy's crotch, then I was onto the second with a flurry of blows that left him unconscious on the cobblestones.

After that I ran, just far enough to get into the shadows, figuring I could walk then, turn up some alleys, things like that.

I worried about my warrior muse, for letting me walk into that kind of situation.

I didn't figure to hear any more from the three po-licemen, but I was wrong. It must have been the one with the broken elbow. Anyway one of their whistles began to shrill, loud and piercing enough to hear for a kilometer in the quiet night. I decided I'd better run again.

But not toward the arena. That way led through town, and already I could hear two other whistles answering more or less from that direction. Instead I turned right at the next alley and started toward farmland—hedgerows and cornfields. I'd just have to miss the Lizard ceremony.

Once away from buildings, I kept to the shadows of hedgerows as much as possible. Where there were gaps, I could see the dome of bluish light that had to mark the Lizard ship, but I gave it little attention.

A kilometer out of town, I took shelter in a cornfield. I saw no more police and heard no more whistles, but from the crowd at the arena, I heard a series of roars that reached me at least three kilometers away. There were several over a period of a half hour or more; they stuck my attention to them and made me shiver.

Then I heard another roar, a sound entirely different, and suddenly I began to race between the corn rows toward the east edge of the field. In half a minute I was standing by a worm fence, watching a firework climb the sky, staring as it arched upward. Then it exploded, with a burst of light that dazzled my eyes.

I stood there and wept bitterly, not knowing why.

The tears flowed for two or three minutes, I guess, and when it was over, it was over. I wiped my face, took a deep breath, and began trotting southward along the fence, feeling cold and deadly, and not knowing what that was about either. What I did know was, it was time for action. And Tom's instructions could go to hell; I was following my muse now. It was the Lizards I was going to get, not the Chairman of the PDR. Dietrich would get along without me or not at all.

I didn't even argue with myself. My warrior muse had never come on so strongly before.

THIRTY-ONE

After I'd gone south far enough, I cut east across fields to the road I'd first entered Eisenbach on. I found the hedge I'd slept behind, and my sword, then started for the dome of flickering blue light.

The land around the skyship hill was pasture. It had been wooded pasture, but the trees had been logged off not too long since. A road with some kind of hard smooth surface crossed it and climbed toward the ship. At the bottom of the hill, I sat down on a white oak stump and sized up the situation. The dome of light only partly obscured the hilltop. The ship that sat on it looked like a wavery silver gravy boat turned upside down. It looked huge, the ship, maybe sixty or seventy meters long.

But nothing I saw told me anything helpful, so after looking it over for a minute or two, I started hiking up the hill, on the road. It seemed to me that someone had to be on watch, but I couldn't see them to do anything about them, so I just kept going, depending on my warrior muse, hoping he knew what we were up to, what we had to do.

There didn't seem to be any door in the dome, but I didn't know if I needed one. Maybe I could just walk through. I stopped at its edge, having no idea what it might do to someone touching it. Up close it looked as smooth as glass, glass with a thick layer of flashing blue water flowing over it. Flowing up, not down.

I'd already drawn my sword. Now I touched the light with it. It knocked me on my back with pain I wouldn't have believed. I got off one scream, couldn't get breath for another one, twisted and writhed and actually thought I was being burned in fire. After a few seconds though, the pain slacked off. If it hadn't, it might have killed me. In another few seconds it was over entirely, and I lay there panting.

Panting was about all I could do. My arms and legs would barely move, and my eyes wouldn't focus at all. Pretty soon someone—more than one—grabbed me by the ankles and hauled me feet first along the hard-surfaced road. Lizards I supposed. I felt myself dragged up a long metal ramp, down a curving corridor, pulled over a sill of some kind, and let flop. There was a brief buzzing sort of feeling then, and I passed out.

They used pain to wake me up. Simple old-fashioned pain; they kicked me a few times in the ribs, hips, and legs. Not hard enough to break anything, but enough to worry me, and enough to hurt; I was going to be black-and-blue. I'd been right before: they were Lizards, the first real ones I'd seen. When they were done kicking me, they dragged me by my feet again, quite a ways.

I felt like I could move now, if I only had the will. But I was too tired; it was too much trouble. I was seeing again, too, the ceilings of corridors, the tops of doorways. They pulled me into a small room, then we stopped as if we were waiting for something to happen. For a moment I felt a subtle pressure that I didn't understand. Then the doors slid back and they pulled me out again, down the corridor, whose ceiling seemed to have changed from gray to light blue, and into another room, a large one this time.

I experienced all this as if I were someone else, observing through other eyes, interested but impersonal.

They let my feet drop, and I heard someone speak in a language that was new to me. The voice was like—I'd never heard one like it. As if the speaker was far superior to whoever he was talking to, and both of them knew it. One of the Lizards that had dragged me answered in a crisp, almost mechanical voice.

Then nothing, except for two voices talking quietly, as if they were chatting about crops or the weather. One of them was the one that sounded like the overlord here, but now he was talking with someone a lot closer to his own level.

The overlord voice ordered again. I was grabbed painfully by the shoulders and upper arms, fingers digging my flesh, and slammed violently into a chair. Something I couldn't see and hardly felt held me upright in it, like in the airboat seat but tighter. And now I could see someone—two someones—sitting in front of me.

I didn't have any trouble recognizing which was the overlord. For one thing, his seat reminded me of a throne. Also he was big—close to two meters tall, I'd guess, and built to scale. A big Lizard with a bluish crest and red-amber eyes, wearing robes and jewelry that would break the royal treasury to pay for. He had an amused smile that didn't hide his boredom, a boredom I read as chronic and long-standing. In the privacy of my mind I decided to label him Satan.

The one sitting near him was only a little bigger than me. He thought I was amusing too.

Satan said something in Deutsch, his voice sounding pleasant now. No one said anything back and he said something more. Suddenly my feet were plunged in fire, and I discovered I could scream again "Ah-h-h-h-h!!! Ich spreche nicht Deutsch!!!"

He'd been talking to me and I hadn't answered!

"Ah!" he said, "but it seems you do speak it. A little at least. What do you speak ordinarily? American?"

The fire had been quenched. Now it felt as if my feet

were in cool water. "Merkan," I gasped. "Loving God! Please don't do that again."

He laughed with delight. That's the only way I can describe it: delight. "And what is your name?"

"Luis. Luis Raoul DenUyl." My voice was shaking. All of me was shaking. I no longer felt like someone else. I was me, and what had happened, was happening, could hardly be more personal.

"Well, Luis, my name is not 'Loving God.' I am Targoth. Targoth Himplanthor. Can you say Targoth Himplanthor?"

I hadn't gotten all of it. "Targoth Him—" I stuck there. He frowned, and a long needle thrust unexpectedly into my left knee joint. I screamed long and hard, my eyes blurred with tears.

"HIM-planthor," he said. "HIM-planthor. Targoth HIM-planthor. Try it again. I'll help you if necessary."

My voice, when I was able to answer, shook worse than before. I didn't want any more help like that. "Targoth Himplanthor," I said.

There'd been no needle in my knee, just as earlier there'd been no fire, no smell of charred flesh.

"Very good," said Satan. Or Targoth Himplanthor. "What did you come to our hill for, Luis?"

I'd let them think I was PDR, and see what happened. "You've been corrupting my nation," I told him. "I came here to kill some of you. As many as I could before you killed me."

His brow rose. "Indeed! That was not very wise of you; we would never allow that. And surely you knew we wouldn't simply kill you. We will cause you great pain, again and again and again and again, until finally you die."

Needles began to prick my feet. I'd have squirmed if I'd have been able to. Targoth Himplanthor and his lieutenant watched me with little smiles. The needles pricked deeper, making the sweat start. Abruptly a terrific pain slammed through my teeth, my jaw, and I screamed again. My impulse was to grab my face, and my arm muscles spasmed more strongly than I'd have thought possible, weak as I was. But whatever it was that kept me upright held my arms on the arms of the chair.

Then the pain was gone. When I'd been feeling the needles, I'd seen Targoth's finger move on an arm of his throne. That was, or seemed to be, where the pain came from—his touching something on the arm of his throne.

"How long do you think you could stand pain like that?" he asked pleasantly.

"I don't know." My voice was weak.

"You will find out, Luis. You will."

A finger touched. Pain exploded in my groin. I screamed again, puked what was left in my stomach, then gagged on the dregs. I felt the invisible bonds loosen on my upper body, letting me slump forward, coughing and spasming, clearing my throat of vomit. Tears poured from my eyes. Nothing more happened for a couple of minutes, till my invisible bonds drew me back upright, holding me there. I looked blurrily at Targoth.

"Now," he said, "I have some questions I want you to answer. First I must tell you that I do not believe you are from the People's Democratic Republic, as you implied. You are from Israel, and you have confederates. Am I correct in this?"

I could barely talk, but managed to shake my head. "I was born in Hoozh," I croaked, "and I came here to find work. I'd heard they pay better . . ."

I saw the finger move again, and he saw that I saw. The needles began to prick my feet once more. "I heard they pay better here," I insisted. The needles pricked harder. *What do you want me to do?*" I shouted. "*Lie?*"

"Hmm." His eyelids had lowered, as if he was considering something. "Grilth!" he said. The words that followed were in Lizard, in the tone he'd used earlier as if talking to dirt. This time he was talking to someone I hadn't noticed before. Someone who stood off to one side, a Lizard no bigger than Dietrich, with a piping kind of voice that made me wonder if he'd been castrated. Its owner hurried to a door and left.

After that, nothing, except for little movements of Targoth's fingers as a kind of heat prickled here and there over me. My skin began to twitch, as if it were trying to escape my body. All he had to do was push the wrong little buttons to show me how badly I could hurt. Then Grilth came back with a set of black clothes. Targoth spoke again and Grilth held them out, letting them unfold to full length. They were Jamila's, beyond a doubt. Now Targoth spoke to me.

"Do you recognize these?"

"Where is she?" I asked.

"Ah. So you *are* an Israeli. I thought you might know her. You share with her a certain . . . air. A certain character." He looked at me, speculating. "Would she happen to be your mate?"

"She hasn't committed herself yet. Where is she?"

Targoth steepled his fingers in front of him. I hoped he'd keep them there. "She was injured," he said, "though not seriously, while resisting arrest by constabulary. She was to be part of a multiple public execution. But there was a difficulty: They wanted information from her first, and it seems she refused to tell them anything, even under torture."

Under torture.

"They concluded that they could torture her to death without getting answers to their questions, so they asked me to question her. A satisfying expression of their confidence, wouldn't you say?

"Obviously word leaked that she'd been brought here, and you came to see what you could do. A quixotic, suicidal act, Luis. You are an interesting—an intriguing person. I shall enjoy you to the dregs."

He tilted his head, pursing thin lips. "Remarkably, I had no more success with the woman than the local authorities had." He shook his head at me. "Oh, I could have, if I'd wished to take the time. But another possi-

bility occurred to me. To make other use of her, her
strength and tenacity."

He looked blandly at me, as if waiting to see what I
might say. "Where is she now?" I asked him.

"She is dead.

"You see, it was time for us to make a public display.
To reimpress the local people. They'd become used to
the sight of our ship, and of our air scouts coming and
going. They were losing their awe of us, and it was time
to renew it. So we arranged to sacrifice her publicly to
our greatest god, ah—" He turned to his lieutenant.
"What was it we decided to call that god, Zarrmok?"

The question was in Merkan so I'd understand. "Yug,
Your Worship," Zarrmok answered.

"Ah yes. The Great God Yug." Targoth turned back
to me, eyes hooded. "Perhaps you'd like me to describe
the sacrificial ceremony for you," he said.

I shrugged, barely, as much as my bonds and my
weakness allowed.

"She'd been rather crudely handled before we re-
ceived her, and we were impressed with her emotional
resilience. She was quite a brash young woman, as well
as remarkably uncooperative. Resistive, Jamila." He
peered as if trying to read my thoughts. "She told us
her name, you know. She *would* talk. She just wouldn't
tell us what we wanted to know . . . Jamila." He paused
over the name as if tasting it. "Rather aesthetic, wouldn't
you say?"

I didn't answer. He gave a slight shrug, a human
gesture, and went on. "We could have gotten everything she knew by questioning her under a drug. It is
quick and certain, though boring. Unfortunately, an
aftereffect, especially on your species, is a somewhat
prolonged anesthesia which would have spoiled her for
other uses.

"Besides, realistically she could hardly harbor knowledge of major importance to us. To the PDR perhaps,
but not to us. And if their Security Ministry could not
get it from her themselves, they hardly deserved it.

"So we proceeded with the ceremony as scheduled. The sacrifice. Surely you'd heard about that?"

This time I nodded. "I heard. But I never thought . . ."

"You never thought it was your lady love we would sacrifice. Yes." He shook his head. "I must confess, I compromised our art. The procedures were selected primarily for their visibility before a crowd, and for their value in entertaining and impressing it. Highly painful of course, and overwhelming to a lesser person than your Jamila. But unrefined. Technically crude. Like the people there."

He smiled at me then. "I won't bore you with a verbal description. I'll let you see it all in . . . Ah, I'll have it shown to you with full sound and color. The thrilling screams, the wild struggling—all of it, as if you were there, a few meters distant." He peered at me. I didn't give him the satisfaction of a visible reaction. "We can do that, you know—show it to you after the fact. There are many things we can do, beyond your wildest imaginings.

"I do want to tell you, though, how she ended. At a time when she was undoubtedly in the process of dying from her injuries, and should have been in a stupor from shock, she directed at me what I presume was the vilest of insults. Though the real significance may have escaped me. She called me *a poor sack of shit!* Isn't that remarkable?"

He peered at me intently. And I stared back at him, seeing something now that I hadn't before. That's what this chief of devils was—a poor sack of shit!

His eyes saw something of my reaction. "I see its meaning did escape me," he said. "Hmm. Well! I'd had our engineer, ah . . . I believe 'jury-rig' is the term, isn't it? But you'd hardly know. The term would have died here after the reprogramming. Yes. I had a rocket prepared from an exhausted oxygen tank; I'm sure you know about rockets. Some of your people on this planet shoot small rockets—fireworks—into the air during celebrations. As our finale, we attached Jamila to a rocket and sent her to Yug in heaven. And when it exploded, about two kilometers up, the only sound was a sort of collective gasp from the crowd. They stared, and left impressed."

I would have expected his story to enrage me. Somehow it didn't. "Do you suppose *she* was impressed?" I asked.

"She? Impressed? I'm not sure I understand. The explosion blew her apart. In fact, she may well have been dead before that, considering the acceleration and her severely damaged condition."

"She knew what you were getting ready to do, didn't she?"

"Oh yes. I made sure of that. And injured though she was, her mind seemed quite clear, quite sane."

"What about you?"

"What do you mean? Was I sane?"

"No. Were you impressed?"

"With the rocket? That was nothing; a show for the crowd. Good theater, though. And it required a bit of ingenuity, given our limited materials and inadequate machine shop here."

"I mean, were you impressed with *her*? With Jamila."

His face went serious. "Ah! With Jamila. Yes, very impressed. We subjected her to a great deal of agony here, you know. In that very chair you're sitting on. I've never seen an Earthling, or perhaps anyone, take pain as she did and retain their personality. She screamed very powerfully—a very strong young woman—but she showed a remarkable refusal to answer meaningful questions, and an even more remarkable psychological resilience."

Targoth had been looking at his memories. Now his eyes focused on me again. "So. And now we have you. You've shown considerable promise yourself tonight; you may even equal your would-be mate." He paused thoughtfully. "I suppose I should make use of the assembly room, where we can entertain the entire crew with you. It would be good for their morale." He turned to Zarrmok.

"Zarrmok, let us now entertain our guest with the holo of the evening's ceremony."

Zarrmok opened a cabinet, took something out that unfolded into a table with wheels, and rolled it over near me. Then he swiveled my seat to face it. After that— After that, Targoth did something that made it impossible for me to move my head, even a centimeter. It just wouldn't budge.

"Make sure of the eyes," Targoth added. Zarrmok knelt in front of me. "Luis," he said, "close your eyes."

I tried and couldn't. Suddenly he jabbed a finger at them. I couldn't even flinch, couldn't blink. Whatever power the torment seat had to keep my head from moving, could also be used to control my eyelids.

"He is ready, Your Worship."

"Good. Begin."

I'd had no idea what was going to happen. Suddenly, above the table, there seemed to be a floor of sand, the arena, with an altar, as if seen from a dozen meters away. Then Jamila was frog-marched out and fastened down. For half an hour I watched, watched the whole thing, ending with the rocket climbing the sky. Before that night I might have gone berserk at what I saw. But now, somehow . . .

And I heard her say it myself while Targoth supervised her being fastened to the rocket: "Targoth, you're a poor sack of shit."

Her voice was hoarse from screaming, but not hard to understand. And she wasn't cursing him. She was telling him what she saw. I saw it too, though I don't think I would have if she hadn't said it.

When the show was over, Targoth released my head, and I watched Zarrmok put the table away again.

"What did you think of it?" Targoth asked me.

"She was a superior being, Targoth," I said. "Superior to both of us. What do you think?"

It had seemed to me, when I said it, that it might break his bored calm. That he might decide to finish with me right there, might poke at his buttons till my heart burst. But he didn't even say anything. He just got up, a slight frown on his face, and walked out of the room. Two other Lizards came in, probably the two that had hauled me in earlier. Zarrmok let me go to the privy—helped me get there in fact—which surprised me. The privy surprised me too. It was not only indoors—just off the room they'd tortured me in—but was made with steel, along with stuff I don't have any words for.

After what had happened to me, it took three or four minutes for my water to start.

Afterward, the two Lizard guards dragged me down corridors, in and out of the strange little room again, and to a small cell, probably the one I'd been dumped in before. Then they slugged me around where it would hurt but not break bones or cause bleeding. I was lucky I'd already pissed. After beating me up, they flopped me onto a low shelf, on a pallet that was there, and pointed a thing at me as if it was some kind of gun. A sleep gun. That's the last I knew for a while.

THIRTY-TWO

The next day I woke up sore, outside and in, from the kicking and beating and from spasming in Targoth's guest chair. With maybe a little left over from working out at Dietrich's place. Interesting that I'd felt so feeble I could hardly move, yet my spasms had been so strong.

And my bare feet were red, almost as if they'd really been burned, although they were only a little tender.

From Targoth's point of view, the torment chair had the advantage that his victim would last longer, though I didn't doubt your heart could quit in it. I could even imagine the soul being driven from the body by extremities of pain. Although maybe it works the opposite way—maybe pain locks it in the body. An unpleasant thought.

Be thankful, I told myself, that the torment chair didn't give the kind of injuries I'd have had under typical torture. If I ever got loose, I'd probably still be able-bodied, assuming the chair was all they used on me. After watching the torments of Jamila, it was obviously they'd quite happily do anything, cut off body parts if it suited them, to give a person additional anguish.

I got off my shelf and knelt beside it—I'd been lax about praying lately—and asked the Blessed Virgin to have Jamila released from Purgatory. Lemmi and Yakov too, if they were dead. And if they were still alive, I went on, let them be safe. And God willing, let me be His instrument in cleansing Earth of the torturers. Finally I prayed that the Lizard Ben, if he was in Purgatory, be let rise to the Blessed Host around God.

Then I examined my cell. There was a small washbasin sticking out of the wall about waist-high. I turned a handle, and water ran into it from a curved pipe. I could use it to drink out of my hand, as well as wash in it. There was even a little sticking-out thing that, if you pushed on it, a sort of soft green soap oozed out. Also there was a big steel nightpot fastened to the floor, like the one I'd used the night before. I tried it out. It had a foot pedal at one side, and when I stepped on it, water swirled and foamed around inside the pot to clean it and carry the waste away. Next to the pot was a thing to straddle, judging from the shape and height. Straddle bare-assed. Then you pushed on a little lever with your hand, and warm water came up in a spray to wash your rear! Next to it was a place where, if you pushed a little knob, papery stuff like soft cloth came out, to dry what you'd washed. There didn't seem to be any place to throw the used paper except in the night pot, so I did, then stepped on the lever again and watched the paper disappear.

About that time I got the notion that the Lizards could watch me in my cell, and as soon as I thought it, chill bumps started running over me. I looked around for a peek-hole or something like that. I couldn't see any, but I still had the feeling.

Well, to hell with 'em. If they wanted boredom, let 'em look.

Anyway it was a pretty fancy cell. Made me wonder what kinds of interesting stuff Tom and Dave had where they lived.

Tom. It seemed to me that my only real chance to leave this place alive was for him to capture it and let me loose. But I couldn't see him getting through the dome, even if he had the whole Order plus all the samurais and monks of Adirondack with him. Sorcery like the Lizards' seemed too much for swords and guns.

Unless he could put the ship under siege and starve the Lizards out. And he couldn't do that with the men he had; the PDR wouldn't allow it. Not under Chairman Hiffenstahl. Of course, I was supposed to kill Hiffenstahl. But instead of staying with Dietrich and working on it, I'd come here and gotten myself captured, and I couldn't see any way I was going to get out of it.

Time was I'd have let myself go round and round in my head about that, the problem getting bigger as I chewed on it. Now, though, I stopped right there. My warrior muse had brought me here, I reminded myself; I'd realized that when it was happening. And I wasn't going to second-guess him this time. Your warrior muse, if you've got one, or whatever muse you have, can't guarantee you'll pull off whatever he leads you into. If you're a warrior, you need to expect death, in battle or apparently sometimes under torment. I'd learned that from Bhatti, and sometimes it was real to me; it was now. Be at peace with Jesus if you can, and go for it. If you get killed, well, Purgatory isn't forever. Besides, after Targoth's torment chair, I was in training for it.

So if Tom and his little army—not even a full platoon, the last I knew—didn't seem likely to rescue me, then it was me or no one. I was alive and still able-bodied. Targoth had left with a fly in his ear, and Zarrmok hadn't done anything bad to me; he'd even been considerate.

Able-bodied. Maybe now was the time to try something, while I *was* able-bodied. I wondered when the guards would come for me. If they came in with their hands empty and I met them with feet and fists, I could probably kill them both. I'd enjoy that. Had they carried weapons the night before? I couldn't remember; hadn't noticed. Of course, they'd had the sleep guns— they were a sort of weapon—but I might be quick enough that they wouldn't have a chance to use them.

If they did have weapons, real weapons, and I killed them, I'd be loose in the ship and armed. But if they didn't, I'd have warned the ship of the only weapon I had: my deadliness with hands and feet. And they'd treat me as dangerous.

At least that's how it seemed to me. Bhatti and Soong had both told me that your muses (aspects of yourself, remember) will make the decisions if you let them; that most people, if they pay any attention at all to their muses, generally don't go along with them unless they can explain those decisions to themselves; and that more often they talk themselves out of it.

Whatever. I felt better when I could explain things to myself.

Aside from my nightpot and so forth, the only furniture in my cell was my sleeping shelf and a low metal stool. It was the stool I chose to sit on. Because now I knew how I could greet my guards when they came for me: attack them with the stool. That way, my hand-foot skills would still be secret.

I'd hardly more than thought it when my door opened, almost without a sound. Two guards were there, not the same two as the night before. Each had a sleep gun in his hand. They didn't scare me, but I never made a move against them when they came in. I didn't realize why till they'd finished roughing me up: it wasn't time yet, and my warrior muse wanted me to be thought of as passive, nonviolent, till the right time came. If it came.

When the two guards were done punching me around, they shot me with one of the sleep guns—either a light dose, or I was getting hardened to it. They left me strength enough to walk, slowly and weakly, and took me to Targoth's torture chamber on my own bare feet.

And now I realized what that weird little room was for. It took us up and down to different corridors, different levels in the ship.

Targoth wasn't there yet, but Zarrmok was. After the guards had slammed me back into the seat, Zarrmok did whatever it was they do to have the seat hold you upright in it. He didn't say anything, though. He was waiting to see what his captain had in mind, I supposed. Targoth was more than just the captain here. He was His Worship, Lord Targoth.

While I'd still been on my feet, I'd seen that Targoth's chair arm, and Zarrmok's too, had things like buttons on them. Zarrmok played a little tune on his for me, of mixed pleasure and misery. The pleasure feelings scared me as much as the pain, or maybe more.

When Targoth did come in, his mood was different from the night before, as if he'd come to some kind of decision. Or maybe, I thought, he was always different in the morning. If this was morning.

"So," he said, "and how is our prisoner today?"

"Not bad," I told him, "considering how my two guards slugged me around last night and this morning."

He laughed. "Crew need pleasure too, Luis, and these are more than crew. They are my, umm, lesser brethren, and while they recognize my Lordship, the least of them stands above your kings. That's why I not only stage an entertainment for them from time to time; at least weekly I give them a captive to play with as they please."

Smiling, he looked at me through half-closed eyes. "We are a bit like a church, you know. And I am like a Pope to them."

He sat down on his throne. "But enough of this. I have questions to be answered." His gaze became intent. "Last night you witnessed a holo recording of the torments and death of your would-be mate. And you seemed unhorrified. Almost unmoved. This behavior is unlike most Earthlings. Explain."

"I can't undo what you did," I said. "And she is with God now, beyond pain."

"With God?" Targoth laughed, shaking his head. "You Earthlings have so little understanding, Luis, so little real knowledge. And you can't blame that on the reprogramming. In important respects you were just as ignorant before.

"Ah well. Meanwhile I find myself still curious about

what Jamila said to me—what she meant by 'poor sack of shit.' I am familiar with each of those words: *poor, sack, of, shit*. But taken together—it seems to me there must be a meaning that escapes me."

"She was pitying you."

He really did look surprised at that. "Pitying me? I don't understand. I'm sure I know what *pity* means, and it was she to whom pity might apply."

I nodded. "It might or it might not, but it applied to you. A person may feel pity for someone who suffers from great pain or great loss, *and also for someone who is seriously lacking in something*—maybe legs or eyes—if that lack prevents them from knowing happiness.

"But to truly feel pity for someone, one must first feel at least a little love for them. Someone who has no love cannot feel pity or understand it."

"Love! Interesting. Love has also been something of a mystery to me. I have heard the term used to mean sexual coupling, but I have also heard it used seemingly in other senses that I find unclear."

"There can be sexual coupling without love," I said, remembering Lise-Lotte, "and there can be love without sexual coupling. Basically, love is a willingness to share the feelings of another person and to have that person share yours."

I didn't know whether that was right or not, or even whether it felt right to me. I just said it. Targoth pursed his mouth and gazed at me. "That does not sound like much," he said.

The bonds of my chair allowed me almost to shrug, a twitch of the shoulders. "Love isn't like a cow or tree or rock to point to and say 'that's love.' And if you've never experienced it, no description can tell you what it feels like. Any more than you can describe seeing to someone born blind."

Targoth's face was locked in a frown, and I wondered if he'd take it out on me with pain. I had him interested, though; I needed to keep his attention on it.

"The barrier to your understanding," I went on, "is

the failure to know that other people are like yourself. They are of the same essence, life, with much the same kinds of feelings. Some people feel this kinship with everyone. They are called saints. Most people feel it for others who outwardly aren't too different from themselves. Some feel it for only a few people."

I wondered what Father van der Bijk would think, back in Aarschot, if he could hear me say that. Would he approve or be indignant?

"Some, like yourself, feel it for no one. They feel as if they were the only one, and other people were put here as furniture for them.

"Jamila saw that it was this way with you. She could sense what it must be like to lack, as you lack, that sense of kinship, of common essence with other people. And she wished that you *could* know that sense of kinship, not for her sake but for your own happiness."

Targoth's frown had deepened to a scowl. His fingers walked, and suddenly I felt as if my skin were being peeled off all over my body while I writhed against my invisible bonds, shrieking. Then my body began to pull apart at the joints. I passed out.

When I woke up, I was still in the torment chair, totally exhausted, used up. My skin felt like I was sunburned, and my throat as if I'd swallowed a wood rasp—from all the screaming, no doubt. Targoth was gone. Zarrmok still sat there. "Lord Targoth has important matters to attend to," he said. "Here." His fingers moved and a flood of comfort flowed over me, even soothed my throat. He spoke in his own language then, and the two guards came over. I felt the bonds let me go. They lifted me off my seat and supported me all the way to my cell.

This time they didn't beat me up, just flopped me on my sleeping shelf and shot me with the sleep gun.

THIRTY-THREE

I didn't know how long I'd slept, but I woke up on my own. Sorer than before, from spasming in the torment seat. My voice was hoarse and raspy, as if I had a bad cold, and my stomach reminded me of how long I'd gone without food.

Hungry or not, I sat down on my shelf to meditate. Surprisingly, considering how sore I was, and how hungry, it went better than usual. The thoughts that drifted across my mind took root less and less, till the vines of mental monologue, as Bhatti called them, faded and disappeared.

I was interrupted by the door opening. One guard set a tray with food on my floor, while another stood behind him, I suppose with a sleep gun ready. Then the door closed and I ate breakfast. The food wasn't that much different from what I'd eaten at Dietrich's, which surprises me now that I look at it.

When I'd finished, I put my tray beside the door, drank at my wash basin, lay down, and thought about the sabbatical I was supposed to have, when and if I got back to Mizzoo. The odds looked close to zero, and that was generous. I wondered whether Jamila was looking down at me from Heaven. Or was she still in Purgatory? If she was, it was probably because of me, which reminded me to pray for her soul. And hope she'd pray for mine.

After praying, I lay back down and went to sleep again. I can generally go to sleep pretty much any time I want, and there wasn't a lot else to do.

When I woke up, my tray was gone, and it seemed like a good time to get some physical exercise. I spent about twenty minutes doing mostly stretching exercises, kinds that wouldn't make anyone think of the fighting arts and didn't look impressive, in case my feeling had been right and I could be watched here some way or other. The soreness wasn't enough to keep me from doing them, and stretching would help get rid of it. With food in my belly, a place to sleep, and the opportunity to exercise and meditate, life, I decided, could be worse. And probably would be, all too soon.

All too soon it was: two guards came, gave me a light dose of the sleep gun, half walked and half dragged me barefoot to Targoth's, and seated me roughly, as usual. This time Targoth was waiting and Zarrmok wasn't there.

There was something different about Targoth today; he wasn't giving off that sense of boredom. I sat for half a minute before he said anything.

Then he ordered everyone else out of the room except Grilth, his valet—Grilth who apparently didn't understand Merkan.

"Luis," Targoth said, "I am interested in experiencing love. And you will help me."

"Okay," I said huskily. "Tell me about it."

"I have witnessed people in love, though admittedly not on Earth, and it is clear that love has a considerable emotional content. Sometimes it seems to be a complex that includes jealousy, resentment, and anger. At other times it seems simpler and subtler. And normally there is a strong sexual aspect, especially when one is male and one is female, but sometimes when both are of the same sex. Not so?"

So now I was counselor to the chief Lizard. It was

better than being tortured. "The jealousy and resentment and anger things aren't really part of love," I told him. "They're adulterations, sort of like, uh, rat turds in the flour. They degrade love. As for sex—there are different kinds of love. One kind includes sex. While sex between two men or between two women complicates love and endangers the soul."

Targoth sat there with his chin in his right hand, looking at me. "And does love never grow out of sex? Sex preceding and love resulting?"

"I'm sure it does, sometimes." I decided to take a different tack. "Let's look at a few questions that might help. How did you feel about your mother?"

He pursed his mouth thoughtfully. "Hmm. My family was the Himplanthors of Trenfoldh, on Araknol. My mother was a Marksudhi, another family of very high rank. When I was a small child, my mother, and occasionally my father, saw me for half an hour before dinner. Then I ate with them. And occasionally my mother had me with her from dinner until my nurse put me to bed. When I was older, I saw them mainly at dinner."

"I see. Did you like being with your mother?"

"Perhaps when I was small I did. Later— Often she'd have a new toy for me, and watch me play with it. I have the notion that she didn't know quite what to do with me."

"How about your father?"

"My father was a large stranger with unrealistic ideas about how children should behave. I resented him except when he brought me major gifts, which was rather often."

I felt sure that Bhatti could do this a lot better than I was. "Have there been any women you've had an interest in?"

"I've broken some by torture, but I suppose that's not what you have in mind. And when I was young, quite a long time ago, I had sexual experiences with several. But there was no emotional involvement, noth-

ing one would think of as love. I must say that I had
more emotional feeling for Jamila than for any other
female I've known, even though she was a simio-homid
instead of a sauro-homid.

"I became involved with the sado-hedonist movement when still quite young. Since then, women have
lost their attraction for me, except as subjects for torture. My desire to have sex seems to have disappeared
long ago.

"Until today. Today I awoke with the hypothesis that
love can grow out of sexual affairs. I propose to pursue a
sexual affair with someone I find interesting, and see if
love grows out of it. If it does, then I will know what
love is like."

"Hmm. Do you have any female crew members?"

His brow furrowed halfway to his crest. "Female
crew members!? Ah, but you're ignorant of the sado-
hedonist culture; you'd hardly know how inconceivable
that is. Female crew members! No, my dear Luis, it is
you I will take as a lover. Each of us will benefit."

Oh Jesus! I prayed, *spare me this!*

"It will provide me a chance to find love," Targoth
went on, "or at least to test my hypothesis. While you
will escape torture, at least for the duration of our
affair. And if I succeed in experiencing love, I promise
you I will never have you tortured."

"Why not Grilth?" I said. "Him you wouldn't need to
keep tied up. With me it'd be inconvenient for you."

"No," he said, "not Grilth. Grilth is not interesting. I
could never learn to love someone like Grilth." Targoth
came over to the torment seat then. "First," he said,
"you will kiss me."

It was a long evening, and we had time for quite a lot
of talking. Targoth wasn't allowing outside interrup-
tions. Early on, a tiny red light had started flashing on
his chair arm, and another on a thing a little like a desk.
After a few seconds, a small sound began—"beep, beep,
beep . . ." He put up with it for about a dozen beeps,

then said something that I suppose was swearing in
Lizard, went back to his chair, and did something that
made it stop. The little red light he let keep flashing. I
suppose someone had a report to make or a question to
ask him.

Targoth told me things I doubt he'd ever told anyone
else, and taken all together, it gave me a picture more
or less like this: when he was young, almost everything
he asked for, and a lot that he didn't, had been given to
him. Things were so easily come by that he didn't find
much satisfaction in them. He got so he was reaching
for more and more intensity of satisfaction. Always more
intensity.

One thing he discovered early: most animals and
people tried to withhold themselves from pain. They
tried very earnestly and very intensely. And when they
couldn't, their reaction to it was extreme. So he found
his thing in life—producing pain in people.

In his youthful sexual affairs, orgasm had felt to him
like a kind of pain, while on the other hand, in his
experience, other people didn't try to withhold themselves from orgasm. For both reasons, sex had not been
pleasant for him. Except for rape. Rape had been fun
for a while; people tried to withhold themselves from
being raped or treated painfully. But he had ways of
giving a lot worse pain, so his interest in rape didn't last
long.

When he took me as his sex victim, inflicting pain was
just an incidental part of it for him. That's just the way
things were. He was big and thoughtless, and used
to people yelling.

"Targoth," I told him afterward, "love is sure as hell
not going to develop when you hurt people like that. Not
unless the person loves to feel pain, and not many do."

He peered at me quizzically. "But that's not the
point. I'm the one who is intended to experience love,
not you."

"It *is* the point," I said. "Part of feeling love is to
want the other person to feel happy."

From his expression, the idea was a new one to him.

"They're not going to feel love for you if you give them pain," I added.

"Hmm." He noticed the flashing red light again. "Always they want advice and orders!" he said, tight-mouthed. "They cannot think for themselves. Well, I am done with you for now."

While he was putting his clothes back on, I told him I'd only been given one meal that day. He didn't answer, just sat down on his throne, and pushed a button. A minute later a door opened and Zarrmok and two other officers came in. Zarrmok looked at me, firmly bound down on a table Grilth had brought out for Targoth's little game. Targoth started ranting in Lizard right away, and two guards came in too. They came over, and I felt the binding force let go of me. One picked up my breeches, and together they stood me on my feet. The sleep gun effect had pretty much worn off, but I pretended to be wobbly, almost fell. They half carried, half dragged me out of the room and down to my cell, to flop me onto my shelf, then threw my breeches on top of me.

One advantage rape has over death, I told myself, is that when you're raped, you just might have a chance to get even. A natural enough feeling, wanting revenge, but not Christian, and I wasn't going to lie there and fantasize it. I got up, making it look as if I could just barely do it, then knelt and prayed. Our Order isn't much for ritual prayers—mostly we make up our own as we go—but when your heart isn't in it, ritual prayer can help a lot. So I did Hail Marys for a few minutes. Then I crawled back onto my shelf and sorted things out in my mind.

I may not have liked what had happened to me that evening, but I *was* alive. And by sending Zarrmok and the guards out, Targoth had jeopardized security procedures. The guards who'd brought me back to my cell assumed I was in a lot poorer shape than I was; with the sleep dose pretty much worn off, I might have been able to take them. Just possibly.

Maybe, I thought, I should have. There might not be another . . . No, I'd assume that my warrior muse was guiding me along the path of best possibilities. When I made my move, I could expect to be killed. And I wouldn't have accomplished much if I only took a couple of guards with me. My main objective had to be to kill Targoth. My next one—I'd worry about the next one when the chance came.

My door opened and a guard set a tray of food down inside, while another stood behind him. Then they stepped back and the door closed again.

After I'd eaten, I knelt again and prayed. I prayed to Saint Higuchi, prayed for the help of all the Christian martyrs, prayed for Jamila's soul. And then somehow I prayed for Targoth. It seemed to me that if he really wanted to know love, there might be something redeemable in him. Finally I meditated. It works best when it's not done so soon after eating, but I wasn't all that full. It took longer to quiet my mind than it had the night before, but eventually it worked.

THIRTY-FOUR

I woke up to a meal tray being delivered. I didn't
know what time it was or how long I'd slept, but I felt
pretty much slept out. After I'd eaten, I didn't have
anything to do, so I prayed and meditated again. It
went pretty well. After that I exercised the body—did
some more mild stretching, then push-ups and things
like that, making myself look a lot weaker than I was,
just in case. Afterward I did my squares up to 30-squared
equals 900. I'd only memorized them up to 15-squared,
so it took a lot of multiplying in my head. Bhatti would
have been proud of me. Sister Perfecta wouldn't have
believed it.

With one thing and another, I filled the time till the
next tray of food arrived. After what seemed like a long
time, a third tray was brought.

It wasn't too long after that, maybe an hour or so,
when two guards appeared again, gave me a light dose
of the sleep gun, and hauled me to my next session
with Targoth. When I'd been secured on the table, he
asked, "How long does it take before love sets in?"

"It takes as long as it takes," I told him. "Sometimes,
they say, it comes at first sight of the loved one. Or it
can take years." Then, not wanting to discourage him, I
added, "Usually though, a few days are enough, if it's
going to happen at all."

After he'd finished an inning, he said, "I'm not sure, Luis, but it may be starting to work. I actually found that pleasurable."

"For you, maybe," I said. "For me it's degrading to be fastened down like this."

I could have raised my head to look around, but I lay with my cheek on the table, to look weaker. I could tell by his voice that Targoth had gone to his throne. "Perhaps," he said. "But you came here to kill; you admitted it. So obviously I have to keep you immobilized."

"Not necessarily, but I can see your problem. Why not have Grilth stand by with a sleep gun?"

"A sleep . . . ? Ah, you mean a stunner! Grilth is of the servant caste. It would be inappropriate."

"How about Zarrmok then?"

"He is my second in command, and just now he is busy. When I am occupied, he needs to be available to the junior officers for whatever orders and advice they need."

"They can't get along without him?"

"He is the only other member of the command caste."

"I see." What I saw was that if I could kill them both, things might get pretty confused here. And something else. Two nights earlier, Zarrmok hadn't been needed; they'd been together in this room when I was first brought here. So what was different? Were Tom and Keiji operating nearby with their warriors? Had Dietrich made his strike?

"Well then, could I be back on a chair till you want me like this again?"

He didn't answer, but I heard the soft sound of the door opening, and Targoth's voice commanded in Lizard. Two guards hoisted me off the table and dumped me in the torment seat. Targoth's finger on the arm of his throne bound me upright. The guards had backed off a few steps, and they stood at rest with their hands on their sleep guns, their stunners.

"So, Luis, what do we do while I rest further?"

"I have given to you. Now it's time for you to give to me. Love involves giving by both sides."

"Indeed! What would you have me give?"

What I asked took me totally by surprise. "Tell me a story," I said. "A true one. Tell me what the world was like before the Shuffling."

Like probably just about everyone else, I'd wondered from time to time but I'd never expected to hear. And somehow it seemed to me that Targoth would know, would even tell me the truth.

The Church told us, simply and briefly, that human-kind had sinned almost beyond imagination, and nearly destroyed itself. And that God, in his mercy and power, had erased the worst of the past, renewed the Earth, and dispersed its remaining people.

Targoth cocked an eye at me. "Interesting that you should ask that. I'd assumed that the desire to know had been programmed out. Hmm. Well—"

The story he told me fitted Scripture, pretty much. He told me of a world with billions of people, and of a terrible war with weapons that really were beyond imagining. Of the dying of billions during the war and of more billions afterward from plagues and starvation that swept the Earth, and from despair and exposure. Then God—like Tom, Targoth called him "the Proprietor" —had "reprogrammed the matrices." When I asked what that meant, he used almost the same words as the Church had: the Proprietor had "renewed the planet." For instance, about where Eisenbach now stood, there'd been a much bigger city, but even so, it had been thought small. There had been a dozen great cities, before that terrible war, that combined had as many people as the whole world did now. The reprogramming had left no trace of them, or of any town.

"Why did you come here?" I asked.

"It is—a playground for us. This building we are in, or fortress, or however you think of it, is actually a ship that can sail the sky, out among the stars."

I tried to look startled, then stunned. "The . . . stars?" I knew from what Tom had said that Targoth had told only part of the truth. They'd come here for refuge.

And their ship couldn't fly anymore; they used our world as a play ground because they didn't have any other and couldn't leave.

I knew what I had to say next. "Will—will you take me with you? When you go back out there? For my Lord Targoth, I must tell you that—that I do not want to be apart from you."

May God forgive me for saying it.

Targoth stared at me for a long moment. "I must think," he said. "Such a thing would be unprecedented. But never before have I known someone I could talk with as I talk with you." Sharply then he spoke in Lizard. The two guards did an about-face and left. He spoke again and Grilth came forward from his corner. Targoth gave him his stunner and got up.

"Can you stand?" he asked me.

I nodded. "I think so. With your help."

Without hesitating, he came over to me, a hand out as if to raise me up. I wasn't as recovered as I'd liked to have been, and he was strong, and a lot bigger, but now was the time. I reached out my right hand. He took it and pulled to help me stand. Then I hit him in the throat with my left, with a blow we call a knife hand, and drove a foot into his crotch. He was still collapsing backward when I scrambled over him and went for Grilth.

I wouldn't have given you a whole lot for my chances, but Grilth reacted slowly. And stupidly. He went for Targoth's chair and its buttons, probably to open the door and bring the guards in, when all he needed to do was point the stunner and press the thumb stud. He'd hardly turned when I reached him from behind. Even mostly recovered, I didn't have the confidence to try a kick or punch from the back, not with him moving away from me, and me not sure where his kidneys were. So I rode him down. He squealed. I slammed his face against the floor, scrambled for the stunner he'd dropped and shot him with it.

Then I stomped his throat. Barefoot it gave me the willies, but it was a quick kill.

After I'd done the same to Targoth, I looked around to see what else I could do. The closest thing to a weapon I could see was the stunner in my hand. The guards, I knew, wore holstered pistols that I supposed were beam guns, and I decided to go for them next.

First though I put my shirt back on, and my breeches, then hoisted Targoth onto his throne—it wasn't easy—and propped him up the best I could. It wouldn't fool anyone for more than half a second, but that half-second could be vital. Then I dragged Grilth back to his corner.

The action or the excitement, or both, seemed to have helped me; I felt stronger than I'd expected. And Targoth's corpse, which I'd manhandled onto his throne, must have weighed a hundred and forty kilos.

I examined the push buttons on the arm of his chair. What I needed to do next was open the door, then try to get to it before the guards started in—shoot them with the stunner before they shot me. But the symbols on the push buttons were a mystery to me.

So I went to the door, figuring I'd stand there by it until someone opened it from outside to come in—Zarrmok maybe. And found two buttons in the wall beside the door. I pushed the top one and the room went dark. Briefly I thought to leave it dark and push the other. If the door opened, the guys outside wouldn't see me right away. But with the room dark, they'd know before the door was open half a meter that something was wrong. So I pushed the same button and the room was light again. Then, standing beside the door, against the wall, I pushed the other.

One of the guards stepped in as soon as the door was open wide enough. I let him through before I shot him, dropped into a monkey crouch as I swung into the doorway, and shot the second, then dragged him inside and closed the door again. When the door had closed, I stomped their throats too, then transferred one gunbelt to my own waist and the holster from the other guard to that belt. The holsters were interesting: they fastened onto the belts with what you could call a spring clip.

The pistols were beam guns—they had no bore—and looked as if they'd operate like the one I'd had before, but I shot one into the torment seat to make sure.

I'd done pretty well for a start, it seemed to me, but it was only a start. Now I had another decision to make. Tom had said the place to do the quickest damage was in the command room, and I didn't know where it was, or where anything was except my cell and the little up-and-down room, and a stairwell we'd passed each time they'd brought me here.

The best thing that I could see to do was to go down the corridor and find out where it took me. So I dragged the guards off to one side, drew a pistol, made the room dark again, and opened the door. When it had opened all the way, I jabbed the button again and got out before the door closed.

There was no one in the corridor. I turned left, nervous, moving quickly. It seemed to me that the command room would be on the top level, but I wasn't sure this was the top level. At the stairs, the ones that went up were narrow and ladder-steep. They didn't look like something intended for Targoth to use. Meanwhile I heard voices from around a curve in the corridor, so I quickly went down a level.

There, next to the stairwell, was what had to be the entryway to the ship. I was tempted to try opening the door and getting out, but I needed to cause damage first, a lot more damage than just killing Targoth and a few others. Besides, there'd still be the dome to keep me from escaping. So I started down the corridor. Faintly I could hear voices behind doors, which made me feel awfully darned exposed, so when I came to a door with another steep stairway, open on one side, I took it down into a large room filled with things like nothing I'd ever seen before.

I got the idea that here was the machinery that made things work, the things that pumped water, made light— things like that. It was full of quiet hummings, and smells I'd never smelled before. One of the walls had

little panes of dark glass with moving lights, some of the
lights forming what seemed to be numbers and words.
If there had been windows in the room to see out of, I'd
have thought this was the command room, even down
in the bottom of the ship like it was.

A Lizard was standing with his back to me, watching
stuff on the wall. Over the hummings, he hadn't heard
me. I drew a beam gun and shot him from close up. He
fell without a sound.

This looked like a good place to do damage, and in a
rack I saw a heavy, tapered steel bar more than a meter
long, along with some other heavy tools. Not knowing
what might happen, I took the bar and, after a moment's uneasy hesitation, smashed it against the biggest
pane of dark glass, one with a moving line of light on it.
Shards flew, and sparks, and from somewhere in the
room a loud, rough, ugly sound bracked at me, like an
accusation. It stopped me, too, while it lasted—maybe
three or four seconds. Then I started smashing anything
else of glass on the wall. There were more sparks, and
smoke, and snapping sounds. The light in the room
started to flicker; I was definitely doing damage!

There was a box on a stand, with a lot of labeled
buttons on it and an upright pane of dark glass that
glowed with more words and numbers. I smashed it
too, the box and the glass both. In mid-swing, a loud,
wild ringing noise started, in the room I was in and also
from above in the corridor. It lasted three or four
seconds too, then a voice jabbbering Lizard startled me
darn near out of my skin, and I wheeled, dropping the
bar, jerking out a Lizard gun. But no one was there.
The words were coming out of the wall!

Lizards would be arriving in a hurry, I knew. I could
either take a position here and wait to shoot whoever
started down, or I could go look for more damage to do.
I chose damage; that's what Tom had wanted, and what
I'd come to the ship for. My eyes hit on a door in one
side of the room, and picking up the steel bar again, I
ran and opened it. The room I found was a lot smaller

and seemed to have no other door. Most of it was taken up by a large network of metal tubes without sound or movement, surrounding a big ball about a meter and a half in diameter that pulsed with milk-white light. Closing the door behind me, I began to swing the bar again.

Tubes gave, broke. I used the bar like a short spear then, smashing it hard against the sphere, and at that instant the place went completely dark—the room I was in and the larger one I'd left. Dark and abruptly silent. But only for a moment. Then light and sound returned, the light weakly, the sound with a new and stronger hum. The big ball remained dark. I swung the bar some more, briefly, battering more of the tubes, then stepped back into the larger room.

Footsteps, several sets of them, pounded along the corridor above, hardly leaving me any time to smash more things before they arrived. With all my strength I swung at a box on the wall, and the lights went out again. The humming stopped. Somewhere just above, someone shouted what might have been orders.

There were more distant shouts, too, as if on some higher level, but at the head of the stairs it was quiet for the moment. I threw the bar across the room to bang against a steel wall, then crash onto the deck. Then barefoot, pistol in my teeth, I started silently up the stairs on hands and knees.

Until I touched someone. He screamed, kicked clumsily, blindly, his boot grazing my head but hardly hurting. I almost dropped the pistol, then shot him, and he pitched over me and down the ladder-like stairs. From not three meters away, a pistol went off, not a beam gun but a powder-and-ball gun, firing a whole string of shots in the darkness like a dozen guns in one, the bullets spanging and singing below. I almost shit my pants! I fired a short jolt at the muzzle flashes and they stopped; it sounded as if the guy fell under the handrail and off the side. I followed him. The stairs were a dangerous place to be.

I landed on the last guy I'd shot, turning my right

ankle, and fell down, but it didn't feel like a real injury. A line of hard green light speared the inky dark, crisscossing the stairway: a beam gun. It seemed to me I was about at the end of my luck, and I hoped the damage I'd done was serious enough. Footsteps hammered again in the corridor above. There was urgent shouting. It seemed to me that every Lizard on the ship was coming.

The light came back on then, dimly, unexpectedly, with a different humming this time, and I scuttled for the small room where I'd wielded the bar against the network of pipes. There were more shouts, and more gunshots, outside the stair door. I didn't hear any bullets. Ducking inside, I slammed the steel door and turned its handle, then found there was no way to lock or bar it, so I moved well to one side, a beam gun in each fist.

After a minute I saw the door handle move, the door open, and I shot at the leg that shoved it. Someone bellowed with pain and the leg disappeared. No one else came in. I could smell burned meat. I heard feet on the steel ladder, and somewhere voices were shouting.

Then someone outside my door threw an unstoppered metal flask into the room with me, something that fumed and reeked. My eyes stung and began to water. Already wobbly, I went to the flask and threw it back out, then reached and slammed the door again. My head was swimming now, and I stared stupidly at the deck, where some of the flask's contents had spilled into a puddle. Bullets spanged as I turned the handle then hung onto it, intending to hold it down. That was the last thing I remembered.

THIRTY-FIVE

I woke up gradually over a period of time, aware in a vague, eyes-closed kind of way, of a splitting headache, more or less wrapped in dreams about pain in the head. I would come up a little closer to waking and try to back out of the pain into sleep again. Then there'd be a period of dreaming, followed by another climbing toward consciousness. Finally I couldn't put it off any longer. I woke up, aware of groaning, opened my eyes, and after a few seconds closed them.

The question of where I was, or where I might be, didn't occur to me right away. My attention was on my headache. After a minute or two, though, other thoughts drifted through the pain: I'd opened my eyes to darkness, but there'd been moonlight, and someone beside me.

And I was lying on the ground, slightly lumpy ground. Something seemed peculiar about that, not right. I felt around with my fingers: dirt.

Let's see. I'd been in a stoneyard and . . . No, that was a while ago. I'd come to a hill, a hill with a dome of flickering blue light that seemed to . . .

Suddenly it was all there for me, like it or not, the torment seat, Targoth, killing him, smashing things up with a steel bar. And passing out alone in a little room with a steel deck, the piercing reek of something in my nose and eyes and head.

I opened my eyes again. A roof slanted from overhead down to the ground, and I'd been right about the moonlight. I raised my head, and a moment's piercing pain stabilized again to just a savage headache. A little way off someone called: "It looks as if he's driving a prisoner along ahead of him."

The voice wasn't one I recognized, but it seemed to be human. It had spoken in Merkan, and the accent wasn't right for a Lizard. The person who'd been by me had crawled partly out into the moonlight. Now he called back to the man who'd spoken: "Oi suppose he's got somethin' in mind to use him for."

"Paddy!" I croaked it out loud, and the Connemaran turned, then crawled back to me.

"Luis! Ah, Jesus Christ! Yer all right! Aren't you? Moira Moira Moira! I was so afraid ye'd die on us!" He shouted then, the words like hammer blows to my head. "Milo! Luis is awake!"

Milo. One of the Brothers who had caught up with us on the road, after the monastery. He trotted back to the slanting roof and was peering in beneath it when a loud voice called from some distance off, in Lizard. Not a natural voice, but like the one that had come out of the wall in the ship.

After half a minute it called again, in Merkan this time. "Milo! Be ready to receive a prisoner!" Milo left.

The voice had to be Tom's. And I realized now where I was: under the entry ramp to the ship. There was a big piece, a very, very important piece of time that was missing for me. I remembered the hubbub then, the yelling and shooting, in the minute or so before I'd passed out. "Paddy," I said, "can you help me out of here?"

He did, and helped me stand up. Again pain split my head, a moment's knee-buckling agony through the hard background pain, and I braced myself against the ramp.

"Oi'll be back," Paddy told me, and went over to stand by Milo. Outside of weakness and the headache, a grandfather among headaches, I seemed to be all right. My curiosity was stronger than the pain, and I looked around, swiveling my head carefully. The dome was gone, the entry door open, and I saw an airboat flying slowly toward us, a few meters above the ground, with a Lizard trudging along ahead. Milo stood waiting, sword at his waist and a gun in his hand.

The airboat didn't look like the one I'd ridden in to Israel. It looked like the Lizard airboat at the farm outside Kings Town, in Allegheny. Apparently Tom was flying it.

I sat down on the edge of the ramp where my feet could rest on the ground and watched Milo receive the Lizard. Milo said something, then Paddy grabbed the prisoner and threw him on the ground, easily if a little roughly, and held a sword to his back. Milo turned and trotted up the ramp, into the ship. The airboat disappeared onto, or maybe into, the top of the ship. A long minute or two later, Milo trotted back out with cord of some kind and tied the Lizard's wrists behind his back. Then Paddy lifted the prisoner as if he only weighed about forty kilos, and stood him on his feet. Milo marched him up the ramp, and Paddy came over to me.

"Are ye sure yer all right?" he asked.

"Except for feeling worse than my first and only hangover." It was easing a little.

"Shall we go inside?" he asked.

"I'll be better off outside for a while," I told him. "But if you've got something to do inside, go ahead."

"Tom told me to take care of you."

"Let's walk around then. That'll do me more good than anything else."

It was a beautiful night, with a lopsided moon looking about three nights into the second quarter.

We started out slowly, my head throbbing in time with my footsteps. "What happened?" I asked. "How did you guys get here? And take over?"

"We walked," he told me. "We walked all night, night after night, as fast as ever we could, and by day we hid in thick places. We were all together for a while, with Keiji in charge. Then Tom came back and we split up, the Brothers and me with Tom and the others with Keiji.

"We didn't even cook anymore after you left us; we left the pot and the bakin' sheet by the road. A couple of times we killed a sheep, but mostly, when we'd make camp, Tom would go off with one or another of us and come back with some cabbages and bread and cheese, and maybe a sausage."

I interrupted him. "How did you get inside the ship?"

"There's a story to that. The last couple of nights we walked, there wasn't very much woods; mostly just patches. Finally we hid out in a brushy little stand of pine and red maple, on an island in an alder swamp, three or four kilometers from here. Then Tom sent two of us to spy in Eisenbach and two to hide on a hilltop with spyglasses—spyglasses that see in the dark!—and watch the dome of light. Oi don't know what-all they told him—they had radios, you know. But the ones watchin' the dome saw you—anyway they thought it was you, and oi guess it must have been—walk up to the dome and touch it with a sword and get knocked on yer ass. Then the dome disappeared, and some Lizards came out and got ye, and after a minute, there was the dome again."

I interrupted to tell him I needed to sit down. I was tired already. When we'd sat, Paddy picked up where he'd left off. "Oi didn't see any of this, of course, but Tom told us."

He paused a moment. "And the spies in town . . ." he started, then stumbled and stopped in mid-sentence, turning away from me, looking at the sky, not finishing.

I finished for him. "The spies in town told him Jamila had been killed."

He nodded without saying anything, still looking away. After a minute he recovered himself and went on. "Finally Tom called his spies in from town, and the whole squad of Brothers went sneakin' through the dark to the ship hill. And glad of it, after layin' up for days and nights in one little brush patch, drinkin' swamp water and fightin' flies. Keiji's people come slippin' up another way from wherever they'd been hidin'.

"Everyone tryin" to be invisible but me. The last couple of kilometers oi came by myself, openly up the road with a gun in me shirt and a pitchfork in me hand. Oi was supposed to go up to the dome as if I was a local with something wrong with me head, and jab the dome with the fork. Tom told me it wouldn't hurt, that the wooden handle would protect me, but oi was to throw meself down anyway, and lie without moving till the Lizards came out to get me. He even showed me how to do it. So oi threw meself backwards on the ground, and lay there like you had.

"We thought the dome would turn off and some Lizards would come out and drag me in the way they did you. Then, when they got me inside, oi was to pull me gun from me shirt and shoot the Lizards draggin' me, and any that might try closin' the door, while Tom's bunch and Keiji's come runnin'.

"But the dome didn't turn off and no one came out. Oi must had lain there the better part of an hour, and nothin' happened till all of a sudden the dome disappeared! Still no one came out. So after a minute or three oi got up and went to the door with me pitchfork. And it not bein' shut tight, oi pried it open with the tines, which wasn't hard, and went in.

"And it was dark inside! By the moonlight through the door, oi could see oi was in an entry room, and oi went on into a hallway. It was really dark there, but oi could hear people—Lizards—up ahead somewhere, makin' a lot of noise. There was even what sounded like gunshots, all in a string.

"The others, when they saw me start for the door, they all come runnin' up the hill from where they'd been hidin'." Paddy paused, as if the good part was coming next. "Well, when they came in behind me, oi started down the hall, feelin' me way along the wall. And then—suddenly there was light, and all kinds of things started happenin'. Some of it oi saw and some oi heard, but most I did neither; they happened in places I wasn't. Tom can tell ye about 'em. 'Twas him that found you, too. He said 'twas you must have turned off the dome, and raised all kinds of hell while you were at it. We killed some Lizards and they killed some of us, and Tom carried ye outside himself, with Milo and me along to take care of ye.

"He showed us how to blow in your mouth, nice and easy, but I'll tell you: The way ye looked, and no breath we could feel—oi was afraid ye'd . . ."

He choked up again, which embarrassed me so I didn't say anything. It had never seemed to me that Jamila and I had done that much for him. We did save his life, I guess, back in Galway Town, but it hadn't really taken much to do it.

Paddy and I got up then and walked around a little more. My headache was still pretty bad, but nothing compared to what it had been. Paddy told me there were a lot of Lizards without guns who'd locked themselves in rooms in the ship. I didn't want to go aboard her anymore, so I asked Paddy to bring me another Lizard gun, and then I crawled back under the ramp to bed down. Before I went to sleep, Paddy was back with two guns and two bedcovers, one for me and one for him. He was *not* going to leave me by myself. Whether that was entirely his idea or Tom's too, I don't know.

I couldn't have slept more than two or three hours when Tom woke me up. Woke both of us, actually; Paddy'd learned to sleep lightly. We crawled out from under the ramp. Tom had another Brother with him, Brother Reini, whom I'd met at the monastery in Adirondack. Reini was there in case someone was needed who could speak Deutsch.

"Luis," Tom asked, "do you feel well enough to go somewhere with us?"

"I don't know. On foot?"

"Flying. To Eisenbach. I take it you know your way around there somewhat."

I nodded without any ill effect; my headache was just that now—a dull ache, a shadow of what it had been. "I'll go," I answered. "And yeah, I know my way around some. I also know some local people who were working on assassinating Chairman Hiffenstahl. Their boss is named Dietrich; that's his given name."

"Fine! Come on then."

We went in a Lizard airboat. It wasn't a lot different than the one the angels—the monitors had—but it was a little bigger. I had a lot of questions I wanted to ask Tom, about how he'd captured the starship, but it wasn't the time for that; he was busy telling us what he had in mind. In three or four minutes we were flying over the edge of night-shadowed Eisenbach.

I told him the government used Merkan, which he already knew, that it headquartered in the Fortress, and that Hiffenstahl lived there. So the Fortress was where we went. He let the airboat settle down to three or four meters above the courtyard. Several rooms had lights in them—more than I would have thought, as late as it was.

Tom talked into what he called a "loud hailer," the thing that made his voice sound loud outside. One of the things he'd told Reini and me was that he wanted the PDR people to think he was a Lizard; he didn't want them to know there were other people around who could do what the Lizards could—fly airboats and things like that.

I was surprised how much Tom sounded like one. "Humans!" he called. "Come outside! I have something important to tell you!"

We waited for a couple of minutes and no one came out. Tom looked over the sort of sloping shelf in front of him, with little glass things and glowing buttons all over it, and he pushed one of them. An awful sound came from somewhere on the outside of the airboat. It sounded ugly inside; it must have been a lot worse out there. Less than a minute later, several people came out into the courtyard with hands over their ears, and Tom stopped the racket. I wondered if they could see us through the airboat windows or if it was too dark.

Then I realized who one of the people was—the one in front: Dietrich! I whispered it to Tom.

"What is your name?" asked the voice of "Tom the Lizard."

"Dietrich Müller." I could hear him perfectly, his voice coming from a place near Tom's head. "I am the acting head of government; Chairman Hiffenstahl died this evening. Tomorrow we will have a new, official head of government—Clark Bannister."

So Dietrich had pulled it off! Probably none of the guys with him would know if Tom called things differently than Targoth had.

"Very good," Tom said. The way he said it, it sounded like congratulations. "Tonight there was a change of government on our skyship, also. A faction headed by myself now rules there. I have come to tell you that we are leaving your republic. Within a few days, most of us will have returned to our home in the sky. The others will be sent to Hell, to suffer there forever.

"We shall leave our old ship here. We do not want it anymore. But we will leave it locked so that no one can enter. Our previous rulers are dead. Any agreements they made with your government are no longer in force."

While Tom talked, a thought had come to me. From my muse, I suppose; I couldn't think of anyone else, or any*thing* else it could have come from. I whispered it to Tom now.

He nodded, then spoke to Dietrich again. "Who specifically killed Chairman Hiffenstahl?"

Dietrich frowned. I could guess what he was wondering: Will these Lizards want to punish the killer, or reward him, or what? After a few seconds he said: "A man named Lemmi Tsinnajinni, an Indian from Israel."

"Can I talk to Dietrich?" I whispered to Tom. His eyebrows lifted but he nodded, pointing to a round place on the sloping shelf. I aimed my voice at it.

"Dietrich," I said, "this is Luis. Congratulations on getting rid of Hiffenstahl. I helped the Lizards who won at their ship, and they have promised to take me home. "Lemmi is my friend. Let me talk to him."

Dietrich's face turned worried; the moonlight showed it. "Luis, I know he is your friend. Someone mentioned you—Karl it was—and Lemmi was very glad to hear of you. But—he is not here. He was here, and then awhile ago he was gone. No one knows where."

I could see why he might worry: I might think they'd done something to Lemmi. And they might have, but I doubted it. For one thing I'd developed a feel for Dietrich, and it didn't seem like the sort of thing he'd do. And for another, Lemmi was hard to do something to—probably even harder than I was. "We'll find him," I said. "Or if we don't, and he comes back, tell him I'm all right. And that Tom, who rules the Lizards now, is taking me home. That name is Tom."

I nodded at Tom then—he was grinning—and the airboat rose up out of the Fortress and startled slowly toward Ship Hill. Slowly for an airboat, that is. Tom flew us one or two hundred meters above the ground, and all the way he kept calling through the loud hailer for Lemmi to report to Tom at the starship. We must have wakened up hundreds of people down below, or thousands, and God only knows what they thought was happening.

Lemmi was already on the hill. He'd snuck up to scout it, and seeing humans go in and out, he'd moved in close enough to recognize some of them. I'd never seen him grin any wider than he did when we got out of the airboat. I was grinning myself; somehow everything had gotten done.

Then my grin slid off. Jamila was dead, and I'd forgotten! And it seemed a terrible and treasonous thing to have been happy just then.

THIRTY-SIX

There were still nearly three dozen Lizards locked in their quarters aboard the ship. Actually they weren't locked in. We were locked out. They could come out any time they wanted to. But before we'd flown into Eisenbach, Tom had told them, over what he called the "ship's comm," to stay where they were until ordered otherwise, or be killed. That an armed force under the command of monitors had captured the ship and both remaining scouts. He'd told them this in Lizard, and the surviving Lizard from the airboat, a junior officer, had backed him up.

He'd also told them that all surviving Lizards would be evacuated, by compartment, to an island until an expected Monitor Service ship, a starship, arrived to take them home. What he hadn't told them was that the ship wasn't expected for twelve years, and that "home" was the "Rehabilitation Projects Service," a place more or less like prison, where they'd have to do things to "rehabilitate" themselves. Whatever that meant. I considered them lucky not to be executed.

Two ship's officers had made a break for it and been killed. So had a petty officer. But that was all.

We still had problems, though, Tom told me. Nothing like the problems we'd had twelve hours earlier, but problems. I'd done such a good job of busting up things in what he called the "engine room," that the "life support system" was down to "one functioning air circulator," and enough water pressure to get water into crew and officer quarters. But not enough for sewage processing. Their quarters would be smelling pretty foul by now, and get worse.

So Tom was busy with the most interesting things! I followed him around like some kind of mascot. First he went down to the engine room and found what he called "welding gear," and "spot-welded" the doors to crew and officer quarters so they wouldn't open except by cutting. The Lizards probably didn't have any weapons, he said, but there were more of them than of us, and if the "emergency power system" failed, he didn't want them coming out and attacking our people in the dark.

I didn't have much trouble understanding the stuff he told me, even if some of the words were foreign—Old American, he said.

While he was welding the doors, he asked what had happened with me while I'd been a captive. I told him. All of it. Like Bhatti and Soong, he was easy to tell things to.

When I'd finished, he told me I'd done amazingly well—"Just as I knew you would," he said. Not well enough, I thought; Jamila was dead. I knew as I thought it that I was being unreasonable, but it was how I felt, and reasonable had nothing to do with it.

I'd intended that when I'd answered all his questions, I'd ask him some. Like how they'd captured the ship. But an airboat came with Dave and three other monitors, including one named Charley, and his time was pretty much taken up with them for a while. Charley was a Lizard like Ben, and he gave a long spiel in Lizard over the ship's comm, which Tom told us was to keep the prisoners from suiciding. He said some of them would anyway, that that's the way sado-hedonists are, but the monitors wanted to keep it down as much as they could. I commented that a bunch of Lizard suicides would save a lot of trouble, then reminded myself to be careful how I talked about Lizards, with Charley around.

Tom agreed about suicides saving trouble, but said it was more ethical this way, and that ethics were important, even when dealing with S-Hs. I'd be learning a lot about ethics pretty soon, he told me, and about a lot of other things.

I thought I knew what he meant by "pretty soon." When Soong had picked me for the mission, Bhatti had agreed, on the condition that when I came back, I'd get a year's sabbatical to raise my spiritual level.

It was getting well on toward dawn by then, and I was feeling pretty used up. A Brother told me where the locker was that held bedding, and I got a cover to hold out the chill and went outside and bedded down next to the ship. I'd already found my sword, and others were taking their turns sleeping out there, so I fell asleep right away.

Tom, it turned out, is the commander of what he called the Northwest Quadrant Monitor District. In the morning he left Ship Hill in charge of Charley: Charley was to fix the damaged Lizard scout, and then they'd use both Lizard scouts to ferry wounded and prisoners to wherever they were taking them. Tom took Lemmi and me and the four of our people with the worst wounds, and we left in the Monitor airboat. He took us way up high, four kilometers he said, high enough that no one on the ground would notice us if they happened to look up.

The wounded with us—two Brothers and two monks— were asleep from some medicine they'd been given.

Flying in the daytime was a lot different from flying at night. It seemed like I could see forever! After awhile we flew over what Tom said was the Huron Sea, and after that the Sea of Mishgun, and some of the country we crossed looked as wild as the Adirondacks.

But I'm getting ahead of myself. More interesting

than the country and the seas was what Tom told us about capturing the starship. For the first few minutes after we'd gone up into the air, he didn't have much attention to give us. Then he did something to his seat and it swiveled around so he was facing us, as if expecting my question. I asked, and he asked me what I already knew. I told him what Paddy had told me.

"Okay," Tom said. "The reason we waited to attack, when we were so close to the ship, was to learn what we could of the possibilities and problems. Did they shut off the dome sometimes? They did, but only now and then, and only in the daytime, so far as our people saw. Did scouts fly in and out at predictable times? Because it wouldn't do to be spotted and attacked from the air. What we found out was that we'd just have to take our chances, have someone do more or less what you did, and hope it worked."

Tom grinned and shook his head. "I'll admit I didn't feel very comfortable, making our move the way we did, after the dome had shut off but with the door still shut. Because if the door stayed shut and the dome came back on . . . but Paddy had gotten up and was going for it, and my muse said to trust him. Paddy's developed a remarkable channel to his warrior muse, and without any real training."

That wasn't clear to me, about a "channel," but I didn't interrupt. Bhatti and Soong had said that each muse was really the man himself, a part of him he couldn't see. That hadn't been clear to me either.

"When we got inside the ship," Tom was saying, "and into the corridor, it was so dark at first that we literally couldn't see anything. We did hear talking and shouts and some shooting ahead, but that was it.

"Incidentally, you know why it was so dark, don't you?"

I nodded. "Something I broke with the steel bar made the lights go out, I suppose. That must have been what made the dome go out, too."

"You've got it. So I started feeling my way along the

wall and found a companionway, a stairwell leading up, and sent Keiji with his sixteen people up it to the second level. I knew the command room would be up there somewhere, and it was important to capture it if we could. And Keiji's group was bigger than mine by seventeen to twelve.

"Right after they started up, the lights came on—dimly, but they seemed bright after the darkness we'd been in. And ahead of us, where the corridor turned right, I could see Lizards bunched up—by the engine room companionway, it turned out. I was up front with a beam gun, and while the Lizards, the S-Hs, weren't looking our way at the moment, one of them was almost sure to turn and see us. . . ."

I interrupted. "Why didn't more of you have guns? Or all of you? Like Lizard guns, I mean. I'm sure you have them where you live."

Tom nodded. "You'll learn about things like that pretty soon. But what it comes to is, we're not supposed to give you things you don't already have for yourselves, like radios, rapid-fire guns, and beam guns. That's part of the rules we're bound by. I'd stretched and bent them pretty badly just by being down here working with you, but I can justify that to a board of review because an off-world force, the S-Hs, was involved. The sado-hedonists. They'd already shown themselves, their boats, and their ship to a lot of people here. And I'm pretty sure I can get away with having given Paddy a gun, because he was already familiar with the one you took from the Lizard droid. But it's more than whether I did those things or not. It's also a matter of whether I used wisdom and restraint when I did it."

His eyes were calm but intent. "Does this give you some sense of things?" he asked.

"I think so. What it amounts to is, God has rules for his angels beyond man's understanding." .

"Yes and no. There are rules, but they're not beyond human understanding. You'll comprehend them soon enough.

"Anyway, I shot into the Lizards I could see ahead—there were others around the corner—and we charged. Three of them ran—around the next turn, up the corridor on the other side of the ship, and up the companionway there. But we didn't know about them; we were too busy hacking up the ones who didn't run. Those of us who hadn't been shot—seven out of twelve. It was a mess, believe me.

"When it was over—it probably lasted ten seconds at most—several of us had guns. Mostly semiautomatic projectile pistols, bullet guns. Bullet guns have an advantage for on-ship security: they do less damage to the ship.

"Meanwhile, on the second level, Keiji's crew had come out into the starboard corridor, the right-hand side of the O. He split his group up, half going each way, and he'd started forward when a Lizard came around the turn ahead of him, saw him and yelled, fired two or three wild shots from his pistol, and ducked back into the command room. Keiji's other group rounded the O into the port side, the left-hand side, just in time to see the three Lizards that came up from the first level—see their backs— heading for the command room.

"Some of Keiji's men had brought their bows in with them, and I have to admit I doubted they'd be worth much aboard the ship. They were carrying them with arrows nocked and bows half-drawn, and seeing three Lizards hurrying down the corridor away from them, they let fly and knocked down two of them. The other one got around the turn at the forward end of the corridor just in time to meet Keiji and his group coming around from the other side. Before they cut him down, he'd fired several shots from his pistol, killing two of Keiji's men and wounding three. That's why Keiji was wearing a bandage on the side of his head; a bullet grooved his face and bobbed his left ear."

"Wait a minute," I said. And saw Lemmi flash a grin. I knew why: I always had a mouthful of questions; all he had to do was sit back and listen. "You were on a shipful of Lizards," I went on, "sado . . ."

"Sado-hedonists. People who live for pleasure. And their passion, the only thing they really enjoy, is causing pain and grief. They're very good at it."

Somehow his saying that made me remember Jamila. A wave of feeling—loss and emptiness—washed over me. How could anyone do what they'd done to someone like her? I pushed through it—I'd look at it later—and went on. "You were on a shipful of Lizards, and all that yelling and shooting was going on, and—how come all you ran into was a handful or two of them?"

"It was thanks to you," Tom said. "I'll bet you heard an alarm go off before we came on board. Right? A sound like maybe"—and he made a noise kind of like a throaty howl to show what he meant.

I shook my head. "Two noises," I told him, "while I was down in the bottom of the ship, busting stuff up with a steel bar. The first noise was kind of like this"—I did my best to imitate it—"and a minute later a wild ringing kind of noise, with a Lizard voice coming out of the wall right afterward."

Tom nodded. Lemmi was grinning again, as if something had really tickled him. "What's funny?" I asked.

Lemmi chuckled. "There was a whole ship full of devils—S-Hs—with all their guns and power, and one single prisoner without even his pants on to start with, who ends up killing their captain and his guards and tearing up their ship, all by himself. And it never occured to that prisoner how amazing that was."

I felt my face get hot. Grinning, Tom bailed me out. "Lemmi's right," he said. "Now about those noises you heard: The first one would have been an alarm signaling a system failure. Off-world somewhere it would have caused a lot of excitement. Sitting here on Earth, only the command and engine rooms would have paid much attention to it at all. The second noise—that would have been when someone discovered their dead captain, and that you were missing. The bells would have gotten everyone's full attention. Then whoever was in command . . ."

"Zarrmok," I told him.

"Zarrmok would have announced an escaped prisoner on board. That's the voice you heard. He'd have ordered his people—everyone not on duty at that time of night—to stay in their quarters and keep the corridors clear for security personnel. And maybe to lock their doors. When the shooting started, they would definitely have locked their doors. They didn't know what was going on, wouldn't have had weapons in quarters, and wouldn't want to give cover to whoever was running loose in the ship. Probably no one on the ship, other than people on duty, had a weapon at hand. Their small arms were kept in a locker off the command room; we found them when we got in.

"Anyway, Keiji's people had cleared the second-level corridor, and most of the killing was right there by a big double door that he guessed correctly led into the command room. He gave the three captured guns and spare ammunition clips to some of his people, with a ten-second briefing and demo on how to use them. Then he tried the command-room door.

"It was locked, of course. So he set the three of his people with guns where they could command both sides of the corridor and the command room door, and hid ambushers with swords and bows inside the doorways of equipment lockers, the wardroom, the kitchen, and the companionways. Any Lizard who stuck his nose out anywhere on the second level was likely to get it cut off, even if he was quick on his feet.

"One of Keiji's men even explored up the companionway to the hanger deck, and reported that the door up there was locked."

"Where were you all this time?" I asked.

"I'm coming to that. After we cleared the corridor on the first level, there were seven of us left, including Paddy, who was in a locker by the entry, watching the corridor with a beam gun in his hand. I passed out the guns we'd taken from the dead Lizards, left three people to help Paddy cover the corridors, and took the other two with me down into the engine room. We

picked up two more guns from bodies there, guys you
must have killed. There were a couple of doors in the
forward bulkhead—the front wall—and I opened one of
them, kicked it, and jumped back. Someone inside
fired half a dozen rounds out through it, and I dove in
and shot him. He was no warrior; I doubt that any of
them were. He'd emptied his weapon at an empty
doorway, so fast that recoil had sent some of the slugs
into the overhead.

"The room there was a machine shop, and behind it
was the ship's main storage locker; nothing we were
interested in just then. So we went back in the engine
room. We didn't check the door where you were. In a
side bulkhead like that, I just assumed it was a locker of
some kind. And what I was looking for"—he paused to
grin—"what I was looking for was the droid room I
knew had to be somewhere on board. It was. It was
through the other door in the forward bulkhead. We
took the bar you must have used—tapered steel about
twelve hundred centimeters long—and a couple of heavy
wrenches, and smashed up the function control mod-
ules on the vats where they grew their droids. And on
the stasis chambers where they stored them. Nothing
in them could survive that, though they might have
lived a few minutes.

"If the Lizards had come down on us then and somehow wiped us out, they'd still have been crippled and
badly demoralized. I doubt they had either the materials or the technical people, the artisans, to repair most
of the damage we did and you did.

"When we'd finished off the droid room, we went
back into the engine room, and that's when it struck me
that no one had found you. If they had, I'd have been
told. And why the crowd and the uproar and shooting
around the head of the engine room companionway?
The why was you; it had to be. So I looked around and
headed for the door we hadn't tried yet. And there you
were.

"There was still enough smell in there to tell me

what had happened. It was a good thing the air system wasn't down entirely, or you'd have been dead. As it was, I could barely find a pulse. So I carried you up, and took Milo and Paddy, and we went outside in the fresh air, where I gave them a quick practical course in mouth to mouth . . . I taught them what to do to bring you back among the living. And left them to do it.

"Because the S-Hs still held the command room. And the one in charge—"

"Zarrmok," I said again. "He was the only other command level officer besides Targoth. Maybe they'd heard about Hiffenstahl being assassinated. That may have been why Targoth had posted him in the command room."

Tom nodded. "Could be. So with the command room under siege, he would have called in any scout, any airboat, that was out. And with a scout hanging around outside, we wouldn't be able to leave the ship.

"We knew one was out, but I suspected one was in, too, in reserve. And I wanted it.

"Zarrmok was thinking about that too, and how he could get to it. Because if he could, he could escape."

Tom grinned and cocked a furry white eyebrow. "Do you remember old Mitsuru, the little holy man who joined us north of the monastery?"

I nodded. I hadn't remembered his name, but the man wasn't someone you'd forget.

"He explored up a companionway that went to the hangar level, but the door was locked, just the way it had been reported to Keiji. Locked and airtight. But Mitsuru noticed a panel of control buttons on the wall near it, and without knowing why, or what they were, he touched them in the correct sequence. And the door opened, so he went in.

"I still haven't figured why it worked. There has to have been a master control in the command room. And I'd suspect that as soon as he thought of the scouts, Zarrmok would have made sure no one could open it the way Mitsuru did. Maybe Zarrmok had a convenient mental lapse—convenient for us. Whatever. Open it did. There was hangar space for three scouts, but only one was there. While Mitsuru was looking around inside, he heard a noise that seemed to come from a wall. He listened and decided it came from an air grille. Not that he knew what an air grille is."

Tom paused. "You see, there's no air out among the stars. Even just a dozen kilometers above the ground, the air's too thin for breathing. You'd suffocate out there unless you took a supply of air with you. So there's a system to circulate air throughout the ship, and the air can be cleaned and used over and over. There're one or more air grilles into each room.

"And Zarrmok had sent someone crawling and climbing through the air ducts to get into the hangar.

"There are controls in the command room—there have to be—and Zarrmok would have opened the duct to the hangar, if it was sealed off. And there was Mitsuru, listening while the guy came right up to the grille. Then he'd have smelled hot metal, because the Lizard in the duct cut his way out with a beam torch. After a minute, the grille fell out on the deck, and a couple of minutes later, when the cut had cooled enough, a Lizard's head came out, and his shoulders and chest. That's when Mitsuru killed the guy with his knife. Sank it into the back of his neck, into the spinal column. It's a lot tidier than cutting off the head.

"Then he pulled the body out, belted on the Lizard's gun—a beam gun—and crawled into the duct himself. A person could have gotten lost in the ductwork, I suppose—the Lizard would have studied a diagram first— but getting lost wasn't what Mitsuru got in there to do. And Mitsuru is as close with his muse as anyone you'll find. He crawled until he saw light ahead and heard voices, Lizard voices. Then he pulled out the beam gun, crept very quietly to where the grille into the command room had been removed, and sliced down everyone there."

Tom chuckled. "Meanwhile I'd left you in the care of

Paddy and Milo, and gone up to the second level to see
if I could get into the hangar. Keiji told me the door
was locked, but it seemed to me there ought to be a
way, so I went up the companionway to check. And
found the door open! It wasn't too dark in there. There
were windows, dirty of course, but they let in a lot of
moonlight, and I could see one scout and two empty
docks. One would be for the scout that Ben shot down.
The third scout was out there somewhere in the night.

"With the shadows as dark as they were, though, I
almost didn't notice the Lizard. Actually I stumbled on
him, looked down, and made out what was there: a
body with a crest on the head. And the open duct. I
didn't need anyone to tell me what had happened; I
just didn't know who had done it. One of Keiji's,
obviously.

"Then I went aboard the scout, lit up the controls,
and found out they weren't much different from what I
was used to. Those things are pretty much standard
throughout the Commonwealth—the Commonwealth of
Homid Space that is, not the Commonwealth of the
Lakes. I could even recognize what most of the symbols
meant on the keys, and what the readouts were. . . .
Anyway, I powered it up and decided I could fly it. All
I lacked was a gunner, and I could operate the gun,
too, if I didn't have to maneuver at the same time. A
big if."

He cocked an eyebrow at us. "Have I got you totally
confused?"

I shook my head. "You could fly it, and you could
shoot its gun at—at a target on the ground, for example." I remembered what the gun on a Lizard airboat
could do.

He nodded and grinned. "You've got it. So I decided
I'd better fly it out of there, but one thing I hadn't
found was how to open the exit door of the dock. The
control had to be there on the console in front of me.

"I recognized the radio key, though, and pressed it,
and immediately heard Lizards talking in the command

room. Obviously they'd left their radio open. They were discussing whether to order their people to come out of their quarters and attack the intruders. It sounded to me as if they weren't going to, though—as if they'd only do that if they couldn't escape in the scout.

"They were interrupted by the other scout. It was approaching the hill, and the pilot asked for instructions. They hadn't started to give them yet when all of a sudden I heard yelling, about two or three seconds' worth, cut short. Mitsuru was shooting them from the air duct. After that there was nothing for a few seconds. The pilot of the scout would have heard all that too, of course. You can imagine how alarmed he must have been."

I could have imagined it, all right, but just then the only feeling I had was satisfaction. Tom went on:

"After a few seconds he got his answer, though it wasn't directed at him. I, and he, could hear Mitsuru calling cheerfully in Japanese to his friends outside the door. A few seconds later I heard other voices talking happy Japanese; he'd gotten the door open and let them in. I assumed that would get them access to the arms locker. It also probably meant we could lock or unlock other ship's doors, including doors to troop quarters, if we could find out how. Which we didn't until after I'd spot-welded them.

"Anyway, I narrowed down my candidates for the instrument panel key that opened the hangar door, and the first one did it. What I needed to do next was shoot down the other scout before he could shoot me down. But he'd have a gunner. So as I came out of the hangar, I radioed in Lizard, 'Coming out. Wounded. Need help.' I assumed that if I kept it brief and desperate-sounding, he wouldn't notice my accent, or if he did, he'd blame it on pain and excitement.

"Whatever. He apparently didn't suspect a thing. I let her wobble as I flew her, and didn't lift more than twenty meters above the ground, as if I were afraid of losing consciousness and control. I set it down in a pasture a kilometer away. The other one landed about thirty meters from me, its door opened, and two Lizards jumped out and started trotting toward me.

"Right away I swiveled my gun, locked it onto their boat about where the pilot and copilot would sit, and pushed the firing stud. Held it down for a few seconds, then lifted at once to about ten meters. For security; I hadn't found how to keep my own door from being opened with the outside control.

"The gun was on *pulse,* which caused more damage to their boat than I'd have liked, but it meant a surer kill. I didn't have to hit them directly—hit their bodies— the way I would have on *beam.* The two Lizards on the ground heard and saw what had happened, of course, and started to fire their side arms at me. Not that they could do much; it was just a reaction. I tilted around and brought my gun to bear on one of them—they were about five meters apart—and shot him. Blew him pretty much to pieces. The other one threw his gun away and flopped spread-eagled on the ground in surrender. Using the loud hailer, I told him to get up and start walking to the ship, and you know the story from there on."

Tom turned back to look at his shelf of little glass panes and lights, and I looked out a window. What I saw was wilderness, and what looked like a sea. Tom said it was actually a bay of the Huron Sea. We spent quite a few minutes crossing it, the Huron Sea I mean. It was beautiful in the sunshine, rich blue and cold-looking. After we'd crossed it, I asked Tom how wide it was and he told me 200 kilometers on the line we'd taken. That's when I realized how fast we were going! Two hundred kilometers in minutes!

While we were crossing it, something occurred to me that had bothered me a little, at times. "Tom," I said. "how many Brothers are there in the Order?"

"In Merka, going on three hundred."

"How many were sent to Adirondack?"

He turned, and I could see he knew what was on my mind. "About thirty," he said.

"Did the rest of the thirty get as little information as I did, about where they were going and what they were supposed to do?"

He nodded. "Right."

I gathered my thoughts. "I can see why you wouldn't want to leave the Brother houses shorthanded. If you'd sent all three hundred or whatever, you still couldn't have stormed the ship, or even gotten them that far. You did well to get there with—how many?"

"Eleven Brothers including Paddy, fourteen monks, and three samurais. Add you and Lemmi and I and there were thirty-one of us, all told."

"But if everyone you'd sent had had full instructions . . ." I stopped then, because I could see the answer to that one, too.

"That's right," Tom said, as if he'd read my mind. "The only ones I wanted to take with me were the ones who could get to the monastery with no more than that."

"The only way I got there was with your help," I pointed out. "And *I* was the key to winning."

It wasn't easy for me to say that; it sounded like bragging. But it was true, and it rebutted his statement.

"There were special circumstances," he answered. As if it wasn't important. "You'll see them later, for yourself."

I examined his statement, then set it aside. "Do you suppose the others will get back to their Brother houses?"

"Most of them. Probably all."

We were crossing what looked to me like pine forest— flat land, or nearly so, with lots of small lakes and swamps scattered around, but mostly pine forest. Then, pretty quickly, we were crossing forest of mostly leafy trees, on low hills, and up ahead I saw another sea. The Sea of Mishgun, Tom told us. Shy Town was near the Sea of Mishgun. Shy Town, that Jamila would never return to now.

I knew I'd die someday too; everyone would. I suspected even Tom would. Monitors might be actual angels, but they weren't—didn't seem to be—the same kind of beings the Bible told about. Of course, I'd always felt a little skeptical about some things in the Bible. Had when I was a little kid, and that never changed. I decided the way to look at it was the way Jamila had: The monitors were the real angels, and the ones in the Bible were inaccurate descriptions.

I wouldn't tell that to Father van der Bijk though. No use making someone mad for nothing.

I began to feel eager to see Aarschot again. As fast as we were going, we couldn't be more than an hour or two away. They wouldn't fly me there, of course—wouldn't want people to see the airboat. Tom would come down in some out-of-the-way place, maybe in the dark, and I'd walk from there.

Which made me wonder about the wounded; they wouldn't be walking anywhere. I didn't recall where the two Brothers were from, but the monks had to be from back in Adirondack, and clearly he wasn't taking them to their monastery. It looked like he was taking them home with him.

We were over the Sea of Mishgun by then, and I saw a couple of ships on it, each with its tall mast, its big triangular sail and a small one. I wondered what they hauled. I would have thought them big, before I'd seen the starship.

Then we were over land again, and before long passed over a river so big, it had to be the Mississip. Not long after that I saw a patch of prairie ahead—a few hundred hecters—reminding me of Kansas, where I'd been on mission once. I also realized that Mizzoo was far south of us, and that we were still traveling west, or mostly west.

"Tom," I said, "where are we going?"

"Home," he answered. "Not to the world I'm from, but to where I live on this one. In the foothills of some mountains called the Sangre de Cristo—the Blood of Christ. In a kingdom called Mora; used to be part of New Mexico. You'll like it there."

I wasn't surprised, but it shut me up for a minute. "Will we be there long?" I asked.

"You and Lemmi will. Long enough to be trained as masters. The two of you did outstandingly well on this mission, and we're always watching for Brothers who are good master material."

That made even Lemmi sober. Before long we were over real prairie, a vast ocean of grass with the only woods growing in narrow ribbons along the rivers. Now and then we'd see a big herd of dark cattle; herds so big, they had to be wild. Nobody could manage, control, herds like those.

I passed the time imagining myself being a master, training people the way I'd been trained. And if I ran into a young girl like Jamila had been, eleven years old and orphaned, and if she seemed right, I'd take her in and train her. Then I wondered about the monitors who'd train us, and if any would be Lizards.

Later the rivers got farther and farther apart, and then we saw a mountain as tall, I thought, as any I'd seen in Adirondack. But flat-topped, its top and upper slopes mostly black with trees, its feet in grassland. I decided it must be the Blood of Christ, because there was a redness to the rock.

But we flew over it, and then, ahead on our right, I saw—real mountains! So big they made the other seem puny. The closer we got, the bigger they looked, a long, long line of them with pointy tops that looked bare and rocky, with heavy forest blackening the slopes below. I even saw patches of white on some of them, which had to be snow! I hoped we'd go there.

Tom pointed. "The Sangre de Cristo," he said.

"Why do they call them that?"

"I suppose because from October till June, the upper slopes are snow-covered, and at sunrise and sunset the snow looks pink. But the actual reason might be something else."

They were so beautiful that as we approached them my heart almost stopped, just from looking. "Where?" I asked.

"Not up there. Too much snow for too many months. In the foothills."

I realized he'd said foothills before; I'd just wanted it to be up there. We were over foothills covered partly with grass and partly with pines. Creeks flowed through deep ravines that Tom called canyons. The hills were rounded, the pines short and sprawling, with deep grass around them. We came to earth between two ridges. I couldn't see a building, a road, or anything that looked as if people lived there. Our door opened and Lemmi and I followed Tom out, wondering.

Then five men appeared out of nowhere! Actually nowhere! Suddenly they were just there, pushing stretchers ahead of them that floated in the air. In a sort of daze, Lemmi and I helped load the wounded, and still the stretchers floated. Then the men, grinning at us, started pushing them back toward nowhere; the last man winked at me as he went by. They disappeared right where they'd appeared at, maybe twenty-five meters away.

I stood there next to Lemmi, not scared but a little unsure. Tom was grinning at us like he so often did. But now there was a softness to the grin, and stepping between us, he put his thick arms over Lemmi's shoulders and mine, and we started walking after the stretcher men.

"I think you'll like it here," he said.

An excerpt from MAN-KZIN WARS II, created by *Larry Niven*:

The Children's Hour

Chuut-Riit always enjoyed visiting the quarters of his male offspring.

"What will it be this time?" he wondered, as he passed the outer guards.

The household troopers drew claws before their eyes in salute, faceless in impact-armor and goggled helmets, the beam-rifles ready in their hands. He paced past the surveillance cameras, the detector pods, the death-casters and the mines; then past the inner guards at their consoles, humans raised in the household under the supervision of his personal retainers.

The retainers were males grown old in the Riit family's service. There had always been those willing to exchange the uncertain rewards of competition for a secure place, maintenance, and the odd female. Ordinary kzin were not to be trusted in so sensitive a position, of course, but these were families which had served the Riit clan for generation after generation. There was a natural culling effect; those too ambitious left for the Patriarchy's military and the slim chance of advancement, those too timid were not given opportunity to breed.

Perhaps a pity that such cannot be used outside the household, Chuut-Riit thought. Competition for rank was far too intense and personal for that, of course.

He walked past the modern sections, and into an area that was pure Old Kzin; maze-walls of reddish sandstone with twisted spines of wrought-iron on their tops, the tips glistening razor-edged. Fortress-architecture from a world older than this, more massive, colder and drier; from a planet harsh enough that a plains carnivore had changed its ways, put to different use an upright posture designed to place its head above savanna grass, grasping paws evolved to climb rock. Here the modern features were reclusive, hidden in wall and buttress. The door was a hammered slab graven with the faces of night-hunting beasts, between towers five times the height of a kzin. The air smelled of wet rock and the raked sand of the gardens.

Chuut-Riit put his hand on the black metal of the outer portal, stopped. His ears pivoted, and he blinked; out of the corner of his eye he saw a pair of tufted eyebrows glancing through the thick twisted metal on the rim of the ten-meter battlement. *Why, the little sthondats,* he thought affectionately. *They managed to put it together out of reach of the holo pickups.*

The adult put his hand to the door again, keying the locking sequence, then bounded backward four times his own length from a standing start. Even under the lighter gravity of Wunderland, it was a creditable feat. And necessary, for the massive panels rang and toppled as the rope-swung boulder slammed forward. The children had hung two cables from either tower, with the rock at the point of the V and a third rope to draw it back. As the doors bounced wide he saw the blade they had driven into the apex of the egg-shaped granite rock, long and barbed and polished to a wicked point.

Kittens, he thought. *Always going for the dramatic.* If that thing had struck him, or the doors under its impetus had, there would have been no need of a blade. *Watching too many historical adventure holos.* "*Errorowwww!*" he shrieked in mock-rage, bounding through the shattered portal and into the interior court, halting atop the kzin-high boulder. A round dozen of his older sons were grouped behind the rock, standing in a defensive clump and glaring at him; the crackly scent of their excitement and fear made the fur bristle along his spine. He glared until they dropped their eyes, continued it until they went down on their stomachs, rubbed their chins along the ground and then rolled over for a symbolic exposure of the stomach.

"Congratulations," he said. "That was the closest you've gotten. Who was in charge?"

More guilty sidelong glances among the adolescent males crouching among their discarded pull-rope, and then a lanky youngster with platter-sized feet and hands came squatting-erect. His fur was in the proper flat posture, but the naked pink of his tail still twitched stiffly.

"I was," he said, keeping his eyes formally down. "Honored Sire Chuut-Riit," he added, at the adult's warning rumble.

"Now, youngling, what did you learn from your first attempt?"

"That no one among us is your match, Honored Sire Chuut-Riit," the kitten said. Uneasy ripples went over the black-striped orange of his pelt.

"And what have you learned from this attempt?"

"That all of us together are no match for you, Honored Sire Chuut-Riit," the striped youth said.

"That we didn't locate all of the cameras," another muttered. "You idiot, Spotty." That to one of his siblings; they snarled at each other from their crouches, hissing past barred fangs and making striking motions with unsheathed claws.

"No, you did locate them all, cubs," Chuut-Riit said. "I presume you stole the ropes and tools from the workshop, prepared the boulder in the ravine in the next courtyard, then rushed to set it all up between the time I cleared the last gatehouse and my arrival?"

Uneasy nods. He held his ears and tail stiffly, letting his whiskers quiver slightly and holding in the rush of love and pride he felt, more delicious than milk heated with bourbon. *Look at them!* he thought. At the age when most young kzin were helpless prisoners of instinct and hormone, wasting their strength ripping each other up or making fruitless direct attacks on their sires, or demanding to be allowed to join the Patriarchy's service *at once* to win a Name and household of their own . . . *His* get had learned to *cooperate* and use their minds!

"Ah, Honored Sire Chuut-Riit, we set the ropes up beforehand, but made it look as if we were using them for tumbling practice," the one the others called Spotty said. Some of them glared at him, and the adult raised his hand again.

"No, no, I am *moderately* pleased." A pause. "You did not hope to take over my official position if you had disposed of me?"

"No, Honored Sire Chuut-Riit," the tall leader said. There had been a time when any kzin's holdings were the prize of the victor in a duel, and the dueling rules were interpreted more leniently for a young subadult. Everyone had a sentimental streak for a successful youngster; every male kzin remembered the intolerable stress of being physically mature but remaining under dominance as a child.

Still, these days affairs were handled in a more civilized manner. Only the Patriarchy could award military and political office. And this mass assassination attempt was ... unorthodox, to say the least. Outside the rules more because of its rarity than because of formal disapproval. ...

A vigorous toss of the head. "Oh, no, Honored Sire Chuut-Riit. We had an agreement to divide the private possessions. The lands and the, ah, females." Passing their own mothers to half-siblings, of course. "Then we wouldn't each have so much we'd get too many challenges, and we'd agreed to help each other against outsiders," the leader of the plot finished virtuously.

"Fatuous young scoundrels," Chuut-Riit said. His eyes narrowed dangerously. "You haven't been communicating outside the household, have you?" he snarled.

"Oh, *no*, Honored Sire Chuut-Riit!"

"Word of honor! May we die nameless if we should do such a thing!"

The adult nodded, satisfied that good family feeling had prevailed. "Well, as I said, I am somewhat pleased. If you have been keeping up with your lessons. Is there anything you wish?"

"Fresh meat, Honored Sire Chuut-Riit," the spotted one said. The adult could have told him by the scent, of course, a kzin never forgot another's personal odor, that was one reason why names were less necessary among their species. "The reconstituted stuff from the dispensers is always ... so ... *quiet*."

Chuut-Riit hid his amusement. Young Heroes-to-be were always kept on an inadequate diet, to increase their aggressiveness. A matter for careful gauging, since too much hunger would drive them into mindless cannibalistic frenzy.

"And couldn't we have the human servants back? They were nice." Vigorous gestures of assent. Another added: "They told good stories. I miss my Clothilda-human."

"Silence!" Chuut-Riit roared. The youngsters flattened stomach and chin to the ground again. "Not until you can be trusted not to injure them; how many times do I have to tell you, it's dishonorable to attack household servants! Until you learn self-control, you will have to make do with machines."

This time all of them turned and glared at a mottled youngster in the rear of their group; there were half-healed scars over his head and shoulders. "It bared its *teeth* at me," he said sulkily. "All I did was swipe at it, how was I supposed to know it would die?" A chorus of rumbles, and this time several of the covert kicks and clawstrikes landed.

"Enough," Chuut-Riit said after a moment. *Good, they have even learned how to discipline each other as a unit.* "I will consider it, when all of you can pass a test on the interpretation of human expressions and body-language." He drew himself up. "In the meantime, within the next two eight-days, there will be a formal hunt and meeting in the Patriarch's Preserve; kzinti homeworld game, the best Earth animals, and even some feral-human outlaws, perhaps!"

He could smell their excitement increase, a mane-crinkling musky odor not unmixed with the sour whiff of fear. Such a hunt was not without danger for adolescents, being a good opportunity for hostile adults to cull a few of a hated rival's offspring with no possibility of blame. *They will be in less danger than most,* Chuut-Riit thought judiciously. *In fact, they may run across a few of my subordinates' get and mob them. Good.*

"And if we do well, afterwards a feast and a visit to the Sterile Ones." That had them all quiveringly alert, their tails held rigid and tongues lolling; nonbearing females were kept as a rare privilege for Heroes whose accomplishments were not *quite* deserving of a mate of their own. Very rare for kits still in the household to be granted such, but Chuut-Riit thought it past time to admit that modern society demanded a prolonged adolescence. The day when a male kit could be given a spear, a knife, a rope and a bag of salt and kicked out the front gate at puberty were long gone. Those were the wild, wandering years in the old days, when survival challenges used up the superabundant energies. Now they must be spent learning history, technology, xenology, none of which burned off the gland-juices saturating flesh and brain.

He jumped down amid his sons, and they pressed around him, purring throatily with adoration and fear and respect;

his presence and the failure of their plot had reestablished his personal dominance unambiguously, and there was no danger from them for now. Chuut-Riit basked in their worship, feeling the rough caress of their tongues on his fur and scratching behind his ears. *Together*, he thought. *Together we will do wonders.*

From "The Children's Hour" by Jerry Pournelle & S.M. Stirling